THE
DOOMSDAY
BUNKER

THE
DOOMSDAY BUNKER

William W. Johnstone
with J. A. Johnstone

PINNACLE BOOKS
Kensington Publishing Corp.
www.kensingtonbooks.com

PINNACLE BOOKS are published by

Kensington Publishing Corp.
119 West 40th Street
New York, NY 10018

PUBLISHER'S NOTE
Following the death of William W. Johnstone, the Johnstone family is working with a carefully selected writer to organize and complete Mr. Johnstone's outlines and many unfinished manuscripts to create additional novels in all of his series like The Last Gunfighter, Mountain Man, and Eagles, among others. This novel was inspired by Mr. Johnstone's superb storytelling.

All Kensington titles, imprints, and distributed lines are available at special quantity discounts for bulk purchases for sales promotions, premiums, fund-raising, educational, or institutional use. Special book excerpts or customized printings can also be created to fit specific needs. For details, write or phone the office of the Kensington sales manager: Kensington Publishing Corp., 119 West 40th Street, New York, NY 10018, attn: Sales Department; phone 1-800-221-2647.

This book is a work of fiction. Names, characters, businesses, organizations, places, events, and incidents either are the product of the author's imagination or are used fictitiously. Any resemblance to actual persons, living or dead, events, or locales is entirely coincidental.

PINNACLE BOOKS and the Pinnacle logo are Reg. U.S. Pat. & TM Off.

ISBN-13: 978-0-7860-3605-9
ISBN-10: 0-7860-3605-2

First printing: October 2017

10 9 8 7 6 5 4 3 2 1

Printed in the United States of America

First electronic edition: October 2017

ISBN-13: 978-0-7860-3606-6
ISBN-10: 0-7860-3606-0

America was not built on fear. America was built on courage, on imagination, and an unbeatable determination to do the job at hand.
—HARRY S. TRUMAN

Americans never quit.
—DOUGLAS MACARTHUR

BOOK ONE

BOOK ONE

Chapter 1

May 24

"**I**n other news, there are unconfirmed reports that North Korea conducted further missile tests today. The missiles involved in these tests are said to have the potential to reach the continental United States. With the recent increase in North Korea's nuclear development, these reports have caused grave concern in some circles in Washington, but the President, in a statement today, referred to that concern as 'fear-mongering' and said that there is no reason to believe North Korea may be considering aggressive action, despite heightened tensions with South Korea and the U.S."

As a commercial came on for the season finale of *Singing for Dollars*, Patrick Larkin picked up the remote and pushed the mute button.

"See?" he said to his wife Susan.

"You're just fear-mongering," she said.

Larkin rolled his eyes.

"And don't roll your eyes at me," Susan added. "You're talking about a lot of money, Patrick. A hell of a lot of money."

He grimaced and said, "Yeah, I know. We've got it, but it would sure take a big chunk out of our bank accounts."

"It would wipe out a couple of them."

Larkin nodded. The remote was in his right hand. He slid his left arm around his wife's shoulders and pulled her closer against him.

"You're not getting ideas, are you?" she asked.

"Not the kind you're thinking about," he said with a sigh.

He was in his late forties, but the only signs of his age were a few streaks of gray in his thick dark hair and a slight weathering of his features. Also, he wasn't in quite as good a shape as he had been when he retired from the Marine Corps a few years earlier, but he liked to think he hadn't lost too much of that conditioning.

Susan, with her honey-blond hair and classic good looks, didn't show her age, either. Even after all the years of marriage, it didn't take much encouragement for him to think about turning off the TV and taking her to bed. Unfortunately, watching the news was as much of an antidote for that as a bucket full of ice water dumped over his head would have been.

Too late now, he thought as she said, "It's back on."

"West Nile, Zika, and now Hydra. No, we're not talk-ing about comic book villains. The Centers for Disease Control has confirmed three more cases of the Hydra virus, so named because of the way it reproduces. This brings the number of confirmed cases in the United States to seventeen. The latest victims of the disease have been identified as refugees from the Middle East who were resettled in Houston, Texas."

"Good Lord," Larkin said. "It's in Texas now, not just Florida and the East Coast."

"Shh," Susan said.

"These patients are being held in strict quarantine,

and Houston's mayor stated today that the situation is under control and there is no danger of the virus spreading. The patients are listed as being in critical condition, and the prognosis for their recovery is uncertain."

"Uncertain, my ass," Larkin said. "Hydra's killed everybody else who came down with it. And how can that windbag politician say there's no danger of it spreading? The doctors and scientists don't *know* how it spreads. And now it's in Texas. You think it's not coming up I-45 toward us right now?"

"They'll get it under control. They did with all the other new viruses, didn't they?"

"Well, there hasn't been another plague that wiped out half the country yet, but give it time."

"I swear, Patrick, you sound almost like you wish that would happen."

"No," he said, "I just wish people would wake up to the fact that it *could.*"

"Widespread demonstrations prompted by last week's incident in Cedar Rapids, Iowa, erupted in violence today as police and peaceful protestors clashed. Riots broke out in Des Moines, as well as in other cities in Illinois, Ohio, California, and New York. The Cedar Rapids incident, in which two alleged armed robbers were gunned down by police, is under investigation by the Justice Department, and the officers involved in the shooting have been placed in protective custody after their homes were destroyed by firebombs. No arrests have been made in those bombings.

"We'll have news of the latest celebrity breakup right after—Wait. What? Where . . . Breaking news. There has been an explosion in downtown Chattanooga, Tennessee. Reports are coming in of serious destruction

*and numerous injuries, although there are no confirmed
fatalities at this time . . . We'll try to find out more—"*

"That's enough," Larkin said as he pushed the power
button on the remote this time.

"I might have wanted to see that, you know," Susan
said.

"Why? You know what's going to happen. All the
talking heads will speculate about who's responsible for
that explosion, and they'll mention everybody *except*
who it turns out to be."

"You don't know who's responsible."

Larkin just gave her a look.

"Well, you don't."

"Maybe I'll be proven wrong. The history of the last
thirty years says I won't be, though." Larkin shook his
head. "Let's face it, you could write the script for the
news every night before it comes on. Some dictator on
the other side of the world rattles a sword, and our guy
waves it off and accuses his political opponents of fear-
mongering. So-called peaceful protestors start burning
and looting because they can get away with it, while
cops trying to do their jobs have to worry not only about
being shot but about their families being threatened as
well. Some athlete spits on the country that made him
a millionaire. We've conquered all the diseases except
the ones that have mutated to the point that we *can't*
do anything to control them. And people can't go about
their business without having to wonder if there's some
suicidal nutcase with a bomb standing next to them in
a crowd. Isn't that what we see, night after night?"

"Maybe, but what good is ranting going to do about it?"

"Ranting? This is not *ranting*. I haven't even come close
to working up to a good *rant*—"

Susan stood up. "Good night, Patrick."

"That's it? Good night?"

"Yeah, I think so. I'm tired. I still have a job, you know, and it was a long shift in the ER today."

He made a face again and said, "Sorry. I guess I do get a little wound up sometimes."

She went behind the sofa, leaned over, and kissed his ear. "You're passionate about things," she told him. "I can't complain too much about that." She straightened, started to walk toward the bedroom, and then paused to add, "I just hate to see you get so worked up over things you can't do anything about. Really, Patrick, this is just . . . the new normal."

The new normal, he thought as she left the room. He supposed she was right about that.

God help us all.

Chapter 2

Two weeks earlier

"It's out in the country west of here," Adam Threadgill said. "You know, so it would be handy to the Air Force base." He shrugged. "Back when there was still an Air Force base."

"There's still a base there," Larkin said. "It's just a reserve base now."

"Yeah. So they don't have any need for nuclear bombs, do they?"

"I thought you said this place you're talking about was where they kept missiles."

"They had *missiles* to protect the *bombs*."

"I get it," Larkin said, although he wasn't sure he did. "But now the installation is empty?"

"Yep," Adam said. "For now. But not for long, if this guy I'm telling you about has his way."

"Okay, run it past me again," Larkin said as he reached for his glass of iced tea. The plate in front of him was empty except for a couple of tiny smears of barbecue sauce, all that was left of his weekly lunch with his fellow retired Marine.

The two men were in what looked like a hole-in-the-wall dump of a restaurant, but actually it had some of the best barbecue to be found in Fort Worth. Located near the big aircraft plant, the place was usually packed with guys Larkin could tell were engineers just by looking at them. It was popular with retired military, too, and there were a lot of them in this area.

"Okay," Threadgill said. He had let himself go more than Larkin had, but you could still kind of see the tough, squatty noncom he had been. "The Air Force had this secret underground base out in the hills west of town where they stored all the nuclear bombs they'd stockpiled for the B-52s and B-58s that flew out of the regular base. This was in the early Sixties, you know, when the Cold War was at its height. Everybody was afraid the Russians were going to try to bomb the hell out of us at a moment's notice. Considering there was a stockpile of nuclear weapons here, this whole area was considered a prime target for the Russkies. So they put in Nike Hercules missiles to guard the place. In fact, there were missile bases all around the Dallas/Fort Worth area, but the one I'm talking about was *secret*. You can't find out anything about it even on Wikipedia."

"Then how do you know about it?"

"You forget, I grew up around here. My dad worked at General Dynamics, right across the runways from the Air Force base. All the kids whose dads worked at GD knew about the missile base. And it scared the shit out of us thinking that the Russians had painted a big bull's-eye on the whole area."

"So your dads who worked on the flight line knew about it. Wow, that's some really top-notch military security there."

"What can I say?" Threadgill shrugged. "The Russians

never bombed us. Maybe they didn't know about it, after all."

"They should have put a few sleeper agents into the elementary schools around here."

"Anyway, the empty silos are still there, and so are the bunkers where the warheads were stored, along with all the fire control and administrative areas. It's almost like an underground mall, but there's nothing in it. It's been sitting there like that for all those years, just waiting for somebody to come along and put it to good use."

"Like this guy Moultrie you were telling me about."

"Yeah. Graham's got *vision.*"

Larkin was pretty sure Threadgill was quoting something Graham Moultrie had said. In his experience, he was a little suspicious of anybody who claimed to have *vision.* All too often, a businessman who said that was just after a buck. A politician who started spouting about it was after power . . . and a buck. None of it ended well.

"Moultrie bought the property?"

"Yeah. From the way he talks, the government was glad to get rid of it. It's kind of a white elephant. It's never been sold to a real-estate developer because then they'd have to disclose the fact that nuclear material used to be stored there. Otherwise, if somebody bought the property and covered it with McMansions, they'd be opening themselves up to lawsuits for not revealing that. But in Graham's case, he knew what had been down there and bought it as is."

"Complete with radiation contamination."

Threadgill shook his head. "No, the place is clean.

He's had it checked up one way and down the other. It's perfectly safe."

A dubious frown creased Larkin's forehead. "Yeah, but if he's trying to sell shares in the place, he's not going to admit that it might give you radiation poisoning, is he?"

"He's going to live there himself, if that day ever comes, God forbid. He wouldn't move into a place he knew would kill him, would he?"

"I suppose not," Larkin admitted. "It wouldn't be much of a survival bunker if it was going to kill you."

Survival bunker . . . It said something about the state of the world that such a term had even come into being. Of course, back when he was a kid, Larkin had heard people talking about fallout shelters, even though the craze where everybody wanted one in their backyard had passed more than a decade earlier. Even most of those had been nothing more than glorified storm cellars, a place where you could go to hunker down safely until a tornado blew over. You couldn't wait out a nuclear war in one of them, though.

A survival bunker was different. He had read up on them, even before Adam Threadgill got interested. Most of them were set up in abandoned military installations like the one Threadgill was talking about, underground bases hardened against not only nuclear blasts but also electromagnetic pulses, chemical and biological warfare, and any other hideous threat the modern world could dish up. They were big enough to hold more than just a family; most could house hundreds of people in relative comfort and were self-sustaining with generators to provide power, plenty of room for stored rations, equipment to supply clean water, and even gardens to grow food hydroponically in case the rations ever ran low. Theoretically, people could live safely under the ground for years no matter what went on above them on the surface.

What would they find when they came up, though?

Larkin pushed that thought out of his head. Always a practical man, he said, "What's it going to cost to buy some space in there?"

Threadgill's beefy shoulders rose and fell. "I don't know exactly. I'm not sure Graham's figured out the price yet. He said he's putting at least twenty million into developing it, though. So that's fifty K per person just to recoup his investment. I figure he's going to be asking somewhere in the neighborhood of $75,000 each to cover contingencies and allow him to make a little profit."

"Twenty million?" Larkin let out a low whistle. "If he's got that kind of money, what's he doing getting mixed up in a thing like this? Why doesn't he just build himself a bug-out space and call it good?"

"Because like I told you, he's a visionary. He wants to help people. Besides, we're talking worst-case scenario here, right? The end of the world as we know it. What's the point of escaping that if you're the only one left? Well, I mean, he's got a wife, but you know what I mean. They don't want to open a hatch and find the world devastated with no way to start over. So he needs enough people to have a real community. That way the human race has still got a fighting chance."

"I guess that makes sense. Still, seventy-five K . . ."

"To ensure that you and Susan survive. Doesn't sound like much then, does it?"

Larkin squinted at his friend and said, "You're not gettin' a kickback on this, are you?"

"Me? No, I—" Threadgill stopped, frowned at Larkin for a second, and then laughed. "You're kidding me, aren't you?"

"Mostly."

"No, I don't have a piece of the deal. There's no discount for drumming up new customers, either. I'm trying to scrape up enough for me and Luisa and the kids."

"That's a lot of money."

"I'm thinking my daughter Sophie and her husband can kick in some. I know they're not rich and haven't been married long, but they're both working."

"Kids aren't known for worrying much about the future."

"Well, they'd better start," Threadgill said. "The way things are going . . ."

"Yeah," Larkin said with a sigh. "There's that." He had a daughter, son-in-law, and grandkids of his own, and that was a real concern.

"Anyway, you want to go out and take a look at the place?" Threadgill slid a business card across the table. "There's Graham's number. He's got a website, too, so you can look it up and check it all out before you call him to set up an appointment. Just don't wait too long."

"At those prices, I don't think the place is going to fill up in a hurry."

Threadgill glanced at the TV mounted on the wall of the barbecue joint. Set to one of the cable news stations, at the moment it was showing live footage of flashing lights and cops in riot gear and smoke billowing from a building, with a graphic across the bottom that read *NEW TERRORIST ATTACKS IN LONDON.*

"The bunker filling up isn't what I'm worried about," he said.

Chapter 3

Larkin hadn't had a job lined up when he retired from the Marine Corps. He had a dream instead.

He was going to be a writer.

Such a crazy idea had never occurred to him when he was growing up, or during his first few years in the Corps. He enjoyed reading but never gave much thought to the people who actually produced the books.

Then he met an older Marine who edited and wrote for the base newspaper and who had been a journalist before enlisting. The guy had invited Larkin to submit something to the paper, and that had been the start of it. Larkin had discovered right away that he enjoyed putting words together and had even sold a few short stories and articles, mostly about military history, to paying markets. That had planted enough of a seed to make the dream grow.

Along the way, he had also met and married a beautiful blond emergency-room nurse. They'd had a daughter, Jill, now married with kids of her own. Larkin and Susan were soul mates and best friends, and when he'd retired from the Corps they moved back to her hometown of Fort Worth, Texas, where their daughter and her family lived. Susan's salary, along with his retirement pension, had supported him while he took a crack at writing books.

Five years into that effort, he had done fairly well: six books sold, thriller novels under a pseudonym that had done decent numbers without being big bestsellers. Maybe he would break through to that higher level someday, maybe he wouldn't, but either way he was having fun and doing what he wanted to do. It would be nice to make enough money so that in a few years Susan could retire, too, but they'd have to just wait and see about that.

Problem was, all those plans were moot if the world went to hell . . . as it was looking more and more like it was going to, with each passing day.

That was why he found himself getting out of his SUV in front of a large steel gate attached to a massive stone and concrete pillar on each end. A brass plate was mounted on one of the pillars, and on it were etched the words THE HERCULES PROJECT. That was all it said.

A Jeep was parked on the other side of the gate. Behind it, a paved road ran up into gently rolling hills dotted here and there with live oaks and post oaks and cottonwoods. At this time of year, the scenery was green and beautiful, almost like a pastoral English countryside except for the occasional clump of cactus that made it unmistakably Texas. A few low structures were visible among the hills, mostly screened from the road by trees.

A man got out of the Jeep and lifted a hand in greeting. "Patrick?" he called through the bars of the gate.

"That's right," Larkin replied. "You're Graham Moultrie? I talked to you on the phone."

"You bet," Moultrie said with a smile. He was a wiry, medium-size man with close-cropped silvery hair and a little goatee. He wore a khaki shirt and jeans and looked more like somebody who would run a lawn-care service instead of an entrepreneur with the ability to sink twenty million dollars into something like the Hercules Project.

He took a small, square remote from his shirt pocket and pressed a button on it. Almost noiselessly, the gate began to roll back.

"Drive on in," Moultrie invited when the gate was open. "You can park your SUV here and we'll take the Jeep up to the office."

Larkin did what Moultrie said. As he got out of the SUV after parking it at the side of the road, the gate began to close again.

"Feels a little like a prison," he commented.

Moultrie laughed. "Just the opposite. We want to keep people out, not in."

"Will that gate do it?"

"You could ram through it with a tank, if you've got a spare one in your garage, I guess," Moultrie said with a shrug. "Anything short of that and it ought to hold up."

Larkin pointed at the high chain-link fence that ran along the front of the property. "Wouldn't take a tank to go through that."

"No, but we'll have some extra defenses put in place soon." Moultrie didn't explain what those defenses were, but he added, "For now, it can be electrified with a flip of a switch in the office or the push of a button on this remote. That's enough to keep most intruders out."

Larkin nodded. It still felt a little like a prison to him, but at least the fence wasn't topped with coils of razor wire. Yet.

Moultrie waved him into the Jeep. They started along the road, weaving easily through the hills.

"You know the history of this place, I guess?" Moultrie asked.

"Yeah, mostly. My buddy told me about it."

"Adam Threadgill." Moultrie nodded. "Seems like a good guy. I hope he's able to join us."

"Us meaning you and the people who have already signed up with you?"

"That's right. We'd all like for you and your family to be part of the Hercules Project, too. You said you were married?"

"That's right."

"Any kids?"

"A grown daughter. She's married and has a little boy and girl."

"Grandkids," Moultrie said. "That's great. I don't have any children myself, and I wish I did. There's something about being able to see the continuity of the family. Kids and grandkids are like . . . a physical manifestation of the future."

"Assuming we make it to the future."

"Well, yes," Moultrie said, "there's that." While he drove, he moved his head to indicate their surroundings. "That's why we have the Hercules Project."

"Named after the missiles that used to be here, I suppose?"

"That and because Hercules is a symbol of strength. That's what we're doing here. We're making a stronghold to ensure the future of humanity."

"You really think that's necessary?" Larkin asked.

"I hope every day that it's not . . . but I'm a practical man. Practical enough to recognize that the possibility exists, and it's not going to go away, no matter how much most people want to ignore it."

Larkin nodded. Moultrie was a salesman, all right . . . but that didn't mean he was wrong.

Moultrie drove around a clump of trees and pulled into a gravel parking lot in front of one of the squat, tan brick structures Larkin had caught a glimpse of from the gate.

"This is the office," Moultrie went on. "We'll stop in here for a minute and then walk on up to the bunker's main entrance."

Inside looked like hundreds of other offices Larkin had seen in his life, with a couple of desks, computers on each one, filing cabinets, and a water cooler. Two things were different: an oil painting of a big missile with flame blasting from its tail hung on one wall, presumably one of the Nike Hercules missiles that had been kept here . . . and behind one of the desks was a drop-dead gorgeous redhead who looked more like a fashion model than a secretary.

Turned out she wasn't a secretary, or not just a secretary, anyway. Moultrie smiled and said, "This is my wife Deb. Deb, this is Pat Larkin. I told you about talking to him. He and his family are considering joining us."

In some circumstances, Larkin would have corrected Moultrie. He would answer to Pat if he had to, but he had always gone by Patrick. Right now. it didn't seem worth bothering with. Deb Moultrie stood up, extended her hand across the desk, and said, "It's nice to meet you, Mr. Larkin."

Larkin was just old enough and just enough of a re-actionary that he had never been completely comfortable about shaking hands with women, although for the most part he had gotten used to it in the service. He took Deb's hand and had to admit she had a good grip. Looked a guy in the eye, too, which he liked.

"Anything going on since I left earlier?" Moultrie asked his wife. Deb was a good twenty years younger than him, so Larkin had to wonder if she was a second or third wife, or a trophy wife. Not that it was any of his business or really mattered.

"Some emails for you to answer when you get a chance, that's all."

Moultrie nodded. "I'll do it later. I'm gonna show Pat around the place. You want to come along?"

"No, I'm still making some calls. You go ahead." She smiled at Larkin. "You wouldn't believe how many contractors and sub-contractors and sub-sub-contractors you have to deal with in order to get a place like this in shape."

"I'll bet," Larkin said.

Moultrie gestured at a rear door and said, "We can go out here."

The door opened onto an asphalt walk that led slightly uphill for about a hundred yards to a cinder-block building that looked like a garage. It had a garage door built into it, in fact, along with a smaller steel door.

Moultrie unlocked the smaller door with his remote before they got there. Larkin said, "You seem to depend a lot on that thing. What happens if the battery goes dead?"

"There are redundancies built into everything," Moultrie said. "In this case, you can use a key card to get in, or if it comes to that, there's a manual override operated with a regular key."

"You think of everything."

"We try." Moultrie opened the door and motioned for Larkin to go ahead. He stepped into a room the size of a foyer. On the other side of it was a steel wall painted battleship gray. Set into the wall was a heavy steel door with a simple handle.

"It's not locked . . . now," Moultrie said as he stepped around Larkin and grasped the handle. He pulled the door out, and a light set into a recessed fixture in the ceiling beyond came on, evidently activated by the door opening. Sharp LED illumination washed down over a wide set of concrete stairs with steel rails on both walls. At a landing one floor down, the stairs turned back and continued to descend. Moultrie held on to the door with one hand and extended the other toward the stairs like a tour guide as he said, "Welcome to the Hercules Project."

Chapter 4

Larkin hesitated slightly. There was something about descending into the bowels of the earth with someone he didn't really know that made the skin on the back of his neck crawl. But he was four inches taller and probably fifty pounds heavier than Graham Moultrie, plus he had all that training from his career as a Marine and had seen combat in the Middle East.

Besides, Moultrie wanted at least 150 grand from him. The guy wasn't likely to try to kill a potential customer unless he was crazy.

Of course, in this day and age, *anybody* could turn out to be crazy . . .

Larkin didn't pause more than a heartbeat. He started down the stairs with Moultrie behind him. Out of habit, he listened to Moultrie's steps. A break in the rhythm might be a warning sign.

Nothing happened except they went down two flights of stairs. At the bottom of the second flight was an even thicker, heavier metal door.

Larkin twisted the handle. He grunted with effort as he pushed the door open and stepped into a concrete walled chamber eight feet wide and twelve feet long. A similar door was at the far end.

Moultrie followed him and pointed to a wheel on the back side of the door Larkin had just opened. "This is a blast door that will stand up to just about anything short of a nuclear explosion. It's equipped with a mechanism like a bulkhead between compartments in a submarine. Turn that wheel and you can seal it off so completely nothing can get through. The door at the other end is identical." He pointed with a thumb at vents in the ceiling. "This chamber can function as an airlock. We can pump out all the air in it, pump it back in, and open either door by remote control."

"Just in case there's something in the air outside that shouldn't be inhaled?"

"Yep." Moultrie opened the second blast door. "This leads into one of the main corridors."

They stepped into a wide, tile-floored hallway that stretched for a hundred yards in either direction. Numerous doors opened from it, some closed, some standing ajar. Again, the lighting was recessed and LED.

Moultrie saw Larkin looking at the lights and said, "That's one of the first things we did. The original lighting was fluorescent. This is more energy-efficient and easier on the eyes. Anybody who has to stay down here may be staying for a long time."

Directly across from the blast door leading to the stairs was a corridor running at right angles to the main one. Larkin could tell it ended at another cross corridor about fifty yards away.

"These main halls are laid out in the shape of an H," Moultrie explained. "There were four missile silos, one at each end of the long sides of the H. They go down considerably deeper, so we're dividing them up into five levels with a separate apartment at each level." He pointed to a sliding door and went on, "That's an elevator leading down to the big storage bunker one level below this. We're going to be turning it into more of a barracks type of living quarters. The quarters on this level"—he waved a hand toward the doors along the corridor—"are a more family and small-group type of arrangement, with six or eight bunks in each unit, along with a small kitchen and bathroom. Not a great deal of privacy, granted, but still more than there will be down in the lower level. We anticipate that most of the residents who will opt for that will be single people."

"Are you splitting up the single male and female residents?" Larkin asked.

"No. Everyone here will have to be a grown-up and police their own actions to a certain extent." Moultrie smiled. "Except the actual kids, of course, and they'll be with their parents. But we're not going to impose any sort of litmus test on potential residents. Gay, straight, any race, creed, or color, as they used to say, everybody is welcome here."

"If they have the money."

"Well . . . I created the Hercules Project because I think it's the right thing to do, but it *is* a business venture, too."

"Say it *is* a worst-case scenario," Larkin mused. "There's some sort of disaster and you and the people who have signed up with you have to come down here for a year or two, or longer. When you finally do go back up to the surface, what good is the money going to do you?"

"Probably not a damned bit." Moultrie laughed. "I'm fully aware of that possibility, Pat. If that's the way it plays out, I still have the satisfaction of knowing that I helped save the human race. That's worth something, isn't it?"

Yeah, Larkin thought, *if you've got a God complex.*

Then he told himself that maybe he was being unfair. Maybe Graham Moultrie really was as altruistic as he was trying to make himself sound.

"Anyway, to get back to what we were talking about, what I envision down here is a meritocracy," Moultrie went on. "What can you do, and how good are you at it? That's what's really going to count. And because of that, at some point I probably will have to do some picking and choosing as to who gets in here. Now, take you for example . . ."

"I'm a writer," Larkin said. "I'm not going to be much good to you."

"Yes, but you're also an ex-Marine."

Larkin had to correct that. "Former Marine. There are no ex-Marines."

"Once a Marine, always a Marine. Sorry. I knew that. Slip of the tongue. The important thing is, you have an exemplary military record. You've been in combat, you've commanded men, you know how to get the job done, whatever it is."

"You're going to have a military force down here?"

"A security force," Moultrie said with a shrug. "I'd like to think that everyone will be on their best behavior at all times, but I'm realistic enough to know that won't be the case. It's possible we'll have to step in and restore order now and then. When and if that happens, I want men I can count on. I think you could be one of those men, Pat, along with your friend Adam."

"Sounds like you know quite a bit about us," Larkin said as suspicion stirred again in his mind.

"An arrangement like this requires trust on both sides," Moultrie said. "And you know what they say . . . There aren't many secrets left in the world." He smiled and gestured again. "Let's look around some more."

They walked along the main corridor, Moultrie opening doors to show Larkin storage areas and a dining area with a large kitchen attached to it. "We'll provide meals for people who prefer that, or people can cook in their own units, sort of like an assisted-living center for the elderly. Everyone's food consumption *will* be kept track of, though, either way. There'll be enough rations stored down here to keep the population alive for a number of years, plus we intend to grow crops hydroponically—that area is down on the lower level, too—and we'll be raising both rabbits and chickens, as well, to stretch our food supplies. But it's unlikely we'll be able to feed ourselves indefinitely."

"Your population will grow, too," Larkin pointed out.

"Undoubtedly. And we probably won't have many elderly residents, so they won't die out at the same rate as babies are born. But we'll deal with that as it happens."

Larkin pointed through an open door into a room lined with sturdy-looking cabinets. "What's this?"

"Our armory. We'll have some weapons to start with, and residents will be allowed to bring along their personal firearms, at least a certain number. But they'll all be kept here and used only for practice and in emergencies."

"Some people won't like giving up their guns."

"We're talking about a situation where there are a lot of things people don't like."

"Armageddon," Larkin said.

Moultrie shrugged. "Or a reasonable facsimile."

"You have medical facilities?"

"An infirmary and an operating room, plus a large supply of every drug we can think of. A woman like your wife will be a very welcome addition to our ranks, Pat."

That nickname was getting under Larkin's skin, but he still suppressed the urge to say anything about it. Instead, he said, "So you know she's an ER nurse."

"Of course. A very highly regarded one, too. Honestly . . . you two are just about perfect. I couldn't ask for a better couple to join us."

"We'll have to do a lot of thinking and talking about it," Larkin said. He added grudgingly, "I have to say, though, you seem to have thought of everything. This looks like a viable operation."

"Just as viable and self-sustaining as I can make it," Moultrie said. "You have my word on that."

"Where are your generators?"

"Down on the lower level as well. We actually have our own power plant, as well as equipment to recycle both air and water."

"So we'll be drinking our own piss."

"You're already doing that if you have any sort of municipal water supply. We just—you'll pardon the expression—streamline the process." Moultrie pointed up. "There will be sensors in place on the surface to instantly detect any sort of radiation or unusual chemical or biological activity. We can monitor that around the clock and keep the shelter completely sealed off as long as there's the least bit of danger. Food, clean air and water, sustainable resources, and enough hardened steel and concrete to withstand anything up to a ground zero nuclear hit . . . what more could you ask for when it comes to survival, Patrick?"

The guy was good, Larkin had to give him that. Moultrie must have noticed the slight tightening of his mouth when he called him Pat and adjusted accordingly.

"You say there are separate apartments in the old missile silos?"

"That's right. Twenty in all, with full kitchens, two bedrooms, and two baths. I wouldn't exactly call them luxurious, but they're very comfortable. If it weren't for the lack of windows, you'd think you were in a nice apartment house."

"How much?" Larkin asked bluntly.

"I'll give you our price list when we get back to the office," Moultrie said.

That didn't bode well, Larkin thought, if it cost so much to get in here that Moultrie didn't want to say the numbers out loud. Or maybe it was just easier to hand out a price list. Larkin supposed he would find out.

"Also, you don't have to come up with the entire cost at once," Moultrie went on. "You can put down a deposit to hold your space and pay it off either in installments or in a lump sum when everything is complete and the place is ready to move into."

"But once it is, you've got to be paid in full to get in if the shit hits the fan."

"That's the way it works," Moultrie said quietly.

"Survival on the layaway plan," Larkin said.

Chapter 5

May 25

As Larkin was driving away from the Hercules Project, he had the satellite radio in the SUV tuned to a news channel. The announcer was talking about a series of riots in Indonesia that had resulted in more than a hundred deaths before being broken up by a typhoon that swept in and killed several hundred more. Meanwhile, one of the socialist countries in South America was descending further into chaos and starvation, one more domino toppling in a seemingly endless chain. Larkin grunted and switched the station to some music. He didn't care what kind of music it was; he just wanted to hear something other the constant litany of death, discord, and destruction.

As he drove through the countryside west of Fort Worth, it was hard to believe there was so much terrible news in the world. The landscape was green and beautiful, with nice houses tucked in among trees and cows and horses grazing in the fields. From some of the hills, he could see the downtown skyscrapers about ten miles away, shining in the sun.

A vision suddenly appeared in his head: those buildings disappearing in an instant, in the searing fireball of a nuclear explosion. Adam Threadgill had mentioned growing up in this area and being scared of such a thing when he was a kid. Larkin's childhood had been spent in Kansas and Nebraska, without any military targets nearby, but even so he could remember what that Cold War paranoia felt like.

Only it wasn't paranoia if somebody was really out to get you, he reminded himself, and for a while there, the United States and the Soviet Union hadn't been all that far from actually launching nukes at each other. Larkin had been born a few years after the Cuban Missile Crisis, so he didn't remember that incident himself, but it had had enough of an effect on the nation's consciousness that he had been aware of it for as far back as he could remember. He remembered hearing fear in his father's voice when he talked about the Russians . . . and in young Patrick's mind, his dad had been invincible, never afraid of anything. If *he* worried about being bombed, there must be something to it.

Then that anxiety had receded after the fall of the Soviet Union, only to resurface with new faces behind the bombs. It wasn't missiles people worried about now, but rather truck bombs or suitcase nukes or drone payloads being wielded by Islamic terrorists. As so-called "refugees" from the Middle East continued to flood into the country over the objections of nearly everybody except the politicians in Washington, people couldn't help but wonder how many of those young men came to America seeking not sanctuary but rather an opportunity to sow carnage.

The trouble didn't necessarily have to come from overseas, either. Plenty of it was already here in the form of homegrown terrorists, the children of legal immigrants from earlier generations who had been corrupted by a ceaseless barrage of hate coming from their Middle Eastern cousins. And so there were bombings, shootings, stabbings, all sorts of violence, and the worst part of it was . . . you never knew where it was coming from. No wonder people were stressed out.

Throw in the racial unrest relentlessly stoked by politicians, so-called community leaders, and the media, and it was hard to leave home without thinking, *Well, this might be the time when I don't come back.*

That didn't even take into account all the little things that could kill you, like some new superbug resistant to any treatment, or the rising tide of cancer—God, Larkin couldn't even begin to count all the friends and acquaintances he had lost to one form or another of cancer!—or the dementia that seemed so much more prevalent than it used to be, or an allergic reaction to some common, everyday food or item, or the stress and depression that led people to medicate themselves into a stupor until it finally seemed that ending it all was the easiest way out . . .

Were there still good things in the world? Sure, logically Larkin knew that there were. But sometimes it was hard to pick them out from the tsunami of crap that seemed to be washing over everything.

By the time he got back to his nice, comfortable house, he was feeling anything but comfortable. Graham Moultrie had made plenty of good points, and from what Larkin could tell, the Hercules Project was being developed into the sort of safe, secure place where somebody really *could* ride out all sorts of catastrophes.

He glanced down at the brochure lying on the seat beside him. The prices were high, but not out of reach.

One of those apartments in the old missile silos could be had for $80,000 per person. The more spare accommodations along the main corridors went for $60,000 per person, and space in the barracks-like lower level was 50 grand per. Kids under the age of fifteen were half-price. The down payment/deposit was 20 percent of the total. It could be done, Larkin thought as he parked in the garage and then picked up the brochure from the seat.

Susan's sedan was parked in the garage, too. He had left the house before she was awake, but she would be up now, getting ready to head to the hospital for her shift. He went in through the garage, into the kitchen, and found coffee in the old-fashioned coffeemaker. He'd never cared for those new ones with the plastic cups and pods and things.

As he poured himself a cup, she came into the kitchen fully dressed in her scrubs but toweling her hair dry. "I saw your note saying you'd gone to run an errand," she said. "Get it taken care of?"

"Yeah, maybe."

"What's your plan for this afternoon? Going to get some pages done?"

"Thought I would."

"Maybe you could unload the dishwasher, too?"

"Sure," Larkin said. After everything he had seen and thought about this morning, worrying about dirty dishes seemed almost trivial beyond belief, but Susan was right: life went on, and that included all the mundane chores that went with it.

Yeah, life went on . . . until it didn't.

"If you've got a few minutes, there's something I'd like to talk to you about."

Susan looked at him and frowned. "This isn't a *situation*, is it? I hate situations."

Larkin laughed and shook his head. Any time one member of a couple announced that they had a "situation," it almost always wasn't good.

"No. You know I went to lunch with Adam Threadgill the other day."

"You have lunch with Adam every week unless something comes up."

"Yeah, but this time he was telling me about this new place west of town—"

"A new place to eat? Ooh, I like the sound of that."

Larkin made a face and shook his head. "Well, they have food there, but it's not exactly a restaurant."

"A bar? I'm not much on bars, you know that."

"It's more of a place you go and stay."

"A bed and breakfast? A resort? Those places are expensive. Although, if you wanted to call it, like, a second honeymoon . . ."

Larkin sighed and held out the brochure to her. "Just take a look and think about it, all right. I took a tour of the place and can tell you all about it."

Susan glanced down at the brochure, which had a mushroom cloud on the folded front. She looked right back up and said, "No. This is some sort of crazy fantasy, Patrick."

"I wish it was."

She pushed the brochure back in his hand and snapped, "I have to get to work."

"Then we'll talk about it later—"

"There's nothing to talk about. However much this costs, we can find better ways to spend the money."

"Better ways than survival?"

She just looked at him, shook her head, and walked out of the kitchen.

That was the way it had been ever since, Larkin bringing up the subject from time to time, Susan refusing to even talk about it . . . but gradually getting less steadfast in her refusal. Larkin hoped that was because some of his arguments, even the snippets of them she listened to, were getting through to her. The fact that the news seemed to be getting worse and worse all the time probably had an effect, too.

In making the arguments to her, he realized he was making them to himself as well. When he'd driven away from the Hercules Project, he had been undecided about what was the right thing to do. Moultrie had made a compelling case, and so had the things Larkin had seen with his own eyes. But he'd been raised to be frugal, and spending a chunk of money that big just went against the grain for him, even when it was in a good cause. He'd had doubts about nearly every big purchase he had ever made in his life, he recalled, and most of them had turned out just fine. Not just fine, but in some cases downright great. So history told him—in more ways than one—that he didn't have any reason to drag his feet about this.

No reason other than getting Susan to see the practicality of it, too.

After their conversation about "the new normal" the night before, he hadn't said anything else about the idea.

This morning he had coffee and breakfast—pancakes, scrambled eggs, and bacon—ready when she came into the kitchen. He wasn't trying to suck up to her; since retiring, he had discovered that he actually liked cooking . . . as long as it was basic stuff and didn't get too complicated.

She was still in her nightgown and looked great to him. He enjoyed the casual intimacy of their decades-long marriage. He was about to say good morning to her when she walked through the kitchen and on into the living room. The open-concept design of the whole living area allowed him to watch her as she picked up the remote and aimed it at the TV. The big screen came on.

"I had the TV on in the bedroom," she said as she glanced over her shoulder at him. "This was on."

"—shooters' motive is unknown at this time," a solemn voice was saying over an apparent live shot of what appeared to be a mall somewhere. A graphic listing the town of Pembroke Pines, Florida, was at the bottom of the screen. Emergency vehicles were parked around the mall, but that was all that could be seen because members of the media were being kept back a considerable distance. *"There are reports of multiple fatalities, and at least a dozen injured have been transported to nearby medical facilities. There appear to have been at least three shooters, and as far as we know they are still active inside the mall. Police have cordoned off the area, and we believe that SWAT teams have gone in— Oh, my God! What was that?"*

The live shot bounced on the screen as the camera was jolted. Larkin gripped the edge of the counter hard as smoke and flames erupted from the mall and people screamed and shouted. The view tilted and careened as the person with the camera fled. For a split second, the camera caught sight of a massive fireball rising and enveloping the mall. Larkin felt sick.

Susan muted the sound on the TV but left the picture on, although there was nothing to see but chaos. She turned, looked at Larkin, and said, "That place out in the country . . . I'm ready to talk about it now."

Chapter 6

The destruction in Florida was massive, even though the newscasts kept harping on the fact that it hadn't been a nuclear explosion that had destroyed the mall and killed the hundreds of people still inside it when the blast went off. The fact that it was a conventional bomb didn't make them any less dead.

Since all the security cameras inside the mall had been destroyed as well, it was thought at first that the exact chain of events would remain unknown. However, within hours of the attack, cell phone video shot and sent out from inside the mall during the incident began to surface. Although the footage was often shaky, naturally enough, since the innocent people taking it had been terrified, it was clear enough to show the three young men of Middle Eastern descent opening fire on shoppers with semi-automatic pistols. No one else in the mall seemed to be armed; no one returned the fire anyway. People screamed, ran, and tried to hide instead.

Mall security guards showed up and engaged in a gun battle with the shooters. One of the men was hit and apparently killed. The others retreated into a store. Emergency personnel began to arrive and evacuated some of the wounded. The mall was effectively in lockdown, however, with most of the customers who'd been in there when the violence started still there, hiding, afraid to venture out and maybe become a target. Then the police had lobbed in tear gas and stormed the store where the remaining shooters had holed up . . .

And all the streaming video ended at that point.

Eventually the investigation into the attack determined that the three suspects (they were seldom, if ever, referred to in the media as terrorists) had parked a rental truck at the loading dock of one of the mall's anchor stores. It had been packed to bursting with explosives and had been triggered with a remote detonator. The horrific blast destroyed more than half the mall, including the area where the attackers had taken shelter. It was a classic suicide bombing on a huge scale. If they hadn't been trapped, if they had gotten away somehow, they might have waited until they were clear to trigger the bomb, but the consensus was that they'd had no real intention of surviving.

Identifying the three men hadn't taken long, either. Two were Syrian refugees; the other had been born and raised in Encino. But all were fervent jihadists, according to their social media pages. All had predicted their own deaths.

And all had vowed that the bloodshed would go on no matter what happened to them, until a worldwide caliphate was established that would usher in peace.

The country was shaken. The previous holiday season, another mall had almost been destroyed in a terrorist attack. The pattern was forming. When it wasn't even safe to go to the mall anymore . . .

The attack was the top story for a week. Then the North Koreans staged another nuclear test that put the entire Far East up in arms. The Iranian government issued a stern warning to the United States not to respond to the North Koreans' action. The Hydra virus ramped up, with scores of new cases reported and a 90 percent mortality rate. Seven police officers were ambushed and killed in Kansas City, Missouri. The President made a speech from the Oval Office saying that in order to quell the rising tide of violence in the country, some constitutional rights might have to be suspended, but only temporarily, of course.

And the winner of *Singing for Dollars* was announced: Jodie Swain. Leading to immediate howls of protest that Taneesha Hamilton should have won and had been robbed because she was not only black but transgender. That story trended even more than any of the others.

In Texas, Patrick Larkin took his wife Susan to visit the Hercules Project.

"I have to say, you're an absolutely perfect candidate for residency here, Susan," Graham Moultrie said after taking them on the same tour of the project that Larkin had gotten a couple of weeks earlier. "It's vital that we have people in the community with hands-on medical experience."

"She's got plenty of that," Larkin said. "Fifteen years as an ER nurse. I'd say she's seen just about every kind of medical emergency there is."

"Hardly," Susan said. "I'm sure there are all kinds of things I've never encountered."

"But you've seen plenty," Moultrie went on. "And it's not like you'd be in charge of our medical unit. We already have several doctors and their families signed up. You'd be joining a great team."

"Assuming that we'd ever have to take shelter down here."

"Of course," Moultrie said. "And we hope that never happens, don't we? Just like we buy car insurance and home insurance to protect us against things that we hope will never happen."

"So this place"—Susan gestured at their surroundings—"is nuclear war and plague insurance."

Moultrie looked like he was thinking it over, then he nodded. "You could call it that, I suppose. I prefer just saying that it's survival insurance, because there are all sorts of things out there that could threaten our survival."

Larkin thought about everything that had been happening in the world recently and knew Moultrie was right about that, anyway. There was no telling which direction catastrophe would come from next. But there were getting to be so many potential civilization-ending disasters that the odds were tipping further and further in favor of *something* bad happening.

Susan looked around the main corridor where they were standing and said, "Well . . . it does seem like you've thought of just about everything."

"We tried," Moultrie said modestly. "And it's not just Deb and me, either. I've hired some of the top survival experts and futurists in the country as consultants, to make sure we haven't overlooked anything. I know that having a place down here isn't cheap. One of our goals is to make sure that each of our residents gets his or her money's worth."

"Of course, who would anybody complain to?" Larkin asked. "If it's bad enough on the surface for everybody to come down here, there won't be any Better Business Bureau left."

Susan said, "Patrick, that was rude."

"No, not at all," Moultrie said quickly. "Your husband is right, Susan. Ultimately, there's only one person to be held accountable." He poked a thumb against his chest. "Me. That old saying about where the buck stops is true. It's right here. The Hercules Project is *my* baby, no one else's."

A moment of silence went by before Moultrie resumed in his usual affable tone, "Well, what do you think? Can we sign up the two of you?"

"I don't know," Susan said. "It's a lot of money."

"It is," Moultrie agreed with a solemn nod.

Larkin said, "We have our daughter and her husband and our grandkids to think of, too. I'm not coming down here without them. If things are bad enough to need a place like this, there's no way I'll abandon them."

"That's absolutely right," Susan said. "Our family is, well, a package deal."

"Just the way it should be," Moultrie said without hesitation. "Honestly, I'm not sure I'd want anybody down here who could just leave their loved ones behind. We're talking about . . . four more people, I believe you said, Patrick?"

Larkin nodded. "Our daughter Jill, her husband Trevor

Sinclair, and their kids Bailey and Chris. Bailey's twelve, Chris is eight."

"Sounds like a fine family," Moultrie said. "There'll be quite a few other kids down here, so they'll fit right in. And if you're worried about their education, I knew starting out that I'd definitely have to recruit enough teachers so that we can have our own school. If the world falls apart, it's going to take educated people to put it back together again."

"I couldn't agree more," Susan said. "Let us talk to Jill and Trevor and see what they think."

"Of course."

Larkin said, "Aren't you going to warn us not to wait too long to make up our minds?"

Moultrie smiled. "You're a smart guy, Patrick. I know you're not going to be rushed into anything, but at the same time, you're not going to drag your feet when it's time to take action. I trust you to figure out what's right for your family."

"Fair enough," Larkin said.

"So, unless there's something else down here you'd like to see . . . ?" Moultrie looked at Susan and raised his eyebrows.

She shook her head, "No, I think you've covered everything very well."

"Let's go back up to the office and have a cup of coffee, then. Deb makes *great* coffee."

"He's really slick, isn't he?" Susan asked as they drove away from the Hercules Project in Larkin's SUV.

"Slick as snot," Larkin agreed.

"Don't be crude. And yet he's not really as oily as . . . as . . ."

"A snake oil salesman?" Larkin supplied.

"That's right. I've always wondered, though . . . who would buy snake oil in the first place?" Without waiting for Larkin to answer, Susan went on, "He's a salesman, no doubt about that, but he also seems very sincere. I can usually tell when somebody's just trying to talk me into buying something."

"Exactly. Moultrie really believes in what he's selling."

"And his wife is lovely."

"Is she?" Larkin said.

Susan laughed. "Don't try acting like you didn't notice. I know you have a thing for gorgeous redheads."

"I'm not sure I'd say she's gorgeous—"

"She's considerably younger than Graham, though. I suspect she's not his first wife."

"And I suspect that's none of our business," Larkin said.

"And it really doesn't have anything to do with whether we sign on the dotted line."

"Not a thing."

"We need to get Jill and Trevor to come over for dinner so we can talk to them about this."

Larkin nodded. "I agree completely. They're smart kids. We'll lay it all out for them and see what they think."

"If they come in on it with us, though, we're going to have to pay some of the cost. I won't have them raiding the college funds they've set up."

"We can do that. Of course, if we all wind up down

there, they won't be worrying about college, probably for a long time."

Susan looked out the passenger side window at the beautiful countryside rolling past. "Don't remind me. We're talking about the end of the world, aren't we?"

"Yeah," Larkin said. "And I don't feel fine."

Chapter 7

Jill Sinclair lined up the sights of the Walther CCP 9mm pistol she held, and in a deliberate fashion, not rushing the shots, put four rounds center mass. The spread at ten yards was six inches. Not bad, she thought as she lowered the pistol, but it could be better. Accuracy could always be improved upon.

She dropped the eight-round magazine, set the Walther on the shelf in front of her, and started reloading. With ear protectors on, she didn't hear the step behind her, didn't know anybody was there until a hand lightly touched her shoulder. She had thought she was alone on the range.

She closed her left fist around the partially reloaded magazine, ready to bring it around and punch if she had to. She resisted the impulse to do so blindly and looked over her right shoulder instead. Probably a good thing she did, she thought. Her husband wouldn't have appreciated it if she'd punched him in the face and broken his nose.

She pulled the ear protectors down so they hung around the back of her neck and asked Trevor, "What are you doing here?"

He pushed his glasses up on his nose and said, "I was on my way home from work when your mother called me. She's been trying to get you."

Jill nodded toward her range bag. "My phone's in there. I didn't hear it."

"Yeah, I told Susan that's what I guessed."

"There's not anything wrong, is there?" Jill caught her breath a little. "The kids—"

"The kids are fine. I talked to Bailey just before I left the office."

"Oh. Okay. What did my mother want, then?"

"Your folks want us to come over for dinner."

Jill looked down at her outfit: running shoes, yoga pants—she'd never been to a yoga class in her life, but she loved the pants—and T-shirt. "Not like this," she said. "I'll have to go home and shower and change."

"Your parents wouldn't care."

"Maybe not, but I would. What's going on? Is there some sort of urgency about this invitation?"

Trevor shrugged. "I don't know. Your mom didn't sound like there was anything *wrong*, exactly, but she did sound like she and your dad want to talk to us about something."

"They didn't just get the urge to have dinner with us and the kids, then."

Trevor frowned and said, "Actually . . . she said it would be a good idea if it was just you and me, without Bailey and Chris."

Jill raised an eyebrow that matched her long, light brown hair pulled back into a ponytail. She had inherited a blend of her father's dark hair and her mother's blond.

"No kids? That sounds sort of ominous, don't you think?"

"Maybe they've got some news they don't want the kids to hear. Like something about . . . illness, maybe."

Jill caught her breath. "Oh, God, one of them has cancer."

"Now, don't jump to any conclusions—"

"What else could it be?"

"All sorts of things," Trevor said. "Maybe they're getting a divorce."

Jill gave him a disgusted look. "That's ridiculous. My parents couldn't last a month without each other, and you know it."

"Well, that's the way it seems, but you never know."

"Yeah. Sometimes you *do* know."

"All right, but just because it's not divorce doesn't mean it has to be cancer."

Jill sighed. "I suppose not. There's only one way to find out. What did you tell her?"

"I told her I'd have to talk to you. I saw your car when I was driving by here and thought it'd be better to stop and let you know now, instead of waiting until we met up at home."

Jill nodded and said, "Good idea. I'll call her, just in case she was worried."

"I think that'd be a good idea."

"And Bailey can make something for her and Chris for supper."

"We could see if Marisol can come over—"

"They don't need a babysitter, Trev. They're too old for that."

"Chris is only eight."

"And Bailey's twelve. My parents didn't helicopter me, and I'm not gonna helicopter my kids. They're going to be self-reliant."

"Just like their gun-toting mother."

Jill gave him a look. She didn't want to have this . . . argument wasn't the right word. Discussion, maybe. Trevor wasn't opposed to guns, and he had never told her she shouldn't carry one. He just didn't feel that comfortable with them himself. She had persuaded him to try shooting a few times, and honestly, he wasn't very good at it. In his case, it was probably better that he didn't carry.

Jill, on the other hand, never left the house without her Walther, or her Baby Glock, or her S&W Shield . . .

"Let's just head home," she said. "I'll call my mom on the way and let her know we'll be there. I can shower and change pretty quickly."

"Okay."

Jill packed her gear away in the range bag and led the way out through the pair of doors, one closing before the other opened. She smiled at the guy behind the gun shop's counter and said, "Since when do you let non-shooters back on the range, Ed?"

"Since you were the only one back there and the guy's married to you, I figured it would be all right."

"Yeah, it is," Jill said. "Just kidding."

"I'm just glad she didn't shoot me," Trevor said.

"Not a joke to make here," she told him solemnly.

"Sorry," he muttered.

* * *

Jill and Trevor lived about five miles from her parents, both homes being on the west side of Fort Worth but in different suburbs. When her dad retired from the Marines and they made plans to move to the area, Jill hadn't been sure she liked the idea of having her folks so close by. She didn't want to fall into the trap of using grand-parents as built-in babysitters, as so many people did, and she didn't want them judging her, either.

As it turned out, though, things had been good. Her parents had given them plenty of space, although every-one was close enough that it was easy to pitch in and help out whenever needed, not just with babysitting but with anything else that came up. And with modern life the way it was, something *always* came up. If the day-to-day stress level ever went down too much, Jill wasn't sure she would know what to do.

Trevor parked his hybrid sedan in the driveway of the Larkin home. Looking presentable again, Jill got out and went up the walk with her husband. Her mother must have been waiting for them, beause she opened the door before they got there.

"Come on in," Susan said. "Dinner's almost ready. Your father made meatloaf."

Jill smiled. "I never would have thought Dad would turn out to be a cook."

"It shocked me, too, to be honest."

From behind the island that separated the kitchen from the living room and dining room area, Larkin raised a bottle and called, "Want a beer, Trev?"

"Sure," Trevor said as he walked into the kitchen.

Larkin got a beer from the refrigerator, opened it, and handed the bottle to him.

Susan and Jill sat down on the sofa. The TV was on, with the sound down. Susan turned it off and said, "There's no point. All the news is bad these days."

"I expect people have been saying that as long as there's been any sort of news being reported."

"Probably," Susan replied with a shrug. "I appreciate the two of you coming over on such short notice."

Jill looked back and forth between her parents and said, "This isn't about bad news, is it? Because if it is, I'd just as soon not postpone it until after we've eaten."

"No, not bad news. Although, in a way . . ."

"Neither one of you is dying from some kind of disease, right?"

Susan looked surprised by that blunt question. "No. Not that I know of, anyway. Why in the world would you ask that?"

"And you're not getting divorced?"

"What? No! Certainly not."

"I'm glad to hear that," Larkin said from the kitchen. "Although if that's what it was, I would have hoped that you'd tell me first."

"Don't be ridiculous," Susan said.

"And I don't have cancer?" Larkin asked.

"How would I know that? You haven't even been to the doctor in months."

"Wives know things," Larkin said with exaggerated gravity.

"Stop that," Susan said. "You know good and well why we asked Jill and Trevor to come over here."

"Well, yeah, I guess I do," Larkin admitted.

"It was your idea."

"No, it was *Adam's* idea."

"Wait a minute," Jill said. "I'm confused. Your friend Adam Threadgill? What's he got to do with anything?"

"He's the one who told me about this place."

"Oh, man," Trevor said after he took a pull on his beer. "This isn't some timeshare deal, is it?"

"No," Larkin said. "It's more of an . . . end of the world deal."

Chapter 8

After that cryptic statement, of course, there was no way Jill and Trevor were going to wait to hear what this get-together was all about. Dinner was ready, though, so they ate as they talked, and pending apocalypse didn't make for the most appropriate conversation.

"Don't you think the whole thing is really . . . far-fetched?" Trevor asked when Larkin had laid out the facts about the Hercules Project. "I mean, I can understand being worried about some of the things going on in the world, but you don't actually believe anything really bad is going to happen, do you?"

"I can't guarantee that it's not going to, either," Larkin said.

"And you can't guarantee that the sun's not going to go nova tomorrow, either."

"Actually," Jill said, "there aren't any signs to indicate that the sun will go nova in the next billion years or so."

"And if it does, even a place like Moultrie's got out there won't do any good," Larkin added, "so that's one thing I'm *not* worried about."

Trevor tapped the brochure that was lying on the table next to his plate and said, "Okay, given that the world is a dangerous place these days—"

"That's putting it mildly," Jill said.

Trevor ignored the interruption and went on, "How do you know this . . . refuge or whatever you want to call it . . . will offer any real protection?"

"We've both gone out there and taken a look at it," Larkin said. "I've been there twice."

"And you've seen what the owner *wants* you to see and listened to what he wants to tell you."

Larkin inclined his head in acknowledgment of his son-in-law's point. Trevor was a smart guy, a likable guy. Larkin had gone through a little of the usual dad's feeling that nobody was good enough for his daughter, but logically, he knew that Trevor was. The two of them were a fine match.

"Yeah, but I took a good look around and asked a lot of questions. Maybe you two should go out there and do the same thing."

"And the cost of it . . ." Trevor said.

"Yeah, it is pretty expensive," Jill added.

"True. But you don't have to pay the whole thing up front, and if you needed it, we thought we could maybe help you out with the down payment."

"Oh, no," Trevor said instantly. "We couldn't do that."

"Why not?" Larkin asked. "We've never loaned you a dime. There's not many people our age who can say that about their kids."

Jill made decent, but not spectacular, money as a pharmacist. Trevor made decent, but not spectacular, money working for a computer consulting company. Together, their incomes had allowed them to live comfortable lives, although in recent years it had become more of a challenge because of constantly rising taxes and the cost of everything else going up as well. Still,

Larkin figured they were doing all right. But probably not all right enough to come up with the chunk of money the Hercules Project would require.

"We have the money," Susan said. "Helping you out wouldn't be a hardship. Well, not enough of one to worry about, anyway."

Jill looked at her mother and said, "What do you really think about all this, Mom? You're the most level-headed person I know."

"Hey," Larkin said.

"You're level-headed most of the time, Dad, but we all know you can go off on a tangent now and then."

"My tangents always turn out to be right. Well, nearly always." Larkin reached over and picked up the brochure, held it up as he added, "This is one time I really hope I'm wrong, but I'm not sure we can afford to take that chance."

Jill was still looking at her mother. Susan said, "I started out telling your father it was far-fetched, just like Trevor did. I even said it sounded paranoid."

"She did," Larkin said. "Took great pleasure in it, too."

"But I don't know," Susan went on. "After what happened in Florida . . . that terrible attack and the people responsible for it promising there would be more . . . I just wasn't sure what to think anymore. I started listening more carefully to the news, and there are just a *lot* of things going on in the world that could cause a real catastrophe. I mean, there are at least two countries with nuclear bombs that would like to see the United States blown off the face of the earth. Then when you think about the terrorists who might be able to get their hands on a nuclear device, or some biological weapon . . ."

Trevor said, "They make movies about that stuff. In real life, the government always finds a way to stop such things from happening."

"Yeah, the same government that runs the IRS and the VA," Larkin said, "and all the other alphabet soup agencies that can't quite seem to do their jobs. If you want to put all your faith in the government, Trev, you go right ahead. I've dealt with them too much to do that."

"Dad's kind of got a point," Jill said. "The FDA and the other agencies we have to deal with have put some good safeguards in place, but they've also weighed the whole process down with so many needless, contradictory regulations that sometimes I think it makes the public *less* safe in the long run by wearing out the people who have to cope with the bureaucracy."

"See?" Larkin said. "I raised a smart girl."

"You say that because she's agreeing with you," Trevor said.

"What more proof do I need?"

Trevor sat back in his chair and raised both hands as he said, "Look, objectively, intellectually, I have to agree with you that the world is a dangerous place. Anybody would have to have their head completely buried in the sand not to realize that."

"Or stuck up somewhere else. I believe the technical term is Rectal Cranial Inversion."

"But casting your lot with these . . . survivalists . . . I'm not sure that's a good idea, either. I mean, they're kind of extremists, aren't they?"

"Some people might say that. Some people might wish they'd been a little more extreme themselves, if things really go as bad as they could."

"I guess I can understand stockpiling some food and water—"

"Won't do you much good in the case of a nuclear explosion or a virus that's going to wipe out ninety percent of humanity."

"Maybe not, but what if none of those things happen? Then you're stuck with some really expensive real estate that's under the ground."

Jill said, "Look, we can go around and around in circles like this all evening and not get anywhere. Maybe what we should do is make an appointment to go out there and look at the place."

Trevor gave her a surprised look. "Really?"

"It can't hurt anything, and if my folks feel this strongly about it, maybe it's not a bad idea."

He shrugged and said, "Well, sure, if that's what you want. Maybe this weekend?"

Jill nodded. "I'll call and see if I can set it up."

"You want us to come with you?" Larkin asked.

"No. We can make up our own minds, Dad. But we'll take everything you've said about it into consideration."

Susan said, "That's about all we can ask."

Trevor said, "Have you actually signed up yet, Patrick?"

"Not yet," Larkin said. "We wanted to talk to you two first."

"Because we wouldn't want to live in a world without you and our grandchildren," Susan added.

"Well," Trevor said as he lifted his wineglass, "I'll drink to that."

They were on their way out to the Hercules Project that Saturday afternoon, listening to NPR—Jill often got annoyed with the station, but Trevor liked it—when a news bulletin came on. Jill was driving—they were in her crossover—so she thumbed the button on the steering wheel to increase the volume.

"—*reports that the North Korean missile destroyed an American fishing vessel in the Bering Sea. The North Korean government issued a statement a short time after the incident declaring that the firing of the missile was only a test, not an aggressive action, but it stopped short of apologizing for the loss of life and the destruction of the vessel. Nor did the statement actually say that the American vessel was struck by accident.*

"*With tensions already in a heightened state, the Pentagon immediately placed the American fleet in the Pacific on high alert. The President, in a statement from the White House, said that it would be a mistake to jump to any conclusions and that a full investigation of the incident will be carried out. In the meantime, he assured the North Koreans that the United States will not overreact to this incident.*"

"Overreact?" Jill said incredulously. "They blow one of our boats out of the water, kill who knows how many Americans, and the President practically falls all over himself telling them not to worry about it, it's all good, we won't do anything about it!"

"He didn't actually *say* that," Trevor pointed out.

"He might as well have."

"You're starting to sound like your father. The President said we were going to investigate the incident fully."

"And when we find out that they did it on purpose— which it sure sounds like they did—how are we going to react? Are we going to go in and blow up a few things, too?" Jill snorted. It wasn't very ladylike, but there was no other way to express her contempt. "You know good and well that's not going to happen. If anything, the guy in the White House will apologize to the North Koreans because our boat got in the way of their missile!" She took a deep breath. "And here's what really worries me . . . If that missile reached the Aleutian Islands, it wouldn't take much more for it to make it to Alaska. That's the United States, Trev. You want that dictator lobbing nuclear warheads at the United States?"

"Nobody said anything about nuclear warheads. I'll bet the missile was unarmed, if it was just a test like the North Koreans say. Just the impact was probably enough to sink the ship."

"You think they'd have a missile that they couldn't put a warhead on if they wanted to?"

"I don't know. I'm no expert on nuclear armaments."

Neither was Jill, but even so, the latest incident was enough to make her glad they were taking this little excursion today. If nothing too terrible ever happened, at least it was a pleasant drive in the country.

If worse came to worst, though, it might wind up saving their lives . . .

Chapter 9

The tour of the Hercules Project went a little better than Jill anticipated. She didn't mind Trevor asking hard questions of Graham Moultrie. The man had to expect those and be able to provide honest, complete answers if he was going to ask people to invest that much money. She had been concerned that Trevor might be a little obnoxious about it, though. Sometimes he could come across as condescending and arrogant. In point of fact, he often *was* the smartest guy in the room, and he'd been known to act like it.

As it turned out, however, Trevor was on his best behavior. That might have had something to do with Deb Moultrie going along with them on the tour. The redhead was distracting, to say the least. Trevor was able to focus on what Moultrie was saying, but he couldn't work up the energy to be annoying. That was Jill's theory, anyway.

Anyway, Deb wasn't *that* much more attractive than her, Jill thought, so there was no need for her to feel threatened by Trevor's reaction.

They went through the place from top to bottom, seeing everything there was to see, as far as Jill could tell. She knew from talking to her parents that they were thinking about getting an apartment in one of the missile silos. Those were more expensive, and Jill wondered if she and Trev and the kids wouldn't do just fine in one of the four-person units along one of the main corridors. The lower level barracks-style arrangement was out of the question. There would be little enough privacy in the four-person unit.

When they were finished with the tour and had paused near the staircase leading back up to the surface, Trevor said, "Can I ask you one more question, Mr. Moultrie?"

"Sure," Moultrie said with a smile, "if you call me Graham like I asked you to."

"All right, Graham." Trevor waved a hand at their surroundings. "This is a big operation. When you get right down to it, it's a real-estate development."

Moultrie thought it over and nodded. "I think it's fair to say that. What's your question?"

"Every real-estate developer I've ever run into has had salesmen working for him, trying to move the property. I didn't see anybody around here except you and your wife. Where are your salesmen?"

"I don't have any," Moultrie replied without hesitation. "Don't need 'em. The Hercules Project is my baby. Well, mine and Deb's. You see, Trevor, a guy who buys a big piece of property, cuts it up, and slaps fifty or a hundred houses on it, he's looking to do one thing: make money. I want to make money, too, but for a different reason. I want to funnel that money back into this place and make it even better. Because in the long run, the goal is to save humanity. You might say we're trying to save humanity from itself. I know people talk about climate change and natural disasters, but my gut feeling is, if things ever get bad enough to need something like the Hercules Project, it's going to be because of a war or a man-made plague or something else that we've done to ourselves out of sheer greed and stupidity and lust for power."

Jill said, "That makes it sound like you don't have a very high opinion of people in general."

"That's absolutely right," Moultrie said, again without missing a beat. "I don't. No offense, Jill, but you and Trevor aren't old enough to remember the way things used to be. People had some common sense that's missing today."

"Every generation says that about the generation that comes after them," Trevor said.

Moultrie shrugged. "More than likely. But think about politics. Neither side is willing to admit that the other has any good ideas, isn't even willing to consider that possibility. If one side does something, the other side says it's the worst thing that could ever happen. Then they switch around and the dance goes on. They're so consumed with that and their never-ending quest for power that they've let our place in the world slip."

"You mean nobody fears the United States anymore."

"It's not fear so much that I'm talking about. It's respect." Moultrie chuckled. "But I'll be honest with you . . . a little good old-fashioned fear isn't a bad thing for your enemies to have, either."

"Wouldn't it be better not to have enemies?"

"Now you're just denying human nature. There will always be people who hate and resent the United States. As messed-up as we are now, as little of a threat as we've become compared to what we used to be, there are still plenty of them out there, just hoping something terrible will happen to us. And if they can nudge along whatever that is, they'll do it, gladly. We've seen plenty of evidence of that today."

"That North Korean missile hitting our fishing boat," Jill said.

"Exactly," Moultrie said. "That was a test, all right, but it wasn't an accident. They aimed that missile right where it landed, just to see how far they could push us. And based on Washington's reaction so far, now they know: they can push us a little farther."

"You could be jumping the gun," Trevor said.

Moultrie shook his head. "I wish I was. But I don't believe that I am. And that's why I believe in this place enough to handle every aspect of its development myself. Because things are just going to get worse, a lot worse, before there's ever a chance of them getting better."

A strained silence settled over the four of them for a long moment before Deb said, "That's enough doom and gloom for right now. Let's go back up to the office. I've got a nice bottle of wine. Maybe we could have a drink and talk about something pleasant."

"Like getting us to sign on the dotted line?" Trevor asked. The bluntness of the question made Jill wince a little. She was usually the more outspoken of the two of them.

Moultrie answered smoothly, though. "Not at all," he said. "I don't want you making any decisions today. This is an important step, a very important step, and I want anyone who decides to join us in the project to be absolutely certain they're doing the right thing. Because who knows . . ." He smiled again. "I could turn out to be totally wrong about the direction the world is headed."

Jill might have hoped that was true, that Moultrie was totally wrong.

But looking back over everything that had happened, she was afraid he wasn't.

Bailey and Chris were smart kids. They knew something was going on. The way their mom and dad had gone to their grandparents' house for dinner on such short notice, the trip out on Saturday afternoon without any explanation of where they were going . . . Those things were just enough out of the ordinary to tell the kids that something was up, and there was a strong chance it wasn't anything good.

Jill could tell that from the way they looked at her. She hated keeping them in the dark, but she couldn't bring herself to tell them that Mom and Dad were trying to figure out what to do in case the world came to an end. Kids had enough . . . kid things . . . to worry about without piling that on top of them as well.

She and Trevor hadn't talked much on the way home. Despite how pleasant Graham and Deb Moultrie had been, the whole experience was a sobering one, starting with the North Korean missile incident.

Jill ordered pizza. They sat around and watched some cheesy old monster movie on TV. Just a pleasant Saturday evening at home. Then Bailey and Chris, both of them yawning, had gone off to bed. Trevor got a beer out of the refrigerator, carried it into the living room, and sat down next to Jill.

"We have to talk about this," he said.

She was watching the news with the sound off. The police in Ohio were digging up some guy's backyard and had found seven bodies so far, with the prospect of more to come.

"Has the world really gone mad," she said, "or are we just better informed?"

"You mean because we have twenty-four-hour news and more social media than anybody can keep up with?" Trevor shook his head. "I don't know. I'd really like to believe the world isn't worse than it used to be, but I just don't know anymore."

Jill couldn't keep a certain savagery out of the gesture as she pushed the button on the remote to turn off the TV. She said, "We have to do it."

"What? Buy space in that . . . project? We need to talk about it, sure, but—"

"We talk things to death, Trev. We debate, we ponder, we mull, we think it over. And usually we don't pull the trigger on anything."

"That's not true. We've built a fine life for ourselves." He waved the bottle he held. "Just look around. Nice house, good jobs, great kids."

"And all of it could go away in a flash. Literally."

Trevor swallowed some of the beer, sat back on the sofa, and frowned. "We live in Tornado Alley, you know. There's a lot more of a chance that an F5 will come along and blow us all away than there is of nuclear war."

"And there's a safe room in the garage, isn't there?" The bedrock in their neighborhood was less than two feet under the ground. The cost of blasting it out and building a storm shelter was prohibitive, or at least they had decided it was. The safe room built into the back corner of the garage was a viable alternative. "A tornado might destroy the neighborhood, but with even a little warning, we can at least survive and rebuild. But if there's some worldwide disaster, or even something that was confined to this country, there won't be any rebuilding for a long time. You know what they say: The people who are killed right away in a nuclear war will be the lucky ones."

"Nobody knows that for sure. It's all theory."

"One that I'd just as soon not test," Jill said. "Just before the story about the serial killer came on, they were talking about how the Russians and Iranians have warned us not to overreact to what happened with the North Korean missile. Not that we were going to do anything anyway, but now they've put us on notice that if we take action against North Korea, they'll take action against us. Can't you see where this is going?"

"It's not going anywhere," Trevor insisted. "Even in the old days, before our government started apologizing for everything it's ever done or ever might do, all that would happen is that we'd talk tough, and then the Russians would talk tough, and then we'd all move on to something else. It's a game. A show." He laughed. "A game show. *Who Wants to Rule the World?*"

"Also not funny."

"It was a *little bit* funny."

Jill didn't say anything. Her phone was lying on the coffee table in front of her. She leaned forward and reached for it.

"I've made up my mind," she said. "You can do what you want."

Trevor took a deep breath. "I'm going to do what I always do," he said. "I'm going to be with you."

Chapter 10

June 5

Writing a check that big was painful for Larkin. Literally painful, because he was gripping the pen so hard it made the little touch of arthritis in his thumb joints twinge.

But he wrote it anyway, then tore it out of the checkbook and slid it across the desk to Graham Moultrie. He and Susan had already signed a big stack of forms that came from the printer wirelessly connected to Deb's computer. Larkin hoped the check for $68,000 would be the last thing he'd have to sign today.

"That should do it," Moultrie said as he picked up the check and put it in a desk drawer.

"You understand that covers Susan and me, plus Jill and Trevor and their kids," Larkin said.

"Of course. When they came in to sign their contracts, they explained that you'd be writing one check for the entire family. That's fine, Patrick. However you want to arrange things like that, it makes no difference to me."

"I just don't want there to be any question about, uh, who gets let in. You know, when the time comes."

"If the time comes." Moultrie smiled. "We all hope and pray it never will."

"Sure. But you know what I mean."

"Of course." Moultrie tapped the fingerprint scanner on his desk. "That's why we have everyone's prints in our system now. That's your key to get in, so to speak, if there's ever any question."

"What if there's a power failure?" Susan asked. "Or an EMP that knocks out all the computers?"

"That's why our mainframes and servers are all down below, behind not only digital firewalls but literal walls hardened against electromagnetic pulses. I want our systems to be as secure as the government's systems." Moultrie grunted. "Actually, more secure, I'd hope, considering how many times the government's computers have been hacked in the past ten years. However, in the unlikely event that everything goes down, we'll have a master hard copy list of all our residents. Nobody who's supposed to be here will be turned away, you have my word on that."

"Turned away," Susan repeated quietly. "I hadn't thought about that. If things go bad . . . really bad . . . people may try to take shelter in here."

With a solemn expression on his face, Moultrie nodded. "That's true. It's liable to be a very unpleasant situation."

"Like people fighting over lifeboats on a sinking ship," Larkin said. "Could get ugly in a hurry."

"That's one reason our outer perimeter is so secure," Moultrie said. "You remember, Patrick, we talked about that the first time you came out here."

Larkin nodded. "Yeah, you thought of that, too."

Moultrie clasped his hands together on the desk and

said, "I can tell what you're thinking, Susan. You're thinking, how can we just turn people away in case of a disaster? How can we refuse to let them in when it means they'll probably die?" He shook his head. "I don't like that possibility any more than you do. But there's a term that someone used once as the title of a story . . . "The Cold Equations." Numbers have no emotion. They add up, or they don't. You can't negotiate with them and convince them to mean anything other than what they do. Only so many people can survive down here. One or two might not make a difference. An extra hundred means that everybody starves to death a couple of years earlier . . . and that couple of years might make all the difference. That's assuming that overconsumption might not cause the air and water recycling plants to break down. Everything is figured to a certain tolerance level. Go much beyond that level and it's not going to work."

"I understand that," Susan said. "But I'm in the business of helping people and saving lives."

"That's exactly what I'm trying to do here, too. I know it sounds cold-blooded as hell, but yes, I'll turn people away—whatever it takes to do that—in order to save the people who are depending on the project for their survival. I've been aware of that possibility right from the start."

A grim silence settled over the four people in the room. It was easy to talk about the end of the world in abstract, Larkin thought, harder to accept just how much death and destruction might be lurking out there in the darkness, waiting to strike senselessly and wantonly.

"All right, that's enough brooding," Deb said. "Maybe

nothing happens except that Graham and I get rich and everybody goes on living."

"That's the spirit," Moultrie said with a chuckle. "You've got the installment-payment paperwork?"

Larkin tapped the stack of documents on the desk in front of him. "Got it, along with all the other disclaimers and waivers and guarantees and indemnifiers."

"You're all set, then." Moultrie stood up and extended a hand. "Welcome to the Hercules Project. Come visit us any time you like while we continue working on the place, and we'll all hope and pray that visiting is all you ever have to do."

"Amen to that," Larkin said as he stood up and gripped Moultrie's hand.

The death toll from the destroyed American fishing boat was seventeen men. Their bodies were never recovered from the icy Bering Sea. A memorial service was held for them, but the President did not attend. He issued a statement that expressed his regret for the incident, then went on to deplore the rhetoric employed by members of the opposition party who considered the boat's sinking to be an act of war, rather than an unfortunate accident in the cause of furthering scientific research. The President did not call on the North Koreans for an apology, nor did they offer one.

Reports were that they were readying for another missile test.

The death toll in Ohio rose to fourteen as authorities continued to recover remains from the backyard of Lorenzo Stanwick. Forensic tests revealed that some of the recovered bones bore teeth marks, as if from gnawing . . . by human teeth.

The death toll from the Hydra virus climbed to eighty with more patients in Texas and Florida succumbing. The surviving patients were under strict quarantine, but it was still uncertain how long the virus was communicable before symptoms began to appear. Spokespersons for the Centers for Disease Control were always grim-faced when the subject of vectors came up at news conferences.

In the aftermath of the mall attack and explosion in Florida, more bodies were discovered during the cleanup. Other, smaller attacks by young, Middle Eastern men followed in the wake of that tragedy, taking place in Boston, Atlanta, and Denver, and in each case the attackers had posted material on their social-media pages linking them to Islamic terrorist groups. The administration and news media barely acknowledged this fact.

A ship in a French port was sunk by a suicide bomb carried next to it in a motorboat by a pair of Syrian brothers.

Russian troops massed on the border of one of the former satellite states of the Soviet Union. Officials of that government appealed for help but received no reply.

Rocket attacks were carried out on Israel. The American President blamed the Israelis for bringing it on themselves.

Iranian troops advanced on the Turkish border. Missile batteries were moved into position, and satellite surveillance appeared to show increased activity around Iranian facilities supposedly involved in producing fuel for nuclear power plants. The United Nations issued a request for clarifications from the Iranians regarding their actions. The Iranians ignored the request.

Earthquakes rattled the Midwest, causing extensive damage but few casualties. An outbreak of violent tornadoes a week later produced more damage and a dozen fatalities.

A large hurricane made landfall in Mississippi, and two more were percolating out in the Atlantic, taking aim at the East Coast. Rioters began looting in several coastal cities, laughingly declaring in videos posted online that they were just getting a jump on the storm.

Students at a college in New England attacked a writer and historian invited to the campus to give a lecture, claiming that his racist, sexist, ableist, cisgender-normative views of history—he had once written a book about the causes of the Civil War and raised the possibility that other things were involved in addition to slavery—were intolerant and a violation of the safe space the students were owed by the university. The writer was left in a coma, and the student union building suffered heavy damage in a protest prompted by the university's failure to issue a trigger warning about the lecture. The university president immediately issued an apology to the protesting students and filed a lawsuit against the writer, who could try to defend himself when and if he came out of his coma.

Email hacks uncovered a plan by one of the major political parties to create as many as ten million entirely fictional voters before the next presidential election, since steps had been taken in many of the states to make it more difficult for illegal immigrants and dead people to vote. The news media mentioned the story briefly, then ignored it.

The governor of a northeastern state announced that police would soon begin confiscating legally owned firearms, and that if anyone didn't like it, they could sue him.

Russian troops moved into the neighboring country, which put up a bloody resistance for two weeks before collapsing. The U.S. adminstration expressed grave concern over this reckless action. The Russians moved in a large occupation force, then began shifting their troops to another border.

Turkish planes bombed the Iranian missile batteries, destroying them but not before several missiles were launched into Ankara. Those missiles carried conventional warheads, not nukes, but still caused widespread destruction. The United States decried this destruction, then blamed Turkey for provoking the Iranians with the bombing raid.

Rockets landed on Tel Aviv again. There was no comment from the administration.

The turmoil caused the stock market to plummet. Chinese interests moved in, buying up huge blocks of American companies and real estate. By executive order, the President committed trillions of dollars to propping up failing banks. To finance this, an emergency tax would be levied on the "wealthy," with the bottom cutoff for such tax being a $40,000 annual income. The legality of these executive orders was widely debated, with most pundits agreeing that the President had no authority to do such things. But the orders were carried out anyway, as Congress debated but took no action.

The North Koreans prepared for another missile test . . .

Chapter 11

"**D**on't put your hand like that," Jill said. "Slide it up a little. Now move your thumb over . . . Ah, right there. Perfect."

"You're sure?" Trevor said.

"Yes. You're good to go. Just . . . gently. Don't rush it. No, wait—Keep both eyes open. Take a breath . . . squeeze . . ."

The Smith & Wesson M&P Shield 9mm boomed as Trevor fired. Jill had him standing and holding the gun correctly, so the recoil wasn't bad. She could tell that he was a little surprised.

"That was loud," he said, his voice muffled some by the ear protectors she wore. "But it didn't kick as much as I thought it would. What do I do now?"

"You've got six more rounds in the magazine," she told him. "That one hit a little low and to the left." Actually, it was quite a bit low and left, but it wouldn't do any good to tell him that. "Adjust your aim a little."

"Okay." He started to line up the second shot.

"Your arms are too stiff. Bend your elbows slightly."

"How's that?"

"Better. Go ahead."

It had been so long since Trevor had been on the range that this was almost like the first time for him. He'd never practiced enough to have any sort of muscle memory for it. He didn't seem to have any natural aptitude for it, either, so Jill had always figured it was better not to push him.

Since they had taken the big step of committing to the Hercules Project, though, she had started thinking that maybe it would be a good idea to get him a little more familiar with firearms. The fact that the situation in the country, and in the world beyond the U.S., had gotten steadily worse over the past few months made her more determined than ever to be prepared if something terrible happened. At her father's suggestion, she had prepared bug-out bags containing nonperishable food, first-aid supplies, extra clothing, blankets, water, and weapons for her and Trevor: a pistol, ammunition, and a multifunction knife/tool.

She wasn't going to arm her children. A part of her thought she needed to teach Bailey and Chris how to shoot, too, but at this point, she hadn't been able to bring herself to do it. Maybe that was stupid—well, no maybe about it, she realized when she thought about it coldly and intellectually, but right now that was where her head—and her heart—were.

Trevor fired out the magazine. His shots were so widely scattered that Jill couldn't even think of them in terms of a grouping. He would get better, though, with practice . . . she hoped.

"Okay, push that button right there," she told him. "That releases the magazine. Now you can reload."

"How's that work again?"

She picked up the loader and showed him. "The top of the magazine goes in there . . . push down . . . the bullet goes there . . . release . . . Now do that six more times."

"It takes a while, doesn't it?" he said as he struggled with some with the technique.

"That's why you have multiple magazines and keep them loaded. You can switch them out and release the slide in a second or so."

"Maybe you can."

"You'll get it," she said.

"You think so? Is it really so important that I can do this?"

"Well, if you never need to, you haven't lost anything except some time."

"And maybe part of my hearing," he muttered.

"But if it ever comes down to you being able to shoot in order for you to save your life . . . or to save the lives of me and the kids . . . wouldn't it be better for you to know what you're doing?"

He looked at her for a long moment, then started to slide the loaded magazine into the pistol's grip.

"Finger away from the trigger first," she reminded him. "Finger never goes in until you're ready to shoot."

"Now you're just talking dirty."

"Slide that on in there, big boy," she told him, "and let's go."

Larkin had grown accustomed to writing the checks to the Hercules Project. He still winced at the amounts, but just like the mortgage on their house, they were paying off the debt in big chunks and would have it off their back sooner, saving money in the process. It was the prudent way to handle things. Of course, thrift was no longer in fashion, starting right at the top with a government that spent money in mind-boggling amounts, faster than seemed humanly possible.

The work of finishing the Hercules Project had continued. Several times, Graham Moultrie had invited the people who had signed up as residents to come out and take a look at what had been done. Larkin had to give him credit for transparency. He had never really warmed up to Moultrie, but the guy seemed to be genuinely devoted to what he was doing.

Moultrie had made his money in commercial real estate, Larkin had discovered through doing some online research into the man's background, so this was hardly the first big project he had tackled. It was maybe the biggest and most important, though. Building a shopping center didn't really compare to the survival of the human race.

Those visits to the project had given Larkin and Susan the chance to meet some of the others who would be there in case of an emergency. Larkin was glad to see that his old friend and fellow Marine Adam Threadgill was among them, along with Threadgill's wife Luisa, their daughter Sophie, and Sophie's husband Jack. If it ever came down to something bad enough to need the refuge, it would be good to have friends there.

In the meantime, life went on, including mowing the lawn, and Larkin was doing that when his next-door neighbor Jim Huddleston pulled into the driveway separating their yards. The door on the Huddleston garage started rolling up, but Huddleston stopped his car in the driveway and got out.

Huddleston waved and looked like he wanted to talk, so Larkin cut the engine on the lawn mower. Huddleston's wife Beth hated that lawn mower, claiming that it was not only noisy but produced an incredible amount of pollution. Larkin had tried to explain to her more than once that he kept the engine tuned up so it worked efficiently, but she drove one of those tiny electric cars, so there really wasn't any reasoning with her. He hoped Huddleston wasn't about to scold him for using the mower. That seemed unlikely. Huddleston tolerated his wife's opinions but had never come across as passionately devoted to them.

"How long have you been out here mowing, Patrick?" Huddleston asked as he walked over.

Maybe he was wrong, Larkin thought. Maybe his neighbor was going to gripe at him after all.

"Fifteen, twenty minutes is all," Larkin said. "I'm almost done."

"Then you haven't heard." Huddleston scrubbed a hand over his face and looked tired. "I'd just left one of the stores when there was a news bulletin on the radio."

Huddleston owned a regional chain of pizza restaurants, one of which was close by and was the "store" he referred to, Larkin knew. He was about Larkin's age, with a brush of sandy hair and the still handsome face of an aging frat boy. Larkin liked him well enough. They'd been to barbecues at each other's houses, drank beer together, gone to the same Super Bowl parties. It was a typical suburban friendship, more of a casual but extensive acquaintance than anything else.

"News bulletins these days are never good," Larkin said.

"There's been another terror attack. Somebody crashed

a light plane filled with explosives into the stands at a college football game in Michigan."

Larkin took a deep breath as his jaw tightened. "Good Lord," he said. "I'm sure there were fatalities."

"More than a hundred so far, they said on the radio. Could go as high as a thousand, people are speculating."

"What the hell is *wrong* with those bastards?" Larkin burst out. "What are they trying to accomplish?"

"They're trying to scare us," Huddleston said. "And they're succeeding. Any time, anywhere I'm around a crowd these days, I worry that something's going to happen. Whether it's a crazy terrorist or a kid who's had his mind messed up by ADHD drugs and video games, it seems there's always *somebody* out there who wants to hurt innocent people."

"Yeah, it sure seems like it," Larkin said. "But hell, you can't just curl up in a little bubble and stay there. You've got to keep on living your life."

"I know. But then you think about the Russians and the North Koreans and the Iranians, and you never know what *they're* going to do, and I tell you, it just . . ." Huddleston shook his head, unable to find the words. "Sometimes I just want to give up and go crawl in a hole, that's all."

The irony of what they had both just said hit Larkin hard. Was that what he and Susan were doing by their involvement with the Hercules Project? Giving up and crawling into a hole?

No, he told himself. It wasn't the same thing at all. The project was a last-ditch option, never to be used unless the shit really did hit the fan. It wasn't like they would be going down there just in case something happened. Disaster would have to be imminent.

The place wasn't a damn resort, after all.

But when he looked at Huddleston, a thought suddenly hit him. He hadn't said one word to the man about the Hercules Project. Huddleston probably didn't even know about it. Graham Moultrie had mentioned that he was relying on word of mouth to inform people, because he wanted to have some control over who applied for residence there. As Moultrie had pointed out, there had to be balance as far as skills and occupations went in order for the community to function.

Huddleston was a good guy, though, competent and dedicated enough to be quite successful in the difficult restaurant business, and his wife Beth, though annoying in some of her opinions, was an experienced elementary school teacher. They were going to need teachers in the Hercules Project, Larkin recalled Moultrie saying, and probably Huddleston would be good at whatever job they gave him. He could always cook pizza, if nothing else, Larkin thought.

All that went through his mind in a second while Huddleston was still standing there shaking his head gloomily over the latest terrible news. Larkin reached out, put a hand on his neighbor's shoulder, and said, "Listen, Jim, there's a place I want to tell you about . . ."

Chapter 12

October 5

"**W**hat a horrible thing," Beth Huddleston said with an expression of revulsion on her face. "Jim, you can't be serious about actually taking part in such madness."

"I don't think it's a bad idea," Huddleston said. "Patrick explained everything to me in detail. Surely it wouldn't hurt just to go take a look."

Beth glared over at Larkin, who was sitting in a recliner across the living room from where the Huddlestons sat on a sofa, and said, "I think even considering such a cruel, callous thing coarsens our culture and harms the country's collective consciousness."

Larkin managed not to grimace, both at what Beth said and the way she said it, but he had to work at controlling the reaction. He'd had plenty of practice, though. He was, after all, white, straight, middle-aged, and retired military, to boot, which meant he was to blame for everything bad that happened anywhere in the world . . . at least in the eyes of some people.

"Look, it's like having insurance," Huddleston said to his wife, unknowingly echoing one of the arguments

Graham Moultrie had used. "You don't think having insurance is bad, do you?"

"It's a manifestation of white privilege, but I suppose it could be considered a necessary evil."

"And you've got to admit, with the way things are going—climate change, pollution, and all that—the world could be in for some rough times."

Huddleston knew the right buttons to push, Larkin thought. Bringing up terrorism and rogue nations overseas wouldn't do any good, because that would just prompt Beth to launch into a tirade about how all that was the fault of the United States and how the rest of the world would leave us alone if we would just leave them alone . . . while continuing to funnel billions of dollars of aid and outright payoffs to them, of course.

"I don't think there's anything wrong with trying to make sure that we survive, do you?" Huddleston went on.

"I suppose not." Beth frowned. "But what about everyone else? How many people can this . . . shelter . . . hold?"

Huddleston looked at Larkin, who wished the guy had left him out of this discussion. Huddleston had insisted that Larkin come into the house with him, though, and help him talk to Beth. If it was a good cause—and Larkin truly believed that the Hercules Project was—then he supposed he had to try.

"The project is designed to support approximately four hundred people," he said.

"Four hundred?" Beth stared at him, as obviously aghast as if he'd just taken a dump on their carpet. "Four hundred? What about all the millions of other people in this area?"

"Well, Beth, they won't all fit in there."

Her glare darkened even more. "Are you making fun of me, Patrick?"

"No, not at all," he said. "It's just a simple fact. The room for people and supplies is limited, and so is the capacity of all the equipment necessary to make those quarters livable. You're talking about physics and math. You can't make numbers stretch any farther than they do."

"So everybody else except your select few can just *die*, is that it?"

"Nobody knows what's going to happen. People just want to have a place to keep themselves and their families safe. That's just human nature."

Beth sniffed contemptuously. "Animal nature is more like it. And people should be trying to rise above that, not pander to it." She looked at her husband and shook her head. "No, Jim, absolutely not. We won't have any part of this, and honestly, I'm a little offended that you would even bring it up. I had a higher opinion of you than that."

Well, that was pretty cold, Larkin thought. Huddleston looked like he might be used to it, though. He shrugged and said, "We can talk about it later—"

"No, we can't." Beth stood up. "I'm not talking about such a disgusting thing ever again."

She stalked out of the living room, casting a glance at Larkin as she went out that told him very plainly he fell into that "disgusting thing" category.

It was good that he didn't give a crap how Beth Huddleston felt about him, or he might have been offended.

"I'm sorry, Patrick," Huddleston said. "I should have kept you out of it. She didn't have to be so . . . so . . ."

"Don't worry about it," Larkin said, as much to save

his neighbor from having to come up with an accurate word to describe his wife as any other reason. "Beth just has strong opinions, that's all. Nothing wrong with that."

"It's nice of you to see it that way. I was hoping I could appeal to her logic. You actually can convince her to change her mind if you can point out logical reasons for it."

Larkin couldn't recall Beth ever changing her mind, or even modifying an opinion slightly, about anything, but he didn't see any reason to mention that. He just stood up and said, "Hey, you gave it a try. That's all you can do, right?"

"Maybe." Huddleston frowned. "Maybe not. I'll work on her."

"Well, good luck." Let the guy take that however he wanted to.

"In the meantime, I can go out there and have a look at the place myself, right?"

"I don't see any harm in that." *As long as Beth doesn't find out about it,* Larkin added to himself.

"There are still units available?"

"I'm pretty sure there are. The project's getting pretty close to being finished, though. You'd have to come up with a big chunk of change in fairly short order, I think."

Huddleston waved a hand. "Not a problem." He laughed, but there wasn't much humor in the sound. "Not compared to some I'll have."

Huddleston had his own problems. So did Larkin. The world might be falling apart, but he still had a book due. He retreated to his office every morning and after-noon to get some pages done, and the manuscript slowly progressed toward completion. It was a little difficult writing about super-competent characters who never seemed to have any trouble solving their problems when most of the time he looked at what was going on in the news and felt utterly helpless to change anything . . . but that was the nature of the game. Dramatic license, he told himself.

The death toll from the attack on the football game in Michigan leveled off at 937. Of course, there were still people in the hospitals who'd been critically injured and might still die. Some of the survivors were maimed for life, and it was unlikely that anyone who'd been in the stadium on that fateful Saturday afternoon would ever be the same. Larkin knew that if he'd been there, any time he heard an airplane he would start looking for cover. He supposed people who had been in Manhattan on 9/11 were the same way.

Nine-eleven seemed relegated to the dim, distant past now. Kids who hadn't even been born then were adults. The attack that had seemed so horrifying, so beyond belief, was now only noteworthy because those who hated the United States hadn't been able to achieve anything of quite the same magnitude again, although the mall bombing in Florida didn't lag that far behind. It hadn't been as visually spectacular, though.

But the hatred, the vicious lust to deal out death and suffering to innocent people . . . that was just commonplace now. People were still shaken when there was a new attack, like the one in Michigan, but then they shrugged their shoulders and asked what did anybody expect when the country had thrown itself wide open to welcome such killers, and then they went on about their business.

The New Normal. Larkin shuddered every time he heard that phrase, but he didn't doubt its truth.

He was surprised to answer the doorbell one afternoon and find Jim Huddleston standing there. Huddleston looked excited and scared at the same time.

"I did it," he said without waiting for Larkin to say hello or invite him in.

"Did what?"

"Got a place for Beth and me at the Hercules Project."

Larkin couldn't stop his eyebrows from climbing pretty high. He said, "Really? I thought Beth was completely opposed to the idea."

"She doesn't know."

You poor, dumb son of a bitch, Larkin thought. But he said, "Come on in and have a beer."

When they were sitting on stools beside the kitchen island with beers in hand, Huddleston said, "I went out there and had a good look around the place, like I told you I was going to."

Larkin nodded and said, "Yeah, sure." He hadn't given the Huddlestons much thought, since he'd had his own work on his mind.

"That guy Moultrie is really impressive. Definitely smart and dedicated to what he's trying to do."

"And he has a good-looking wife."

Huddleston laughed. "Well, yeah. But that's not enough to make me plunk down a hundred and sixty grand."

"You got one of the silo apartments?"

"That's right. Silo A, Apartment Three."

"That's right below us," Larkin said. He wasn't sure

he wanted Beth to be that close by, but hey, he told himself, they were next-door neighbors now, so things wouldn't really change that much. "You didn't tell your wife?"

Huddleston took a long drink from the bottle, as if fortifying himself, and said, "I'll tell her tonight when she gets home from school. She won't like it, but damn it, Patrick, this is important. Especially after what the North Koreans did today."

Larkin frowned. "I've been in my office, working. I don't know what you're talking about."

"The attack on South Korea."

Larkin looked blank and shook his head.

Huddleston took a deep breath and said, "Seoul has been nuked."

Larkin rocked back on his stool like he'd been punched.

"And they've warned us to stay out of it," Huddleston went on. "They claim they have missiles armed with nuclear warheads that can reach the West Coast. There's no proof of that, but—"

"What are we going to do?"

"I don't know. There hasn't been any official response yet, but the Russians have told us to butt out . . . So I imagine that's what we'll do."

Larkin figured as much, too, given the timidity that seemed to run from top to bottom in the administration. Still, if anything was going to shake Washington out of its lethargy, it seemed like an actual nuclear attack might be the thing to do it . . .

Something penetrated his consciousness as he was thinking that, something that made him frown and lift his head. He frowned and said, "You hear that?"

Huddleston said, "No, I . . . Wait a minute. I *do* hear something. Is that . . . the tornado sirens?"

Larkin turned his head to look out the kitchen window, saw the bright fall sunshine spilling over everything, telling him there wasn't a cloud in the sky, and said with a hollow note in his voice, "No. Not tornadoes."

Chapter 13

Jill was working on a prescription when one of the clerks came over to her and said quietly, "People are saying the North Koreans dropped a nuclear bomb on the South Koreans."

Jill's hand jerked a little, causing some of the pills she was counting to scatter across the counter in front of her. "What?"

"It's true," the clerk said. "Well, I don't know if what they're saying is true, but they're really saying it."

Jill swallowed hard. Eighty years had passed since anyone had dropped a nuclear bomb in anger. Her parents hadn't been born the last time it had happened. Her grandparents had barely been teenagers. It had happened countless times in fiction, but in reality it was the stuff of history.

As Jill's heart slugged in her chest, she wanted her kids. She felt an instinctive need to put her arms around Bailey and Chris and draw them to her. She thought about Trevor, too, mere seconds after that, but the kids came first.

"What are we going to *do*?" the clerk asked, her voice a nervous whisper.

"We can't do anything," Jill said. "Even if it's true, it happened on the other side of the world."

"The fallout—"

"The fallout from one blast won't get this far. It might have some effect on Hawaii. And of course, Japan, Taiwan, the other countries over there, I don't know what will happen in them." Jill stiffened her back. "But right here, right now, we have people waiting on their prescriptions, Mandy, so we're going to go ahead and fill them."

Despite the fact that what she really wanted to do, more than anything else, was to run out of the store, jump in her car, and head for the kids' schools.

"Oh," the clerk said. "Okay. It's just . . . the whole thing makes me scared."

"Me, too," Jill said. "Me, too."

It was about five minutes later when a man ran into the store shouting that the storm warning sirens were going off. Jill knew good and well, though, that no storms were in the forecast for today.

Trevor was hunched forward in his chair, squinting at the monitor. Bad for the back, bad for the eyes. He knew that. Occupational hazard, he sometimes told Jill.

A little chime announced that he had gotten an email just as the notification sound came from his phone. He hesitated for a second, unsure which to look at first, then went with the phone. There was a text from Jill. When he tapped it, at first he couldn't quite comprehend the words he was reading.

Nuclear attack on South Korea.

What? A nuclear attack? By who? Well, North Korea,

of course, Trevor thought with a little shake of his head. Although he supposed it could have been some other country besides the usual suspect. But not likely.

He was about to respond but decided to check the email first. It was a news alert from one of the sites he subscribed to, and a click took him right to their front page, where there was a bulletin about the same thing, the nuclear bomb that apparently had gone off in Seoul. It was still uncertain whether the bomb had been dropped from an airplane or delivered via missile, although the latter was considered the most likely. Trevor took in that much at a glance.

He saw, as well, that North Korea was also threatening the United States, and so was Russia. Trevor didn't know if the Koreans had any weapons that could reach the U.S., but the Russians did. Russia was still a credible threat.

A *very* credible threat.

Trevor picked up his phone again to respond to Jill's text, but before he could do anything, another message from her came in. It was just one word.

Hercules?

Trevor's thumbs moved swiftly as he answered: *Now? You think?*

There are sirens going off.

The pit of Trevor's stomach suddenly felt cold. He swallowed hard, looked around. He was alone in the office right now. Most of the people who worked for the company did so from home. He did, too, most of the time, but he liked to come into the office some days. It made him feel more like he had a real job. He was alone today, though, as far as he knew.

Jill had better survival instincts than he did. He knew

that, and he trusted her gut. If she thought it might be a good idea to head for the Hercules Project, then maybe that was what they ought to do.

I'm closer to Bailey's school, he texted. *I'll get her.*

I'll get Chris. Bug-out bags in car?

Yeah. We're good.

He wondered how long it would be before he could say that again and actually mean it.

The sudden commotion that ran through the mall made Adam Threadgill take hold of his wife Luisa's arm and pull her behind one of the big pillars next to the entrance of a store. She said, "Adam, what—"

"Stand there," he told her as he tried to look along the mall to see what was happening. The disturbance was up toward the food court.

Ever since malls had started proving to be such attractive targets for terrorists, he hadn't liked coming here. He never set foot in the place without his carry gun being snugged in its waist holster. Not that his lone gun would really make much difference if the mall came under attack by suicidal, homicidal lunatics, but at least he could put up a fight and maybe, just maybe, save Luisa's life.

Of course, these days terrorist attacks didn't have to be large, well-coordinated affairs. It could be as simple as one nut with a gun or a knife, in which case two or three well-placed rounds *could* make all the difference in the world. Threadgill didn't unholster his pistol because he didn't want to start a panic, but his hand was close to it as he told Luisa, "Stay here and I'll find out what's going on."

"Adam, I'm scared," she said as people continued running and shouting.

"So am I, babe," he told her. He leaned close, put his other hand behind her head, and kissed her hard. "I love you."

"I love you, too, but somehow that isn't making me feel better."

Threadgill knew what she meant. It felt like they were saying good-bye forever.

These days, that might be true.

He turned and trotted toward the center of the mall, toward whatever the commotion was instead of away from it. That was a Marine for you, he thought wryly. Too dumb and stubborn to go the other way.

Then he heard someone yell, "Nuclear war!" That put a whole different slant on things. Threadgill grabbed the arm of a guy rushing past him and jerked him to a stop. The man looked like he was about to take a swing at him, but one look at Threadgill's solid form made him pause.

"What the hell's going on?" Threadgill asked.

"Somebody dropped a nuclear bomb on South Korea," the man said, "and they're coming after us next!"

"Who? North Korea?"

"I don't know, man. I just want to get out of here!"

Threadgill let go of the man's arm and stepped back. He didn't have any right to keep the guy from getting to whoever he wanted to reach before the end came. If the end was indeed coming.

And then he thought about the Hercules Project, wheeled around, and broke into a run back toward his wife.

* * *

Beth Huddleston was about to start talking to her third-grade class about fractions when the speaker on the wall crackled into life and the principal's voice said, "Teachers, just to let you we have a code orange."

She probably sounded normal enough to the kids, but Beth heard the little quiver in the woman's voice and knew something actually was wrong. This was no drill. There was a good reason to put the school on lockdown, which was what code orange meant.

After all the shootings over the years, Beth had taught herself not to think about the possibility of something like that happening at her school, but the little twinge of dread was always there in the back of her mind. She was firmly convinced that such things would never happen if the country would just wake up and make it illegal for anyone to own guns except the police and the military—and they shouldn't have nearly as many guns, either.

As it was, the school had an armed security guard on duty at all times during the day, so Beth listened intently for the sound of shots as she tried to keep her voice calm and said, "All right, children, we're all going to stand up and move over on the other side of the room." Forcing herself not to rush and spook the kids, she walked to the door, locked it, and turned the lights off.

"Oh, my God!" one of the little girls cried. "It's a lockdown! There must be a killer in the school!"

"Hush!" Beth told her as she motioned for everyone to be quiet. "We don't know what's going on. We'll all just stand here quietly, and I'm sure everything will be all right . . ."

Her voice trailed off as even through the school's walls, she heard warning sirens begin to wail.

Jim Huddleston tore out of the house like his tail was on fire. Larkin didn't try to stop him. He was too busy calling Susan.

A glance at the clock had told him that it was late enough for her shift at the hospital to have ended some forty-five minutes earlier. At least, he hoped she hadn't had to stay on duty for some reason. Maybe one of the other nurses couldn't come in and Susan was covering for her. Maybe there had been a bad wreck and Susan didn't feel like she could leave with the place swamped. Working in an ER wasn't like punching a clock in a lot of jobs. You did what needed to be done, when it needed to be done, even if it meant staying past the end of your shift. At least, the dedicated nurses did.

Larkin knew that if his wife was still at the hospital with an emergency breaking, she might not leave. She would want to, but her sense of duty might not let her.

He was a little ashamed, but as he called her he was praying that she'd already started home.

She answered when the phone had barely started ringing. "Patrick?" she said. He heard the anxiety in her voice. "What's going on? I hear sirens, and some people are even running around in the street."

"You're on your way home?"

"Yes, I'm like a mile away."

Larkin closed his eyes for a second in relief, then said, "Thank God. Get on back here as soon as you can.

I'll have our bags ready. Grab the spare one from your car when you get out."

"The bug-out bags?"

He didn't answer her directly. Instead he said, "South Korea got nuked."

"Oh, my God."

"And North Korea and Russia say we're next if we do anything about it."

"But we won't . . . will we?"

"I don't know. Lord help me, I don't know."

"So we're not actually in . . . a nuclear war?"

"Not yet. It could happen any time, though."

"Maybe I should go back to the hospital—"

"No!" Larkin forced himself to take a deep breath and calm down. "Come on home," he went on. "Whatever happens, you'll be where there are people who need your help. Just remember that."

"You're right. Of course, you're right. I'll be there in a few minutes."

Larkin broke the connection. He didn't want to—he would have preferred to stay on with her until she got home—but there was too much to do. He hurried through the house, grabbing not only the specially prepared bug-out bags but also his computer bag and a carrying case with several pistols in it. He had already taken a number of rifles and pistols out to the Hercules Project and stored them in one of the gun vaults there, along with a large supply of ammunition. The anti-gunners could call him a gun nut all they wanted to. He didn't care. Being well-armed was a lot more important than what some people thought about him.

As he carried the bags into the garage, he looked down at the one containing the computer. His backup

USB drives were in there, except for the one that was in his pocket. He was paranoid about losing his work and perfectly willing to admit it. He recalled that earlier he had backed up the current manuscript to the cloud.

Would there be a cloud left by the time this day was over? Would there be anybody left to read his books?

Did any of it even matter anymore?

But on the chance that it *would* matter, he was taking his computer with him.

The garage door rattled and started up. He needed to oil it, he thought as he saw Susan turn in at the end of the driveway. Couldn't have a noisy garage door for the apocalypse.

She pulled into the open space next to his SUV. He had already opened the back gate and was piling the bags inside. She got out of her car, opened the trunk, and took out the bag she kept in it. Larkin took it from her and added it to the cache in the back of the SUV.

"Is this it?" she asked, tense but calm.

"I don't know."

"Have you talked to the kids?"

"Figured we'd call them on the way."

"I'm not going in without them, Patrick."

"I know," Larkin said. "Neither am I."

He slammed the SUV's gate closed.

Chapter 14

Jill could hear the sirens continuing to wail as she drove toward Chris's school, counterpointed by the screech of tires as she took the corners as fast as she could without rolling the crossover.

She had to do a lot of dodging, too, because people weren't paying much attention to things like stop signs and traffic lights. In this crisis, everybody had somewhere they wanted to be *right now*. And she was the same way, gunning through intersections if there was enough of a gap in the chaos for her to make it.

The incessant honking of horns assaulted her ears, too. People were just driving down the streets leaning on their horns. What good that was going to do, she didn't know, but obviously they felt compelled to do it.

She veered around a wreck that had the edge of the road blocked. Somebody had lost control of a pickup, jumped the curb, and slammed into a fire hydrant. A plume of water shot into the air, splattering Jill's windshield as she went by. She hit the wipers to clean it off. She had to be able to see.

Chris's school was only three blocks away now, but the road was getting more clogged with traffic. Everybody with a kid there wanted to reach their child or children. Jill had to slow down, then let out a groan as the vehicles in front of her shuddered to a halt.

This wasn't going to work, and she knew it. She couldn't reach the school, and if she stayed here, she'd be trapped in the traffic jam.

But there was a cross street just a couple of cars ahead, and she knew if she could reach it, she could circle around and come up behind the school. A drainage ditch blocked that side of the campus, so she couldn't drive right up to the rear of the school, but she could get close enough to retrieve Chris. She hoped the smaller street back there wouldn't be blocked like this main boulevard was.

That plan formed in her mind in an instant. She wrenched the wheel over and jammed her foot down on the gas. The crossover bumped up over the curb and tore across somebody's front lawn at an angle. Jill was sorry for any damage she did, but every instinct in her body told her it no longer really mattered.

As she jolted off the curb into the cross street, she checked the rearview mirror, worried that other people would follow her example and flock to the back of the school, creating a logjam over there, too. The idea didn't seem to have occurred to anyone else just yet, though. The street was clear of vehicular traffic, although panicked pedestrians ran here and there.

Jill took the next two corners hard and fast. She rammed the crossover ahead on the street that ran next to the drainage ditch. When she could see the school on the other side of it, she hit the brakes and skidded to a stop on the side of the road. She was out of the vehicle in a flash, although she paused just long enough to lock it. One thing an emergency always brought out was the lawless element interested only in looting.

The sides of the ditch were concrete, the bottom covered with a couple of inches of mud and scummy water. Jill slid down, splashed through it with no thought for her shoes, and bounded up the other side. A high chain-link fence separated the ditch from the school's playground. She hit it on the move and scrambled up it, grateful now for all the hours she had spent working out. Thankfully, there was no barbed wire at the top. This was a school, after all, not a prison.

She landed, running, in the playground.

The first door into the school she came to was locked. Of course it was, she thought. As soon as the sirens went off, the place had probably gone into lockdown. Since this was a fairly new school, it had been designed to make it difficult for intruders to break in. She couldn't shatter a window or kick down a door.

Muttering bitter curses, she ran around the building to the front and found chaos waiting for her.

Dozens of parents had made it to the school and demanded to be let in so they could get their kids. From the looks of things, the principal was maintaining the lockdown, though. Men and women yelled and pounded on the glass doors at the entrance. As Jill forced herself into the mob, she peered through the glass and saw several terrified women inside. They had to be able to recognize at least some of the parents, but they still didn't know what to do. The threat of a lawsuit hung over so much of modern life, including the educational system, that anything out of the ordinary tended to paralyze bureaucrats.

Behind Jill, someone screamed and a man shouted, "Get out of the way!"

She looked back and saw the crowd scattering in a frenzy as a van plowed through, picking up speed as the path cleared. Jill scrambled out of the way. The van flashed past her and crashed into the locked doors, blasting them open, shattering glass, spraying shards everywhere. The vehicle came to a stop in the school's foyer.

People fought their way past it, ignoring the carpet of broken glass on the tile floor, and scattered through the school in search of their children. The principal and other administrators screamed at them to stop, but no one paid any attention to them.

Jill certainly didn't as she wedged her way into the school and then dashed along one of the corridors toward Chris's classroom. She knew where she was going, knew this school quite well from all the Meet the Teacher nights, the Open Houses, the field trips, and the special days when the parents could come and read with their kids or eat lunch with them, and she felt a sharp pang of loss as she realized she would probably never experience any of those things again.

There was Chris's room. The door was closed. Jill appeared to be the first parent to reach it. She grabbed the knob and twisted it. Still locked. She slammed her palm against the glass and shouted, "Mrs. Fletcher! Mrs. Fletcher! It's Jill Sinclair. I have to get Chris. Let me in!"

A middle-aged woman with eyes so big they seemed about to pop out of her head appeared on the other side of the glass. She looked past Jill, maybe to make sure no one was forcing her to do anything, and then reached down to throw the bolt on the door. She stepped back quickly as Jill flung it open.

"Is it true?" the teacher said. "Is it a nuclear attack?"

"Maybe. We don't know yet. But you have to let me take Chris." Jill thought about the Walther in its holster inside the waistband of her slacks and had a crazy vision of her sticking the gun in Mrs. Fletcher's face to force her to back off and give her her son.

It didn't come to that. Mrs. Fletcher turned her head and said, "Chris! Grab your things and go with your mom!"

Jill's heart pounded hard in relief as she saw Chris hurrying toward her. Then she looked at all the other kids, who were scared out of their minds, and wished she could take all of them with her.

But the only thing she could do was grab Chris's arm, look at Mrs. Fletcher, say, "Good luck to you," and then run along the hall toward a door that led out onto the playground. Like most of the school doors, it would open from the inside even though it was locked from the outside. The two of them burst through it and started at a run toward the drainage ditch.

"You're gonna have to climb, kid," she said as they approached the fence.

"Mom . . ." Panting a little. "Are we gonna be all right?"

"You bet."

The sirens still howled. Jill looked at the sky. Clear, blue, beautiful. No sign that devastating, fiery death might lurk up there.

Behind them, the cry of the mob mixed with the sirens.

In the third-grade hall, Jim Huddleston thought he saw Larkin's daughter Jill going out the back door with her son, but he only caught a glimpse of them as he started hammering on the door of Beth's classroom.

"Beth, open up!" he shouted through the glass. "It's me!"

She jerked the door open while he was pounding on it, so suddenly that he stumbled forward and bumped into her. He grabbed her, held her to him.

"Thank God! Are you all right?"

She didn't answer. Instead she said, "What is it, Jim? I heard people yelling, and those awful sirens . . . The principal said something about an attack—"

"The North Koreans and the Russians are threatening to nuke us," Huddleston said. "We've got to go."

"But . . . but surely the President will do something . . . This can't be happening . . ."

"The President is an incompetent asshole! He always has been. You just can't see it with those blinders you wear!"

"Jim! Everyone has a right to an opinion, but talking like that isn't productive."

Huddleston wanted to rage at her, but he caught hold of his surging emotions and put his hands on her shoulders.

"We have to go," he said again, trying to stay as calm and reasoned as possible because that's what Beth responded to.

"Go where?"

"The Hercules Project."

Her eyes got big in a way that even the threat of nuclear annihilation hadn't been able to accomplish. "You went against what I told you to do?"

"Damn right I did, and now I'm glad. We've got a

place to go. We can live through this, but you've got to come on, now!"

"But I can't . . ." She turned her head to look at the children huddled against the far wall. "I can't leave the class."

"Their parents will get them." Huddleston couldn't help himself. He gave her a little shake. "If we stay here, we'll *die*!"

For several seconds that seemed like an eternity, she just stared at him. Whether she didn't understand or just refused to accept what was happening, he didn't know. Finally, she said, "I'm sure if we just try to talk to them—"

"The Russians and the Koreans?" Huddleston laughed and heard the hysterical edge in the sound. "They don't care! This is the excuse they've been waiting for to blow us off the face of the earth!"

All the children were crying in terror now. Huddleston knew he was scaring them, but he didn't care. He damn well wanted to scare his wife right now.

"Oh, God!" Beth cried in a broken voice. She threw her arms around his neck. "We're going to die!"

"Not if we get out of here now," Huddleston said grimly.

She pulled back a little and asked, "There's a chance?"

"Yeah. Maybe."

"Then let's go!"

She shoved him out the door, followed him from the classroom, and never looked back, even though several of the children were screaming her name.

Chapter 15

Trevor was halfway to Bailey's school, fighting crazed traffic and looking for shortcuts every foot of the way, when his phone rang through the car's Bluetooth system. He saw Jill's name on the dashboard display, although he would have recognized the ringtone he had given her anyway. It felt like his heart was at least halfway up his windpipe and trying to crawl the rest of the way as he thumbed the button on the steering wheel and said, "Jill! Are you all right?"

"I'm fine," her answer came back, stopping his heart from its ascent, at least for the moment. "I have Chris, and he's okay, too."

"Oh, thank God, thank God," Trevor said. He had never been much of a religious person, veering from agnostic to atheist and back again, but right at this moment he believed every word he said. Today, the whole world was a foxhole.

"We're on our way to the project," Jill went on. "I heard from Mom and Dad. They're heading out there, too."

"I'll be there as soon as I can get Bailey. The traffic is insane!"

"I know. I went through the same thing around the

elementary school. Just be careful, okay? People are getting more panicky by the minute, and when people panic, they get desperate."

"Yeah. It might help if they'd turn off those awful sirens. Surely everybody knows by now what's going on."

In point of fact, though, *nobody* knew what was going on, he realized, and that made things even worse. It was still possible this crisis could blow over. The President would find the right words to say to the Russians and the North Koreans, and things would calm down. It was a shame about Seoul and all the South Koreans who had been killed, of course, but even so, that wasn't sufficient reason to plunge the entire world into a nuclear holocaust . . .

"Trev." He shoved those hopeful thoughts away as he realized she was still talking to him. "Trev, you've got the Shield in the car, don't you?"

"Shield? What—Oh, the gun! Yeah, I have it. It's in that little case under the seat."

"You should have two loaded magazines with it. I put them in there. Get it out and load it. Release the slide."

"But then it'll be ready to shoot." He remembered that much from the trip to the range.

"That's right. Keep it handy in case you need it. But *don't* act like you're going to use it unless you're really ready to use it. You don't want to start waving it around just to scare people, because they're liable to *get* scared and start shooting at *you*. So be sure of what you're doing."

He shook his head, even though she couldn't see him. "I don't like this, babe—"

"Nobody does. *But you bring me my daughter, whatever it takes.* Do you understand?"

Trevor swallowed. "I understand." He'd been driving

while they were talking, gunning the gas, slamming the brakes, trying to take advantage of every opening in the traffic he could find. "I'm getting pretty close to the school now—Oh, crap."

"What is it?"

"Looks like traffic's at a standstill up ahead."

"I encountered the same thing. Go around, Trev. Find a back way. Get as close as you can, stop somewhere it looks like you can still get out, and then go the rest of the way on foot if you have to."

"All right. I understand. Once I have Bailey, I come straight to the project?"

"That's right. Don't stop for anything—or anybody."

Trevor swallowed again, even harder this time. That was maybe the most difficult part of this whole terrible thing. Knowing that so many people would be left to whatever fate had in store for them. Logically, he knew he couldn't save anyone except his daughter, but at the same time, that knowledge gnawed at his guts.

"I love you," he said.

"I love you, too. Get our daughter."

"On my way," he said. "I'll call you when I have her."

He broke the connection, then yanked the wheel hard to the left and roared along a side street. He didn't know these roads around the school as well as he should have, considering all the times he and Jill had been here for various activities. He didn't have the greatest memory for directions and landmarks, though.

Frustration was mounting in him when he spotted the school between two houses. Somehow, he had managed to get close to it. He stopped and stepped out, leaving one foot in the car. All he had to do was cut through a side yard, climb a fence, and he'd be on the school grounds.

He reached back into the car, cut off the key, and was about to head for the school when he remembered what Jill had said about the gun.

Trevor looked around. Some people were running in the street in the next block, but there was nobody close to him. He didn't think he'd need the gun, but still he hesitated. She had told him to load it and keep it with him, and she was usually right . . .

He sat down behind the wheel again, reached under the seat, and found the hard-plastic case that held the 9mm pistol and two magazines.

It didn't take him long to slide one of the loaded magazines into the gun. He was about to release the slide when he realized he didn't know how to put the safety on. He didn't want to carry around a loaded gun that could go off with just a little pressure on the trigger. Better to leave the slide locked back, he decided, than to take a chance on an accidental discharge.

When he stood up again, he started to tuck the pistol in the waistband of his jeans. Texas was an open-carry state, so he wouldn't be breaking the law by doing that. Or would he? He seemed to remember that open carry was legal only as long as the weapon was properly holstered and secured. He didn't have a holster, and sticking the gun in his pants didn't seem very secure. Maybe if he pulled his shirttails out and let them hang over, that would count as concealed carry. He could try to look it up on his phone, he supposed . . .

"Hey! Hey, buddy, I need your car! I gotta get outta here!"

Startled, Trevor swung around and saw a man running toward him. The man's face was twisted and grotesque, and for a second Trevor had the wild thought that this wasn't a nuclear war, it was the zombie apocalypse.

But then he realized the guy was just scared out of his wits, and the stranger suddenly looked even more terrified as he stumbled to a halt, threw out his hands toward Trevor, and started backing away. "Don't shoot, please don't shoot!" he cried.

Trevor looked down and realized he had the Smith & Wesson in his hand, gripped firmly and pointed in the direction of the man who'd accosted him. Evidently the man hadn't noticed that the slide was locked back. He turned abruptly and sprinted the other way, obviously figuring it would be easier to steal a car from somebody else.

"Huh," Trevor said.

He shoved the pistol into his waistband, slammed the car door, and locked it. Then he hurried through the side yard toward the fence that ran along the school property.

Jill would have been up and over that fence in a matter of seconds, he thought as he struggled to climb up, threw his leg over, and make it down the other side without falling and breaking his neck. He let go and jumped the last couple of feet, stumbling as he landed. People were running around the school from the front. Trevor joined them. One man had what looked like a tire tool of some sort. He jammed it into the gap next to a door lock and heaved on it. Two more men rushed to help him. With a grinding squeal, the door came open, and there was a chaotic stampede into the school as people shouted for their children.

Trevor realized belatedly that he had no idea where Bailey would be at this time of day. He stumbled along in the mob thronging the hallway, hoping he would spot her, when instead he caught a glimpse of a girl named . . . Ashley? No, Amber. That was it. She was one of Bailey's best friends. He lunged and caught hold of her arm.

She screamed and tried to pull away, but he hung on and raised his voice to say, "Amber! Amber, calm down! It's Mr. Sinclair! I'm Bailey's dad, remember?"

She ought to remember. She had gone to enough ice cream parlors and pizza places and bowling alleys with them for various parties. She stopped jerking against his grip when she recognized him.

"Mr. Sinclair! Have you seen my mom or dad?"

Trevor didn't recall what either of Amber's parents looked like, so he just shook his head. "Where's Bailey?" he asked. "Do you know where I can find her?"

Amber pointed with her free hand. "I think she was in math class, but she may not be there now."

If she wasn't, he was screwed, Trevor thought. He would just have to keep searching for her.

Because there was no way he was going to the Hercules Project without her.

"Go find your folks," he told Amber as he let go of her and started toward the classroom she had pointed out. It was like swimming against the tide, but he made it eventually.

The door was wide open. Half a dozen kids were still inside, looking scared and lost, but no adult. The teacher must have cut out as soon as he or she got a chance.

"Dad!"

The cry made Trevor's heart jump. He turned and saw Bailey running toward him from a corner. He opened his arms and she came into them with a flying leap. She hugged him tight, and he returned the embrace, holding her so that her feet were off the floor.

Then she wiggled a little and said, "Dad, what's that?"

He realized he had her pressed up against the gun. Quickly, he set her down and said, "Don't worry about that, let's just go."

"That's one of Mom's semi-automatics. Why do you have a gun? What's going on? Is it really the end of the world?"

"What? No! Not the end of the world, not at all. But we've got to go now. We need to meet up with Mom and your brother."

"At that place out in the country? The one where we're supposed to go if anything really bad happens?" They had told the kids a little about the Hercules Project, without going into all the details that might prove to be too disturbing.

"That's right. We may have to stay there for a while."

"Then it *is* the end of the world!"

"Not if your mom and I have anything to say about it, honey," he told her, wishing that he was really as confident as he was trying to sound. If Jill had been here, she could have said it and meant it.

But then he realized that he *did* mean it. Whether he was cut out for things like this or not, he was going to get his daughter to safety, one way or another.

Chapter 16

"Thank God," Susan breathed as she lowered the phone from her ear. "Jill just talked to Trevor again. He has Bailey, and all four of them are headed out here."

"That's good," Larkin said as he turned the SUV's wheel and veered around a car stopped on the side of the road so that half of it stuck out into his lane. Nobody was around or inside it, as far as he could tell. He had seen a surprising number of stopped, apparently abandoned vehicles. He wasn't sure why the threat of nuclear war seemed to make cars quit running, but evidently it did.

Maybe there were so many people driving, it was just a matter of averages. He had traveled on this winding country road hundreds of times and never seen it like this, almost bumper-to-bumper heading away from town. At least the cars were moving on, although at a much slower speed than usual. The line of traffic stretched as far ahead and behind him as he could see. People honked from time to time, but it wasn't the cacophony Larkin might have expected.

"This is like that time we were down at the coast and the hurricane came in," Susan said. "Everybody just wanted to get away from there as quickly as possible."

"Yeah. People figure big cities will be the main target

in a nuclear attack, so they're heading for the sticks. Not sure they can get far enough away in the time that we've got, though."

Susan leaned forward slightly in the seat and turned her head to peer out through the passenger window at the sky. "It looks so peaceful," she said. "Nothing up there but a few fluffy white clouds." She looked over at Larkin. "But we won't see anything coming until it's too late, will we?"

"We probably won't see anything coming at all," he said.

"Well, that doesn't make me feel the least bit better."

A humorless grin stretched across his face. "Another couple of miles and we'll be there. Then I'll feel better."

"I won't. Not until Jill and Trevor and the kids are there with us."

Larkin nodded. She was right about that. As long as their loved ones were out there, unaccounted for, he couldn't rest easy. And just because Susan had talked to their daughter didn't mean they would all make it safely to the project.

Another vehicle was stopped on the side of the road ahead, this time a pickup. At least, with everyone trying to get away from the city, there was little if any traffic coming the other way, so there was room for the cars to get around the ones that were stopped.

In this case, though, three men ran out into the road just as Larkin started to go around. They were yelling and waving their arms, and Larkin had no choice except to hit the brakes unless he wanted to run over them.

One of the men hurried around to the driver's window. All of them were in their thirties, dressed in jeans and work shirts. The pickup had a sign on the door for a landscaping company, and a zero-turn mower and other pieces of equipment were in the back.

"Thanks for stopping, man," the one who came to the window said. Larkin had lowered the glass a few inches. "You wouldn't believe how many times we had to jump out of the way of people who didn't. We need a ride."

"Wouldn't do you any good," Larkin said. "We're not going very far."

"Not going very far?" the man repeated as he stared in disbelief. "You need to get as far away from the Metroplex as you can! They're gonna nuke the place!"

Larkin wasn't about to tell this man about the Hercules Project. The fewer people who knew about that, other than the residents, the better. He was starting to wish he'd kept going and made these guys jump out of the way again.

"We don't know that they're going to nuke anybody. Anyway, you'll have to get a ride with somebody else."

"You got room in there, man. We can see that." The man's face twisted angrily. "And we're gettin' tired of bein' ignored. We got a right to live just as much as anybody else."

"Patrick," Susan said in a low, worried voice.

Larkin glanced in her direction. Through the glass on her side, he saw that the other two men had taken shovels out of the back of the pickup and assumed vaguely threatening stances. This was just a standard SUV. A few swings with those tools would break the windows out.

Larkin turned his head back toward the man on his side and started to say, "Sorry—" when the man reached his hand in through the gap, fingers clawing at Larkin's face.

Larkin hit the button that raised the window, pinning the man's arm. He howled in pain and outrage, the sound blending with the impatient honking that came from the vehicles stopped behind the SUV. Larkin's foot came down hard on the gas. The SUV leaped forward, and the man whose arm was caught in the window had to run and try to keep up or lose his balance and be dragged. At the same time, his two companions lunged at the SUV and swung the shovels. Larkin's quick move had caught them unprepared, however. Instead of hitting the windshield or the passenger window, the shovels clanged off the vehicle's top.

Larkin kept accelerating. The man just a few inches away on the other side of his window was screaming now. Larkin pushed the button again, and as the window lowered, the man's arm came free and he fell and rolled on the asphalt, out of control from his momentum. Something banged off the back of the SUV, and when Larkin checked the rearview mirror he saw a shovel lying in the road. One of the men had flung it after them in fear and rage.

The man who had tried to grab Larkin through the window was still on the ground. One of his friends ran up to him and started trying to haul him to his feet. Both of them had to scramble to get out of the way of an accelerating car.

Larkin couldn't see any of them after that and turned his attention ahead again.

Susan was breathing hard. Her eyes were wide. "They

were going to hurt us," she said. "They were going to hurt us and take the SUV."

"Yeah," Larkin said. "They would have tried."

He glanced down at the Colt 1911 .45 lying on the seat between them. He hadn't reached for the gun back there . . . but he would have if he'd needed to in order to shed themselves of the would-be thieves.

What was troubling was that a few hours earlier, those guys probably weren't thieves at all and wouldn't have been so quick to grab tools and try to turn them into weapons. They were just guys who'd gone to work that morning not worrying about anything other than getting through the day and then going home to their families, if they had them, or spending their evening however they usually did. Nobody got up thinking, *Well, the world's going to end today and there's not a damn thing I can do about it.*

After the brief stop, Larkin had caught up to the traffic in front of him. Now the vehicles ground to a halt in the road. Susan, recovered a little from her fear, leaned forward and asked, "What is it?"

"Don't know," Larkin said. "I can't see." As he watched, though, peering up the line of cars, he spotted figures reeling back and forth between some of the vehicles. Men flailed at each other with fists. "Oh, crap! It's a fight. Somebody else must have tried to take somebody's car."

"There's no way around this, is there?" Susan asked, her voice tight with anxiety.

"No, this is really the only road in. Moultrie probably didn't think about that, since everything else about the site is perfect."

"I didn't mean that, necessarily. I meant . . . there's no way to keep people's worst nature from coming out in a crisis, is there?"

Larkin grimaced. He had thought the same thing, but he said, "That's not always true. It depends on the person. Think about all the disasters, natural or man-made, where people rise above what they usually are and perform great acts of heroism. Sometimes they save a lot of lives, even at the cost of their own."

"But even in a hurricane or something like that, people know it's not the end of the world."

"If you don't make it, it's the end of *your* world. That doesn't stop most people from pitching in to help."

"But some don't. I mean, look at all the looters every time there's a riot. Some people are always out just for themselves, and that just gets worse when there's an emergency."

Larkin couldn't argue with that. He just said, "That's why we're prepared . . . and why we'll do whatever it takes to save our family."

Susan sighed. "I wish they were all with us right now."

"So do I, babe. So do I."

A few minutes of tense silence went by while Larkin watched the brawl up ahead. If the violence spilled in their direction, he wouldn't take any chances this time. He would grab the 1911 and be ready for trouble.

More men got out of their vehicles and shoved a stalled car out of the way as the battle moved onto a grassy hillside next to the road. Larkin wondered if the stalled car was what had started the fight. The traffic began to move forward again. Overall, the clog was getting worse, though. They measured their progress now in feet. At this rate, it might soon be inches.

And it might take too long to reach the Hercules Project. Larkin glanced up at the sky, wondered what was up there. What might be speeding toward them at this very second . . .and the news on the local radio stations was scrambling to stay on top of the different scenarios, some accurate, some fake . . . but it was impossible to know the difference.

"The hell with this," he muttered. "There's gotta be another way."

"Can you get around on the shoulder?"

He shook his head. "Too many stalled cars. The ground drops off too much on this side, and there are too many culverts. We'd get stuck if we got too far off the road."

"Maybe the other shoulder?"

The lack of traffic inbound toward Fort Worth made that a possibility, Larkin thought. There was a double line of outbound traffic now, but as far as Larkin could see, the far shoulder was at least partially clear. If he took off over there, other people were bound to follow him, and that would just create *three* lines of traffic. It wouldn't be long before that third line stalled for some reason, too.

But it wouldn't matter if he and Susan could get close enough to the project before that happened. They could get out and carry the bags and guns if they had to. He'd been stashing extra food and supplies in their apartment for the past few weeks, ever since the place was close enough to completion for him to do so, so they hadn't had to bring too much with them on this last mad dash for safely . . .

This mad dash that had turned into a crawl.

Larkin checked his side mirror, saw an opening, hauled the wheel over. Somebody honked as he veered left, but nobody ran into him, so he didn't care. Let 'em get mad. It didn't matter anymore. When he got over in the second lane, he could see the other shoulder even better. It was empty.

He hit the gas and popped out, still only moving about ten miles an hour, but it seemed faster as he passed the other vehicles. In the rearview mirror, he saw others following his example, as he had known they would.

"We're on the wrong side of the road now," Susan said. "I guess we should have thought of that. We'll never be able to get back over and turn into the gate."

"Doesn't matter," Larkin said. "We'll ditch the SUV and go in on foot. We can take everything with us that we really need. If things get as bad as it looks like they might, we won't be driving anywhere for a long time anyway."

"You're right." Susan took a deep, shuddery breath. "Oh, Patrick, I'm so scared. I keep thinking that at any second there's going to be a bright, blinding light, and then . . . and then . . ."

"Try not to think about it," he told her. "I know that's hard, but we're alive, the kids are alive, and nothing's really happened yet—"

The windshield exploded inward, shattering and spraying glass at them.

Chapter 17

It wasn't a bomb, because he was still alive. Some small part of Larkin's brain knew that. The blast wave from a nuclear explosion would have killed them, possibly even vaporized them. But other than shock and some stinging pain on his face and hands where flying slivers of glass had cut them, he seemed to be all right. Instinct and reflexes had closed his eyes in time to protect them.

Susan was screaming, though, either in shock or pain or both. He forced his eyes open and reached over to grab her, fear making his heart pound as he saw the blood on her face.

Before he could get his hands on her, something else crashed into the driver's side window and sprayed him with more glass. Larkin flinched away from it, but something made his hand drop to the seat and scoop up the Colt.

He twisted toward the window, bringing the gun around and shoving down the safety with his thumb as he did so. A man stood there, a long tire iron gripped in both hands as he swung it back to strike again. The window was already broken out, so this time that blow would be aimed at Larkin.

Larkin shoved the Colt at the man and fired twice. The shots were deafening inside the SUV.

The two rounds struck the man in the body and knocked him away from the vehicle. He landed on his back and slid down into the ditch. Larkin jerked his head around to look for any other threats but saw none. He turned back to Susan.

"I'm all right!" she cried before he could ask if she was hurt. "Just drive! Go!"

Larkin punched the gas and lurched ahead before any of the other vehicles could pull out in front of him. He gripped the wheel with his left hand and kept the pistol in his right.

"The blood—" he said without taking his eyes off what was in front of him.

"The glass cut me in a few places, that's all. You have blood all over your face, too, Patrick."

He did? A glance in the mirror told him she was right. He looked pretty gruesome, too. He lifted his right arm and sleeved some of the gore from his face. Susan found some tissues and wiped at her face, but he didn't care about getting his shirt blood-stained.

"Why did that awful man do that?"

"I guess he wanted a ride," Larkin said. "Or to kill us both and steal the SUV."

"You . . . you killed him."

"We don't know that."

But the chances of anybody surviving two rounds from a 1911 at close range in the midsection like that were pretty damned small, Larkin realized. It was almost a certainty that he *had* killed the guy with the tire iron. He knew that he'd been acting in self-defense, and in defense of his wife, too, and he had killed the enemy during wartime . . .

But this wasn't a war, and that guy hadn't been an enemy, at least not when the day started. He'd just been another Texan until terror had driven him to lash out.

Dear God, was this what they were all doomed to become? Animals rending and clawing at each other?

Larkin shoved that thought out of his head. This was no time to debate morality, even with himself. The only thing that really counted was survival. His survival, and that of his loved ones.

Everything else could be hashed out later . . . if there was a later.

A couple of times he was forced to swing far enough out that his left-hand wheels were off the shoulder and coming dangerously close to either a drop-off or a culvert. But they had covered at least half a mile this way before people ahead of him saw him coming in their mirrors and began to pull out, following his example even though they were in front of him. Larkin glared futilely.

"You can't blame them," Susan said. "They just want to get to somewhere safer, too."

"I know, I know."

She had slipped off a shoe and used it to brush broken glass off the seat between them. Little trails of drying blood gave her face a striped look. She leaned over and reached toward him. "You've got a little piece of glass stuck in your cheek . . . hold still . . ."

She plucked it free. He said, "Ouch."

"Don't be a big baby."

"Yes, ma'am. You're a trained medical professional, though. It shouldn't have hurt."

"Just be thankful I'm not picking broken glass out of your butt. I've had to do that at work, you know."

"Could be interesting, depending on whose butt it was."

"Trust me, it wasn't the least bit interesting."

Larkin grinned tightly. It said something for the human spirit that they could banter like this when they'd been under attack just a few minutes earlier—and when the ultimate doom could fall on their heads at any second, with no warning. But what good would it do to curl up in a ball and cry? Wasn't it better to keep fighting?

One of the cars up ahead got too close to a culvert. Its left front wheel fell in with what must have been a bone-jarring thump, and the car came to a dead stop, tilted so its right rear tire was off the ground.

"Oh, hell!" Larkin said as he smacked his left hand against the steering wheel in frustration. Enough of the car was still on the shoulder that no other vehicles would be able to get by.

"Can't they back out of there?" Susan asked.

Larkin shook his head. "Not with that wheel off the ground. If somebody could get a jack under the front . . . or maybe enough guys lifting . . ." He looked around, then turned the .45 and extended it butt-first toward his wife. "Here, take this."

"What?" Susan stared at the gun. "I don't shoot."

"The safety's off. All you have to do is point it and pull the trigger. Hold it with both hands if you have to fire it. It's got a kick to it. And *don't* fire it unless you're absolutely sure you need to."

"Patrick, what are you going to do?"

He opened the door. "See if I can get the way cleared so we can go on. And I'm counting on you to stand guard while I'm doing it."

Susan looked like she wanted to argue, but Larkin was already out of the SUV. There was a woman behind the wheel of the car that had gone into the culvert, and she had several children in there with her. Larkin turned to the vehicles in line behind him and waved, then pointed to the stuck car and shouted, "Come on! We've got to get it out of there!"

For a couple of seconds, nothing happened. Then a few doors swung open and several men climbed out of their vehicles. "Come on!" Larkin called again, and they trotted forward.

Larkin led half a dozen men to the culvert and pointed to where they needed to stand. As they positioned himself, he gestured to the driver for her to roll down the window. She looked like she didn't want to because she was so shaken and frightened, but after a moment she complied.

"We're gonna lift on the front end," Larkin told her. "Watch me, and when I nod, you put it in reverse and give it some gas. Not too much, though. There's not a lot of room between you and the car behind you. When you're out of this hole, you can cut your wheels back to the right and ease around it. Understand?"

"I . . . I think so," the woman said. "I didn't mean to cause trouble—"

"It's okay. Just keep an eye on me. You'll get out of here."

Whether that would be enough to save her life and the lives of the kids in the car with her, Larkin had no idea. Like everybody else out here, all the woman could do was hope.

Larkin took his place among the other men, reaching under the car's bumper and finding a place to grab hold. "Ready?" he asked, and got nods and grunts of acknowledgment. "Lift!"

More grunting as they put their backs into it. Larkin felt his muscles straining and creaking. But the car's front end came up, and he could tell that both rear wheels were on the ground again. He nodded to the driver.

She was too nervous to follow his advice about taking it easy. She tromped the gas hard, and the car lurched backward, banging heavily into the sedan behind it. The driver of that car, an older guy who hadn't gotten out to help, opened his door and leaned out to yell, "Hey!"

One of his headlights was broken, but Larkin didn't figure that was going to matter. He and the other men let go of the car and Larkin checked to make sure the bumpers hadn't locked. They hadn't, so he thumped the top of the car a couple of times and told the woman through the open driver's window, "You're good to go, lady. Just be careful."

"Thank you!" she called. She eased forward, missing the edge of the culvert this time.

"What about the damage to my car?" the older man said.

"If that's all that happens to it," Larkin said, "consider yourself one lucky bastard."

Larkin ignored the glare the man gave him and walked back to the SUV while the other men who had pitched in returned to their vehicles. He brushed more glass off the seat and then got in.

Susan heaved a sigh of relief and said, "I was afraid someone would try to jump you while you were out there, Patrick. I . . . I don't know if I could have shot anybody."

"Not even to protect me?" he asked with a grin.

"Well . . . even if I tried, I don't know if I could have hit them. I might have shot you instead."

"Don't think I didn't worry about it," he said as he took the Colt back from her. His smile took any sting out of the words, but there was some truth to what he said. He really should have insisted that she go to the range with him more often.

The slow procession rolled on.

There was plenty of news on the radio, of course, but at the same time, there was no news. Nobody seemed to know anything about what was going to happen. The South Korean army and air force had tried to strike back against the North, resulting in an all-out war between the two countries, but from what Larkin could gather, the nuclear strike had been such a crippling blow that South Korea wouldn't be able to muster much of a fight. It was likely the "war" would be over in a day or two.

What worried Larkin was the tone of everything the Russians said. The statements had a threatening stridency to them, as if the U.S. had already declared that it was going to attack North Korea and the Russians were foaming at the mouth to jump in. Washington's official stance was that the "incident" was "still under investigation." As with any crisis, the administration wanted to pretend to investigate until the problem went away on its own. With the attitude coming from the Russians, though, Larkin had his doubts about this one going away.

As they started slowly down a hill, Susan pointed and said, "I can see the gate up ahead!"

So could Larkin. The entrance to the Hercules Project was about a quarter of a mile away now, close enough that they could walk the rest of the way if they had to. Part of him wanted to climb out now and start in that direction, figuring they could move faster on foot.

But they had quite a few bags, including the gun bags, and he didn't want to load Susan down with any more of a burden, for any farther, than necessary. So they stayed where they were for the moment, with the SUV rolling forward a foot or two at a time.

Finally, after what seemed like an eternity, they were just about even with the gate. Larkin could see Graham Moultrie's Jeep parked on the other side but no sign of Moultrie himself. The man had to be somewhere close by, though. Larkin couldn't imagine that Moultrie would be anywhere else under these circumstances. The project was the man's baby. He would want to protect it and see that everything functioned the way it was supposed to.

"Good enough," Larkin said. He turned the wheel to the left and ran the SUV out onto a grassy, fairly level spot clear of the shoulder so others could get by. "Let's get the gear."

He stepped out of the vehicle and holstered the .45 on his right hip where he had clipped its holster earlier. Susan got out of the other side and joined him at the back of the SUV. Larkin opened it and started taking out the bags, slinging the heavier ones on his shoulders and handing the lighter ones to her.

"Are we just going to leave the car here?" she asked.

"It's no good to us in there," he said. "If nothing happens, maybe we can retrieve it later. If it's gone, well, I'll trade a stolen SUV for the world being safe."

"You're right. There are a lot of things it just doesn't make sense to worry about anymore, aren't there?"

"Almost everything," Larkin said.

They were both pretty weighed down when they started across the road toward the gate, stepping between the barely moving cars. Larkin hurried them along as much as he could, wishing there were some way they could do this without drawing attention to the gate that was their destination.

No one tried to stop them. The AR-15 he carried, the .45 on his hip, and the grim look on his face probably had a lot to do with that. But it was inevitable that someone would notice him and Susan, and sure enough, he heard somebody shout, "Hey! Where are those two going?"

Someone else yelled, "They must know where it's safe!"

"Follow them!" a third voice chimed in.

"Shit," Larkin muttered. He told Susan, "Come on, fast as you can."

Ahead of them, with a faint rumble of its motor, the gate started to open, the two halves sliding apart. Larkin and Susan broke into stumbling runs. Behind them, angry shouts and howled curses filled the air. Larkin heard footsteps rapidly slapping the ground as people ran after them.

Graham Moultrie appeared from somewhere, a weapon of some sort in his hands. He shouted, "Come on!" to Larkin and Susan, then the gun he held began to chatter and spew flames.

Chapter 18

Moultrie was off to one side, so he was able to fire through the iron bars past Larkin and Susan as they hurried toward the gate. Larkin threw a glance over his shoulder, thinking that surely Moultrie wasn't mowing down the people from the road. They were all fellow Americans, after all.

The slugs from the automatic weapon chewed up the asphalt in front of the charging mob and made them all throw on the brakes. Some of them might have been hurt by ricochets or chunks of flying asphalt, but at least it wasn't wholesale slaughter.

Larkin and Susan reached the gate, which was open barely wide enough for them to get through, one at a time. Larkin hung back a step to let Susan go first. She slipped through the gap, one of the bags she carried catching for a second before she tugged it free. Larkin was right behind her. The machine gun had fallen silent, but Moultrie still stood there pointing it at the crowd, and the grim look on his face made it clear that if he had to pull the trigger again, it might not be for warning shots.

The gate began to rumble closed. Moultrie hadn't

moved, so Larkin figured someone else was probably close by with the remote control, probably Deb. She could easily be hidden in the brush close to the entrance.

A man yelled, "You son of a bitch!" and the next instant a shot blasted from the crowd. Larkin looked around to see that the press of people had scattered, leaving one man holding a revolver. Larkin wasn't surprised that somebody else on the road was armed. There were probably plenty of guns out there in those stalled cars.

Larkin didn't know where that lone bullet had gone, but he knew where the burst Moultrie fired in return landed. The handful of slugs punched into the gunman's chest and knocked him backward as blood sprayed from the wounds. Screams came from the crowd as they scattered even more.

"Get in the Jeep and go," Moultrie snapped at Larkin and Susan. He swung the machine gun back and forth, menacing the crowd outside the gate.

Deb raced from the brush and jumped behind the wheel while Larkin and Susan were piling their gear into the back. Larkin hung on to the AR-15 and told Susan, "You go with Deb! I'll stay here and help Graham!"

Deb looked around from the driver's seat and told him, "No need! Help's on the way!"

Larkin looked along the road leading to the project's buildings and saw several more Jeeps heading toward the gate, each with several armed men in it. Rifle and shotgun barrels bristled from the vehicles, and on the back of one of them was mounted . . .

"Good Lord!" Larkin said. "Is that a .30 caliber machine gun?"

It certainly was, he saw as the first of the Jeeps raced

past and then slewed to a stop with a screech of brakes. The gunner on the back fired a long burst over the heads of the mob. People scrambled to get back in their cars and started driving again, closing up the gap that had opened while they were trying to get into the Hercules Project. There were plenty of curses and angry shouts hurled at the gate as the vehicles slowly rolled past, but nobody was willing to face the threat of a dozen armed men and a high-powered machine gun.

A thoroughly illegal machine gun, Larkin thought, but right now he was glad Moultrie had broken that law.

With society falling apart around them, the law of the gun might soon be the only one that counted for anything.

Susan was in the Jeep's front passenger seat. Larkin swung into the back, and Deb punched the gas. She handled the wheel expertly on the winding road.

"Are you two all right?" she asked as she drove. "You look like you need medical attention."

"Just cuts and scratches from broken glass," Larkin said. "A guy busted out our windshield and one of the windows trying to steal our SUV."

"You stopped him?"

"Yeah," Larkin said, thinking about the way the guy had flown backward when those two rounds from the .45 struck him. He was stopped, all right.

"I never dreamed people would act so crazy."

"They're crazy with fear," Larkin said. "I suppose I can't blame them . . . too much. Who were those guys in the other Jeeps?"

"Our security force. They're all residents here. Cops, military, ex-military like you, Patrick. Graham was going to ask you to join, just hadn't gotten around to it yet. And then *this* happened . . ."

"We knew something like it was coming. Otherwise there wouldn't be any need for the Hercules Project."

Susan said, "Our daughter and her husband aren't here yet, are they?"

Deb shook her head. "No, I'm afraid not. I've been trying to keep track of everyone checking in. It went pretty fast at first, before the traffic got backed up so badly on the road. Nobody even seemed to notice that some of the cars were turning in here. What happened to your SUV?"

"We left it on the other side of the road," Larkin said. "Couldn't get through with it, and well, we don't really need it anymore, do we?"

"Not unless this is a false alarm. God, I hope it's a false alarm!"

"We all do," Larkin said. But whether the bombs fell or not, right now the world was an immensely more dangerous place than it had been earlier today, and now that Susan was safe, all he could think about was Jill and her family.

Jill wanted to know what was going on, but she kept the radio in the crossover turned off because she didn't want to scare Chris even more than he already was. He bit his bottom lip and kept looking around like he expected some sort of monster to jump at him without warning.

But monsters weren't real . . . unless you wanted to count the human race. On this day, Jill thought, at least some of humanity definitely fell into that category.

Impatience made her want to bang her hand on the steering wheel. She suppressed that urge, too. It wouldn't make the traffic in front of her move any faster. It had been bad enough on the Interstate and then on the loop around Fort Worth, but once she had gotten off onto the country road that led into the hills west of the city, her progress had slowed down even more.

Trevor and Bailey were somewhere in this mess, she thought. She hoped her mom and dad had already made it to the bunker, but given the geography, it was too much to hope that her husband and daughter were there by this time. They probably weren't even ahead of her. Their cell phones were useless—the wireless networks were likely overloaded.

"We're going to that underground place, right?" Chris asked.

"That's right. We'll be safe there."

"Dad and Bailey will be there?"

"Of course." Jill managed to smile reassuringly—she hoped—as she said it.

"And Grandma and Granddad?"

"Yep. We'll all be there."

"Good. Maybe it won't be too bad, then."

"It won't be bad at all," Jill said. "It'll be fine."

Chris was quiet for a minute, then he said, "You know, this is the first time I'm glad you didn't let me get a dog after all. Because if you had, we were in such a hurry we'd have had to leave him behind in the back-yard to get blown up along with all the other dogs and cats and people."

Jill's heart seemed to twist painfully in her chest. She

swallowed hard and said, "I hope nobody gets blown up, including all the dogs and cats."

"That's what some of the kids said was gonna happen. They said the bad guys were coming to blow us all up. Is that what's gonna happen, Mom?"

"No," Jill said firmly. "We're going to be just fine, Chris. You have to believe that."

He nodded and said, "I'll try." He didn't sound convinced, though, and his obvious fear made Jill feel that awful pang in her chest again.

It just wasn't right. The grown-ups in the world owed it to the kids not to do stupid shit like this. Somebody should have realized what was going on and never let things get this far.

But that would have required the politicians and the media to act like reasonably intelligent adults, she thought bitterly, and nothing in the past seventy or eighty years indicated they were capable of that anymore.

Jill had been out to the Hercules Project several times. She and Trevor had taken a few things out there and stored them in their unit. She knew the roads, knew there was only one way to reach their destination. At this rate, they might not get there in time.

Of course, there was no way of knowing just how much time they had, she reminded herself.

Since they were moving so slowly, she pulled out her phone and opened the maps app. It didn't take long to find the map of the area where they were. She switched to satellite view and zoomed in on the Hercules Project.

What she saw made Jill catch her breath. She zoomed in more just to be sure she wasn't imagining things.

A number of years earlier, with the advent of fracking, a natural gas boom had swept through north central Texas as companies tried to reap the bounty of a geological feature known as the Barnett Shale. That had resulted in scores of gas wells popping up all over the countryside. In order for the gas company trucks to get to those wells, roads had to be put in. Most were just primitive gravel roads, but they crisscrossed the area and didn't show up on maps.

Very few drilling rigs were to be found these days, but the wells already put in were still producing and there were dozens of storage tanks. The companies still needed access to them, as well, so the roads were still there.

Those narrow gravel lanes showed up on satellite view, and Jill saw that one of them led from the road she was on up into the hills alongside the property occupied by the Hercules Project. It came close enough that she and Chris could reach the boundary on foot . . . if they could get in that way.

Jill lifted her eyes from the phone and realized she was almost to the spot where the gas company road turned off. In fact, she could see the gate that closed it off up ahead. The gate was fastened with a lock and chain, but they didn't look like they were meant to keep anyone out who really wanted to get in.

There was only one way to find out.

As she drew even with the gate, which was set back about forty feet from the road, she turned the wheel, poised her foot to press down on the gas, and told Chris, "Hang on, kid."

Chapter 19

"Whoa!" Chris exclaimed as the crossover leaped toward the gate. Jill floored the accelerator to get up as much speed as she could before the front end of the vehicle crashed into the wood and aluminum barrier.

The chain snapped under the impact and the gate flew open. The crossover lurched through and came to a stop as the airbags deployed.

Jill was shaken but still clearheaded. She pushed against the airbag and said, "Chris! Chris, are you okay?"

"Yeah," came the muffled reply. "Dang, Mom!"

The engine was still running, so she pushed the airbag down until she could see again, then started up the gravel road.

"Are you sure you're all right?" she asked Chris.

"Yeah. I saw what you were gonna do, so I was ready when the airbag came out. It didn't hit me very hard."

"Good. I hated to do that, but I think this way will get us to the project quicker. I'm just glad the engine's still running."

There had been a chance the collision with the gate would damage the vehicle so much she wouldn't be able to drive it. The cars on the road were barely moving, though, and her impatience had gotten the best of her.

Trevor had told her many times that she was a little too reckless and impulsive. Under the right circumstances, it could be an appealing quality, but it could also get her into trouble.

This time, the gamble had paid off . . . at least so far.

The little road twisted and turned through the hills with their scattered clumps of trees. It went past leveled-off clearings with three or four or more natural gas storage tanks on them. Those clearings were usually near large, muddy wallows that were the remains of pools where water from the fracking process had been collected. The gas boom had left its scars on the landscape, but right now Jill was grateful for all the drilling. Without it, this road wouldn't be here.

"Can we get in this way, Mom?"

"I don't know, kid, but we're gonna try." Jill thumbed the phone on, and said, "Call Trevor."

All she got was "Call Failed" on the dashboard display.

"Crap."

"That's a bad word."

"I could've said worse. We were probably doing good to stay in touch as long as we did. I've got to let your dad know about this road, though. He may need to take it, too."

"I can try calling Bailey on my phone while you drive," Chris offered.

Jill had never been a strong proponent of giving little kids phones, but everybody did it these days, and for once she was glad she had gone along with a helicopter parenting technique.

"You do that, Chris. This road is narrow and has enough holes in it, it's probably better if I concentrate on where I'm going."

Chris's call to his sister wouldn't go through, either, he reported, but he kept trying. When they had gone a half-mile or so on the gas company road, Jill spotted a high brick wall on her left, a couple of hundred yards away. That had to be the edge of the project's property, she thought, remembering how the terrain had looked on the satellite map.

"Mom, I got her!" Chris said as Jill braked to a stop.

She reached over for the phone, took it from him, said, "Bailey, honey, give the phone to your dad."

"Okay, Mom," Bailey said, and Jill felt a pang of relief just hearing her daughter's voice again. She wished she could have talked to Bailey for a moment and tried to reassure her, but there might not be time for that.

"Jill, are you and Chris still all right?" Trevor asked as soon as he had Bailey's phone.

"Yeah. Where are you?"

"We just passed . . . let's see . . . Verna Trail, but the traffic's barely moving now."

"All right, listen close. In another mile or so, you're going to come to a gas company road on the right side of the road you're on. It had a gate blocking it, but that gate is broken open now."

"Did you do that?" Trevor asked quickly. He knew her pretty well, all right.

"Yeah, I did."

"Jill, are you crazy—"

"I told you to listen to me," she cut him off. "Take that

road, follow it until you come to my car, then get out, bring all the gear if you can carry it, and hike toward the brick wall you'll see off to the left. I'm pretty sure that's the border of the project's property."

"'Pretty sure'? Jill, our lives may be at stake here!"

"Stop that. You're probably scaring Bailey. If you stay on the road until you come to the main gate, it's going to take you an hour or more. You can cut that time in half by coming this way."

"You don't know if you can even get in where you are."

"They're not going to keep me out," Jill said. "Please, Trevor, do like I asked." She paused. "We don't know how much time we have left."

She hated to say that in front of Chris, but it was true.

"Oh, all right," Trevor said. "I'll look for the broken gate— What's that?"

She heard the alarm in his voice. Her hand tightened on the phone. "Trev, what's wrong?"

"The warning sirens . . . they had stopped, but they started again just now."

Jill opened her door and stepped out. She could hear the sirens' howl floating over the hills. She didn't know what they meant, but it couldn't be anything good.

"Hurry, Trevor," she half-whispered. "Please."

"We'll be there as soon as we can," he promised, and then the connection went dead.

Panic tried to well up inside Jill, but she forced it down. She handed the phone back to Chris and said, "Come on. We need to get moving."

They grabbed the bags from the back of the crossover and started walking at a fast pace toward the wall. As they did, Jill thought she heard several bursts of gunfire in the distance, but that wasn't possible, was it?

Of course it was. On a day like today, *anything* was possible.

Deb drove around the administration building to the bunker's main entrance. Scores of vehicles were already parked back here on the wide grassy area to the left, and people were moving back and forth between them and the concrete building housing the stairs, as they unloaded personal belongings they had brought with them. Steady streams of worried-looking men and women came and went from the building's open door.

"The two of you can go on in and unload your gear," Deb told Larkin and Susan as she turned halfway around in the driver's seat. "Don't worry, Patrick. Graham's got everything under control. We're monitoring developments constantly—"

She stopped and lifted her head as the sirens in the nearby housing developments, which had gone silent, started their keening wail again.

"That can't be good," Susan said.

"Wait a second." Deb picked up a walkie-talkie from the console between the seats and keyed it. "Talk to me, Andrew."

"England's been hit!" a man's frenzied voice replied. "Russian missiles! At least five nuclear blasts!"

Susan moaned in horror.

"More missiles launched at our west coast from Siberia and North Korea," the man continued on the walkie-talkie. "Our anti-missile defenses will try to stop them, and we've launched strikes of our own, but this is it, Deb!"

A death-like pallor washed over Deb's face, but her voice was still composed as she asked, "What's the time frame?"

"Not sure. If they do fire any at us, it'll take approximately twenty minutes after launch for them to reach us."

Alarms inside the project began to clamor, and the people unloading their vehicles started moving faster.

"So we have a twenty-minute minimum window," Deb said.

"Yeah. I've advised Graham. He's going to start withdrawing from the main gate. Deb . . . we've got an encroachment along the eastern boundary of the property."

"What kind of encroachment?"

"A woman and a little boy, approaching on foot. Looks like they're carrying go-bags, like they know what they're doing."

Larkin leaned forward sharply when he heard that. He touched Deb's shoulder and said, "Is he watching them on surveillance cameras?"

She turned her head slightly and nodded.

"Ask him what they look like," Larkin urged.

"Description on the two?" Deb said into the walkie-talkie.

"Woman's mid-thirties, brown hair, little boy around ten, blond hair."

Susan said, "That could be Jill and Chris!"

Deb told the man in the command center, "Send a screen cap of them to my phone."

"Will do."

Mere seconds later her phone chimed and she held

up the screen so Larkin and Susan could see it. Susan said, "Oh, my God!"

"That's them," Larkin confirmed. "Our daughter Jill and our grandson Chris."

"They must have taken one of the old gas company roads to get close, then tried to get here on foot," Deb said.

"Can they . . . can they get over that wall?" Susan asked.

"The ground inside it is mined."

Susan groaned in fear and desperation.

Larkin gripped the back of the seat in front of him, hard. "Can the mines be deactivated?"

"I believe so. They weren't activated until Graham turned them on earlier, when things started to go bad. The pressure sensor in them sends a signal to the computer in the command center, and that sends a detonation signal back."

"Turn them off!" Susan cried. "For God's sake, turn them off!"

Deb hesitated. "I don't know . . . I wish Graham was here . . ."

On the walkie-talkie, Andrew said, "Deb, the woman and the little boy are on the wall. The woman's about to jump down inside . . . There she goes!"

Chapter 20

Jill's feet hit the ground. She stumbled a little as she nearly lost her balance. She threw out her arms and caught herself.

There was a little clump of cactus close by. Wouldn't want to fall on that.

She turned back to the wall and said, "Okay, Chris, toss the bags down to me, one at a time." She had left the bags balanced up there until she was down on the inside of the wall.

Chris dropped the bags to her. She caught them and set them aside, then said, "All right, you can turn around and slide off of there. Hang by your hands and then drop. I'll catch you."

"Are you sure, Mom?"

"Of course I'm sure. I've never dropped you, have I?"

"Dad said you did once when I was a baby."

"That's because you were as slippery as a little eel. Now come on." She didn't like the way those sirens had gone off again, and now some alarms inside the Hercules Project had added their clangor to the racket.

Looking pretty dubious about the whole thing, Chris turned around, slid backward off the thick wall, and hung for a second before letting go. The wall was only eight feet tall, so he didn't have far to fall before he landed in Jill's arms. She was braced for his weight, but she still had to take a quick step backward to compensate for it.

From somewhere not far off, she heard what sounded like a car horn honking. She turned and saw that it wasn't a car but rather a Jeep, bouncing as it came across country toward them.

Was that . . .? Yes! Graham Moultrie's redheaded wife Deb was driving, but Jill's mom was in the passenger seat. And peering anxiously between the two women from the rear seat was her dad. His rugged face was as drawn and haggard as Jill remembered ever seeing it.

"Grab one of the bags and come on," she told Chris. "They've come to meet us for some reason."

The Jeep's tires threw up a small cloud of dust as it came to a stop. Susan was out of the vehicle in a flash, throwing her arms around both Jill and Chris, pulling them against her.

"Oh, thank God, thank God," Susan said. "That was so close."

"Close?" Jill repeated. "What do you mean?"

Larkin had gotten out of the Jeep and come over to stand next to them. He put a hand on Jill's shoulder and said, "This area is mined. They have electronic detonators, so the project's command center was able to turn them off, but not before you jumped down from that fence. You were just lucky enough not to land on one."

Jill looked at the ground and felt like her stomach had dropped all the way to her feet. "Mines?" she said, her voice weak.

"Yeah." Larkin squeezed her shoulder. "But it's safe now . . . until they're activated again."

"That's right," Deb said from the Jeep. "So we've got to get out of here. We can't afford to leave the perimeter unprotected for long."

"But I told Trevor and Bailey to come in this way," Jill protested. "They never would have made it to the gate in time by staying on the road." She saw the look on her dad's face and knew there was something else she wasn't aware of, something bad. "What is it?"

"The Russians have nuked England," he said. "And there are missiles from them and the North Koreans targeting the west coast right now. It looks like they may try to march those missiles right across the country."

"You mean right across us," Jill said. Her insides felt more hollow than ever.

"Yeah. We'll try to knock them down with anti-missile defenses, of course—"

"But some of them will get through."

Larkin sighed. "More than likely."

An explosion sounded not too far off, making all five of them jump. It wasn't a nuclear blast, though. Deb looked toward the main road and said, "That was one of the mines along the front of the property. Someone made it over the electrified fence, although I don't see how. We've got to go, so the command center can turn these mines back on."

Susan said, "You mean someone died over there, just because they were trying to get to safety."

"There's nothing right or fair about it," Larkin told her. "But that's just the way things are. If Graham let in all those people out there, then we'd all die. It's that simple."

Susan caught her bottom lip between her teeth. A couple of tears rolled down her cheeks. "I know," she said. "It's just—"

"I'm telling command to activate the mines," Deb said as she held up the walkie-talkie. "Come *on*!"

Larkin pushed Jill and Susan toward the Jeep. "You girls get out of here," he said. "Take Chris with you. Deb, how far back does the mined zone extend?"

"It's fifty yards wide along the entire perimeter."

Susan clutched at Larkin's sleeve. "Patrick, what are you going to do?"

Larkin didn't answer her directly. Instead he told Deb, "Tell command to reactivate the mines, then leave the walkie-talkie with me while you take my family back to the bunker. I'll stay here and wait for Trevor and Bailey. When they show up, I'll call command and they can turn off the mines again until they get over the wall."

Deb looked skeptical. She said, "I don't know if Graham will approve that . . ."

"You've got to give the rest of my family a chance to get in," Larkin argued.

"What if people who *aren't* residents here try to come over the wall?"

Larkin went to the jeep and picked up his AR-15 from the back of it. "I'll stop them," he said.

Susan stared at him in horror.

Jill was more pragmatic. She took her mother's arm and urged her into the Jeep. "Come on, Mom," she said. "We need to get inside while we still can." She had to swallow hard. She was heading for shelter without knowing if her husband and daughter were going to survive. But they were beyond her help now. Their fates were in the hands of God . . . and Jill's father.

They had to make it.

Larkin watched the Jeep jolt off toward the buildings and the entrance to the underground bunker. The worry crossed his mind that he might never see his wife, daughter, and grandson again, but the knowledge that they had a good chance of survival bolstered his spirits some.

Not many had even that much of a chance, he thought as he looked around the hills. He was up just high enough to catch a glimpse of the skyscrapers in downtown Fort Worth poking up from the southeastern horizon, about ten miles away. It was mid-afternoon, and by nightfall the city might be a flattened, smoking, radioactive ruin. These hills could be swept clean of vegetation, all of it burned away by the blast wave. Radioactive fire would consume everything above ground, leaving only ash. Not even memories, because no one would be alive to have them.

From where he was, he could see part of the old gas company road Trevor would have to use to get here. He forced his attention onto that short stretch and kept it there, praying he would see his son-in-law's car come bumping along the gravel lane. Trevor was a smart guy. He would be able to find the road . . .

The walkie-talkie Deb had left him crackled. She said his name.

"I'm here," Larkin replied as he keyed the mike.

"Patrick . . . there are reports that missiles aimed at

Texas have been detected in the upper atmosphere. You have to get back here *now*."

"Trevor and Bailey aren't here yet."

"The bunker will be sealed in fifteen minutes or less. There's no more time."

Larkin felt sick, but Deb was right: there was no time for that. He said, "Are Susan, Jill, and Chris safe?"

"They're all down here, and they won't be allowed to leave."

"Good. I'm staying put for a while longer."

"Patrick—"

"Deb, tell Graham I really appreciate what the two of you have done. And if things don't work out, tell my family I love them."

"Patrick, you need to—"

A flicker of movement from the road caught Larkin's eye. He interrupted Deb again, saying, "Wait a minute! I think I see—Yeah! That's Trevor's car. Tell command to deactivate the mines."

"Are you sure?"

"Yeah, I recognize the car. Please, Deb."

For a moment, there was silence on the walkie-talkie, broken only by the faint crackle. Then Deb said, "The mines are deactivated. But the time is *very* short, Patrick."

"Got it. I'll let you know when we're clear."

"No need. Surveillance cameras, remember? Just get out of there and back here as quickly as you can."

"Will do." Larkin turned the walkie-talkie off. He didn't need any more distractions now.

He got them anyway, as more movement caught his

attention. Trevor's car was out of sight from his position by now, but he could still see that other stretch of road.

And several vehicles had just roared along it, obviously following Trevor, no doubt in the hope that he knew where he was going and that there was some sort of sanctuary at the other end of the gravel road.

Larkin's heart sank even more. For those people, it was a false hope. They were doomed and didn't know it yet. All along, Larkin had tried to keep his emotions hardened against what might be coming. Now that it was actually on the way, that was even more difficult.

Maybe . . . maybe it would be better to stay out here and die along with everybody else. What kind of world was it going to be for the survivors? Empty, devastated, depopulated. Humankind had never dealt with the sort of disaster this promised to be.

Not since the last extinction event, anyway.

But that was why the success of the Hercules Project and other, similar projects was so important. So that this *wouldn't* be an extinction event. So that the torch of humanity on Earth *wouldn't* be extinguished. Even if only pockets of people survived here and there, life would continue and one day the world would be fit for living again. Education, history, some semblance of culture could be preserved. It was all a slim chance, of course . . . but better than no chance at all.

Larkin heard car doors slam not too far off and ran toward the wall. "Trevor!" he shouted. "Trev, over here!"

"Patrick?"

The sound of his son-in-law's voice made a surge of relief go through Larkin. "This way!" he called. "Throw your bags over the wall!"

The heavy canvas bags sailed over the rock wall. Trevor said, "I'll boost Bailey up! Can you catch her on that side?"

"Yeah. Come on, there's not much time!"

Larkin leaned the rifle against the wall as he saw his granddaughter's head appear at the top of it. Bailey scrambled onto the top of the wall, which was about a foot wide, and balanced there precariously with a frightened expression on her face.

"Granddad!" she said when she saw Larkin.

"Turn around, slide off, and drop, honey," he told her. "I'll catch you."

She swallowed, nodded, and followed his orders. Her weight made him stagger a little as he caught her, and he couldn't help but think about the mines under his feet. He hoped whoever was in charge of activating and deactivating them back in the command center was on the ball.

Trevor climbed onto the fence, swung a leg over, and dropped, falling to his knees as he landed. He was up in a hurry, though, grabbing both bags.

Larkin set Bailey on the ground, grabbed the rifle with his right hand, and took Bailey's right hand with his left. "Let's go," he said.

Trevor said, "Patrick, has something else happened?"

Larkin looked at his son-in-law and said, "We've got less than fifteen minutes."

Trevor practically gulped. "Come on, Bailey."

They had just turned away from the fence when Larkin heard a man shout, "Hey, over here! That's where they went."

"Go!" Larkin said as he urged the other two toward

the bunker. "Bailey, stay with your dad! Don't slow down! Both of you keep moving!"

"Patrick, what are you—" Trevor began.

"Just get underground," Larkin said, his jaw tight with strain. He turned around and faced toward the fence again. He gripped the AR-15 in both hands now.

He heard Trevor and Bailey running away and was glad of that much, anyway. More shouts came from the other side of the fence as Larkin backed away from it. He stopped when he was certain the distance was more than fifty yards.

A man's head appeared suddenly at the top of the fence. He pulled himself up and rolled onto the narrow perch.

"Go back!" Larkin shouted at him. "It's not safe!"

That was just about the stupidest thing he could have said, he realized, although it was certainly true.

There was very little safety to be had in the world today. Not enough for all its billions.

The man on the fence ignored him and turned his head to shout, "There's some sort of compound in here. Hurry!"

Larkin lifted the rifle to his shoulder. The man glanced at him but in his terror didn't seem to comprehend the threat. Larkin swallowed. Already, Moultrie and his security force had killed people today in order to protect the Hercules Project. It didn't matter that they had been fellow Americans. As of today, that concept didn't really exist anymore. Once the missiles and the bombers were in the air, there was only *us* and *them*.

And *them* included not only the Russians and the

North Koreans but everyone who wasn't a resident of the Hercules Project.

Larkin's finger was about to take up the slack on the trigger when the man on the fence shouted to whoever was on the other side, "Helen, bring the kids! Now!"

Larkin couldn't shoot.

But as the man swung his legs over the fence and poised to drop, he shouted, "No, don't—"

The man leaped.

Chapter 21

His feet hit the ground and he disappeared in a blinding flash of flame and noise. Larkin flinched away from the blast as rocks and dirt clods sprayed through the air. Other things might be spraying, too, but he didn't want to think about that. A cloud of smoke and dust billowed up from the site of the explosion, hiding the grisly results.

Larkin turned and raced after Trevor and Bailey. There was nothing more he could do here. He hoped the mine going off would discourage anyone else from trying to climb over the fence, but it didn't really matter, he supposed. Die in an explosion now, die in an explosion in ten or twelve minutes, what was the difference?

But all the missiles might *not* make it through, he reminded himself as he ran. Some of them undoubtedly would. The United States would be changed drastically and forever. But would it be wiped out? Would the U.S. and Russia keep lobbing nuclear death at each other until everything was gone?

Larkin had no way of knowing. None of them did. All they could do was try to save what they could. Save *who* they could.

He was aware of the seconds ticking by with each

running stride he took. He couldn't help but glance at the sky, although he knew it was unlikely he would actually be able to see doom descending toward him. If it was all over for him, he wouldn't know it when the time came, unless there was a split second of awareness, the tiniest shaved fraction of time when he felt his atoms being blown apart . . .

There was the concrete building that housed the bunker entrance. The door was still open, with armed men standing around it. Graham Moultrie was one of them. He waved Larkin on. Larkin wasn't surprised to see Moultrie. He figured the man intended to be the last one in, the one to close the door on whatever happened in the outside world.

More explosions sounded from around the property. More mines going off as fear-crazed people scrambled over walls and fences and tried to find shelter from the storm, somewhere, anywhere. Breathing hard, Larkin pounded up to the small group at the entrance. Moultrie gripped his arm and said, "Glad you made it, Patrick."

"My son-in-law . . . and granddaughter . . .?"

"Inside with the rest of your family." Moultrie summoned up a grim smile. "Go and join them. Everybody's gathering on the lower level right now."

Larkin managed to nod. He hesitated long enough to say, "You don't need . . . more help here?"

"We're all right. Go on, Patrick. You made sure they had a place to come, and they all got here. You should be proud."

"The missiles?"

"Some have been knocked down or blown out of the sky. But more than half look like they'll get through."

Moultrie's face was bleak as he added, "I'm giving it two more minutes, then we're buttoning up tight here."

Larkin nodded. A few people were still trying to get things out of their vehicles and carry them into the project, but if they had any sense they wouldn't make any more trips out of the building.

Carrying the rifle, Larkin went into the building and started down the steps. Several people were in front of him, and others followed. When he reached the landing where the stairs turned back, he paused for a second to look back up at the entrance with the afternoon sun shining through it.

How long would it be, he wondered, before he saw sunlight again?

Would he ever? Would anyone inside the Hercules Project?

Larkin didn't know the answer. He took a deep breath and kept going down.

A lot of people were in the lower bunker, but the cavernous space was so large it didn't seem particularly crowded. The noise level was pretty high, though, since plenty of them seemed to be talking at once. Once Larkin had been passed through the double blast doors, including a fingerprint scan to confirm his identity, he searched for his family, his size allowing him to move through the press of people without much trouble.

A hand came out of the crowd and clasped his arm. Larkin looked over and saw Adam Threadgill standing there. Threadgill's wife Luisa was with him, and beyond them Larkin saw their daughter Sophie and her husband Jack Kaufman.

"Patrick!" Threadgill threw his arms around Larkin and pounded him on the back with one hand. "You made it."

Larkin said, "Yeah, and I've got you to thank for telling me about this place, buddy. I might not have known about it otherwise, and we'd still be . . . up there."

Threadgill's face grew solemn. "Yeah. Your family is all here, safe and sound?"

"They're somewhere in this crowd, all right." Larkin put his arm around Luisa's shoulders and gave her a quick hug, then reached past her to hug Sophie and shake hands with Jack. "Good to see you, son."

"Thank you, sir," Jack said. He looked pale and scared, but so did just about everybody else down here. There was a definite undercurrent of fear to the hubbub.

"You haven't seen Susan, have you?" Larkin asked Threadgill.

The other former Marine shook his head and said, "No, not so far. But if you're sure she's down here . . ."

"I am, but I want to see her with my own eyes, and Jill and Trev and the kids, too."

Threadgill nodded. "I know what you mean."

"I'll see you later," Larkin told them. He resumed his search.

Before he found his family, he spotted another familiar face, one he didn't really expect to see down here. He made his way over to the man and woman who stood near one of the walls, talking to each other. The woman saw him coming and frowned.

"Jim, Beth," Larkin greeted the Huddlestons as he

came up to them. "I, uh, didn't know you were going to be here." Even as the words came out of his mouth, he realized how lame they sounded. He might as well have said, *I figured you'd get blown to Kingdom Come.*

"We almost weren't," Jim Huddleston said. "Got through the gate at the last minute."

"Even then I thought some of those goons were going to shoot us," Beth said. "Give a bunch of rednecks guns and some power, and it's a bad situation."

Larkin ignored that. He was sort of a redneck himself, in many ways, but he knew what Beth was like. Instead he clapped a hand on Huddleston's shoulder and said, "I'm glad you're here, Jim."

"It's ridiculous," Beth said before her husband could respond. "Jim got me all spooked with his talk about nuclear war, but now that I've had time to think about it, I'm sure it's not going to happen. Why, the President is *much* too smart to ever allow things to get to that point."

"Then . . . you haven't heard?" Larkin said.

"Heard what?"

"The Russians hit England with at least five nukes. They and the North Koreans launched missiles aimed at our west coast." Larkin thought about how much time had passed. "Some of them have probably struck by now, unless we were able to stop all of them. And the odds of that are pretty slim, as gutted as our defenses have gotten over the past few years."

Beth's mouth tightened. "I don't believe that. You're just using that as an excuse to complain because your side didn't win the last election."

Huddleston said, "Beth, I don't think Patrick would make up something like that just to score political points."

"Of course he would. *Those people* will stop at nothing."

The longer this conversation went on, the more difficult it was going to be to remain civil, Larkin realized. And having a partisan political argument under these circumstances was just asinine. After today, there was a good chance there wouldn't be any more political parties. Not for a long, long time, if ever.

"I need to find my family, so I'm going to keep looking for them," he told Huddleston.

"Thanks again, Patrick."

Beth didn't look grateful, just pissed. Larkin was glad he wasn't going to have to deal with her.

His nervousness grew as he continued searching for his family. Moultrie and Deb had assured him they were safe for the moment, but like he had told Huddleston, he wouldn't relax until he saw them for himself.

Of course, relax was a relative term. None of them could be absolutely certain that the Hercules Project was as safe as Graham Moultrie claimed it was until it was tested. It might turn out that their doom was only postponed briefly. One of those missiles might land right on top of them. Not even this bunker could withstand being ground zero, Larkin thought. But if the end came, he wanted to be with his family when it did.

He still had the rifle in his right hand. Someone took hold of his left. He looked around and then down and saw his grandson there, smiling up at him.

"Granddad," Chris said. "We're over there."

He pointed, and Larkin saw Susan, Jill, Trevor, and Bailey about twenty feet away. His heart slugged like a jackhammer for a couple of seconds as his wife smiled at him. He didn't trust himself to speak as emotion swept through him.

Then he grinned down at Chris and said, "How're you doin', kid?"

"I'm all right. Scared, but . . . you know. There are a lot of scary things in the world, Mom says. You have to live in it anyway."

"Smart girl, your mom. I taught her everything she knows."

"That's what Grandma says. That *she* taught Mom everything she knows, I mean."

"We can hash that out some other time. Right now, let's just go see 'em."

Susan hugged him as he came up to them, then so did Jill and Bailey. Larkin set the rifle on one of the bunks and returned the hugs. The bunks would be occupied later, but for now none of the residents who'd be staying here had claimed a place.

Trevor patted Larkin on the shoulder, an awkward gesture but one Larkin appreciated anyway. The younger man said, "Thanks for helping us out there, Patrick. We couldn't have gotten in here safely if not for you. I guess that's true in more ways than one."

"We're here, that's all that matters."

"Have you heard anything?" Jill asked. "I mean, about what's going on?"

Larkin knew what she meant. Nobody had anything else on their mind today. He shook his head and said, "No, but by now Moultrie's got the place shut up completely. Maybe he'll make some kind of announcement soon."

"All those people out there . . ." Susan said.

Larkin put his arm around her shoulder again and

drew her against him. "If there was a way to save all of them, we would," he said. "All we can do is save what we can."

She nodded in understanding, but he saw the sheen of tears on her face again. A lot of people down here were crying, he saw. How could they help it? The world they had known all their lives was dying, and there was nothing they could do to stop it.

There were little clusters of hilarity here and there, people laughing and joking, celebrating because they had made it into this refuge and at least had a chance to live through the disaster. Those happy notes didn't really ring true, though, Larkin thought. It was easy to be relieved that you might live, harder to act as if the deaths of billions of people didn't bother you.

An abrupt silence fell as Graham Moultrie's voice came from loudspeakers mounted on the walls of the bunker.

"Welcome to the Hercules Project. All entrances are now closed and securely sealed. No matter what happens from here on out, we are all in this together. We are, potentially, the citizens of a new world. The future is impossible to predict, but one thing we do know is that it will be very, very different from the lives that all of us have known until today."

Jill moved up on Larkin's other side and pressed her shoulder against his. One hand reached out and clasped Trevor's hand. Her other hand rested on Bailey's shoulder as the girl stood in front of her, looking up at the speakers. Trevor had his free hand on Chris's shoulder, holding the boy against him.

"I know all of you are anxious for news. Here in the

command center, we've been monitoring all the reports we can from around the world, via the Internet. I will not lie to you: the situation is grave. Within the past half hour, San Diego, Los Angeles, San Francisco, and Seattle have all been hit by nuclear missiles launched from Russian and North Korean naval vessels in the Pacific Ocean. Destruction is widespread, and the loss of human life is incalculable."

Gasps and moans came from the crowd assembled in the bunker. Larkin's arm tightened around Susan's shoulders.

"This follows Russian attacks using high-level bombers as well as missiles on England, France, and Germany. No word has come from any of those countries in the past hour. Total destruction is feared. In addition, Iranian missiles carrying low-yield nuclear warheads have landed in Israel and Turkey, and Iran is now carrying out conventional bombing and missile attacks against those countries. American vessels in the Persian Gulf have attacked Iran but so far have been unable to stop their assault.

"The Pentagon reports that retaliatory strikes by U.S. naval and air forces are being carried out against Russia and North Korea. The President has urged calm from the citizens of this country who have not yet come under attack and has pledged that the United States will be firm and resolute in its opposition to such wanton aggression. He also said that this is not the end of the world."

Larkin was willing to bet that no one down here believed that, and probably no one anywhere else did, either. The President might be clinging to some hope that it would turn out to be true . . . otherwise he wouldn't have anything left to be president *of.*

Moultrie went on, *"I want to express my deep appreciation to each and every one of you for placing your faith in the Hercules Project. You have my word that I will do everything in my power to make sure we all remain safe in these very trying times. As long as there is news to report, we'll keep you informed."*

Larkin knew what he meant by that. Sooner or later, the Internet would go dark and quiet. The infrastructure to support it would be gone. Then, it would be the same as living underneath a dead world, because they would have no way of knowing what was going on above them.

Or else silence would reign because the rest of the world actually *was* dead. That possibility couldn't be discounted, either.

The concrete floor suddenly shuddered under Larkin's feet, the lights flickered, and startled screams filled the bunker. Susan clutched Larkin and said, "Patrick, was that . . ."

"That was a hit," Larkin said. "Close."

Chapter 22

The lights didn't go out, and after a moment the screaming trailed off, but the hubbub was louder and people milled around more. Evidently their growing fear drove them to move, even though those movements were aimless for the most part.

Graham Moultrie's voice came back on the speakers. *"I'm sorry to have to tell you that a missile armed with a nuclear warhead has struck between Fort Worth and Dallas. We're picking up that news from Internet postings elsewhere in the country, via underground cable from servers in West Texas that are still online. The electromagnetic pulse from that explosion has knocked all technology in this area off-line. We have no reports regarding casualties or destruction at this time, but it's safe to assume that both are catastrophic. Whenever we have new information, we'll announce it right away. Until then . . . remain calm. Pray for this country. For the world."*

The speakers went off with an audible click.

Susan shuddered against Larkin. "All those people . . ." she breathed.

He tightened his arm around her shoulders. "I know."

Nearby, a woman sank onto one of the bunks and began to sob. Larkin didn't know if she had friends or family in the blast area or if she was just crying for the loss of life in general, and he supposed it didn't matter. All around the giant, cavernous chamber, more sobs began to be heard. Sorrow thickened in the air like a visible fog.

Bailey was crying, too, although she did it quietly, the tears trickling down her cheeks in silence. Chris sniffled but was trying to be brave. Larkin felt the dampness in his own eyes. He was no more immune to what was happening than his grandchildren were.

Not far away, a man laughed and said, "Biggest bomb to hit Arlington since the Dallas Cowboys."

Another man grabbed him by the shoulder and jerked him around, demanding, "What the hell's wrong with you?"

"Get your hand off me! We're safe, aren't we? Don't expect me to feel sorry for all those losers out there!"

"My brother lives in Grand Prairie!" a third man yelled.

"Not anymore, I'll bet!"

Larkin listened to the interchange and muttered, "Stupid . . ."

The third man said, "You son of a bitch!" and threw a punch

That was all it took. A wild melee erupted in that part of the chamber as men slugged and cursed at each other. Women and kids weren't immune from the madness fueled by fear and grief. Larkin herded his family away from the brawl in case it spread in their direction.

The chaos didn't last long. Members of Moultrie's security force showed up to put a stop to the fighting. They wore red vests and looked like guys who might have been working in a discount store, but they were good at their job, getting between combatants and grabbing the ones they had to in order to settle them down. Within a few minutes, the fight was over.

Moultrie wanted him to be part of that force, Larkin mused. That was probably a good idea. There would be plenty of trouble down here to take care of. That was just human nature. You couldn't put this many people together in a limited amount of space and not expect problems.

He was glad, though, that he didn't have to step in today. He wanted to be with his family as much as he could, this first day of their self-imposed exile.

A woman pushed through the crowd, calling, "Nelson! Nelson! Are you here? Nelson!" Her voice held a frantic, almost hysterical edge. She came up to Larkin and grabbed his sleeve. "Have you seen my husband? His name is Nelson Ruskin."

"I'm sorry, ma'am, I don't know him," Larkin said. "I wouldn't know if he's here or not."

"I have to find him," she said with painfully obvious desperation. "He's supposed to be here. We made plans . . . we had an arrangement . . . If it looked like anything was going to happen, we were both supposed to head out here as quickly as we could . . ."

"There are a lot of people here," Susan said. Larkin could tell she was trying to be as gentle with the woman as she could. "I'm sure you just haven't found each other yet. He's probably looking for you, too."

The woman didn't seem to hear. She turned away and pushed into the crowd again, crying, "Nelson!"

"That poor woman," Susan said quietly as the press

of people swallowed the searching woman. "What if her husband *didn't* make it?"

"Everyone's fingerprints were scanned as we came in," Larkin said. "We'll know soon enough who got here in time and who didn't."

He looked around the big room. He was pretty good at estimating crowds, and he would have said there were almost four hundred people here . . . but not quite. That meant some of the residents of the Hercules Project *hadn't* arrived before Moultrie locked everything up. They'd been left outside to wait for whatever fate had in store for them.

So far he hadn't felt the vibrations from any more nuclear explosions. American anti-missile defenses had been able to take out some of the attackers. Maybe the missile that had fallen between Fort Worth and Dallas would be the only one to strike the area. That would give some hope, however slight, for survivors aboveground, although the fallout and residual radiation might render the entire Metroplex virtually unlivable for years.

The speakers came on again and hummed for a second before Graham Moultrie said, *"We have more news. Multiple missiles armed with nuclear warheads have struck San Antonio and Houston here in Texas, as well as Kansas City, St. Louis, and Chicago. Also, tactical nuclear devices have been detonated in Washington, D.C., New York, Boston, Atlanta, and Miami. It's thought that these devices were planted and set off by terrorists affiliated with ISIS and other Islamic groups. The timing and the planning required to coordinate such attacks indicates that the terrorists were working with Russia and North Korea, and that a concentrated effort is underway to destroy the United States. There are reports that our counterattacks have caused widespread devastation in those countries. In addition, there have been nuclear exchanges between Israel and Iran, and between Pakistan and India."*

Everyone in the now hushed bunker heard Moultrie draw in a deep breath. When he resumed, the strain that they were all feeling was evident in his voice.

"The entire world is at war. There can be no doubt about that. The lines of communication are becoming more spotty with each passing minute. All conventional broadcasting is off the air, likely as the result of nuclear airbursts and the ensuing EMPs. Wireless networks are down as well. Satellite Internet connections are failing, doubtless due to infrastructure damage, but the fact that we've been able to maintain a connection here at the Hercules Project tells us that our aboveground equipment is still functioning. There are also operators sending on old-fashioned ham radio rigs that don't depend on computers, and we have radios in the control center to pick up those transmissions as well. But I won't lie to you, my friends.

"The world is going dark and quiet even as I speak to you now. On the eve of World War I, a British government official said, 'The lamps are going out all over Europe, and we shall not see them lit again in our lifetime.' The first part of that statement is true now for our entire planet. But I refuse to believe we shall not see them lit again in our lifetimes. Certainly, some of us will not. But as human beings, we cannot give up hope. That is why each and every one of us is here: because we still have hope that our world has a future. This is not the end, my friends. The Hercules Project is the beginning."

The speakers clicked off again.

"Do you believe him?" Susan asked as she huddled

against Larkin. "Do you think he's right about there still being a future?"

"What other choice do I have?" he said.

The human mind can cope with only so much tragedy and trauma before retreating into a stunned state. So it was in the vast underground bunker as people began to sit down and talk quietly as they waited to see what was going to happen. There were still some sobs, but the terrified screams and angry shouts had subsided.

Susan, Jill, and the kids sat on one of the bunks while Larkin and Trevor stood nearby. Larkin saw the way his son-in-law kept swallowing hard and wiping at his eyes with the back of his hand. He kept his voice down as he asked, "You're thinking about your folks, aren't you?"

Trevor swallowed again and said, "You know, I tried to get them to move up here so they'd be closer. And then, when the deal with this place came up, I tried again. I wanted them to invest in it. But they didn't want to leave their home. They'd been there for forty years."

"Can't blame them for feeling that way," Larkin said. "And listen, when you stop and think about it, Midland is a long way from where any of the bombs went off. Given the prevailing winds, the fallout might not even be too bad where they are. They can make it through, and when things calm down—"

"They're in their seventies, and the electromagnetic pulses have wiped out technology," Trevor interrupted. "How long do you think they're going to survive once everything goes back to a nineteenth-century level?"

"People in the nineteenth century did okay."

"Did they really? Life expectancy was a lot shorter then. Almost any little thing can kill you without modern medical attention. Besides, people back then didn't know any different. People today aren't equipped, either mentally or physically, to live under those conditions."

Larkin knew Trevor was right about that. "Maybe so," he said, "but I don't think you should give up hoping that they'll be all right."

"I'm not going to. I'm just not sure it's going to do any good."

Larkin didn't know what to say in response to that, but he was saved from having to say anything by a sudden commotion over near the stairs that led down from the upper level.

At first Larkin thought another fight had broken out, but then he spotted a group of people coming down the stairs, led by Graham and Deb Moultrie, who were holding hands. Several red-vested members of the security force followed them.

Moultrie stopped while he was still several steps from the bottom, so he could look out over the crowd. All over the bunker, people moved in his direction, eager to find out what had brought him down here and hear anything he had to say. He lifted a bullhorn to his mouth and his amplified voice filled the chamber.

"Please, gather around, my friends. I have more news, but I wanted to tell you face-to-face."

"Is it over?" a man yelled. "Will there be any more bombs?"

"I can't tell you for sure," Moultrie replied, "but I believe the attacks have ended. The reason for my uncertainty is that we've lost all communication with the surface."

Larkin glanced up. The surface was less than a hundred and fifty feet above their heads, but right now it might as well have been on the other side of the moon.

"All Internet and wireless networks are off-line," Moultrie continued through the bullhorn. "We have no satellite or cable connections, and the ham-radio frequencies have gone silent as well. Our hope is that some of those ham operators will resume broadcasting at some point, so we'll have some idea what's going on in the world, but until then all we can do is wait."

"What about your instruments on the surface?" a man asked, raising his voice to be heard.

"They're functioning. Approximately half an hour ago, immediately following the detonation of the warhead in the Arlington area, thermal sensors detected a temperature spike to just under five hundred degrees lasting fifteen seconds. According to our calculations, our location here should have been on the outer edge of the thermal blast radius. We also detected wind speeds in excess of two hundred miles per hour from the concussion blast."

Susan moaned softly as she stood next to Larkin. She knew as well as Larkin did that nothing living could withstand a heat wave like that. Not caught in the open, anyway. People hiding in basements or storm cellars *might* have lived through such a fiery burst.

But that didn't mean they were safe, because as Moultrie went on, "Our sensors have also picked up extremely high levels of radiation, and while the winds and the heat have subsided, the radiation has not. We're shielded from the radiation here—our internal sensors continually monitor the levels, and we're perfectly safe—but anyone on the surface who somehow survived the initial blast will suffer from radiation burns and poisoning that will prove fatal, probably sooner rather than later."

"You're saying we're the only people left alive!" a woman cried out in a strident voice.

Moultrie shook his head. "No. I'm saying that we can be relatively sure of what happened in *this* area, but we don't know what's happened elsewhere, and unless and until we get word from outside, we won't know anything more. I firmly believe that in the short term, there *will* be survivors from this attack. But with the widespread death and destruction, the collapse of civilization as we know it, the inevitable rise of disease, and the lingering threat of radiation . . . over time, we may well be the last ones left in this part of the world."

People began to cry again.

"I want to assure you that the Hercules Project is secure," Moultrie continued. "All of our equipment is functioning perfectly, just as we designed and intended. We will remain down here, safe and together, until our instruments indicate that it's safe to begin exploring the surface. When the time comes, that will be done on a *very* limited basis until we can be absolutely certain what the situation is. I will not do anything—*anything!*—to risk the security of the project until I'm sure that—"

A woman lunged from the crowd and started up the stairs, hands held like claws and reaching out toward Moultrie as she screamed at Moultrie, "Murderer! Murderer! You left Nelson out there to die!"

Chapter 23

Larkin recognized the woman as the one who had come up to him earlier looking for her husband. Ruskin, that was her name, he recalled. It was obvious she hadn't found Nelson, or else she wouldn't have attacked Moultrie.

As the woman charged him, Moultrie moved quickly and protectively to put Deb behind him, even though the woman's anger was directed at him. He lifted the arm holding the bullhorn to protect his face from Mrs. Ruskin's hooked fingers, but he just shielded himself instead of striking back as she rammed into him and knocked him back against Deb.

By then, a couple members of the security force had moved around Moultrie. They sprang to his defense. Each grabbed one of Mrs. Ruskin's arms and pulled her away from Moultrie.

"Don't hurt her!" he shouted.

Mrs. Ruskin started screaming curses. Moultrie jerked his head toward the stairs and went on to his security men, "Take her up to my office. Somebody stay with her to make sure she doesn't hurt herself."

The woman tried to pull away from the men in the red vests, but they had good grips on her. Moultrie and Deb moved over to the edge of the stairs to give them room as they forced Mrs. Ruskin up the steps. The assembled residents of the Hercules Project looked on in mingled shock and horror. The security men reached the landing and went around it, out of sight. Everyone could still hear Mrs. Ruskin's screamed oaths, though. The staircase muffled them, and after a moment they went away.

Moultrie took a deep breath and heaved a weary sigh. "This is a terrible thing," he said. He wasn't using the bullhorn now, but the bunker was so hushed and quiet that his voice carried to everyone. "You can't blame the poor woman. I certainly don't."

A man near the front of the crowd asked, "Was she right?"

Moultrie smiled, but there was no humor in the expression. It was more like a death's-head grimace. He said, "Do you mean about me being a murderer? I'd like to think she wasn't."

"But her husband didn't make it?"

Instead of answering directly, Moultrie turned to Deb and held out his free hand. She gave him a sheet of paper. He faced the crowd again and lifted the bullhorn.

"As you know, we have the fingerprints of all the project's residents in our files. We've been matching them against those of the people who entered the project today, so it's a simple matter to isolate the ones who are . . . unaccounted for."

"Dead, you mean," a woman said.

"Not necessarily. As I mentioned earlier, we're far enough from Ground Zero that it's possible there were survivors."

"But if the bomb didn't kill them, the aftereffects will," a man spoke up. "That's what you said."

"It's all speculation at this point," Moultrie said. "We don't *know* what the long-term result will be." He swallowed hard. Watching from the crowd, Larkin could tell that Moultrie was almost overcome by emotion. Moultrie lifted the paper and went on, "These are the people who were not able to be with us today. David Ahearne. Melissa Ahearne. Jacob Ahearne. Tamara Bradley. Matthew Beckerman. Teresa Beckerman. John Eldridge. Samantha Eldridge. Peyton Harwell . . ."

He continued reading names, among them Nelson Ruskin. For the most part there was no reaction from the stunned crowd, but at some of the names, someone gasped or cried out, and sobs began to be heard, grim counterpoints to the list Moultrie was giving them.

Finally, Moultrie lowered the paper and said, "That's all. Thirty-three of our residents are unaccounted for. The current population of the Hercules Project is three hundred and seventy-four. Three-hundred and seventy-four souls . . . and God bless each and every one of us." His nostrils flared as he drew in another deep breath. "Right now, my friends, and until we know differently . . . we are the United States of America."

Moultrie and Deb went back up to the command center. Larkin assumed that's where they were headed, anyway. A short time later, Deb's voice came over the loudspeakers announcing that everyone should begin moving to their assigned areas. That was good, Larkin thought, because it gave everybody something to do. They needed something to occupy their minds and their energy, instead of just sitting around thinking about what had happened. He had seen the same thing in combat. All hell could be breaking loose, but if somebody had a job to do—and it had been drummed into them that they should do it, no matter what the circumstances—they were a lot more likely to stay alive and prevail against the enemy . . . whoever that enemy happened to be.

At this point, the enemy wasn't really Russia or North Korea anymore. They had shot their bolt, done the worst they could. The main enemy of the residents of the Hercules Project was fear, ably abetted by grief, resentment, and anger.

Susan said to Jill and Trevor, "Let's find your place first. Your father and I have everything ready in our apartment."

"I could have used some more time to move things into our quarters," Jill said with a sigh. "But I suppose we were lucky to have as much time as we did."

That comment made Larkin think of the old saying about how the lucky ones in a nuclear war would be the ones killed outright.

He hoped that wouldn't turn out to be true in real life.

Several sets of stairs led from the lower bunker to the main hallways above. People began trooping up the steps, mostly couples and families. The ones who had chosen to live in the barracks-like lower bunker were overwhelmingly single. Space couldn't be wasted. Anyone who was single but wanted to live in one of the main corridors or a missile silo apartment had to accept that they would have roommates.

The H-shaped main corridors ran roughly east and west. The quarters that Jill and Trevor would be sharing with Bailey and Chris were in the southern corridor, designated Corridor One. The northern corridor was Corridor Two. The four silos were called Silos A, B, C, and D, starting with the one at the western end of Corridor One and running clockwise. The door of the Sinclairs' quarters was labeled 1A09, which meant it was actually the fifth door on the left, going toward Silo A, directly across the broad hallway from 1A10.

Down at the end of the corridor were wide double doors that opened into a reception area for Silo A. Apartment 1 in Silo A was located at this level, with four apartments underneath it, accessible by both elevator and stairs. Larkin and Susan were in Apartment 2, just one level down, with Jim and Beth Huddleston directly below them. Larkin wasn't too fond of that idea, but he *was* glad that Jill, Trevor, and the kids would be so close.

When they went in, a door on the left opened into a small bedroom with two bunk beds in it. That wasn't the optimal arrangement for the kids, but again, a certain level of privacy had to be given up. Along a painted concrete wall and around a corner, also to the left, was the small kitchen and dining area. A door in the left corner of that room led into the "master bedroom," as Larkin wryly thought of it, another chamber on the cramped side with a full-size bed in it, along with a closet and a tiny bathroom barely big enough for the toilet and the combination bath/shower. Another bathroom and a storage area were beyond the kitchen.

Everything was pretty spartan. No living space other than the kitchen/dining room, but the dining table had space for six at it, so that was a little bigger than what they actually needed. The table would serve as a desk for Bailey and Chris, too, where they could do their homework. Larkin wasn't sure how long it would be before the school was up and running, but he didn't expect Moultrie to wait too long about that.

They could prepare food here, eat, sleep, study, read. The project had a good-size library of physical books, as well as a huge collection of e-books, movies, and TV shows that could be downloaded onto just about any device anyone could think of. Larkin wasn't sure how the kids would get along without the latest popular social media site, but they would figure it out. Kids always did.

Under the circumstances, cramped though they might be, the quarters in the Hercules Project were quite possibly the most luxurious accommodations left anywhere in the world. A crazy thought, but it was true.

The family stowed the gear from their bug-out bags in the storage area, then Bailey and Chris sat down at the dining table and got out their phones. There was no Internet, of course, but Trevor had explained to them that there probably wouldn't be, while they were inside the bunker, so they had already downloaded movies, games, and plenty of other apps to keep themselves occupied for a while. Their parents, along with Larkin and Susan, stood in the doorway watching for a moment, then retreated to the main corridor.

"They look so solemn," Jill said. "Like the weight of the world is on their shoulders. I can't stand it. They shouldn't have to be going through this."

"No one should," Trevor said as he put his arms around her. "But—"

"I know. They're alive. And I'm so thankful that's true. So thankful that . . . that all of us are here and safe, at least for the time being."

"We'll be all right," Larkin said. "Everything's worked just like it was supposed to so far."

Susan said, "Except for the thirty-three people who couldn't get here in time."

Larkin put a hand on her shoulder and squeezed reassuringly as she dabbed at her eyes. The brain couldn't really grasp the millions of people who had died today, but it could understand a number like thirty-three. Thirty-three people who had gotten up this morning to go about their lives and now were nothing more than ashes tossed around on a nuclear wind.

"Come on," Larkin said quietly to his wife. "Let's go on and let the kids get settled into their place."

"That's right," Trevor said. "*This* is our place now. And for who knows how long . . ."

He and Jill went back into their quarters while Larkin and Susan walked on toward the entrance to Silo A at the end of the corridor. People were moving around, but with a little less than four hundred of them spread out through the two main corridors and the huge lower bunker, it didn't seem crowded now. Once folks settled into their lives here, Larkin mused, it would be possible to go for long stretches of time without seeing very many of their new neighbors. He knew from talking to Moultrie and Deb that there would be activities to help maintain a sense of community and social connection, but those wouldn't be mandatory. Larkin had always had to fight the hermit tendency in his own nature, but at least he had Susan to goad him into not being completely antisocial.

Larkin had both of their bags slung over his shoulders and carried the AR-15 in his left hand. The Colt 1911 was still holstered on his hip. All guns were supposed to be locked up in one of the vault rooms except for practicing or if they were needed for defending the project, but no one had asked him for the weapons yet. He supposed they would come around and do that later.

He wanted to talk to Moultrie about volunteering for the security force, too, although the idea of wearing one of those dorky red vests didn't appeal to him that much.

Besides, red made a good target. Somebody needed to talk to Moultrie about that, and maybe advise him about a few other things, too. Larkin wasn't going to be pushy about that, however. Anybody who made too many noises about the way things were done often wound up being put in charge, and he sure as hell didn't want *that*.

They walked through the double doors at the end of the corridor. The entrance to Apartment 1 was directly in front of them. The elevator was to the left. Back in the days when this underground chamber had held a Nike Hercules missile ready for firing, that had been a service elevator, so it was fairly large. Susan pushed the button to open the door, and as they stepped in, Larkin said, "Jim and Beth Huddleston have the place right under us, you know."

"Really?" The door slid closed as Susan went on, "I didn't think Beth would ever agree to getting involved in something like this."

"Jim did it behind her back."

"He did?" Susan laughed hollowly. "I don't mean to be offensive, but I never would have thought that he had the balls."

"They're lucky he did. Beth may come around to seeing it that way sooner or later. From the brief conversation I had with them earlier, she's probably still waiting for the announcement that there really wasn't a war and it was just some dirty, underhanded trick of the right-wingers instead."

Susan sighed. "Do you think that now, down here, people will just forget about all that nonsense?"

"We can hope, baby. We can hope."

Larkin wasn't convinced of it, though. Some prejudices were so deeply ingrained that maybe not even a nuclear war could blast them out of existence.

Not without blasting humanity completely out of existence as well.

Today might have been a good start on that. It was too soon to tell.

The elevator stopped and let them out into the reception area on their level. Larkin set down the bug-out bags to get the chip-enabled key card from his wallet. Residents in the Hercules Project were able to lock their doors, although Moultrie and his security and maintainence staff could get in wherever they needed to, of course. Larkin and Susan went into the apartment. Larkin thumbed a switch on the wall.

The indirect LED lighting sprang to life, revealing a small but comfortably furnished living area. A love seat, two armchairs, a desk. Some framed photographs and paintings they had brought from their house hung on the walls. A bathroom and storage area was to the right, kitchen and dining area straight ahead, and the bedroom and second bathroom to the left.

Larkin heeled the door closed behind them, set down their gear again, and put his arm around Susan's shoulders as she stood there looking at the place.

"Home, sweet home," he said.

Chapter 24

It had been early afternoon, a little after one o'clock, when Jim Huddleston had told Larkin about the North Koreans nuking Seoul. As incredible as it was to believe, not quite three hours had passed since then. Three hours that had changed the world forever.

Larkin and Susan were sitting on the love seat, leaning against each other, quietly drawing strength from the human contact, when the soft chime of the doorbell sounded.

"Are you expecting company?" Susan asked.

"Actually, yeah. Somebody's probably come to tell us that we need to lock up any guns we brought in with us."

"I remember you saying that nobody would ever take your guns away from you."

Larkin frowned. "I know, and honestly, I don't like it very much. But I understand. In such a confined area, under such high stress, Moultrie doesn't want people running around armed. Besides, there's a range down here, and we're supposed to be able to get our guns whenever we want to practice." He paused, then went on, "Actually, it would be a good idea to set up classes so that all the people who don't know how to shoot can learn. There may come a day when we're relying on everybody in here to defend the place."

"From what? You heard the things Graham said about the damage and the radiation. There's no one left up there, Patrick."

"Probably not," Larkin said. "But I wouldn't want to bet my life on it. I especially don't want to bet the lives of you and the kids on it."

The doorbell chimed again. Larkin sighed, stood up, and went to answer it.

A tall, burly black man with graying hair smiled and nodded as Larkin opened the door. Larkin had never seen him before. The man wore one of the red security vests.

"Patrick Larkin?" he asked.

"That's right."

The man stuck out his right hand. "I'm Chuck Fisher. Graham asked me to come and collect you. We're having a meeting in the Command Center."

Larkin shook hands. Fisher had a strong grip, and he also had the brisk air of a military man that Larkin instinctively recognized. Larkin said, "Corps?"

"Army," Fisher replied.

"Dogface, eh?"

"That's right, jarhead."

Susan had come up behind Larkin. She said, "You two aren't going to fight, are you?"

Fisher smiled again and sketched a little salute to her. "Nothing to worry about, Mrs. Larkin. We're on the same side. We're just upholding a long tradition, that's all." He looked at Larkin again. "You need to bring any firearms you have in your quarters as well."

"Yeah, I expected that." Larkin had leaned the AR-15 against the wall near the door. He picked it up and said to Susan, "I'll be back."

"I'll be here," she said, and her tone made it clear enough that she didn't have to add, *Where else would I be?*

As Larkin and Fisher went up one level in the elevator, Larkin commented, "I'm surprised Moultrie didn't just send somebody around to collect the guns. I didn't figure I'd have to turn them in in person."

"It's not just about the guns," Fisher said.

"Then what is it?"

"I'll let Graham explain that."

"You retired or active duty?"

"Retired. You?"

"Same."

Fisher nodded. Larkin felt an instinctive liking for the guy. He came across as tough, no-nonsense, and not the type to waste time with unnecessary talk.

The Command Center was at the eastern end of the upper-level corridors, a huge complex of offices, hallways, and chambers that began between Silos C and D and extended deep under the rolling hills. The generators and air- and water-purification systems were located here, along with the medical and dental facilities, the pharmacy, the hydroponics gardens, even the big warehouse-like space where rabbit hutches and chicken coops were located.

Those animals were not pets. Over the coming months, they would be a vital supply of fresh food. The people entrusted with raising and caring for them had very important jobs. A great deal of nonperishable food had been stored down here, but the chickens and rabbits, along with the gardens, meant the difference between mere subsistence and a truly healthy diet.

The Command Center was also the beating heart of the Hercules Project, where staff members monitored the equipment that measured surface conditions, along with all the life-support systems. They also searched for any signs of life coming from the surface, any communication via Internet, wireless, broadcast, or amateur radio. All the surveillance cameras up top had been destroyed by the blast, so the project was blind . . . but not deaf.

Larkin was able to pick up on that when he and Fisher entered a large room reminiscent of news coverage he used to see on TV of Mission Control at NASA in Houston. Most of the big monitors on the walls were dark. The ones that were lit up displayed data, not visual images. Ranks of computers were set up on tables where men and women worked with them.

"Looks like you could launch a rocket from in here," Larkin commented.

"There was a time you could," Fisher said. "Or a missile, anyway. This was the original fire control center. Graham expanded and updated it, of course, and added a lot of equipment." He pointed to a steel door. "The meeting room is over there."

As they went in, Larkin saw ten men seated at a long conference table that looked like it should have been in some corporate boardroom. The place could have passed for one of those boardrooms, in fact, with its dark paneling and a few sedate landscapes hanging on the walls. All that was missing was a fancy portrait of the chairman of the board and maybe the company president. Graham Moultrie wasn't really the sort to indulge in such vanity, though.

Adam Threadgill was one of the men at the table. He grinned when Larkin came in but didn't say anything. The other men had the same sort of competent, experienced look to them.

Moultrie stood at the head of the table with his hands resting on the back of the leather-upholstered swivel chair positioned there. He said, "Come on in, Patrick. You're the last of the men I've summoned here right now. You can put your rifle over there."

He nodded toward a smaller table next to the wall. Several rifles lay there already, so Larkin assumed they had been brought in by the other men. As he added the AR-15 to the collection, he said, "What about my Colt?"

"Keep it for now," Moultrie said.

Larkin wasn't going to argue with that. Even though he didn't expect to need the .45 down here in the bunker, the whole experience was nerve-wracking enough that it felt good to have the gun on his hip.

"Have a seat," Moultrie went on. Larkin took an empty chair diagonally across from Threadgill. Moultrie stepped away from the head of the table and walked along it as he continued, "I would have gotten around to talking to all of you in the near future, if events hadn't unfolded the way they have. I've been putting together my security force slowly and carefully, making sure that I have just the right personnel. You men will complete that force, if you agree to take part."

This came as no surprise to Larkin. In fact, it was

what he'd expected as soon as Chuck Fisher showed up at his door and told him about the meeting.

"Every man in here is experienced, either in law enforcement or the military. You've dealt with trouble. You've dealt with bad actors. You've put your life on the line to protect others. That's the sort of man I want responsible for the safety of the Hercules Project." Moultrie gestured toward the man standing at the other end of the table. "Chuck Fisher is the director of this group. Chuck was an Army Ranger and since retiring has worked as a private contractor on a number of high-risk operations. He's an old friend and the top man at what he does."

So Fisher was a mercenary, Larkin thought. He had known men who wanted to get into that line of work. Some were as solid as could be, others . . . not so much. Fisher struck him as the solid sort, which was good.

"Of course, you don't have to accept appointment to this force. It's not mandatory, and needless to say, the job doesn't pay anything." Moultrie smiled. "Not financially, anyway. You do get the satisfaction of knowing that you're helping keep everyone safe, *and* you get more leeway in being able to have firearms in your possession. Right now, people are too stunned by what's happened today to cause any trouble, but starting immediately, I want all of you to be armed whenever you're on duty—and you need to have a gun pretty handy when you're *not* on duty, too. Because we're all going to be on call, twenty-four hours a day, seven days a week. Understood?"

Nods came from the men around the table. Moultrie had started pacing back and forth as he spoke, but now he paused and rested a hand on his security chief's shoulder.

"Chuck will be in charge of setting up duty shifts. In this area, he's my second-in-command. He'll get together with all of you and make sure you know the schedule. I'm hoping you'll all see fit to join this effort, but like I said, it's up to you and if you choose not to, it won't be a problem. Anyone who doesn't want to be part of the security force can go ahead and return to your quarters now."

None of the men at the table stood up.

Moultrie grinned and went on, "That's just the response I was hoping for. But I'd understand anybody who didn't want to throw in with us right now. It's been . . . a bad day. Everyone is shaken up. Horrified. Some have lost loved ones. I think it's important for us all to settle into our new routines as quickly as possible, but folks who have been through what we've been through today . . . well, you've got to give 'em a little leeway." He rubbed his hands together briskly, looked around the table again, and asked, "Any questions?"

"Not a question, really, but a comment," Larkin said. "I look around the room, and one thing strikes me right away."

"Go ahead, Patrick. I'm very interested."

"You don't have any women here. Having the security force be a boys' club is gonna cause trouble somewhere along the way."

Chuck Fisher frowned and said, "This is a chance to get rid of those politically correct notions that never really worked but were forced on us anyway."

"But, as a matter of fact," Moultrie added, "there *are*

a couple of female members of the security force. They're on duty now. We didn't set out to exclude females, but you've got to work with the best personnel you have available."

Larkin nodded and said, "In that case, you ought to talk to my daughter Jill. She was out on the gun range with me when she was in elementary school, and she's as good a shot as I am. I raised her to be able to kick my ass, too." He smiled. "She can't quite do that, mind you, but she can give it a good try. Most guys, she could put on the ground without much trouble."

"An excellent suggestion," Moultrie said. He looked at Fisher. "Chuck, you'll talk to Mrs. Sinclair?"

"Sure," Fisher agreed. "If she doesn't have any military or law enforcement experience, though, I'd have to see enough to be sure she can handle herself."

"She's a pharmacist," Larkin said dryly, "but I don't think she'll disappoint you."

Moultrie nodded and said, "Fine. If any of you know anyone else you think would be a good candidate, talk to me or Chuck. We want things to run smoothly down here." He leaned forward and rested his hands on the table. "I don't have to tell you men that it's going to be rough, even if everything works just like it's supposed to. Put this many people in close quarters, throw in all the emotional turmoil they're going through, and there's going to be trouble sooner or later. All of you saw the incident earlier with Mrs. Ruskin."

"Yeah, how's she doin'?" Threadgill asked.

"She's fine. We had to give her a sedative for her own protection. She's in her quarters now, resting. There's a staff member with her to help her in case she needs anything."

A tiny frown creased Larkin's forehead. Moultrie's response sounded reasonable enough on the surface, but it could also be interpreted to mean that Mrs. Ruskin had been drugged to shut her up and locked in her quarters with a guard on her. That was probably stretching things and not giving Moultrie the benefit of the doubt, but at the same time, somebody like Beth Huddleston, with her paranoia, might see it that way.

Susan might, too, Larkin realized, and that thought was even more disturbing.

So far, though, he had no reason to suspect Graham Moultrie of anything except wanting to save humanity.

"If there are no more questions," Moultrie said, "I need to get back to my rounds. I'm trying to keep up with what's going on in all the sections, and also, Deb or one of my other lieutenants will let me know right away if there are any problems. So far, nothing has happened that we didn't expect and prepare for, and I'd like to keep that record going." He started toward the door but then paused. "I'm sorry about the residents who didn't make it here in time. But honestly, I thought the number might be higher than it turned out to be. We're going to be all right, gentlemen. I can feel it in my bones."

With that declaration, Moultrie smiled and left the meeting room.

"You fellows can go back to your quarters now," Chuck Fisher told the men at the table. "I'll be in touch with each of you and give you your duty schedule. I want to echo what Graham said and thank you for stepping up to make things better here."

They filed out, leaving the long guns behind to be locked up, and walked back through the Command

Center to get to the main hallways. Threadgill walked beside Larkin, hurrying a little to keep up with his friend's longer strides. Quietly, he said, "What do you think, Patrick? Is everything going to be all right?"

"Sure," Larkin said, "as long as everybody down here ignores human nature and is on their best behavior around the clock."

Threadgill grunted. "What do you think the chances are of *that* happening?"

"Slim and none, but we've got to try to make it work. For better or worse, this is our home now."

BOOK TWO

Chapter 25

May 16, the following year

Larkin hurried toward the angry shouts, pushing through the crowd in the Bullpen. He didn't know who had given the lower bunker that name, but someone had done so fairly early on, and it had stuck.

"Break it up!" he yelled, the time-honored command of authority wading into a mob.

Resentful faces turned to glare at him. A man said, "It's the Redshirts! Look out!"

That was just wrong on so many levels, Larkin thought. For one thing, the security force wore red *vests*. Larkin hadn't been able to talk Moultrie and Fisher out of that readily identifiable garment, and he supposed they had a point. For another, the man's frightened cry, along with the reactions of the people who shrank away from him, made it seem like he was here to hurt them, rather than doing his job and protecting them. Larkin didn't like being seen as the bad guy.

On the other hand, he *did* have a job to do, and it included breaking up fights before anybody was injured seriously.

Susan, Jill, and the rest of the medical staff had enough

to do without having to deal with broken noses, busted knuckles, and all the bruises and scratches that came with brawling.

The crowd parted enough for him to get through to the area in the middle of the huge chamber where four men were fighting. Two of them rolled around on the floor, wrestling with each other, while the other two stood toe-to-toe, slugging it out. Larkin recognized all of them.

The two on the floor were Chad Holdstock and Michael Pomeroy. The two sluggers were Jeff Greer and Zeke Ortega. Holdstock and Greer were part of Charlotte Ruskin's group of malcontents. They'd probably been mouthing off, and Pomeroy and Ortega had taken exception to it. There was no telling who had thrown the first punch. With tensions in the Hercules Project as high as they were, it could have been any of them.

It didn't matter who started the fight, Larkin reminded himself. His job was to end it.

The pair on the floor grappling with each other were closest to him, and Holdstock was on top at the moment, trying to wrap his hands around Pomeroy's throat. Larkin stepped in, bent over, and grabbed Holdstock from behind, sliding his arms under the man's arms and then locking his left hand around his right wrist in front of Holdstock's chest. With a grunt of effort, he heaved upward and hauled Holdstock off Pomeroy. Turning, Larkin gave Holdstock a shove that sent him stumbling into the crowd.

"I said break it up!" Larkin repeated. As he swung around, he saw Pomeroy scrambling to his feet. The look on Pomeroy's face told Larkin he was eager to go after

Holdstock and continue the fight. Larkin thrust his left hand toward Pomeroy, palm out in an order to stop, and added, "Damn it, back off!"

Pomeroy stopped, but his hands were still clenched into fists.

Larkin moved around him toward Greer and Ortega. Greer had moved into Charlotte Ruskin's quarters in Corridor Two a while back. People's personal lives were their own business. The security force didn't care who slept with who as long as they were peaceful about it. But Greer's relationship with Charlotte Ruskin probably had a lot to do with his dislike for Graham Moultrie and his frequent bitching about the things Moultrie and the project staff did.

Ever since Day One, the day of the nuclear war— that was how they measured time here in the Hercules Project; today was Day 247—Charlotte Ruskin had caused trouble. She hadn't physically attacked anyone again, but she complained constantly about anything and everything. A few months in, she had started holding meetings in the Bullpen, meetings at which she had given loud, angry speeches about Moultrie's leadership. Larkin hadn't attended any of those gatherings, but he'd heard that she was comparing Moultrie to Hitler and his security force to the Gestapo. That appealed to people like Beth Huddleston, since playing the Hitler card had always been one of the Left's go-to tactics in political arguments.

And despite Larkin's hope that they were now beyond all that partisan bullshit—that the residents would understand they were in this together—almost right from the start it had been evident that wasn't going to be the case. Factions had formed almost right away. "Democrat" and "Republican" might not mean much anymore, but now there were Bullpenners, Corridor People, and the Silo-ites—a name that Larkin hated with a passion. Varying degrees of Haves and Have-nots, although anybody who looked at the situation with a clear-eyed, practical bent could see right away that nobody down here "had" much more than anybody else.

Sure, the people who lived in the corridors and the silo apartments enjoyed a little more room and privacy than the ones in the Bullpen, but that had been every-one's choice to make. Nobody was living in the damn lap of luxury, as Larkin had pointed out during more than one argument with Beth Huddleston, who had ap-pointed herself the spokesperson for and guardian of the so-called downtrodden—not that she was just about to give up anything of her own in order to "share their pain."

Charlotte Ruskin, fueled by grief over her husband's death and her hatred for Graham Moultrie, used that festering discontent to stir up trouble. Larkin knew it, Moultrie knew it, and so did everybody else on the security force, but, per Moultrie's orders, there wasn't much they could do about it. This tiny outpost was still America, after all, and people had rights.

But when they started throwing punches . . . *then* Larkin could step in and do what was necessary to keep the peace.

Which was what he did now as he moved toward Greer and Ortega. He had gotten close when Greer hooked a left into Ortega's stomach that doubled him over, then followed with a right uppercut that sent

Ortega flying backward. Larkin braced himself and caught the man.

Ortega hung loosely in Larkin's grip, only semi-conscious. Greer bored in with his fists cocked, evidently so caught up in the heat of battle he didn't notice who had hold of Ortega.

"Hang on to him!" he cried. "I'll teach the bastard a lesson he'll never forget!"

"Damn it!" Larkin turned and pushed Ortega into the waiting arms of the crowd, several of whom grabbed him and kept him from falling. He put his hand out in a warding-off gesture, as he had with Pomeroy. "Back off, Greer!"

The man's chest rammed hard against Larkin's hand, but Larkin was bigger and had set his feet. Greer grunted from the contact and fell back a step.

"Larkin!" A scowl twisted Greer's face. "Come to strut around in your red shirt and give orders?"

Larkin started to say something about how it was a vest, not a shirt, then stopped as he realized how pointless that was. He kept his hand up and said, "I don't know what this is about—"

"He called Charlotte a bitch!"

Maybe if she wouldn't act *like one* . . . The thought started to form in Larkin's mind, but he shook it away. "That's no excuse for going after a guy."

"Isn't it? What would you do if somebody called your wife a bitch, Larkin?"

Larkin knew good and well what he would *feel* like doing in that case. Whether or not he gave in to the urge would depend on other factors, he supposed. He liked to think he could control himself, but if he was being honest, he didn't know if that would always be the case.

"Look, if you and Ortega don't get along, just stay away from each other."

"Yeah, that's easier said than done. You can't exactly go for much of a walk down here, man."

Greer revolved his hand to take in their surroundings. He had a point there, too. This underground chamber *seemed* vast, but when you were stuck down here all the time, it shrunk in a hurry. People could walk around the Bullpen and then go upstairs and walk the full length of both corridors in less than fifteen minutes. It didn't take long to start feeling like the concrete walls were closing in.

"You're gonna have to find some other way to deal with your problems, Greer," Larkin said. "You can't just start whaling away on people."

A man in the crowd yelled, "Yeah, if you do that, the Redshirts will drag you away to jail, Jeff!"

Larkin looked around, unsure who had said that. His jaw tightened. "Nobody's getting dragged to jail—"

"Damn right," Holdstock said from behind him, "because there's only one of you. Where are the rest of your fascist buddies, Larkin?"

Fascist. There it was again. Larkin hadn't been born until World War II was over, but he was old enough to have known men who had fought in it. One of his uncles had been in the 1st Infantry Division, the Big Red One. Another had been on the *Lexington* at the Battle of the Coral Sea and had survived by the skin of his teeth when the carrier went down. A guy like Holdstock could start an argument in an empty room, so he was viewed mostly as a hothead. A lot of muttering came from the crowd. Larkin could tell that some supported Greer and Holdstock while others were on the side of Pomeroy and Ortega. It wouldn't take much for this to go from a fight to a full-scale riot. He didn't want that.

"Look," he said. "Why don't all of you just move on—"

"What's going on here?" a shrill voice demanded. Charlotte Ruskin came through the crowd, pushing people aside. She stopped in front of Larkin, put her hands on her hips, and glared at him. "What are you doing, Larkin? Carrying out Moultrie's illegal orders to harass my friends?"

"My only orders are to keep the peace," Larkin said as he struggled to keep a tight rein on his temper.

That wasn't easy where Charlotte Ruskin was concerned. She was like fingernails on a blackboard. She was around forty, with dark red hair and the sort of looks that used to make people use the phrase "a handsome woman." Not beautiful by any means, but she could be compelling, at least when she wasn't screeching like a harpy.

Now she snorted contemptuously at Larkin's declaration about keeping the peace. "Funny how Moultrie's idea of peace is beating people up and putting them behind bars."

In point of fact, there were several small chambers adjacent to the Command Center where people could be detained, but they were hardly jail cells and there were no bars, just doors. Those confinement rooms were seldom used. Mostly they served as a place where somebody could sleep it off if they got drunk and started causing trouble. Liquor was supposedly controlled— Moultrie had learned quickly that people under as much stress as they were in the Hercules Project didn't need unlimited access to alcohol—but some of them found a way to get their hands on booze anyway. It was an age-old story, Larkin supposed.

"Nobody's getting locked up," he began again. "These guys blew off some steam, and that's the end of it—*if* they'll go on about their business."

Greer bunched his fists and stuck his jaw out defiantly. "What if we're tired of shutting up and rolling over?" he said. "What if we've decided it's time to start fighting for our rights?"

He was just showing off for his girlfriend, Larkin thought. But before he could respond to Greer, the loudspeakers crackled and Graham Moultrie's voice filled the bunker. His tone betrayed his excitement as he said, *"Attention, please. I need your attention, everyone. We've just received a signal—from outside!"*

Chapter 26

That news made everyone in the bunker fall silent—but only for a few seconds.

Then voices erupted in shouts of surprise, joy, and maybe even a little apprehension. During the past eight months, people had settled into a life here, despite its drawbacks.

Who knew what might be going on in the outside world?

For all this time, everything had been silent up there. The Internet, wireless networks, shortwave radio . . . all had been quiet. The project's instruments showed that radiation levels had dropped steadily and exponentially since the day of the war, but the initial readings had been almost off the charts, indicating that the warhead that had fallen on Arlington had been a high-yield and extremely dirty one. The contamination was still bad enough to be dangerous to human life. Moultrie wasn't going to risk the whole project and everyone in it by unbuttoning too soon.

A significant number of the residents were convinced that the people down here were the last human beings on Earth. They had formed their own group and called themselves the Sole Survivors. Their philosophy was a blend of apocalyptic hysteria and religion. Larkin thought their beliefs were a little far-fetched—the chances of the residents of the Hercules Project being the only ones left seemed unlikely to him—but as far as he was concerned, whatever got them through the days and nights was their business.

If there were people still alive on the surface, that would shoot holes in the Sole Survivors' dogma, but they would just have to get over that and move forward. Larkin, like everybody else in the bunker, was excited and eager to hear what Moultrie had to say.

"We've picked up a shortwave radio transmission," the project's leader continued, causing a hushed, attentive silence to fall again. *"It was very brief and fragmentary, probably caused by signal skip in the upper atmosphere. Someone was sending old-fashioned Morse code. We weren't able to transcribe complete sentences, just parts of individual words here and there, so we don't know who they are or where they're located. They were sending in a foreign language, possibly Portuguese, so right now we're speculating that the message may have originated in Brazil. That seems to be the most likely possibility. But even though we don't actually know much at this time, we can be sure of this: we are not alone. There were others who lived through that terrible day, and it's only a matter of time until the human race is reunited again. Until then, God bless each and every one of us in the Hercules Project."*

The loudspeakers clicked off, another second went by, and then another storm of cheers and whistles burst out. People hugged and pounded each other on the back. Some kissed, some even danced around. They were excited and justifiably so. This terrible ordeal they were enduring probably still had a long way to go, but now, for the first time, it was possible to glimpse some hope for the future again.

The fight Larkin had broken up seemed to be forgotten, at least for now, but he didn't fully trust Charlotte Ruskin and her friends. Greer had grabbed Charlotte and was hugging her so tightly her feet had come off the floor. She wasn't a petite woman, so that probably wasn't easy. It showed how excited Greer was, though.

Larkin turned, caught the eye of Pomeroy and Ortega, and motioned with a thumb for them to take off. Putting some distance between them and their former opponents would go a long way toward restoring the peace. Pomeroy nodded and faded off into the celebrating crowd, but Ortega hesitated before moving closer to Larkin.

"Listen, man, you don't know what those two were saying," Ortega said, keeping his voice quiet enough that only Larkin could hear him in the hubbub. "They were talking about how it's time to take control of the project away from Moultrie."

"There are always malcontents, wherever you go," Larkin said. "Those two were just letting out some hot air."

Ortega shook his head. "No, they were saying Moultrie's a dictator and he's got to be overthrown." He leaned closer. "They want to take over and open up the bunker. They say it's time to go back up."

A chill went through Larkin at that. Moultrie kept all the members of the security force updated on surface conditions. Larkin knew it wasn't safe there yet. He understood why people wanted to get back up top and see the sun again, take stock of what was left and what might be possible going forward, but rushing things could spell doom for all of them.

Ortega went on, "Mike and I told 'em they were crazy, and they jumped us. That's what started the whole thing."

Larkin nodded and said, "Thanks for filling me in, Zeke."

"Of course, I guess it's not completely their fault. That Ruskin woman keeps stirrin' 'em up."

"I know," Larkin said. "Maybe this news today will change things."

"I sure hope so," Ortega said, then he drifted off into the crowd, too.

Larkin looked around. More than likely, the excitement that gripped the bunker would keep things relatively peaceful here for a while. Anyway, he wasn't the only security man on duty. He started toward the closest set of stairs leading up to the corridors.

In the wake of Moultrie's announcement, he wanted to see his wife.

Susan had been treating a patient with a cold that was threatening to turn into a sinus infection when Moultrie's announcement came over the public-address system. Colds—good old upper-respiratory viruses—weren't as common down here as they had been in the world before the war, but they hadn't been wiped out because a number of people had been sick when they entered the Hercules Project. In a closed environment like this, it was inevitable that the virus would be passed around. A person couldn't catch the same virus twice, but with more than 200 of the little bastards that caused the common cold, Susan didn't believe the ailment would ever be wiped out completely. Maybe if generation after generation of residents lived down here for the next couple of hundred years . . .

Of course, if it came down to that, they'd probably have lots worse things to think about than the sniffles. Human beings weren't wired to spend their whole lives underground, like worms in the earth.

In the meantime, there wasn't much that could be done about colds. People just had to suffer through them, as they had done before the war. But occasionally the damage done by the virus turned into a bacterial infection, and Susan thought that was the case in the elderly man she was examining today. His nasal secretions were thick and green, and he was running a fever. He was going to need a round of antibiotics. Susan didn't want the infection settling into his lungs and turning into pneumonia.

She'd been about to tell him that when Moultrie's voice came over the speaker, delivering the news of the shortwave transmission that probably had originated in Brazil. That had excited the patient so much he'd wanted to forget about the exam and rush back to his apartment to see his wife.

"Not just yet, Mr. Bardwell," Susan told him. "I'm as thrilled to hear about that as you are, but you don't need to leave until I've written you a prescription for antibiotics. You'll need to fill it today, too. Don't wait until tomorrow to get started on these."

"All right, Dr. Larkin," the man said. "But this sure is great news, isn't it?"

"It certainly is," Susan agreed with a smile. She had

long since given up trying to get people to stop referring to her as "Doctor." Early on, she had been pressed into the role of nurse-practitioner, since a couple of the people who hadn't made it to the bunker in time that fateful day had been MDs Moultrie was counting on to work in the project's clinic. Like most nurses, Susan knew as much on a practical level as most doctors did, at least when it came to general ailments. She'd been able to make up some of the clinic's personnel shortage. Right now, in fact, she was the only member of the medical staff on duty.

Jill helped out now and then, too, when she could find the time between her work in the pharmacy and her duties as a member of the security force. Susan still didn't care for the idea of her daughter being in the middle of trouble when it broke out, but she had to admit that Jill was able to take care of herself.

Mr. Bardwell took the prescription Susan wrote for him and hurried out of the exam room. With the door open, Susan could hear cheers coming from elsewhere in the project. People were excited, obviously.

Jill appeared in the doorway a moment later with a big smile on her face. "You heard that, Mom? You heard?"

Susan said, "I heard. It's wonderful news, isn't it? We're not . . . alone in the world after all." She frowned slightly as she went on, "But I just sent a patient to the pharmacy for some antibiotics. Shouldn't you be there?"

"Sandy Carter is working right now. She should have everything covered. I've got to go find Trev and the kids!" Jill threw her arms around her mother and gave her an exuberant hug. Susan didn't often see her daughter this excited. Normally, Jill was on the cool and reserved side, as quiet and pragmatic as her father.

"The kids will be in school," Susan called after her as Jill started out of the clinic. "You shouldn't interrupt—"

She stopped, realizing that the same sort of excitement gripping the rest of the project was probably on display in the school, as well. The teachers and kids were all human. They would be as thrilled as anyone else to hear that there was other life in the world, that they weren't the only ones left.

The clinic's waiting room was empty. There had been three more patients there earlier. Susan looked at the receptionist, Becky Hammond, and asked, "What happened to everybody?"

"They all rushed out when they heard the news. I don't think we're likely to have any more business today, Susan."

"Well, maybe not. But I'll stay until the end of my shift anyway. If you want to go . . ."

Becky edged out from her little cubicle. "I'd really like to go find my husband . . ."

Susan laughed and waved a hand. "Go."

"Don't you want to see Patrick?"

"If I know my husband, he'll be showing up here before too much . . . Speak of the devil."

Larkin ambled through the entrance. He poked a thumb against his chest and said, "Me? I'm the devil?"

"Of course not. But I was expecting to see you, and here you are."

"Great minds think alike." Larkin took her in his arms and held her. Becky hurried out of the clinic, waving good-bye to Susan over Larkin's shoulder as she left.

After a moment, Susan stepped back and said, "It's wonderful news, isn't it?"

"Sure."

She looked at him, saw the slight frown furrowing his forehead, and said, "What's wrong? You don't sound very enthusiastic, and I can tell that you're thinking about something."

"A possibility occurred to me on the way over here. That was a shortwave message they picked up. Morse code, Moultrie said. My guess is that whoever sent it is looking for signs of human life just like we've been doing. We send out shortwave messages around the clock, too. It's all automated."

"So?"

Larkin sighed. "So what if the message we picked up is the same thing? An automated signal being sent out by some other survivors?"

"I don't see why that would be a bad thing," Susan said.

"Because unless we can answer them and get some response back from them, we don't know that they're really out there. We don't have any way of knowing how long that signal has been going out. The system sending it could be programmed to keep doing so as long as it has power, even if whoever set it up in the first place isn't . . . there anymore."

"You mean dead," Susan said, a bleak note entering her voice.

Larkin's broad shoulders rose and fell. "That's probably not the case, but it could be. Everybody's getting excited about communicating with the outside world, but we aren't, really. Not yet. It could be just . . . a ghost signal."

"You don't know that. It could be that Graham is talking to those people in Brazil or wherever they are, and he just hasn't announced it yet."

"Sure," Larkin said, nodding. "That's what I'm going to hope for. I'm just a little worried that if it doesn't turn out that way, a lot of people are going to be really disappointed. And that's a problem."

"How so?"

"Because when people are disappointed," Larkin said, "sometimes they get mad, too."

Chapter 27

May 23

Living underground like this, night and day didn't mean much. It would have been easy to lose track of time completely. Knowing that, Moultrie insisted on an ironclad schedule. He had programmed the times of sunrise and sunset for the next year into the computers that controlled the lighting in the Hercules Project, and each day at the appropriate time the lights dimmed to almost nothing—many of them went off entirely—or brightened to simulate the dawning of a new day. Large monitors located in various places displayed the date and time. One thing he didn't worry about was Daylight Savings Time, sticking with what it had been when the bunker was closed up.

The temperature went down at night as well, not proportionate to what it would have in an uncontrolled environment, but rather just enough to give a suggestion of what would have been natural. If there had been any way to replicate rain that wouldn't cause too much trouble, he probably would have provided that as well, but some things just had to be done without.

Larkin hadn't forgotten what it was like to feel the

sun and the wind on his face. He hoped they would be outside again soon enough that he *wouldn't* forget, and no one else would, either.

He and Susan were in their apartment in Silo A one evening, watching a movie streaming from the project's library, when a knock sounded on the door. Larkin paused the movie and went to answer it.

Chuck Fisher was there, and Larkin was a little surprised to see that Jill and Threadgill were with the security director. Fisher's expression was grim.

"What's up?" Larkin asked.

"Charlotte Ruskin and her friends are having a rally downstairs this evening. They went around putting up signs about it. They're going to demand a vote to replace Graham."

"They can't do that. This isn't a political system. Graham wasn't elected to start with. How can they have an election to replace him?"

"They seem to have the idea that if they have the numbers on their side, they can do whatever they want."

Larkin grimaced and asked, "What are you going to do?"

"Go down there and put a stop to it," Fisher answered without hesitation.

Larkin glanced at his daughter and saw the worried frown on her face. Threadgill didn't look too sure about this, either.

"Don't you think that confronting them might just make things worse? They stand around and shake their fists in the air and yell a little, and it blows off steam."

"Yelling and shaking their fists in the air like Hitler did? That didn't work out very well, did it?"

Larkin winced this time. He said, "Don't play the Hitler card, Chuck. You never win an argument by playing the Hitler card."

"I'm not arguing," Fisher snapped. "I'm telling you, as the director of security, what I'm going to do. I'd like for you to come along, Patrick, but if you don't want to be part of the force anymore—"

"My dad didn't say that, Mr. Fisher," Jill put in.

Larkin wasn't too happy about that, either. He could express his own opinion without his daughter having to stick up for him.

"Look, Chuck, I never said I wouldn't go with you—"

Susan had come up beside him. She laid a hand on his shoulder and said, "Go where? What's going on, Patrick?"

Larkin turned to look at her. "Charlotte Ruskin's stirring up trouble again. She and her friends are staging some sort of rally downstairs, trying to convince people they can vote to replace Graham Moultrie."

"How can they replace him? He's the one who built this project."

"That's what I said, but—"

"The woman's a danger," Fisher broke in. "It's our job to keep the peace, and she's trying to disrupt it. Simple as that."

In Larkin's experience, not many things in life actually *were* simple if you took a close enough look at them. But Fisher had a point. Charlotte Ruskin's actions were going to cause trouble. That trouble had to be dealt with.

"Fine," he said. "Let's go."

"Get your gun."

Fisher, Jill, and Threadgill were all wearing pistols.

Larkin thought a display of force like that might just aggravate the situation, but on the other hand, they would probably be outnumbered by quite a bit and just the presence of some firepower might keep things from getting out of hand.

"All right," he said. "Give me a minute."

His holstered .45 was on the table next to the sofa where he and Susan had been sitting as they watched TV. He got it and snapped the holster onto his belt. When he returned to the door, he found Susan and Jill standing there talking quietly. Fisher and Threadgill had moved off across the little foyer and into the elevator.

Susan put her hand on Larkin's arm and said in a voice low enough that the other two men wouldn't overhear, "I don't like this very much, Patrick."

"Neither do I. If Fisher gets too gung-ho, Ruskin and her people can turn it around and use it against us. We're the ones who'll come off looking like Nazis."

"Maybe we can keep things tamped down enough it won't come to that," Jill suggested.

"That's what I'm hoping," Larkin said. "Come on, kid."

The four of them took the elevator down one level, which let them out into the foyer in front of Jim and Beth Huddleston's apartment. Larkin had seen both of the Huddlestons fairly often since they'd been down here, although the two families didn't really socialize, just as they hadn't when they'd been next-door neighbors up on the surface. Jim, given his restaurant experience, worked as a supervisor in the kitchen while Beth taught in the school.

Right now, the two of them were just coming out of their apartment as Larkin and his companions emerged from the elevator. Huddleston must have been able to tell from their grim faces that something was wrong, because he said, "Whoa. What's going on?"

Fisher said, "We're going to put a stop to some sort of rally Charlotte Ruskin's holding this evening."

Immediately, Beth said, "You can't do that. We still have rights. What about freedom of assembly?"

"Are the two of you going to it?" Fisher asked, his voice sharp with suspicion.

"As a matter of fact, no," Huddleston said, his tone conciliatory as always. With a wife like Beth, he had gotten used to smoothing over rough patches. "We're on our way to a friend's place over in Corridor Two for dinner."

"But you can't just barge in on a meeting, start waving guns around, and break it up," Beth said. "That's not right."

Although Larkin would never admit it to her, this was one of the rare times he sort of agreed with Beth. He said, "We're going to monitor the rally. There shouldn't be any need for us to take action unless some sort of trouble breaks out."

Fisher frowned, as if he wanted to say that Larkin didn't have the authority to make that statement, but he kept his mouth shut. He had never been acquainted with Beth Huddleston before the war, but like anyone else who came in contact with her, he had learned quickly that it was a waste of time and energy to argue with her. Her opinions were as unmovable as if they'd been encased in a hundred tons of concrete.

"You need to be careful not to violate anyone's rights," Beth snapped.

"We'll do our best," Larkin said.

Beth sniffed, making it clear she thought their best was none too good. She and her husband went into the elevator. As the door slid closed with them behind it, Fisher said, "That man must have the patience of a saint."

"Actually, he's kind of a jerk part of the time," Larkin said. "He was obsessed with his businesses and always hustling to make more money. That's not necessarily a bad thing, but I'm not sure he ever thought about anything else." Larkin shrugged. "It didn't wind up doing him much good in the long run, did it?"

They followed a short hallway from the silo to a metal door with a push bar on it that opened into the vast, barracks-like lower level bunker. The walls were lined with tiers of bunk beds, while rows of single bunks were laid out to cover more than half of the floor space. Short partitions around groups of bunks provided a semblance of privacy. A common area in the center of the bunker had comfortable furniture, computer stations, a snack bar, and other amenities. Showers and restrooms were located at each end of the bunker. Back when he was still in the Corps, Larkin had once had cause to visit a federal minimum-security prison, and this bunker reminded him of that more than anything else.

A few people were in their bunks, but most of the residents who lived down here, plus some from the corridors and the silos, had crowded into the central common area. A lot of talk was going on, but nobody was making any speeches—yet.

Fisher looked around, his head jerking from side to side. Larkin knew he was trying to locate Charlotte Ruskin.

"I don't see her," Fisher said after a moment. "She's bound to be around here somewhere, though."

"Maybe she's changed her mind," Jill suggested.

Fisher snorted in disbelief. Then he bobbed a curt nod toward one of the stairways leading down from the corridors.

"Here she comes. And she's got her entourage with her."

Charlotte Ruskin was descending the stairs with Jeff Greer beside her. Chad Holdstock and three other men followed them. What Holdstock and his companions were carrying made Larkin stiffen in alarm.

Fisher noticed, too, and exclaimed, "They've got guns! They're not supposed to be armed unless they're on one of the ranges, practicing."

The four men had pump shotguns in their hands. As that fact soaked into Larkin's brain, he said, "It's just for show. They can't fire those down here without hurting a lot of innocent people. They're probably not even loaded."

"Are you willing to bet your life on that?" Fisher asked with a scowl.

Unfortunately, Larkin *wasn't* ready to bet his life on that assessment. Even more important, he wasn't willing to risk his daughter's life.

"We'd better tread lightly here, Chuck," he said. "If anybody sets off fireworks, we don't want it to be us."

"I won't have them strutting around here flouting the rules," Fisher said. He started forward, his long strides carrying him quickly toward the large group in the center of the bunker.

The crowd parted to let Charlotte Ruskin and her companions through, but as people looked around and saw Fisher, Larkin, Jill, and Threadgill approaching, they moved closer together and got truculent looks on their faces, as if they meant to block the security force's advance.

"Step aside," Fisher ordered.

"This isn't any of your business," one of the men responded.

"Everything that happens in this project is my business. I'm the head of security."

"There's no trouble here," a woman said. "You're not needed."

"That's right," another man put in. "This is a peaceful assembly. We've got a right to that, don't we?"

"Don't talk to me about—" Fisher stopped and took a deep breath. Larkin figured he'd been on the verge of saying not to talk to him about rights, but then Fisher had thought better of it. As Larkin had pointed out, it was a fine line they had to walk.

Instead, Fisher went on, "Those men are armed. That's a violation of the rules."

"What about the Second Amendment?"

That was another tricky area. Decades of efforts by liberal politicians to circumvent or abolish the right of American citizens to bear arms had failed for the most part, probably because those politicans knew in their guts that if they pushed the issue too hard, more than likely it would result in a civil war—and rightly so, in Larkin's opinion.

However, that was all moot now. Or was it? Moultrie had made it plain that he wanted the Hercules Project to perpetuate American traditions and standards as much as possible, and the right to bear arms was part of that. Regulating that right because of the special circumstances was understandable, but Larkin had always worried about the slippery-slope aspect of that. Now this direct confrontation over the matter made him uneasy.

Charlotte Ruskin's voice came from behind the human wall, saying, "Step aside, please. I'll talk to them."

"You don't have to do that, Charlotte," a man told her as he turned to look at her. "We're not afraid of them."

"No, it's better to get things out in the open," Ruskin insisted. She moved forward, and the people blocking her path stepped out of the way.

"What is it you're doing here?" Chuck Fisher demanded when he was face-to-face with the woman. "And why are those men carrying shotguns?"

"Self-defense," Ruskin coolly answered the second question first. "We have a right to protect ourselves."

"Nobody's going to hurt you as long as you're not breaking the rules."

The woman smiled. "Americans have a long tradition of breaking the rules. It's how the whole country got started, remember?"

"This is different—" Fisher began.

"Is it?" Ruskin broke in sharply. "How is it different, Chuck? We're tired of the rule of an overbearing, despotic tyrant."

Fisher started breathing a little harder. "How the hell can you say that? None of you people would even be alive today if it weren't for Graham Moultrie!"

"That's true," Ruskin admitted. "But that doesn't give him the right to dictate every aspect of our lives."

"Seems to me it does, because he knows more about how this place works than anybody else. And if it doesn't keep working perfectly, that means all of us will probably die."

Ruskin shook her head, blew out a dismissive breath, and said, "You can't possibly know that."

"I don't plan on taking a chance of being wrong. Anyway, you don't really care about anybody's rights. The only reason you're doing this is because you're mad at Graham for closing up the project before your husband got here."

Ruskin's nostrils flared as she sharply drew in air. Her face paled. Jeff Greer had moved up behind her, and he started to crowd forward, his hands tight on the shotgun he carried, as he said, "You'd better shut your damn mouth, you—"

Fisher took a step closer, too, and said, "What were you about to call me?"

"Stop it, both of you!" Charlotte Ruskin said. It didn't look like her words were going to do much good, though, because Fisher and Greer both had their chests stuck out like bull apes ready to do battle.

"Charlotte, what is it you want?" Larkin asked, hoping to steer the conversation back on point and away from violence. "What do you hope to accomplish with this meeting?"

Ruskin glanced back and forth between Fisher and Greer, who were still glaring at each other, and then said, "We want to establish some reasonable reforms."

"Like what?"

"Like giving people a voice in the decisions that are made down here, rather than Moultrie just handing down orders."

"So basically you just want to express your opinion."

"I'd like to see somebody else in charge," Ruskin

said, "but for right now I'd settle for being listened to and taken seriously."

"Yelling and waving guns around isn't the way to do that," Larkin said.

"The hell it's not," Greer snapped. "Nobody ever really pays attention unless they feel like they're being threatened."

"I don't think that's true. Have you tried writing letters, circulating petitions—"

Greer snorted in contempt. "When did that ever work in the past? Don't you know anything about history, Larkin? When did anything ever really change except by force?"

He had a good point there, Larkin thought. There had been some nonviolent turning points in history—but not many.

On the other hand, there had never been a closed system like the Hercules Project before. One could argue that ships at sea were similar, especially back in the age of sail, when there was no long-range communication. Each of those ships had been under the command of a single captain whose word was law, much like Moultrie's was here.

And from time to time, the threat of mutiny had arisen on those ships, too, and sometimes it ended in bloody slaughter. Not the most appealing precedent, Larkin thought.

The tension in the air was growing tighter and thicker. Larkin glanced at Jill and Threadgill. Both of them looked as worried as he felt. They would do their duty as members of the security force, but he could tell they were conflicted, too, about who was right and wrong in this confrontation.

With Fisher and Greer both seemingly eager for trouble, there was no telling what might have happened . . . but at that moment the dynamic changed again. A surprised stir went through the crowd, and since most of them were staring past Larkin and his companions, he half-turned to look over his shoulder.

Graham Moultrie was walking briskly toward them. He stopped about twenty feet away, stuck his hands in the pockets of his jeans, and asked, "What's going on here?"

Chapter 28

For a moment, Charlotte Ruskin gazed at Moultrie as if unable to believe what she was seeing. Then she took a step forward. Since Fisher and Greer were still caught up in their own confrontation, Larkin moved a little to the side so he could intercept Ruskin if she tried to attack Moultrie.

"It's all right, Patrick," Moultrie said. "Mrs. Ruskin is a reasonable woman."

"You bastard," she breathed. "I'll always hate you."

"That's fine. I didn't expect to be loved by everyone down here. I knew there would be hard choices and that some people would be hurt by them."

"Hard choices! You're responsible for my husband's death!"

"That's not fair," Jill said. "There were other people who didn't get here in time. When Mr. Moultrie had to close up the project, he didn't know who was here and who wasn't."

"And if you want to blame somebody," Larkin added, "blame the politicians who started the war in the first place. All of us"—he waved a hand to take in the crowd—"we're just innocent bystanders who got caught in it."

Moultrie said, "I've told you how sorry I am about your husband, Mrs. Ruskin. I wish there was something else I could do, but there just isn't. We can't change what's happened. But we can make sure that we do the right thing going forward. I'd be interested in hearing what you think that is."

"You're lying," Ruskin said. "You're not interested in what anybody else thinks. You believe you're God!"

Moultrie frowned and shook his head. He said, "You're wrong about both of those things. I'm just a guy who did what he could to help. And if you believe you can help me make things better down here, then I damn sure *do* want to hear about it." Moultrie looked around at the crowd. "Tell you what. You've got a good-sized group here. Why don't I go back up to the Command Center, so that you can talk freely among yourselves?"

"Talk about what?" Ruskin asked. "And how can we talk freely with your goons still here?"

"My security people will leave, too."

Fisher frowned and said, "Graham, I don't know if that's a good idea. They've got shotguns!"

Moultrie sighed and nodded. "And that's a violation of the rules, yes. I agree, Chuck. So I propose that if we leave, those guns will be returned immediately to the vault where they came from, since there won't really be a need for them to be down here."

"You'd *trust* these people?" Fisher asked, jerking a hand toward Ruskin and her friends.

"I trust everyone down here," Moultrie said simply. "Otherwise I wouldn't have allowed them to become part of the project in the first place."

That brought a few approving murmurs, Larkin noted.

Moultrie knew how to work a crowd; Larkin had to give the guy credit for that.

"Do we have a deal?" Moultrie went on. "You can have your meeting and say whatever you want to say, but the guns go back where they're supposed to be."

"We'll think about it," Charlotte Ruskin said. She still looked suspicious.

"I suppose that's fair enough," Moultrie said with a shrug. "I hope you'll come to the right decision. And if you'd bear with me just a little longer, I have a suggestion about what you can talk about, too."

Greer said, "We don't need any help from you—"

Moultrie held up a hand to stop him. "My suggestion, since you've got such a good crowd here, is that you talk about electing resident representatives. Nominate five or six people, and have an election. The top two, say, could be your representatives, and any time there's a problem, you can all get together, figure out what you want, and then send the representatives to talk to me. We'll all work together to make sure that everyone's concerns are addressed. That sounds pretty reasonable, doesn't it?"

Again, people nodded and made noises of agreement. Charlotte Ruskin didn't look too happy about the idea, though. Moultrie was stealing her thunder, and she knew it.

"What assurances do we have that you'd actually listen to us?" she demanded.

"All I can do is give you my word. But the only way to find out is to give it a try, isn't it?"

Larkin could tell that Moultrie had won over the crowd. They had let themselves be stirred up by the strident claims of Ruskin and her friends that Moultrie was a dictator, but with him standing right there, talking quietly and calmly to them, his steady presence reminded them that they truly wouldn't be alive today if not for him. Or at the very least, they wouldn't be as healthy and safe as they were. Even if they had survived the nuclear blast somehow, they would still be facing a lingering death from radiation poisoning or starvation.

Ruskin was canny enough to sense that the pendulum had swung. Maybe not against her, but at least back to the center. With a sullen undertone in her voice, she said, "All right. We can discuss electing representatives. But you're not going to be able to put off real change around here, Moultrie. The people have a right to a say in their own lives!"

That prompted a few cheers. Moultrie just smiled faintly, nodded, and said, "Come see me." He turned his attention to Fisher. "Chuck, come with me. The rest of you can go back to whatever you were doing. I assume you're all on duty?"

Fisher said, "No, I rounded 'em up. Didn't want to take any of the regular guys away from their rounds."

"All right, then." Moultrie's smile widened. "Go back to your families, then, and enjoy your evening."

Moultrie and Fisher walked away, heading toward one of the stairways. Larkin, Jill, and Threadgill went the other way, toward the door that led to the elevator.

"Well, that could have gotten really ugly," Threadgill said under his breath.

"It still might," Jill said. "No matter what Mr. Moultrie does, it's not going to satisfy Charlotte Ruskin. She hates him too much for that."

Larkin didn't say anything, but he thought his daughter was right.

Sooner or later, there would be some sort of show-down.

And when it happened, it wouldn't be pretty.

The very next day, notices began to go up around the bunker and along both corridors. An election would be held in a week's time to select two representatives for the residents. Charlotte Ruskin and Jeff Greer were among those nominated for the job, along with three men whose names were only vaguely familiar to Larkin. He figured they were only there to make it look good. There was no doubt in his mind who would actually win the election.

But that was a worry for another day, and anyway, it was Moultrie who would have to deal with them, not him. In the meantime, he had his own job, which consisted of both making rounds of the project and monitoring security equipment.

He also had a side project he didn't talk about much. He had brought several laptops down here in the days before the war, and he always kept an up-to-date file of his current book on a couple of USB drives, one of which he carried around with him at all times. It had been in his pocket on the day everything had gone to hell, and as soon as he'd gotten a chance, he had loaded the manuscript onto one of the laptops and also onto a couple of spare USB drives. Larkin was well aware that he was paranoid about such things compared to a lot of writers, but once he had lost a book that was half written and had to start over, and he didn't want to have to do that ever again.

So nearly every day, he sat down and wrote some pages on the thriller he'd been working on. It was a historical novel now, since it was set in a world that no longer existed, but Larkin didn't care about that. Maybe someday there would be a publishing business again. For untold years, probably as far back as there had been language, people had had stories. It wasn't as vital a need as air and food and water, but that didn't mean it wasn't important. What was life without the human spirit, and what was the human spirit without imagination?

Besides, he was in the habit of writing, and he didn't see any reason to change. Thinking about the book had gotten him through some dark nights of the soul when he might have brooded over everything that was lost, instead.

Several days after the confrontation in the lower bunker, Larkin was working in the Command Center, sitting in the security force's office in front of a computer connected to motion sensors on the surface. A camera at the bottom of the stairs in the main entrance was pointed up at the concrete blockhouse, which appeared to have survived the nuclear explosion twenty miles away relatively intact. It wasn't one hundred percent radiation-proof, however, so the two blast doors at the bottom and the entrance chamber between them were still sealed as a precaution. In places around the project, radiation and atmospheric monitors, as well as radio antennas, had been run up concrete tubes topped with hatches powered by electric motors. Those hatches had been opened within hours of the explosion. The bottom ends of the tubes were sealed and shielded so no radiation or anything else dangerous could leak down through them, and the tubes were too small for anything living to travel through them except insects.

Larkin had heard rumors that fiber-optic cameras had been raised through similar tubes so those in the bunker were able to look around outside, but he had never seen any proof of that. If the rumors were true, it was likely only Graham Moultrie and maybe one or two other people had access to the video feeds from the surface. And it was possible the whole business simply wasn't true.

From time to time, the motion sensors Larkin was monitoring had detected something moving around up there. The movements were brief and seemed totally random, though, so the consensus was that they were caused by bits of debris blowing past the sensors in the wind. It was unlikely any animals were left alive, but it wasn't beyond the realm of possibility. By now they would be pretty sick and starving, though, and if they approached the sensors, it would be by accident, since there was nothing around them to eat.

Like any former soldier who had spent hundreds of hours on boring details, Larkin had developed the ability to pay attention to what he was supposed to be doing and let his mind wander at the same time. He was thinking about some plot developments in his novel when he saw a red light pop up on the grid displayed on the computer's screen. That meant something up there was moving enough to trigger the sensor. Larkin expected the light to disappear as the wind blew whatever it was out of range, but instead it glowed steadily and then was joined by another and another.

Larkin sat up straighter and identified the location

on the grid. It was about a hundred yards away from the blockhouse above the project's main entrance. Several objects were moving around there.

That still didn't have to mean anything. A whirlwind could have whipped several bits of debris into the air. Hell, Larkin thought, it could be a tornado. Did they still have tornadoes on the surface? Nobody really knew. There could be any number of explanations . . .

But even though Larkin knew that, logically and intellectually, a bit of a cold shiver went down his spine. He was no more immune to the fear of the unknown than any other man, and these days, the surface was a *vast* unknown.

A woman named Andrea Marshall was working with him today, checking back and forth between views from the cameras located in various areas of the project. Without taking his eyes off the screen, Larkin said, "Andrea, take a look at this."

"What is it?" she asked as she swiveled around in her chair.

"I've got movement up top, more movement than I've seen before."

"These bogeys don't act like animals."

Indeed, the red dots marking the movement shifted position slowly and deliberately. *Like somebody's walking around up there*, Larkin thought.

Then he sat forward suddenly as more dots appeared, leading in a fairly straight line. The dots at the tail end of the line faded and then disappeared.

Andrea had stood up and moved to look over Larkin's shoulder. She let out a startled, "Holy—! Something's moving fast up there!"

Larkin checked the grid again and said, "It's coming

toward the blockhouse. You've got a camera pointed up the stairs—"

"On it!" Andrea whirled around and lunged back to her station. Larkin stood up and hurried behind her chair. He glanced over his shoulder, saw the bogey was still advancing rapidly, and then Andrea let out a shocked cry.

Larkin looked at the video feed and saw a cloud of dust filling the stairwell. Chunks of concrete came bouncing down out of that cloud.

"Oh, hell, Patrick! What . . . what happened up there?"

"Something just hit the blockhouse."

"You mean another bomb?"

Larkin shook his head. "No. Something rammed it at high speed, something like a truck. Probably aiming to bust the door open."

"But a truck would have to have somebody driving it, or at least aiming it. Who—"

Larkin pointed at the camera feed and said, "I think we're about to find out."

A vaguely human shape had formed in the dust. Now it came down the staircase slowly, step by step, becoming more and more visible . . .

Until Andrea screamed as a monster's face loomed on the screen.

Chapter 29

Only it wasn't a monster, Larkin realized a moment later as Andrea shrank away from the screen, stifling another scream. He leaned closer. The lines of a human face were still there in the thing looking up at the camera, just terribly distorted. The man was gaunt to the point of being skeletal, with his cheekbones pressing so sharply against his skin it appeared they might tear through. Much of that skin had sloughed off, leaving raw, oozing sores in its place. Most of the man's hair had fallen out, including his eyebrows. Only a few tufts remained around his ears. Blood had leaked from his eyes and nose, leaving dark brown streaks. His mouth hung open as he breathed heavily, and Larkin could see that he had only a few stumps of teeth left in pale, dead-looking gums.

"Nosferatu," Larkin muttered, reminded of the vampire in that classic movie. His nerves were stretched taut and his heart slugged heavily in his chest. He wasn't scared by what he saw on the monitor, exactly, but he was definitely shocked.

"What . . . what is that thing?" Andrea had to force the words out.

"Someone suffering from extreme radiation sickness.

The guy lived through the concussion and thermal waves, so he must have been underground somewhere. But he either came out too soon or his hiding place wasn't shielded well enough. He looks like he caught a lot of grays."

"What?"

"The unit of exposure of a human body to radiation. His symptoms look pretty systemic. He's probably got half a dozen tumors eating him up from the inside, as well as what we can see on the outside."

Andrea stared up at Larkin and asked, "How can you be so . . . so calm and analytical?"

Larkin let out a grunt of humorless laughter. "I promise you, I'm not calm at all. I feel like jumping out of my skin."

That was probably a poor choice of words, considering what they were looking at. The thing on the stairs, which wore tattered clothing, clumped on down, mostly out of range of the camera. A bony fist came into view, then fell. The motion was repeated several times.

"He's knocking on the door," Larkin said. "He wants to be let in."

"Ohhh," Andrea said, the sound coming out as a low, choked moan. "He . . . he can't get in, can he?"

Larkin shook his head. "I don't see how. This guy's at death's door, and even if he was in perfect health, he couldn't bust down that door. A SWAT team with a battering ram couldn't bust down that door." He reached for an intercom and pushed a button on it. "Graham, this is Patrick Larkin. You need to come in here."

Moultrie's voice came back from the intercom. "What is it, Patrick?"

For a second, Larkin considered what to say, then settled for, "We have a visitor."

Another second ticked by. Larkin could imagine the stunned expression on Moultrie's face. Then the man said, "I'll be right there."

Moultrie's office was in the Command Center, so it took him less than a minute to reach the room where Larkin and Andrea were monitoring the equipment. He came in fast, not running, probably because he didn't want to attract attention until he found out exactly what was going on, but not wasting any time, either.

The creature that had come down the stairs wasn't visible at the moment. Larkin had a hunch he had slumped against the blast door, exhausted by his efforts. *Hell, he might even be dead*, Larkin thought.

"What is it?" Moultrie asked. He moved up between Larkin and Andrea so he could see the screen. The dust had cleared away somewhat, but the concrete rubble on the stairs was visible. "Son of a . . . What happened?"

Before either of the other two could answer, the diseased man loomed into view again, staggering up a couple of steps and looking back over his shoulder.

Moultrie took a step back and let out a startled, "Shit!" He recovered quickly and went on, "That man is dying of radiation poisoning."

"Looks like he's most of the way there," Larkin agreed.

"How did he get down here? Where did that debris come from?"

"There was an impact up above. The best I can figure, a truck rammed the blockhouse and knocked down the door and part of the wall. Then that fella came down the stairs and started beating on the blast door like he wanted in."

The creature had stopped on the stairs now. He half-turned so he could look directly into the camera.

"He knows we're watching him," Moultrie said in a hushed voice.

As if to confirm that, the man lifted a hand that was little more than skin and bones. It trembled badly, but he was able to control it enough to close all of the fingers into a fist.

Except the middle one, which stuck straight up in an unmistakable gesture of defiant anger.

Then he turned and shuffled up the steps, eventually going out of sight in the dust that lingered in the remains of the blockhouse.

Andrea broke the horrified and astounded silence by asking, "Did a zombie just give us the finger?"

"He's not a zombie," Larkin said. "He's a human being like us . . . except he ran out of luck and we didn't." He turned his head to look at Moultrie. "And judging by what I saw on the motion sensors before things got crazy, he's not the only one up there."

Moultrie's face was stony and so was his voice as he said, "Well, that's liable to be a problem."

Moultrie swore Larkin and Andrea to secrecy. "We need to figure out what we're going to do about this before it becomes public knowledge," he said. "We've known all along there was at least a chance there'd be survivors on the surface. But knowing that intellectually and then seeing that poor devil . . ."

Andrea shuddered and said, "I'll never forget that

face. I'm afraid I'll be seeing it in my nightmares from now on. And what if that man was, well, one of the ones who's in better shape . . .?"

"We'll deal with this, don't worry," Moultrie assured her.

Larkin could tell that Andrea was very shaken up for the rest of their shift, however. As they were leaving the Command Center after going off duty, he asked her, "Are you going to be all right?"

"I suppose," she said, not meeting his eyes. "I just can't stop thinking . . . that could have been any of us, couldn't it, Patrick?"

"Well, yeah, I guess so, although it's more likely that if we'd been caught aboveground when the bomb hit, we'd have been killed right away. Any survivors from around here must have been able to take shelter somewhere underground." Something else had occurred to him. "It's possible that these folks, the ones who rammed the blockhouse, they've come in from somewhere else, farther away from the blast area. But not far enough to escape the radiation. Not only that, the water and anything they could find to eat around here would be contaminated, too, not to mention any dust that's still in the air."

In a small voice, Andrea said, "I've heard that it takes two hundred years for a place to be safe again after a nuclear explosion. We're going to be down here for generations, aren't we? You and I, we'll never live long enough to see the sunlight again."

"I don't believe that," Larkin said with a shake of his head. "That two hundred years figure is way overblown. With proper protection, we ought to be able to leave the bunker and have a look around within another four to six months."

"But you don't *know* that."

He shrugged. "I guess it all depends on what the instruments tell us about surface conditions."

"And when we do go out there, we'll have to face those . . . zombies."

Larkin made a face. "Don't call 'em that. If people start thinking that way, it'll just lead to more trouble. They're not monsters or mutants or anything else from movies. They're just human beings with a disease."

Andrea didn't look convinced, but Larkin didn't spend any more time trying to convince her. As long as she kept her mouth shut about what she'd seen, it didn't really matter what she thought of the radiation-riddled survivors. They might haunt her nightmares, but it wouldn't make any practical difference.

Anyway, the whole thing might well be moot, Larkin thought. By the time an exploratory party from the Hercules Project could go up to the surface, any survivors who had lived through the blast or come into the area from elsewhere would probably be dead. The radiation sickness would not be denied.

Andrea headed back to her quarters in Corridor Two while Larkin returned to his apartment. Susan was still at the medical clinic, he supposed. He sat down and for a while tried to read, but he couldn't get the image of what he had seen out of his mind.

The crude gesture the man in the stairwell had made was one thing. The look in his eyes, deep-set and burning in the gaunt, haggard face, was something else again. Larkin wasn't sure if he had ever seen as much pure hatred and venom in anyone's gaze as he had witnessed there. It was the hatred of someone who was doomed and knew it, directed toward those who still had a chance to survive.

If that man ever got a chance, he would kill each and every one of them, just to take them to hell with him. Larkin was sure of that.

Unable to concentrate, he put his book away and started preparing some supper for when Susan got home. It was nothing fancy, just a bacon and potato omelet, but fancy cooking was pretty much out of the question down here. Some of the people from the lower bunker had the attitude that the ones who dwelled in the silo apartments lived in the lap of luxury. True, they had more privacy, but the other day-to-day aspects of living were pretty much the same.

Susan came in while he was still working on the food. She stepped up behind him, put her arms around his waist, and hugged him hard as she rested her head against his broad back.

"Not that I'm complaining," Larkin said, "but what's that about?"

"Patrick."

Something in her voice made him turn away from the stove so he could look at her. Her face was set in grim lines. He immediately felt a surge of fear that something had happened to Jill or Trevor or one of the kids, but before he could ask, Susan went on, "I know what you saw today. Graham called in some of us from the medical staff and told us."

"Oh. Actually, I'm glad he did. He asked Andrea and me to keep our mouths shut about it, and I know it would have been hard keeping a secret from you."

"Was it really as . . . terrible . . . as he made it sound?"

"It was pretty bad," Larkin said. He turned back to the omelet so he could fold it over. Thinking about what he had seen in the Command Center blunted his hunger a little, but he could still eat. Like any good Marine, it took a lot to kill his appetite completely. He went on, "But it wasn't anything we hadn't considered a possibility all along."

"If people like Beth Huddleston knew about this, they'd be demanding that we open the doors and let those survivors in so we can help them."

"There's not a damn thing we can do for them." Larkin's voice was a little harsher than he intended, but he knew he spoke the truth. "The most merciful thing any of those poor bastards could get is a bullet in the head."

"That's a terrible thing to say, but I'm not sure I can argue with it. The reason Graham called us in was because he wanted to find out if there's anything we *could* do for them, any way we might be able to help them." Susan shook her head. "All the doctors agreed, there's nothing we can do other than giving them drugs to ease the pain a little. Even if we still had access to the best hospitals in the world, anyone as sick from radiation as the man Graham described wouldn't live much longer."

Larkin slid the omelet from the pan onto a plate and cut it in two. A frown creased his forehead as he said, "Maybe they're not all in that bad a shape."

"What do you mean?"

"I saw enough bogeys on the motion detectors to tell me that several people were moving around up there. Our visitor isn't alone. Maybe the others sent him because they weren't sure what he'd find down here and they considered him the most expendable."

"That's a pretty bleak way to look at it."

"Life's a pretty bleak business a lot of the time. Now more than ever."

"Even if you're right, what difference does it make if some of the other survivors aren't as sick as the man you saw?"

"This guy pounded on the blast door, but even if it had been a regular door, he was too weak to do any damage. He wasn't any kind of a threat." Larkin paused. "I wonder if we can say that about the other survivors left up there."

Chapter 30

June 3

Despite Moultrie's orders and the efforts of everyone who knew what had happened, during the next week it proved impossible to keep the developments completely secret. Larkin knew he didn't even hint about the matter to anyone who wasn't already in the loop, and he didn't believe that Susan had said anything, either.

But someone must have, because rumors began to fly, especially in the lower bunker, that *something* was still alive on the surface. No one seemed to know exactly what it was. Speculation ran rampant. Most of it seemed to spring from horror movies . . . from zombies to mutants—or mutant zombies—to animals that had been given super-intelligence by the radiation and were now walking around on two legs and building futuristic weapons, to aliens who had arrived from outer space to investigate the aftermath of Earth's nuclear war. None of those fanciful things approached the grim reality of what Larkin had seen.

The excitement—or apprehension was probably a better word for it—didn't affect the election. Some of the residents from Corridors One and Two had lobbied to be included, and even some of the silo dwellers wanted to be part of it, too. The organizers—Charlotte Ruskin's friends, although not Ruskin herself because she was running for one of the posts—declared the election open to all residents of the Hercules Project who were of voting age. So the turnout was fairly high, but that didn't change the results that Larkin expected. Charlotte Ruskin and Jeff Greer were elected to represent the residents. The fix had been in from the first, to Larkin's way of thinking, and even if two of the other candidates had won, they still would have been taking their marching orders from Charlotte.

However, when Moultrie called a meeting of his senior staff to discuss the situation on the surface, Ruskin and Greer weren't there. They would pitch a fit if they ever found out about being excluded, but evidently Moultrie didn't trust them and didn't care.

Larkin was a little surprised that *he* was invited. He held no official position other than being a member of the security force, but he knew that over the months Moultrie and Chuck Fisher had come to place a lot of confidence in him. Besides, Susan was a member of the inner circle when it came to the medical staff, due to her practical knowledge and tireless efforts to help keep the residents as healthy as possible. Larkin knew from talking to her that at first some of the doctors had resisted bringing a "mere" nurse into their top-level discussions, but the more pragmatic among them had won over the ones with swelled heads.

Maybe Moultrie figured that whatever was discussed at the meeting, Susan would tell him about it anyway, Larkin mused as they walked into the big conference room. That wasn't necessarily true, but he didn't mind being here. He wanted to know what was going on.

Larkin's gaze went around the table where people were talking quietly among themselves. He saw two of the doctors, Jessica Kenley and Stan Davis. A group of engineers and environmental experts, including Doug Liu, Sharon Bastrop, Will Grover, and Larry Milstead, clustered at one end of the table. Curtis Jackson from logistics and supplies sat with his hands clasped on the table in front of him. Down near the other end, Chuck Fisher stood with his hands on the back of a chair and a frown on his face.

Fisher caught Larkin's eye and nodded a greeting. While Susan went to talk to the other medical personnel, Larkin drifted in Fisher's direction.

"Wondering why you're here?" the security chief asked.

"Because no meeting is complete without my good looks and wit?"

Fisher grunted. "Not exactly. You're officially second in command of the security force now."

"I don't recall asking for a promotion."

"You're being appointed, not offered a job. That means you can't say no. Not that I'd expect you to want to."

"You're right," Larkin said. "Thanks, Chuck. I'll try not to let you down."

"If we believed you might let us down, Graham and I wouldn't have made this decision. You've earned it. You've always been there and done anything we've asked you to do. Anyway, you know more about the enemy than anyone else."

"The enemy?" Larkin repeated as a frown creased his forehead.

"You know." Fisher gestured with a blunt thumb. "Up there. You've looked one of them in the eye. It was through a camera lens, but still . . ." Fisher shrugged. "We've seen the footage, of course, but seeing it live is different."

Larkin wasn't sure if he would refer to the people on the surface as "the enemy." What had happened to them wasn't really their fault, other than trusting to luck to keep them alive in case of a nuclear war. And more than 99.9 percent of the population had done exactly the same thing.

On the other hand, Larkin had seen the expression on the mutilated face of the survivor who had come down from the blockhouse. Disease had done more than ravage that man's body. It had turned him mad with resentment and filled him with hate. He would have done harm to the residents if he'd been able to get into the Hercules Project, and in a very real way, that *did* make him "the enemy."

Moultrie came in while Larkin was thinking about that, and the talk in the room immediately stopped as everyone turned to look at the project's founder and leader. Deb was with him, and both of them wore grim expressions.

"Hello, everyone," Moultrie said as he walked to the head of the table. "Thank you for coming. Please sit down."

They took chairs. Susan came back to sit next to Larkin. Deb sat at one end of the table, Moultrie at the other.

"I'm sure all of you have a pretty good idea why we're here," Moultrie went on. "We need to figure out a plan to deal with the problem facing us. I'll be honest with you. I considered this possibility when I was putting the project together, but I never believed it to be a real likelihood. All the odds seemed to be that no one in the area would survive a nuclear war except us."

No one else looked like they were going to say it, so Larkin did. "Those survivors may have come in from somewhere else. From what we know, there are probably large parts of West Texas that are still livable."

Moultrie leaned back slightly in his chair and said, "It depends on what you mean by livable. There'd be no power because of the EMPs knocking out everything that relies on computers, which is almost everything electronic and mechanical these days. Depending on the winds, the fallout could be dangerous. And twenty-first-century people just aren't equipped, mentally or physically, to deal with an eighteenth-century existence. I suspect the mortality rates have been extremely high all across Texas during the past eight months."

He was probably right about that, Larkin thought. But it still didn't rule out the chance that the survivors moving around up on the surface had come from somewhere else.

But then Larkin had to ask himself if it really mattered one way or the other. He supposed it didn't. The survivors were there and in bad shape, wherever they came from.

"We've had other suspicious readings from the motion sensors in the past few days," Moultrie went on. "The data is too fragmentary to make even a wild guess about how many survivors there might be. At least a handful."

"We could easily handle a few more people," Jessica Kenley said. She had been a pediatrician before the war, although down here there were no real specialists anymore. All the doctors had to treat whatever patients came their way.

"Even if we knew there were only three or four, it would mean opening the project and exposing everyone down here to outside contaminants. I'm not willing to do that yet."

Bald, dour Dr. Stan Davis spoke up, saying, "We've all seen the footage from the stairwell camera. Anyone with that degree of radiation sickness is beyond our help. I agree with Graham that it's not worth the risk."

"And we don't know that there are only three or four of them," Chuck Fisher said. "There could be hundreds of them, maybe more, staying just out of range of our sensors. There's no telling what they might be plotting against us up there."

The mention of plotting struck Larkin as a little paranoid, but unfortunately, none of them had any way of knowing whether Fisher was right.

Or did they? Larkin knew he might be pushing his luck, but he asked bluntly, "Is there any truth to the rumors that you've sent surveillance cameras up to the surface, Graham?"

Moultrie didn't answer immediately, which in a way was an answer in itself. Finally, he said, "We did, but the cameras failed after a short time, possibly due to the high levels of radiation. And I wouldn't give the okay to open the access tubes so they could be taken out and repaired. But in the time they were operational, we got a look around. There were . . . no signs of life. If you've ever seen an area after a big wildfire went through, that's the way it looks up there now. All the vegetation was burned off. The hills are bare dirt and rock. And there was no sun. You've heard about nuclear winter.

That seems to be what the area is experiencing. The clouds of dust and ash still in the sky are causing a state of perpetual dusk. The temperature hadn't gotten out of the forties, we know that much from our other sensors, even though we don't have eyes up there anymore. It's pretty bleak, my friends. No place for humanity." He paused. "We're better off down here."

"No one's doubting that," Larkin said.

Fisher said, "The important thing is that we don't know how much of a threat those people represent, so we have to proceed as if they're a danger to us. I know you mean well, Dr. Kenley, but we can't open the doors."

"Is that what we're debating here?" she asked.

"It's not a debate," Moultrie said. "I'm not going to risk the safety of everyone down here. My humanitarian impulses ended the day they dropped the bomb."

Susan said, "There are some residents who would say that you calling all the shots makes this a dictatorship, Graham."

Moultrie smiled. "Do you feel that way, Susan?"

"I didn't say I did. As a matter of fact, I don't feel that way. But you know who does."

"Charlotte Ruskin and her friends."

"And people like Beth Huddleston and her husband."

Moultrie arched an eyebrow. "Beth and Jim? Really? I thought they were in agreement with how things have been going."

Beth would disagree that the sky was blue, just to be disagreeable, Larkin thought. But these days . . . well, who could say what color the sky really was, with all those clouds of dust and ash blocking the sun?

"We're losing sight of why we're here," Fisher said.

"We're not letting anyone else in, that's clear enough. But what are we going to do if they try to get in?"

"You mean force their way in?" Larkin asked.

"That's right. They have to be desperate. There's no telling what they might do. They busted into the block-house, didn't they?"

One of the engineers said, "I don't see how they did that. Vehicles won't run without computers, will they?"

Moultrie smiled. "You're too young to remember when cars didn't have computers, Jared, but some of us here aren't. As long as they've got gas to run it and the charge in the battery holds out, an old truck with a car-buretor will work just fine. I'm sure that's what they used to crash into the blockhouse and knock down the door. There may be a lot of other vehicles up there that will still run."

"That's not eighteenth-century technology," Larkin pointed out. "Neither are the weapons they could have."

"Exactly," Moultrie said, nodding. "I have trouble believing they could come up with enough explosives to damage the blast door, and they'd have to get through two of them, not just one. But we can't rule it out, so we have to be ready just in case. We control the venti-lation system in the antechamber between the doors. I propose that if there's ever a breach of the outer door, we pump poison gas into the chamber. In fact, we can flood the whole stairwell with it."

A tense silence filled the room in response to Moultrie's suggestion. Susan and Dr. Kenley stared at him in apparent disbelief at what they had just heard, and some of the technical staff looked uneasy, too. Finally, Dr. Kenley said, "Graham, you're talking about murder."

From the other end of the table, Deb spoke up for the

first time since entering the meeting. She said, "No, he's talking about self-defense. We've already killed to protect the project. Or have you forgotten about some of the things that happened on the day of the war? There's a good chance that if we hadn't stopped people from flooding in here, we'd all be dead by now."

Quietly, Moultrie said, "Deb's right. I won't deny that the idea is distasteful, but it's a matter of survival."

Fisher said, "I don't find anything distasteful about the idea of killing murderous bastards who want to kill us." He turned to Larkin. "You saw that guy who came down here, Patrick. He didn't have anything good in mind, did he?"

"No, he didn't," Larkin admitted. "He probably knew there was a good chance he couldn't get in, but if he'd been able to, I think he'd have tried to hurt somebody."

"Or get help for himself and the other survivors," Susan said.

"They're bound to know they're beyond help," Fisher said. "That's why all they have in mind is revenge."

Dr. Kenley said, "You can't know what's in their minds, Chuck. Hope is a big part of the human spirit. People don't like to give up. They'll cling to hope long past the point that it's reasonable."

"Doesn't change the fact that they're a danger to us."

Moultrie said, "No, it doesn't." He looked at the engineers and technicians. "Start setting up an apparatus to pump the gas into the antechamber and stairwell. Stan, you'll be in charge of actually producing the gas."

Davis nodded. "I can do that."

"We're going to be doubling the guard on the entrances as well," Moultrie continued. "I want to be sure that each man is issued plenty of ammunition. The odds of it ever coming to a fight are pretty slim, but I'd just as soon not take chances."

Moultrie was giving orders now, Larkin thought. The "discussion" was over, and it had been mostly for show, anyway. Before Moultrie ever came in here, his mind had been made up about what he was going to do. Although if anyone had come up with a good argument against it, he might have changed his mind.

Or would he? Larkin had to ask himself that question. As he cast his mind back over the preceding months, he couldn't recall a single occasion when anybody had talked Graham Moultrie out of anything. Moultrie would listen, then do what he wanted to do all along. Maybe the Hercules Project *was* a dictatorship. A benevolent one, at least so far, but still a dictatorship.

Good Lord, Larkin thought. Was he actually *agreeing* with Charlotte Ruskin? He didn't trust her, that was for sure. He didn't trust anybody who ranted about oppression and dictators. As far as he could tell, any time somebody wanted to overthrow a so-called dictator, it was so they could become one themselves.

Before Moultrie could say anything else, the speaker of the old-fashioned wired intercom on the table at his elbow crackled, and an urgent voice said, "Graham, we need you to come to the Situation Room, please, if you can find the time."

Larkin drew in a sharp breath. He recognized that voice. It belonged to his daughter.

Moultrie pushed the button to talk and said, "On my way, Jill." As he came to his feet, he looked at Larkin and Fisher. "You fellows come with me."

Dr. Kenley asked worriedly, "What's going on now?"

"I don't know, Jessica, but I'm going to find out."

Moultrie stalked toward the door with Fisher right behind him. Larkin hesitated just long enough to put a hand on Susan's shoulder and squeeze, then followed them. As they walked along the hallway, Larkin saw the expressions on the faces of the other two men and said, "This isn't good, is it?"

"'Find the time' is today's Code Red phrase," Fisher said. "It means somebody is coming down the stairs from the surface."

Chapter 31

The Situation Room had access to all the same feeds and data from the cameras and monitors that the regular security room did, plus the setup Moultrie used for addressing everyone in the project and override controls for all the equipment. One member of the security force was on duty there around the clock, tasked with alerting Moultrie immediately, at any hour of the night or day, if anything unusual happened. Larkin had done plenty of those shifts himself but had never had to summon Moultrie.

Jill was sitting in front of a bank of monitors. She turned her chair slightly and looked back over her shoulder. She pointed at one of the screens and said, "There he is."

Larkin, Moultrie, and Fisher crowded in around her and leaned forward to peer at the screen. A different man than before stood on one of the steps near the bottom of the staircase. He wore a khaki shirt and jeans, and although the clothes were stained and ragged, they were in better shape than the tatters the first man had worn.

The same was true of the man himself. His long, bony face had an unhealthy pallor to it, and several sore places were visible, but his skin hadn't begun to slough off yet. He still had brown hair on his head, although it was thinning, whether naturally or from radiation sickness, there was no way to tell. He was thin, but not to the point of starvation.

He was looking directly into the camera. His slash of a mouth opened and his lips moved. No sound came from the speakers in the Situation Room.

"No audio feed?" Larkin asked.

"It went down a while back," Fisher said. "And we haven't gone out to fix it."

Larkin could understand that. "Anybody read lips?"

Jill said, "I think he's asking if we can hear him."

"Damn, I wish we could talk to him," Moultrie said. "Maybe he'd let something slip about how many of them there are and what they want."

Fisher said, "I'll tell you what they want. They want in here."

"You're probably right," Moultrie said with a nod. "Wait, what's he doing?"

The man had taken a notebook from a hip pocket of his jeans. He slid a marker out of his shirt pocket, opened the notebook, and began writing something on one of the pages. After a moment, he turned the notebook around and held it up toward the camera so they could read the large, printed letters.

IS MY WIFE IN THERE? IS SHE SAFE? HER NAME IS CHARLOTTE RUSKIN.

"Ohhhh, hell," Fisher said. "He's alive."

"That's Nelson Ruskin?" Larkin said.

Moultrie sighed and said, "It is. I recognize him now. He's changed a lot in the past eight months, of course."

He reached over and flipped some switches on the console in front of Jill.

"That woman can't find out about this," Fisher declared. "She's raised enough hell already, and it'll just get worse if she knows her husband is out there."

Jill looked around and said, "You don't think she has a right to know he's still alive?"

"No, I don't, and you're not going to tell her. That's an order."

Larkin didn't care for Fisher's tone of voice as the man spoke to Jill, but he reminded himself not to think of her as his daughter right now. They were all members of the security force, and Fisher had a point. Charlotte Ruskin was already a troublemaker, and she would go batshit crazy if she found out her supposedly dead husband was right on the other side of the blast doors, alive but clearly not well.

"Anyway," Fisher went on, "he's got the radiation sickness, too. Look at those sores on his face."

Larkin couldn't stop himself from playing devil's advocate. "It's not as advanced a case as that other guy we saw. Maybe we could do something to help him."

"What? Prolong his misery by a few more weeks or months?" Fisher shook his head. "Not worth the chance."

Jill asked, "Isn't there any way we can at least let him know his wife's alive?"

"Not really," Moultrie said. "I suppose we could open the inner door and try to tap out a message on the outer one in Morse code, but there's no way of knowing if Ruskin understands it."

"You wanted to establish communication," Larkin pointed out. "That might be one way of doing it."

"It's too risky," Fisher insisted.

"That little chamber between the blast doors hasn't been contaminated, has it?"

Moultrie rubbed the beard on his chin as he frowned in thought. After a moment he said, "No, it's still fine. The outer door is sealed and hasn't been breached at all. It's pretty thick, but if you took a hammer and banged on it, Ruskin ought to be able to hear it."

"It's a bad idea, Graham," Fisher said. "You don't know what kind of trick Ruskin and his friends are trying to pull."

Larkin said, "Do you really think they have the capability to carry out any kind of trick? It's probably taken everything they have just to stay alive up there. They're not plotting against us."

"You can't guarantee that."

"No more than you can guarantee that they *are*."

"That's enough," Moultrie said. "I *would* like to know more about what's going on at the surface. We need to find somebody who knows Morse code."

"I do," Larkin said.

Jill looked up at him and said, "Dad, wait a minute—"

"It's a good idea, it ought to work, and I won't be taking much of a chance, I can do it, Graham."

"If anything goes wrong, we won't be able to let you back in," Fisher warned.

Jill looked like she was going to protest about that, but Moultrie said, "I'm afraid Chuck's right, Patrick. We can open the inner door and let you into the antechamber, but then we'll have to seal it up again, and if there's any sort of breach—as unlikely as that seems—we won't open it."

Larkin nodded and said, "I understand that. But this

won't be the first time I've volunteered for a job with some risk to it."

"No, I imagine it's not," Moultrie said, smiling faintly. "If you're sure you want to tackle it, we'll give it a try."

"Dad, you ought to go talk to Mom before you do this," Jill said.

"Nah, she knows what I'm like. Besides, she might try to talk me out of it. Better she doesn't know until it's all over and I'm fine."

"But what if—"

Larkin held up a hand to stop her. "I said I'd be fine."

Moultrie turned to Fisher and said, "Find one of the maintenance guys and borrow a hammer. Meet us at the inner door."

Larkin patted Jill on the shoulder and told her, "Just relax, kid. Don't worry about me."

He felt his daughter's anxious gaze following him as he left the Situation Room with Moultrie.

"I appreciate you stepping up like this, Patrick," Moultrie said as they headed for the hallway leading to the main entrance and the blast doors. Along the way, they passed a number of the residents, none of whom had any idea what was going on. Most smiled and nodded pleasantly as Larkin and Moultrie went by. The two men walked at a casual pace, taking pains that their gait didn't reveal anything was wrong.

"Somebody's got to do the job, and I'm not as vital a cog as you and Chuck," Larkin said.

"I don't know about that. I like to think that everyone down here is a vital cog in the way the project functions. We've made it so far."

"But since we've been down here, we haven't really

been tested," Larkin pointed out. "The friction with Charlotte Ruskin and her bunch doesn't really count."

"No, you're right about that." Moultrie sighed. "That grace period may be over. We may be tested sooner than we'd like."

Larkin could understand Moultrie's concern, but at the same time he really didn't see how Nelson Ruskin and any other survivors up on the surface could pose a serious threat.

Along the way, they also passed a set of heavy steel doors. Larkin knew that on the other side of those doors was a short corridor leading to a freight elevator that Moultrie had used for bringing supplies down here during the months before the war when he'd been developing the project. Larkin pointed at the doors with a thumb and said, "What about the elevator?"

"You mean as a way for outsiders to breach the project?"

"That's exactly what I mean."

"Impossible," Moultrie said. "The elevator is down here, and the top of it is solid steel. It would take a week to cut through it. At the top of the shaft is a hatch made of steel and concrete thick enough that a bomb would have to land directly on it to even make a dent. And that hatch was inside a building that's now debris. Outsiders wouldn't even know the elevator shaft is there. Despite all that, just as a precaution we have cameras monitoring it. You know that, Patrick."

"I know, but it's still another potential way in. We should probably have guards stationed there around the clock, too."

"That's actually not a bad idea. Why don't you say

something to Chuck about it when you get back from this job?"

"All right."

"And be sure to tell him it was your suggestion, and I agree with it."

Larkin didn't say anything to that. He didn't give a damn who got credit for an idea, only that it was implemented properly and did what it was supposed to.

He started to say something about another rumor he had heard, that Moultrie had a private elevator somewhere in the project that only he and Deb knew about. Larkin decided not to mention it at the moment, but he would feel Chuck Fisher out about the possibility later. If there was any truth to the gossip, that was another avenue of ingress that would need to be secured.

They reached the corridor leading to the blast doors without attracting any undue attention and went through the regular doors to wait for Fisher, who showed up a couple of minutes later carrying a large, heavy hammer. He held it up and said, "Didn't think you could use a sledgehammer for something like this, but this one's got plenty of heft and ought to do the job."

Larkin took it, weighed it in his hand, and nodded. "That'll work."

Fisher threw a latch that locked the door leading into the hallway from Corridor One. They didn't want any of the residents wandering in here right now. Moultrie went to the control panel next to the interior blast door and began pushing buttons on it as he said, "There's an intercom on the wall in there, Patrick. We'll be able to hear you as well as see you, so you can let us know when you're ready to be let back in. Are you sure you're all right with going through with this?"

"I'm not gonna back out now," Larkin said.

"All right." Moultrie thumbed one more button, and machinery began to hum. That sound built to a rumble, and then with a low hiss that signified the airtight seal was breaking, the blast door began to swing open.

As soon as the gap was big enough, Larkin slipped through it into the antechamber. He looked back and nodded curtly to Moultrie, who returned the nod and began entering another sequence on the keypad. The door reversed itself and settled back into place. Larkin heard the seals tightening into position. Dim, recessed lighting shone from the ceiling as he turned toward the outer blast door.

He was alone now in this steel and concrete bubble between two worlds, the sterile safety of the Hercules Project and the outside that had been devastated by nuclear fire.

He took a deep breath, walked over to the other door, and began tapping on it with the hammer.

Chapter 32

Larkin had learned Morse code when he was a young man, even before he was in the Marine Corps, because he had thought for a while that he might want to be a ham radio operator. He had never gotten very involved in the hobby, but he still remembered the dots and dashes. He was sure he was rusty at it, but he believed that if he took it slow, he could make himself understood.

Provided, of course, that Nelson Ruskin also understood Morse.

Larkin began by tapping out CQ several times, the universal hail for hams. When there was no response, he tried H-E-L-L-O, then Ruskin's last name. The clanging impacts of hammer against steel were loud in the antechamber, but he knew the sounds would be muffled by the time they passed through the blast door. He paused to listen.

Moultrie's voice came over the intercom speaker. "Anything, Patrick?"

Larkin held up a hand in a gesture for silence, knowing they could see him on the monitors in the Situation Room, and leaned closer to the door.

It was faint but there: *Tap. Tap. Tap.*

"I hear him," Larkin said, keeping the excitement out of his voice. "What does Jill see on the camera?"

"Ruskin has moved on down the steps to the door. She can't see what he's tapping with. The heel of his shoe, maybe."

"Yeah, it's pretty quiet, but he's definitely responding. Let me try again."

He hammered out Ruskin's name again, then stopped and listened intently. It wasn't really a tapping he heard but more of a thudding instead, lending credence to the idea that Ruskin might be using his shoe. The sounds came in a steady rhythm. Larkin grimaced. The man on the other side of the door wasn't sending code.

"I don't think he knows Morse," he reported through the intercom. He tapped a query but the only answer was the steady thumping. It stopped abruptly.

Then as Larkin frowned and pressed his ear to the door, he heard something that took him by surprise.

Bump-bump-ba-bump-bump . . . bump-bump!

He straightened, threw back his head, and laughed, unable to suppress the impulse.

"Patrick, what the hell?" Moultrie asked with a tinge of alarm in his voice. Maybe he thought something was wrong with the air in here after all and it was making Larkin crazy.

"He gave me the old 'Shave and a Haircut,'" Larkin said. "That's something I never really expected to hear again, especially coming from outside."

Chuck Fisher spoke up, saying, "This isn't a joke."

"No, but it's human. Ruskin can't understand code, so he doesn't know what we're saying, but he knows there are people in here and he's telling us that he's human, too. Damn it, he's asking for help."

"We've been through this," Moultrie said, his voice flat. "However many people are up there, they're not coming in. Not now."

"Wait too long and they'll all die," Larkin said, then realized that might be exactly what Moultrie was hoping for.

"Can you ask him what he wants?"

"I can ask, but he won't be able to answer because he won't know what I'm saying."

"Go ahead and try . . . Wait a minute." There was a pause, then Moultrie went on, "He's gone back up a few steps so he can write in that notebook and show it to us. Jill's relaying the information to me. He's written . . . *I know you're sending code . . . I can't understand it . . . I'll see if I can find somebody who does.*"

"Then there's more of them!" Fisher said.

"We knew that," Larkin said. He listened at the door again. "I don't hear anything else."

"Ruskin is going back up the stairs," Moultrie reported. "Let's get you out of there, Patrick."

"No, let's give it a few minutes."

"We don't know how long it's going to take Ruskin to find anyone who understands Morse, or if he even will."

"Yeah, but he might get lucky. Let's just wait a little while and see."

"You're the one who's stuck in there," Moultrie said. Larkin could hear the shrug in his voice. "As long as you're not getting claustrophobic . . ."

"I'm still good to go," Larkin said.

"We'll let you know as soon as we know anything."

Larkin stood there waiting, concentrating on his breathing and forcing himself to take deep, regular breaths. He'd never had a problem with claustrophobia, and he wasn't feeling any twinges of panic now. Still, he was aware of the tension ratcheting tighter inside him. He hoped that Nelson Ruskin would be able to locate someone who understood Morse because he didn't want to have to work himself up to start this effort over.

After twenty minutes that seemed much longer, Moultrie said, "Someone's coming back down the stairs. It's . . . wait a minute . . . it's Ruskin and another man. Jill says this one is older, with white hair and a beard. He's wearing . . . an old army jacket. He has something with him . . . looks like a wrench—"

Larkin heard the sharp impact of metal against metal and said quickly, "Hold on!" He didn't need Moultrie talking while he was trying to listen. He leaned closer to the door again.

C-Q-C-Q

Larkin's pulse jumped as he recognized the letters.

The man on the other side of the door followed with *Who goes there?*

Larkin lifted the hammer. His telegrapher's fist was slow and laborious, but he got the message through, letter by letter.

Patrick Larkin. Who am I talking to?

Earl Crandall, U.S. Army, retired.

I'm one of Uncle Sam's Misguided Children.

Dogface!

Leatherneck!

Who you got in there with you, son?

Some friends. Larkin wasn't going to give away any more information than he had to. *How about you?*

Same here. We're in bad shape, Marine. Could use some help.

How many?

Crandall hesitated, then tapped out, *Just a few.*

Larkin didn't believe him. That pause had been telling. The outsiders were wary, too. If there were honestly only a few of them, Larkin didn't think Crandall would have hesitated to say so and might well have provided an exact number.

Sorry, can't open up.

We need help. Women and children sick. Not much food.

Larkin believed that, and his guts twisted a little at the thought of what those people had to be going through. What they had already gone through. He was glad Susan wasn't here. With her instincts, this would be hell on her.

He realized he was the only one inside the project who knew what was going on here, the only one who understood the conversation, at least for now. Moultrie might have equipment picking up and recording the words Larkin and Crandall were tapping out, so they could be analyzed later, but for the moment he was the sole representative of the Hercules Project and could tell Crandall whatever he wanted.

But unless Moultrie agreed with it, those would be only empty words.

Sorry, Larkin tapped again. *No can do.* Before Crandall could respond, he went on, *Nelson Ruskin is with you?*

If Morse code being tapped out by a guy with a wrench could sound surprised, what came back from Crandall did. *Ruskin is here. You know him?*

Tell him his wife is alive and safe.

There was a moment's silence, then Crandall tapped urgently, *Get her. Let them talk.*

No can do, Larkin sent again.

Does she know he is alive?

Not yet. Will tell her. That was a lie, but Larkin didn't see how it could hurt anything.

Thank you. If you can't open up, can you send help or supplies to us?

Will work on it, Larkin replied. Maybe that wasn't a lie, he thought. Maybe the engineers and technicians could work out some way to get a few supplies to the surface. They were ingenious; they ought to be able to do that.

But then his spirits sank again. Even if it were possible to deliver them, Moultrie would never give up any of the project's supplies. Especially when the food wouldn't make any difference in the long run. The survivors truly were doomed if they stayed around here. They would be better off heading for one of the less-damaged parts of the state. If they had any more vehicles, they could get away from the residual radiation here on the edge of the destroyed Metroplex. The chances of long-term survival would still be very slim, but any chance was better than none.

Thank you, Crandall tapped. *Asking again, will you let us in?*

No can do. Larkin was beginning to hate that phrase, but it was the only answer he could give.

After a few seconds, Crandall tapped, *Will check back later. Really need medical assistance and supplies.*

We know. Larkin left it at that.

He didn't hear anything else, and after another short delay Moultrie said over the intercom, "Jill says they're going back up top. What did you find out, Patrick?"

"Get me out of here and we'll talk about it," Larkin said in a voice thick with emotion. Maybe he had never been claustrophobic before, but right now the walls were starting to close in on him a little.

"He wouldn't say how many of them there are?" Moultrie asked once Larkin had returned to the Situation Room, where Jill was still on duty at the monitors. Fisher stood to one side, his arms crossed and a scowl on his face.

"He claimed there are only a few," Larkin replied, "but I didn't believe him. He took a little too long to answer."

Jill said, "That's reading a lot into somebody tapping on a steel door with a wrench."

"I know. But that's the way it seemed to me."

Fisher said, "You didn't tell him how many of us are down here, did you?"

"No. I didn't really tell him much of anything except that we can't help them. He asked if there was any way we could send some supplies out to them. I told him we'd look into it."

"We can't do that," Moultrie said immediately. "We can't risk giving up any of our own supplies."

Larkin nodded slowly and said, "I know."

"You gave him false hope, Dad," Jill said. "Isn't it better if they know the truth?"

"Is it? Sometimes the truth isn't all it's cracked up to be."

For a moment, they were all silent. Larkin considered revealing to the others how he had passed along the information that Charlotte Ruskin was alive and well to her husband. He knew Fisher would complain about that, however, so for now he kept it to himself.

He looked at an image frozen on one of the monitors, a screen capture from the footage caught by the stairwell camera. It showed a man with a leathery face, his permanent tan set off by a close-cropped white beard and white hair drawn into a short ponytail at the back of his head. He wore an old army jacket, as Jill had reported earlier. Earl Crandall didn't look sick. In fact, he looked like kind of a hardass. Larkin knew the type. He'd been accused of it himself.

He wasn't sure if the past eight months had changed him, though. He felt keenly the loss of those millions of people who'd been wiped out in an hour or so of nuclear hell. *Any man's death diminishes me*, John Donne had written. Larkin wasn't sure he would go so far as to agree with that, but millions of deaths made him feel diminished, no doubt about it.

On the other hand, Crandall, Nelson Ruskin, and whoever was left alive up there would have been toughened up, even more than they were to start with, in the case of Crandall. Even worse, they had nothing left to lose.

He couldn't afford to turn into some damn softhearted pile of mush, Larkin told himself. He had to stay as hard inside as any of those people on the surface.

Because sooner or later, it might come down to him

and all the others down here defending their way of life from those who wanted to take it. If many of them were like Earl Crandall, Larkin and the rest of the residents of the Hercules Project might have one hell of a fight on their hands.

Chapter 33

As soon as Nelson Ruskin had revealed who he was, Moultrie had cut the feed to the other monitors in the Command Center so it went only to the Situation Room. His standing orders were that nothing anyone on the Command Center staff learned in there could be discussed with anyone else. Just like Vegas, what happened there stayed there. And the hand-picked staff, devoted to the safety and security of the Hercules Project, could be depended upon to follow those orders.

Usually.

Charlotte Ruskin was on the way to her job in the hydroponic gardens when she heard her name called behind her. She stopped, turned, and saw a man walking quickly toward her, trying to catch up. He looked vaguely familiar, but she didn't know his name, or at least couldn't recall it if she'd ever heard it.

"Yes?" she said. "What can I do for you?"

"Do you remember me, Mrs. Ruskin? My name is Charles Trahn."

"Of course," she said, although she didn't, really.

"I came to one of your meetings and listened to you and Mr. Greer speak."

She nodded and smiled faintly, still not recalling him. She had talked to so many people, and she'd never been that good with names and faces.

"I shouldn't have been there, I suppose," Trahn went on. "I'm Command Center staff."

"Oh. Did Moultrie send you as a spy?"

"What?" Trahn looked surprised. "No! Not at all. I was just curious what you had to say. My grandparents, they came from North Vietnam. They escaped and immigrated to America. But they knew what it was like to live under a dictatorship, and I've never forgotten their stories. I guess that's made me . . . I don't know . . . a little leery of one person or group having too much power."

Charlotte Ruskin's polite smile turned into an ironic sneer. "And yet you work for Graham Moultrie."

"I was chosen for Command Center staff because of my technological skills," Trahn said defensively. "That doesn't mean I agree with everything Mr. Moultrie does. In fact, that's why I came looking for you today."

"If you have something to say, Charles, I wish you'd go ahead and say it. I have a shift in the gardens in a few minutes."

Trahn jerked his head in a nod. "You know the rumors about how there's something still alive on the surface?"

"Everybody has heard about that."

"Well, they aren't just rumors. They're true. There are *people* still alive up there." Trahn paused. "And one of them is your husband."

Charlotte Ruskin felt like she'd been punched. She took a step back and drew in a sharp breath. She didn't dare let herself believe what she had just heard, so she said, "That's not true!"

"It is," Trahn insisted. "I was on duty yesterday and saw him with my own eyes. He came down the stairwell at the main entrance and held up a note for the surveillance camera there. It asked about you."

She shook her head. "You're lying."

"Why would I lie about something like that?"

Charlotte Ruskin cast about wildly in her mind for an answer. She said, "Moultrie sent you to upset me, to distract me."

"That's crazy," Trahn said. "If Mr. Moultrie knew I was telling you this, I'd be in big trouble. As soon as we all realized what was happening, he cut that feed to the regular Command Center monitors and sent it directly to his Situation Room. *Only* there. He and a few of his security people know what happened after that, but they're the only ones. Your husband was there, though, right on the other side of the exterior blast door. I saw him with my own eyes."

A wave of dizziness washed through her. She had to reach out and rest a hand on the wall to brace herself.

"I'm sorry," Trahn went on. "I know it's a real shock. I wrestled with myself all last night and earlier today, trying to decide if I ought to tell you. Finally, I . . . I knew I couldn't keep it a secret. You deserve to know the truth."

Her heart was pounding so hard it felt like it was going to burst out of her chest. All along, she had felt like Nelson was still alive. Logic and reason said that he wasn't, but the connection, the bond between them, was still there. She would have known if it was broken.

Even though, eventually, she had turned to Jeff Greer for comfort because she was a passionate woman by nature, she had experienced pangs of guilt. She had been aware somehow that she was cheating on her husband.

Now she knew that her instincts hadn't deceived her. She'd been right all along.

That is, if she could trust Charles Trahn. He certainly looked sincere, and he looked more than a little afraid of her, too. That was enough to convince her he was speaking the truth.

She reached out and caught hold of his arm. He flinched and tried to pull away, but her grip tightened. Her jaw was tense as she said, "Tell me everything you know."

"I . . . I already did—"

"No, you didn't. How did he look? Is he all right?"

"Well . . . not too bad, I guess," Trahn said. "Understand, I didn't get a very long look at him. Like I told you, Moultrie cut all the feeds except his private one. But your husband . . . Mr. Ruskin . . . looked like he'd had a hard time of it. You know it's bound to have been pretty bad up there on the surface."

Pretty bad was putting it mildly, Charlotte Ruskin thought. *Hell on earth* was more like it.

"Was he sick?"

Trahn swallowed. "Yeah, I guess. He had some, you know, sore places on his face. And I could tell he hadn't had enough to eat for a long time. But he was moving around okay and seemed strong enough. He had, like, a notebook and a marker, and that's how he wrote the message he held up to the surveillance camera. He asked about you. He wanted to know if you were in here and okay."

She had to close her eyes and take several deep breaths. Emotions ran riot inside her. Chief among them was relief that Nelson was still alive, but she also felt a surge of pure rage that Graham Moultrie had known about this and not told her. He would have let her go on thinking her husband was dead. She would have continued mourning for him.

When she opened her eyes, she asked, "What did Moultrie tell him?"

"I have no idea."

"Who else knew?"

"You mean about your husband? Uh, besides me, there was only one other guy on duty at the security monitors right then. A guy named Pierce Watson." Trahn shook his head. "He'll never say anything, though. He thinks Mr. Moultrie is God."

"But you don't."

"He's just as human as the rest of us. He can make mistakes. Or make decisions based on his own self-interest."

"What about the others? Who else?"

"Let me think." Trahn frowned for a few seconds, then said, "I believe Jill Sinclair was on duty in the Situation Room, and I don't remember seeing her come out. Mr. Moultrie wasn't there at first, and he came in, in a hurry, so I guess Jill called him. He had Chuck Fisher and Patrick Larkin with him. Larkin is Jill's dad—"

"I know who he is," Charlotte Ruskin broke in. "So the four of them were in the Situation Room?"

"Yeah. And a minute or so after they went in there, Mr. Ruskin held up the notebook with the message he'd printed on it and then the rest of the feeds went down. So I know Mr. Moultrie had to give the order. That was the time line."

"The bastard."

Trahn assumed correctly who she was talking about and said, "I'm sure Mr. Moultrie felt like he had a good reason—"

"He's a damned tyrant, that's his reason. How dare he keep that from me!"

"Yeah, I didn't feel like that was right. That's why I finally decided to come and find you—"

Charlotte Ruskin took hold of his arm again. "Don't say anything about this to anybody."

Trahn looked confused and scared again. "I thought you'd want people to know."

"Not until I figure out the best way to handle this. Just keep your mouth shut, understand?"

Trahn swallowed and nodded. "Of course."

She let go of him and forced a smile. "Thank you for telling me. I won't forget this kindness."

"Sure. If, uh, if there's anything else I can do to help . . ."

"You've done plenty," Charlotte Ruskin told him.

In fact, he had changed everything.

Jeff Greer knew that Charlotte Ruskin didn't love him. She was still in love with her husband, and that wasn't liable to change any time soon. She seemed like one of those ladies who'd cling to the memory of her dead hubby forever, as if they actually believed in soul mates and shit like that.

No, Charlotte had hooked up with him for two reasons: she needed somebody who didn't mind kicking ass to help her settle the score with Graham Moultrie, and she needed a man to hold her in the night when the loneliness got to be too much.

Greer could accept that just fine because he had his own reasons for being with Charlotte. She was a damned good-looking woman for her age—which was a few years older than him—and he didn't like Moultrie and was glad to go along with anything that would bust the guy's chops. Greer had been in the real-estate business himself, before the war, and he had seen too many guys like Moultrie, golden boys whose projects always came in on time and under budget and made money hand over fist. Greer had done all right for himself—well enough to afford a place in this bunker—but he was nowhere near as successful as Moultrie had been, and that just wasn't fair.

So he was all right with letting Charlotte call the tune. It got him laid, and it meant that sooner or later Moultrie would get what he had coming to him, and those things were just fine and dandy with Jeff Greer.

He hadn't really expected things to come to a head so quickly, though. He frowned as he propped himself up on an elbow and looked at Charlotte.

"We're going to do *what* now?"

"Take over the freight elevator," she said. She had come out of the shower in her Corridor Two quarters with a towel wrapped around her body and another caught up around her dark red hair. "Moultrie has men guarding it, but we can deal with that. You can run it, can't you?"

"A moron could run a freight elevator, or any other kind," Greer said. "There's a hatch at the top of the shaft, though, isn't there?"

"It's controlled from down here. We can get someone to open it."

"You seem mighty sure about that."

"I am."

Greer frowned. "That still doesn't explain why. I mean . . . there's nothing up there on the surface *I* want."

"There's something I want," Charlotte said as she unwound the towel and resumed drying her hair. "You've heard the rumors about there being survivors from the war?"

"Sure. Everybody's heard them. But there's no proof—"

"Yes, there is. And Moultrie and his bunch of goons have been in contact with at least one of them." She paused. "Don't get upset about this, Jeff, but my husband is still alive."

He sat up sharply in the bed. "What! You mean . . . Nelson?"

"He's the only husband I have," Charlotte said with a smile.

"But he didn't get into the bunker."

"That's why he's up on the surface. But he's alive. I've talked to someone from Moultrie's staff who actually saw him just outside the blast doors. There's no telling how many other people are still up there, starving and trying to survive any way they can. They need help."

"Well, yeah, but . . ." Greer's brain struggled to process what she had told him. The light dawned on him, and he said, "You want to go up and get them, don't you?"

"Moultrie didn't have any right to lock them out in the first place. You know what he's like, Jeff. He's a little tin-plated dictator who enjoys playing God."

"Yeah, that's true. I can't stand the guy. But this? This kind of changes everything, doesn't it?"

She came to the bed and sat down beside him. "It doesn't have to."

"Sure it does. If you get your husband back, that's pretty much the end for you and me, isn't it? You won't need me anymore."

"Damn it, I need you for a lot more than this. We've stood up and fought together against Moultrie's heavy-handed rule, haven't we? Nothing's going to change about that. The people are looking to you and me to lead that effort."

"You're talking politics. I'm talking about—"

Her arm slid around the back of his neck as she moved against him. "I know what you're talking about," she said as she leaned in, her face close to his. "And I still say *that* doesn't have to change."

Her mouth found his. His hand went to the towel wrapped around her and pushed it away. In the back of his head, a little voice warned, *She's playin' you, you dumbass.*

I know that, Greer told the voice. But right now, he was still getting what he wanted, and there was really no way to predict what might happen in the future. He would deal with that when the time came, he decided.

"Now," he said in a half-whisper as his arms went around her, "just how is it you plan to get that hatch at the top of the elevator shaft open . . .?"

Chapter 34

Charles Trahn was as American as could be. He had been born in Dallas, grew up in Irving, then gotten a good job in Arlington doing international accounting for a bank. He was lucky he had been in Fort Worth on the day the bomb fell, doing some work at one of the bank's locations over there, so he'd been able to reach the Hercules Project in time to get in. He'd had to get a loan to afford the place—one of his buddies at work had helped him with that—and of course now it didn't matter because he'd never have to pay it back.

Of course, he might never have a regular job or a home or a family, either, but he was alive and he was grateful for that every single day.

Grateful enough that when Charlotte Ruskin cornered him in his quad in the lower bunker, he didn't want to even listen to what she was saying, let alone agree to go along with the crazy idea.

"Look, I never should have said anything to you," he told her, trying to keep his voice steady. That wasn't easy when he kept darting glances at Jeff Greer, who had come with her and now stood behind and to one side of her, arms crossed over his broad chest. He had the look of a guy who had played college football and then tried to stay in shape afterward, without a whole lot of success.

But he was still taller, heavier, and no doubt meaner than Charles Trahn. None of those things would have taken very much.

"You were just trying to do the right thing, Charles. We know that. And I appreciate it more than I can say. Now I need you to do the right thing again."

Trahn glanced around the vast, dormitory-like bunker. No one was close by at the moment. If Ruskin and Greer wanted to intimidate him with their visit—and of course they did—they had chosen the right moment for it. Trahn could yell for help if they attacked him, but Greer could get in several good shots before anybody came running up to stop him. Trahn had always feared physical violence.

"What do you want?" he asked warily.

"You work rotating shifts in the Command Center, right?"

Trahn nodded. "Yeah."

"When's your next middle-of-the-night shift?"

"I've got the midnight-to-six in, uh, three days from now, I think."

"And you have access to the controls that open and close things? Like doors?"

Trahn's eyes got big. "Oh, hell no," he said. "You want me to open the blast doors? I can't do that. It takes a special access card to do that, and I don't have it. Only a few people do. Just Mr. Moultrie and his top staff."

"What about the hatch at the top of the freight elevator shaft?"

"It's the same deal. It takes a card with the right chip on it."

"But if you had that card, you could open it?"

"Yeah, more than likely, but—"

"I'm going to get that for you," Charlotte Ruskin said. "I need to get up to the surface, so I can be with my husband again."

"You're leaving the project?"

"That's right," she said.

"But it's dangerous up there! The radiation—"

"Have you seen the readings from the sensors, Charles? Do you really know what it's like? Does anyone other than Moultrie and his Gestapo? I mean, people are *living* up there, right now. It's been more than eight months, and my husband is still alive. How bad can it be, really?"

"I . . . I don't know . . ."

"Anyway, it should be my choice, shouldn't it?" she argued. "If I want to take my chances to be with him again, why shouldn't I be allowed to do that?"

Trahn looked past her at the silent, scowling Greer. "But I thought the two of you—"

Greer broke his silence by saying, "I just want whatever makes Charlotte happy, buddy. That's good enough for me."

"Well . . ." What the woman was saying made sense, Trahn supposed. While he worried about contamination, just opening the top of the elevator shaft shouldn't expose the rest of the project to too much of whatever was up there. Anyway, the atmosphere couldn't be *too* toxic or people wouldn't be able to live in it. Nelson Ruskin had been exposed to it for more than eight months now, and while he hadn't looked healthy, exactly, he didn't seem to be on the verge of dying, either.

But Trahn was still worried. "I could get in a lot of trouble."

"Hey, I'd have your back," Greer said. "Nobody's gonna give you trouble without going through me first."

Trahn wasn't sure how much that reassurance really meant, but at the same time, he could read the menace in Greer's eyes. If he didn't go along with what they wanted, one of these days Greer and some of his friends might catch him alone, in some isolated part of the bunker, and then there was no telling what they might do . . .

"All right," Trahn said. "I don't think you'll be able to get one of those access cards, but if you do, I guess I can help you. Nobody could be too mad at me for helping a wife get back together with her husband, right?"

"Of course not," Charlotte Ruskin said as she smiled and leaned in. She gave Trahn a kiss on the cheek. He felt his face warming. This was ridiculous, he told himself. She was almost old enough to be his mother. But in spite of that, she was kinda hot . . .

Greer stepped up, grinning, and slapped Trahn on the shoulder. "Way to go, pal," he said. "I knew we could count on a good guy like you."

Trahn swallowed and nodded. He liked the sound of that, too.

"Three nights from now, you said?" Charlotte Ruskin asked.

"Yep."

"Then that's when it'll happen."

Chuck Fisher's eyebrows rose in surprise when he opened the door of his quarters in Corridor Two and saw

Charlotte Ruskin standing there. He recovered quickly and asked in a cold voice, "What do you want?"

"I need to talk to you."

Fisher shook his head. "I don't think you and I have anything to talk about."

"You'd be wrong," she said. "Something's going to happen, and you need to know about it."

Now instead of surprise, a look of suspicion appeared on his face. "Is this some kind of threat?"

"No, it's a warning, damn it!" Charlotte Ruskin said. "It's about Jeff."

"Your boyfriend?"

It was her turn to shake her head. "Not anymore," she said. "He . . . he's taken things too far, Fisher. He and some of his friends, they're going to try to carry out a coup against Moultrie."

Fisher took that seriously, as she had known he would. He was as devoted to Graham Moultrie as a dog is to its master. That was disgusting, as far as Charlotte was concerned, but she planned to turn Fisher's attitude to her advantage.

"Are you sure about this?"

"They were in my place, talking. They thought I was asleep. I heard them planning the whole thing."

Fisher wasn't buying it. "The way you feel about Graham, I'd think you'd be glad to see somebody get rid of him."

"It's not Moultrie I'm worried about," she snapped. "He can go to hell as far as I'm concerned. But if Jeff and his buddies try to do this, innocent people are going to be hurt, maybe even killed. I don't want that." She caught her lower lip between her teeth for a second, then added, "And I don't want to see him hurt, either. Yeah, now that I know Nelson's alive, I feel bad about being with Jeff . . . but I may never see Nelson again, and Jeff's here."

Fisher grunted and said, "Love the one you're with, eh?"

She could have killed him for that, right then and there, but she didn't have what she needed yet. Instead she kept her voice calm and steady as she said, "Just let me tell you about it, okay?"

Fisher shrugged and stepped back. "Sure, I guess it won't hurt anything to listen. I'm still not convinced you're telling me the truth, but maybe you can persuade me."

"If you just listen to me, you'll be convinced, all right."

She walked past him into the small living and dining area. Fisher closed the door behind her. He wore sweatpants and a T-shirt and no shoes, but he didn't look like he had gotten out of bed to answer her knock. Charlotte spotted a tablet lying on a table next to a chair and figured Fisher had been reading or watching a movie.

Her gaze darted around the rest of the room, coming to rest on a key ring that lay on the counter dividing the kitchen area from the rest of the room. Several small plastic oblongs the size of credit cards were next to the keys. Nobody down here needed credit cards anymore, so she knew that one of them had to be what she was looking for.

Fisher walked past her and asked with grudging courtesy, "Can I get you something to drink?"

He was a big guy, ex-military, able to handle himself. She was no lightweight herself, but she didn't have the sort of experience that he did. So she knew she couldn't afford to waste her one chance. She slid the knife out of her jeans pocket, swung her arm around to get up some momentum, and drove the four-inch-long blade into the side of his neck as hard as she could. All the accumulated tension exploded out of her in a yell.

Fisher tried to turn toward her. She caught a glimpse of his eyes bugging out with shock and pain. She still had hold of the knife's handle. She shoved on it as hard as she could, slicing the keen edge across his throat. Blood spurted out over her hand.

Instinct brought Fisher's arm up and around. His forearm crashed against Charlotte's head and knocked her backward, making her lose her grip on the knife. Her back hit the door, bounced off. He came after her and reached out for her with his right hand while his left pawed at his ruined throat. Crimson welled over his fingers and spread down the front of his T-shirt.

Charlotte was half-stunned. She got her arms up and tried to fend off Fisher's attack, but he rammed into her and drove her back against the door again. This time her head hit it and the impact disoriented her even more. She flailed at him, but he got his hand on her throat and closed it. The pressure of his fingers was incredible.

Fisher twisted, hauled her around with him, fell forward. She landed on her back with him on top of her. She couldn't breathe because of his choking grip and his weight pressing down on her torso. He had caught her without much air in her lungs. Frantic desperation welled up inside her. A red haze began to creep over her vision.

She felt the hot splash on her face as more blood gouted from Fisher's throat. He slumped even more heavily on her. His fingers relaxed slightly. Charlotte blinked blood out of her eyes and looked up into his, only a few inches away, as they started to glaze over in death. She clawed at his hand and pulled it away from her throat.

Fisher was a big man. Getting him off her wasn't easy. But the urgency of needing to breathe again gave her strength. She put her hands on his shoulders and shoved as hard as she could while at the same time arching her back. For a second, Fisher's deadweight stubbornly resisted her efforts. Then he rolled to Charlotte's left and wound up on his back next to her, arms slightly outflung, his throat a gory mess.

She pushed herself up on an elbow and lay there gasping for air for more than a minute before her galloping pulse began to slow down. She gathered her strength and struggled to her feet. A few staggering steps brought her to the bathroom. She shuddered as she looked at herself in the mirror.

She resembled something from an old horror movie, with blood splattered on her face and already clotting in her hair. She grabbed a towel from a rack, got it wet in the sink, and started scrubbing desperately. She had come here to kill Chuck Fisher, partly because he was Moultrie's right-hand man and deserved it, to Charlotte's way of thinking, but mostly because she knew he would never turn over that access card and she needed it to save her husband. Even though what she had done was justified in her opinion, actually ending the man's life had shaken her.

But she would kill again if she had to, in order to save Nelson.

Her shirt had a lot of blood on it, too. She pulled it off and dropped it on the bathroom floor. She looked in Fisher's bedroom and found a sweatshirt in his closet. It was too big, of course, but nobody would pay any attention to that. She pulled it on, and with most of the blood washed off, she didn't think anyone would notice her.

She didn't know which of the access cards she needed, so she stuffed all of them in her pocket, along with the ring of keys. Might come in handy, she told herself. She didn't want to approach Fisher's body or even look at it, but he had pulled the knife from his throat and it lay beside him. Charlotte came close enough to pick it up and wipe off the blade on his sweatpants. She slipped it back in her pocket as she turned toward the door.

It wouldn't be much longer now, she told herself. She would be reunited with her husband.

And Graham Moultrie's reign as dictator of the Hercules Project was about to be over.

Chapter 35

Jeff Greer was waiting for her at the east end of Corridor Two, near the entrance to the Command Center. He had argued against her being the one to steal the access card, but Charlotte had been insistent. Fisher wouldn't have trusted Jeff enough to let him close to him. But Fisher was a Neanderthal and hadn't given "a mere woman" enough credit for being dangerous, just as Charlotte had predicted.

It was late enough, after midnight, that no one else was around. Moultrie's imposition of a regular day/night routine wasn't exactly a curfew, but it was strict enough that for practical purposes it served as one. The Hercules Project never actually slept, but not many people were out and about in the middle of the night.

Greer stepped forward to meet her with a worried frown on his face. "Are you all right?" he asked, then abruptly reached out to take hold of her shoulders. "My God, Charlotte, is that *blood* on your face?"

"What?" Charlotte was annoyed. She swiped a hand at her face. She had believed she got all the gore off. "It's not mine," she went on.

"Fisher's," Greer breathed.

Charlotte shrugged, signifying her agreement with

what he said and getting his hands off her at the same time. She patted her pocket and said, "I've got his access cards."

"Is he going to—"

"He's not going to do anything to cause us a problem. Ever again."

Greer stared at her. He liked to think he was a tough guy, and he didn't back down when it came to a fistfight. She wasn't sure he could have killed Fisher, though. He might have hesitated at just the wrong second. He wasn't driven by the same sort of hatred she was.

After a moment, Greer drew a deep breath and nodded. "All right. I guess that means you're ready to do this."

"More than ready," Charlotte said. She turned to the door with its card-reader slot. Taking the access cards from her pocket, she began trying them one by one until the small light set into the door's handle turned green. She grasped the handle and twisted it. The door opened and they walked into the Command Center.

A guard was on duty just inside the door, but he wasn't used to seeing anyone come in who wasn't supposed to be there. A lot of Moultrie's security force were the postapocalyptic version of rent-a-cops, not all that vigilant or even competent. This one just glanced at them, then did a double-take when he realized they were intruders and started to reach for the semi-automatic pistol on his hip.

Greer's fist crashed into the man's jaw before he could complete the draw. The punch knocked him back against the wall. Greer used his left hand to grab the man's wrist and prevent him from pulling the gun. At the same time, Greer closed his right hand around the guard's throat and banged his head against the wall. The man was already stunned and couldn't muster up his wits enough to fight back. Greer rammed his head against the wall several more times until the man's muscles went limp. He slid down the wall to the floor, leaving a slight bloody smear behind him from the contusions on the back of his head.

Charlotte bent down and pulled the pistol from the man's holster. Greer was already armed with a short-barreled revolver stuck behind his belt at the small of his back.

Charles Trahn had sketched the layout of the Command Center for them. There was a central hallway with large rooms opening from both sides of it. Inside the rooms to the right were the controls for all the environmental and life-support systems, as well as access to the generators and the actual air- and water-filtration equipment. To the left were all the monitoring stations, including the big room where Trahn worked keeping track of readings from all over the project, as well as the sensors located on the surface. There were security camera feeds in here as well, but at this time of night only one person kept an eye on them. The Command Center operated on a skeleton staff during the nighttime hours. There were only two people in the main room with Trahn tonight, a man and a woman, Charlotte saw as she and Greer walked in carrying the guns.

Greer immediately leveled his revolver at the other two, who started to get up but sat back down, looking scared as the revolver's muzzle menaced them. The man said, "What the hell?"

Charlotte pointed the pistol she had taken from the

unconscious guard at Trahn. He had insisted that they treat him like the others, so no one would suspect he was actually helping them. She said, "You! Open the hatch at the top of the freight-elevator shaft!"

Wide-eyed with fear that was probably real because he wasn't sure what Charlotte might do, Trahn stammered, "I-I can't do that! It takes a special access card—"

With her other hand, Charlotte slapped the cards she had taken from Fisher onto the control panel in front of Trahn. "Find the right one and use it," she ordered. "And if you try any tricks, I'll kill you!"

As she said it, she more than halfway meant it.

With shaking hands, Trahn sorted through the plastic cards and picked up one of them. He tapped out some numbers on the keyboard in front of him, then inserted the card into a reader. A green light appeared on the screen in front of him. He swallowed hard and said, "I can access those controls now."

"All right." Charlotte picked up the other access cards. "Wait until one of us tells you to open the shaft." She knew that once the hatch at the top of the shaft began to open, it would set off an alarm. She wanted to wait as long as possible before that happened so she would be ready for the next part of her plan. She glanced over at Greer, who still covered the other two technicians with the revolver. "You have this?"

"Of course I do," he told her.

"I knew you would. Thanks, Jeff." For a second she thought about going to him and kissing him, but she didn't want to waste the time, and besides, the gesture might distract him. They both had to stay focused on what they were trying to do.

The female technician said, "You're trying to leave the project? That's crazy! It's dangerous up there."

"People live up there," Charlotte snapped. "*My husband* lives up there. Moultrie is lying to all of us about how bad it is. We can go back up and start our lives again any time we want to, and I'm going to prove it!"

She turned and ran out of the Command Center.

During the past few days, Charlotte had walked from the Command Center entrance to the freight elevator several times, counting off the seconds in her head and coming up with an average time. She had known she would be hurrying tonight, so that would make a few seconds' difference, but she also had to locate the right access card for the elevator and there was no way of knowing how long that would take. So she and Greer had left the countdown the same and now those seconds were ticking off in her head as she approached the elevator.

Two men in red vests stood in front of it, talking.

Charlotte almost stopped short at the sight of them, but managed to keep moving because she thought an abrupt halt might make them even more suspicious than they normally would be when they saw her. She had expected perhaps one guard, or even none at all in the middle of the night like this. The double guard took her by surprise.

But the plan had come too far for her to abandon it now. She would just have to adapt.

She hurried up to the guards, who looked at her warily. All the members of the security force knew who she was. She held up her hands, palms out, and said, "Hey, I'm not looking for trouble."

"What do you want, Mrs. Ruskin?" one of the men asked.

"And what are you doing out at this time of night?" the other guard added.

"I don't sleep that well, so I go for walks at night," she said. "I was doing that just now when I was around by the Command Center and saw some sort of commotion going on. I don't know what it was about, but you guys might want to go make sure you're not needed over there."

"If they needed us, they would have called us on the walkie-talkie," the first guard said.

"Maybe the walkie-talkies aren't working," Charlotte suggested. The numbers were still ticking off in her head, getting closer and closer to zero. "I'm just trying to be helpful."

Both men looked skeptical about that.

"Think whatever you want about me, but I just want what's best for the project," Charlotte snapped. "Besides, you may have forgotten, but I was elected to be a resident liaison and work with Mr. Moultrie. I'd just as soon put all the problems behind us."

Neither guard looked like he believed that.

"At least one of you should go and see what's happening," Charlotte said.

"Look, Mrs. Ruskin, go on back to your quarters, or keep taking your walk, or do whatever you want to do, but stop trying to interfere with things that are none of your business. You let us worry about—"

The man stopped short as they all heard a faint rumble from somewhere up above.

Both guards turned to face the elevator doors and tipped their heads back, even though there was nothing to see except the ceiling. It was a natural instinct, though. That was the direction the unexpected sound came from.

The countdown had already hit zero in Charlotte Ruskin's head. Now she reached behind her back, pulled the compact 9mm semi-automatic from the waistband of her jeans where the sweatshirt she had taken from Chuck Fisher's quarters had concealed it, and put the muzzle an inch away from the back of the nearest guard's head. She squeezed the trigger. The blast was painfully loud. Fire from the gun's muzzle charred the man's hair. The bullet shattered his skull, bored through his brain, and blew out through his face where his nose had been. The other man was stunned for the half second it took Charlotte to swing the gun over and shoot him through the head, too.

Both of them hit the floor within a heartbeat of each other.

The noise of the shots, the sight of blood and gray matter dripping from the elevator doors, the sheer knowledge that she had just killed two more men left Charlotte disoriented. Before the war, she had been just a normal person. She had worked in an insurance office, for God's sake! And now she was . . . What *was* she, anyway?

A woman who had spent months stewing in grief and hatred, that's what she was, she realized as she shoved the gun down in her waistband again. A woman who'd had the love of her life taken away from her, only to learn that he was still alive but she couldn't be with him again.

Well, they would see about that.

She pulled the access cards from her pocket and began trying them in the reader next to the door. The third one turned the indicator light green. Charlotte pushed the button that opened the doors. They slid back.

Somewhere not too far away, someone started shouting. Charlotte knew that alarms would be going off in various places to let people know the hatch at the top of the elevator shaft was opening. Back in the Command Center, Greer had done the same countdown she had and at the right time had ordered Trahn to activate the hatch.

Now it was up to her.

She stepped into the elevator. Greer had told her what she needed to do, but she would have been able to figure it out anyway. "G" was Ground—the surface—1 was the level they were on, 2 the lower bunker.

Charlotte pressed her thumb on the button marked "G." The doors closed and with a slight jerk the elevator began to rise.

The fifty feet or so that separated the upper level of the Hercules Project from the surface was the longest ride of Charlotte's life. The elevator's progress was smooth and steady. It was as old as the rest of the installation, dating back to the early 1960s when the missile base was built, but Graham Moultrie had made sure that everything was in good working order. If it wasn't, he had it repaired and refurbished until it was good as new. The smoothness of the elevator ride didn't matter to Charlotte, though. It still seemed to take forever.

Finally, after seconds that had passed more like hours, the elevator came to a stop with just a slight bounce of the floor under her feet. The door might have opened automatically, but she didn't wait to see. Instead she jammed her thumb down on the DOOR OPEN button.

With the same slight hiss as before, the doors parted.

Charlotte caught only a glimpse of flames flickering before hell poured in on her and she screamed.

Chapter 36

Larkin was sound asleep next to Susan when the walkie-talkie on the table next to the bed squawked. He came awake fully and instantly—a habit left over from combat days that he had never lost—sat up as he swung his legs out of bed. Adam Threadgill's voice came from the walkie-talkie. "Patrick!"

Larkin snatched it up, thumbed the button on the side, and said, "I'm here, Adam. What's up?"

"Somebody's opened the hatch at the top of the freight elevator. I'm on duty in the security office and got the alarm. I'm heading for the Command Center. Can you check out the elevator?"

"On my way," Larkin said. He bit back a curse. He had warned Moultrie that the elevator might be a vulnerable point. Moultrie had told Chuck Fisher to double the guard, but Larkin wasn't sure that was enough. Moultrie was a technophile; he relied on all the built-in security measures. He might not be as aware as he should have been, though, that sometimes the best defense was a wall of well-armed soldiers.

Of course, most of the members of the security force weren't soldiers at all, but they were the closest thing available down here, Larkin thought as he shoved his feet into the work boots next to the bed. He slept in socks, sweatpants, and T-shirt, so putting the boots on was all he needed to do in order to be dressed and ready to move.

"Patrick, I heard that," Susan said from where she had sat up on the other side of the bed. "What's wrong?"

"Don't know, but that elevator hatch shouldn't be opening." He stood up and reached for the belt with the holstered 1911 attached to it.

"This is going to compromise the sealed environment down here."

"Maybe. If the elevator doors stay closed, it might not."

"The hatch wouldn't be open unless somebody was trying to use the elevator."

The same thought had occurred immediately to Larkin, followed by a question.

Was somebody trying to get in . . . or out?

"Keep your pistol close until we find out what's going on," he told his wife as he buckled on the gunbelt. "I'll be back."

"Patrick, be careful," she called after him as he hurried out.

He would have told her he always was, if they hadn't both known that wasn't strictly true.

Larkin hurried out of the apartment and into Corridor One. The short hallway leading to the freight elevator opened from Corridor Two, so he had to run halfway to the other end of the project to reach the hall forming the crossbar in the giant letter "H." He pounded along it toward Corridor Two, not knowing what he was going to find but feeling deep in his gut that it wasn't going to be good.

He came out, swung to his right, and saw that people were milling around, obviously upset by something. Larkin paused and asked a man in pajamas, "What's going on?"

"Somebody said they heard gunshots," the man replied.

That made Larkin's heart slug even harder. The next second, a woman screamed, kicking his adrenaline even higher. He bulled his way through the crowd and came to the hallway leading to the freight elevator. People were sobbing and cursing now. Larkin waved them back. His jaw clenched as he looked along the hall. Twenty feet away lay the bodies of the two men who had been posted here on guard duty. Pools of blood around their heads told him they'd been shot.

The elevator doors were closed, but Larkin didn't believe for a second that they had been that way all along. The only reason to kill the guards was because somebody wanted to use the elevator. Charlotte Ruskin's name sprang into Larkin's mind. He couldn't know for sure that was the truth, of course, but it was a strong hunch. Would Ruskin do something as crazy as going up to the surface to find her husband? Larkin didn't doubt it for a second.

"Shouldn't you get help for those men?" someone in the crowd asked.

Larkin knew from the way the guards were sprawled and the amount of blood that had welled from their head wounds that nothing was going to help them now, but he didn't want to say that in front of these people. Instead he pulled the walkie-talkie from his pocket, keyed the microphone, and said, "Medical personnel to the freight elevator, ASAP!"

Then he stiffened as he heard something. He thrust out his left arm in a peremptory gesture and rested his right hand on the Colt at his hip.

"Shut up! Everybody be quiet!"

"What is it?" a man asked.

The faint rumble Larkin heard could mean only one thing.

He waved the left arm at the crowd and shouted, "Get out of here! Clear out! Everybody move!"

The elevator was coming back down from the surface.

Inside the Command Center, alarms klaxoned. Spooked by the loud, raucous noise, Jeff Greer grabbed Charles Trahn, jerked him around, and ground the barrel of his gun against the terrified technician's cheek.

"What the hell!" Greer said.

"I told you there'd be alarms!" Trahn practically wailed.

"I didn't know it would be like that! Can't you turn them off?"

"No, I'm sorry, I—"

Trahn didn't get any further before the other male technician gathered up his courage now that Greer wasn't pointing the gun at him and the woman anymore. The man leaped out of his chair and charged.

Greer heard the slap of shoe leather on the floor and wheeled around. He pulled the trigger and the gun boomed, flame lancing from its barrel. The slug tore through the other technician's shoulder, but the man's momentum carried him forward so that he crashed into Greer and knocked him back into Trahn. All three of them sprawled back against the console where Trahn had been working earlier.

Trahn screamed and frantically grabbed Greer's wrist so he could point the gun away from him. Greer's trigger finger jerked spasmodically. The weapon blasted twice more. Both bullets smashed into the gauges and controls in the console. Sparks flew with an electrical crackling.

Greer rammed a fist under Trahn's chin and jerked his head back. Trahn went limp and slithered to the floor. Greer shoved the other man away, which gave him enough room to swing the pistol and slam it against the man's head. The wounded technician went down, too.

Greer turned to look for the woman. She was gone. The door was open. He cursed as he realized she had made a run for it while he was tangled up with the two guys.

But it didn't matter. Charlotte would be on her way to the surface by now, and no one was going to stop her. He supposed there were overrides on the elevator, but he wasn't sure they would work anymore, considering the damage his shots had done to the controls.

Charlotte hadn't known what she was going to find when she got up there, but her plan was to locate her husband and bring him and some of the others back down here. She would have to do it quickly, though, otherwise Moultrie would freeze the elevator at the surface. Greer's hunch was that most of the survivors would be close to the project's entrances, hoping for some miracle that would let them come down to safety.

At worst, Charlotte would be with her husband again, and since that was what she wanted more than anything else, Greer was willing to go along with it. Sure, he would miss her once she was gone, but there were plenty of other single women—legitimately single women—down here. Well, maybe not plenty, and some of them weren't really that good-looking, he amended, but there were *some*.

A chance was all he'd ever asked for in life.

"Hey!"

The shout snapped Greer out of the momentary reverie. He looked up, saw the stocky figure of a guy he recognized as Adam Threadgill. The security man had a gun in his hand, so Greer didn't stop to think about it. He just fired his own gun and saw Threadgill rock back a step as the bullet punched into him.

Then flame blossomed from the muzzle of Threadgill's gun and Greer felt the hammerblow of a bullet. It knocked him back. He tripped over the unconscious Charles Trahn and fell to the floor. A wet heat flooded through his body. He couldn't seem to get his breath, and his muscles just flopped uselessly when he ordered them to get up.

He was able to lift his gun, though. He pointed it at the dark figure coming toward him, knowing it had to be Threadgill. Greer was trying to pull the trigger again when the world split apart in orange flame.

That was the last thing he knew.

Except for a fleeting image of Charlotte's face.

It was like something out of a horror movie. Twisted, grotesque faces leering at her. Skeletal hands clawing at her clothes and face. Gaunt bodies slamming against her, driving her against the back wall of the elevator.

No wonder terrified screams ripped Charlotte's throat raw.

She flailed at the attackers flooding into the elevator. Panic gave her strength. She knocked several of them away from her. Sickness twisted her stomach as she felt her fists slide off faces that were little more than oozing sores.

The relatively close quarters of the elevator worked in her favor. With her back pressed to the wall, the maddened survivors couldn't surround her. As soon as she had enough breathing room, she reached behind her and closed her hand around the gun. There were several rounds left in the magazine. She hoped that would be enough to drive these lunatics away.

Before she could fire, another gun went off somewhere nearby. The dull boom sounded like a shotgun. The attackers flinched from the sound and then began to shrink away from her as a man shouted, "Get out of there! Get back, damn it!"

Instantly, Charlotte knew those tones. She had expected never to hear them again. She cried, "Nelson!"

Her husband waded into the knot of people still blocking the elevator's entrance and flung them aside with one hand while his other held the shotgun he had just fired. Charlotte saw him and felt her heart practically leap up her throat. Still holding the shotgun, he threw his arms around her and pulled her against him.

"I thought I'd never see you again," he rasped.

Charlotte just cried, unable to find words anymore.

Another man shouted, "Back off!" The rest of the survivors cleared the elevator. The newcomer stood in the door, brawny and broad-shouldered, with a white beard and white hair pulled into a short ponytail. Like Nelson Ruskin, he held a pump shotgun.

After a moment, Nelson turned toward the other man, put his arm around Charlotte's shoulders, and said in a voice thick with emotion, "Earl, this is my wife."

The man called Earl gave her a curt nod. "Ma'am." He looked at Nelson and went on, "Looks like your hunch paid off. You said the lady would get to you one way or another, if it was possible at all."

"And now we've got a way down there."

A frown creased Earl's forehead. He said, "I'm still not sure that's a good idea."

"None of our people are going to survive up here. You know that."

"Maybe, maybe not. Some of 'em are still in pretty good shape. Could be it's time to move on, like those folks down there suggested."

Charlotte could tell that this argument between the two men was nothing new. She looked around, saw that they were below ground level in what appeared to be the basement of a collapsed building. Rubble from that structure had fallen around them. This had been a warehouse at one time, she realized, probably for the supplies Moultrie had taken down into the project. The flames she had seen were from a large campfire about fifty yards away. The ragged, emaciated, diseased survivors had retreated toward it. Charlotte saw men, women, children, all in bad shape. Many of them looked like pictures she had seen of prisoners from Nazi concentration camps, only worse if that was possible.

She looked up at her husband and said, "You've been waiting for me?"

"That's right," Nelson said. "I knew you'd come if you could. And I knew that you'd save us all."

Earl just shook his head and stepped away, as if declaring that he wasn't going to have anything to do with this. Charlotte supposed that he was Nelson's friend, but right now she didn't care. All that mattered was that the two of them were together again.

"How much time do we have before they shut off the elevator?" Nelson asked.

"I don't know. I have a friend holding the Command Center. He'll give us as much time as he can."

"A friend?" Nelson asked the question, then gave an abrupt shake of his head as if realizing that it didn't matter right now. He lifted a hand, put a couple of fingers in his mouth, and gave an old-fashioned, piercing whistle that carried through the dark night.

Charlotte's eyes widened as more ragged figures began to drop down into the ruined basement. The dancing firelight threw shadows back and forth over them as they swarmed toward the elevator. Although gaunt and obviously sick, they appeared to be in better shape than the hapless, unarmed creatures who had rushed the elevator.

All of these people carried weapons. Most held firearms. Charlotte saw a variety of pistols, shotguns, and rifles. A few brandished axes or pitchforks. The firelight glittered on knife blades, too.

Even though the survivors had listened to Nelson and followed his orders earlier, the sight of this small but lethal army made Charlotte step back as fear welled up inside her.

"Don't worry," Nelson told her. "They're your friends now. They know you came to save them."

Charlotte wasn't sure what those disease-ravaged brains knew. As more and more of the survivors crowded into the big elevator, she and Nelson were forced back into a corner. The stench of corrupted flesh filled the air and made her want to gag. She forced down the reaction.

"I . . . I thought you might want to leave here and go somewhere else," she said. "Just the two of us."

Nelson shook his head and said, "We wouldn't make it. We need what's down there, Charlotte."

"But these people . . ." She suddenly felt queasy about what she had done and the possibilities she had opened up. Keeping her voice at a whisper only her husband could hear, she went on, "Most of them aren't going to live."

"Maybe not, but they'll have more of a chance. And there's something that's more important, anyway."

"What's that?" Charlotte asked as someone at the front of the car pressed the button that closed the doors. Howls of outrage came from those left outside, but the doors cut off the sound.

"Revenge," Nelson replied. "Revenge on Graham Moultrie and everyone else who turned their backs on us and left us up here in this hell."

"You mean—"

"We're going down there to kill as many of the bastards as we can. If we can manage it, we'll kill 'em all."

With a lurch, the overloaded elevator began to descend.

Chapter 37

The alarm went out over the walkie-talkies that had been issued to every member of the security force. The strident ringing brought Jill Sinclair up out of the bed she shared with her husband. Trevor was left behind in the rumpled covers, sitting up and looking confused as Jill dressed rapidly and buckled on the belt that had her holstered Glock attached to it. Several loaded magazines were slid into pouches on the belt.

"What is it?" Trevor asked.

"Don't know," Jill said as she raked her hair back and put a band around it to keep it out of her eyes. "But that's the general alarm, so it's bad."

"Like a red alert?"

"Yeah." Jill opened the drawer in the nightstand on Trevor's side of the bed and reached into it to bring out the 9mm Shield. She set it on the table and said, "Here. Get dressed, hang on to this, and put a couple of loaded magazines in your pocket."

"I'm coming with you?"

She shook her head. "No, you're staying here and readying for trouble."

"I can come along—"

"No. I need to know that you're here, protecting Bailey and Chris."

"Of course I'll protect them," Trevor said as he stood up. "I'd die before I'd let anyone hurt them."

Jill gave him a grim smile and said, "I'd rather you make any son of a bitch trying to hurt them die instead." She leaned in, pressed her lips to his for a second, and then turned to run out of the bedroom.

Trevor picked up the little semi-automatic, looked at it, and took deep breaths as he tried to control his wildly hammering heartbeat.

Adam Threadgill leaned against the console and ignored the pain from the bullet wound in his side. It was bleeding heavily, but he was pretty sure the slug had bored through without hitting his ribs or nicking any internal organs. If that was the case, he wasn't going to die, although he might pass out from blood loss.

He knew he couldn't afford to let that happen. Not yet, anyway.

He bent down, fought off a wave of dizziness that threatened to overwhelm him, and grasped Charles Trahn's shirt collar. He hauled the groggy technician upright and propped him against the console.

"Trahn!" Threadgill said urgently. "Trahn, come on, damn it. Wake up."

Trahn muttered something Threadgill couldn't make out. Threadgill didn't know if the guy was speaking Vietnamese or was just incoherent from being knocked out.

That thought made Threadgill glance at the man who had battered Trahn into unconsciousness. Jeff Greer lay on the floor almost at their feet, his face a bloody ruin from the shot Threadgill had fired just in time to keep the man from shooting him again.

Threadgill knew he couldn't worry about that now. He grabbed Trahn's shoulder and gave him a shake.

"Come on! You gotta tell me what's going on here. Has that elevator started back down?"

Trahn shook his head, pawed his hair back away from his face. He swallowed hard and looked at the readings on the console.

"The system shut down from the . . . from the power spike when Greer's shot made it short out. Everything's rebooting."

"How long is that gonna take?"

Trahn looked at Greer, then shuddered. In a choked voice, he said, "I don't know. It should be further along than it is." He pointed a trembling finger at a status bar on one of the screens. "It looks like it may have gotten hung up somehow."

Threadgill suddenly felt cold inside. "You mean the environmental systems aren't working?"

"Nothing's working," Trahn said.

"Well, *fix* it! Without that life-support equipment, we'll all die."

Trahn leaned both hands on the console, obviously as dizzy as Threadgill was. "No. We have several days' supply of usable water stored, and the air won't go bad for hours."

"Hours! What if it's days before the computers start working again?"

"It won't be. They may have to restart again, but they'll boot back up in time, I'm sure of it. There are enough fail-safes and redundancies—"

Threadgill grabbed his arm. "What if they don't?"

"Then we . . . we'll have to get up to the surface somehow."

"But the surface is poison!"

Trahn shook his head again. "As far as I know, there's never been any sign of biological contamination in the air. The only real threat is the radiation."

"But the air's still bad, right?"

"It'll keep us alive right now. We don't know what the long-term effects would be. That's better than suffocating to death in a matter of hours, though."

Threadgill slumped into Trahn's chair, unable to stand up anymore. Already the atmosphere seemed stuffier and hotter to him, but that might be his imagination running wild, he told himself.

"You can't stop that elevator from coming back down?"

"I told you, I can't do anything."

Threadgill brightened slightly. "But if the computers are down, whoever's inside it can't open the doors."

Trahn made a face. "That's not strictly true. The motors that control everything about the elevator, including the doors, run off electrical power, but they're not computer-operated. Our generators are still working." He pointed to a glowing display as proof of that, but the numbers didn't mean anything to Threadgill. "You need an access card to get *into* the elevator, but you don't need one to get *out*."

"Holy crap," Threadgill said. "The project's about to be under attack."

Trahn nodded and said, "I think there's a pretty good chance of it."

* * *

"Get out of here!" Larkin yelled at the crowd that had been drawn by the gunshots and the grisly sight of the guards' dead bodies. "Everybody get away from here now!"

He didn't know who—or *what*—was riding on that elevator, but he was convinced it wouldn't be anything good.

He pulled the .45 and leveled it at the elevator door in a two-handed grip. There was no light to indicate the elevator's progress, and he couldn't hear it anymore because in addition to stampeding, the people in the crowd were yelling and screaming as well. It was chaos behind and the unknown in front, and standing between, as it had been so often in human history, was a rough man ready to do violence.

Larkin glanced over his shoulder as the tumult subsided slightly. The mob of nightclothes-wearing residents had cleared out of the immediate vicinity.

That was good, because when he looked at the elevator again, the doors started to open.

Gunshots erupted before the gap was more than a couple of inches wide.

Larkin opened fire as he backed away. The people in the elevator had to be survivors from the surface, and clearly, they didn't come in peace. Aiming between the doors as they slid apart, he emptied the .45's magazine. The thunderous roar from the Colt was deafening, especially in these closed spaces. The barrage brought screams from inside the elevator, and the shots stopped for a moment.

That gave Larkin the chance to duck around the corner at the end of the short hallway, back into the main area of Corridor Two. The bystanders were really scattering now that an actual battle had broken out.

But help was on the way, although Larkin wasn't all that glad to see it. Jill ran toward him, gun in hand and an anxious expression on her face.

Larkin waved her toward the wall on the other side of the opening. She veered and put her back against it. Several men Larkin recognized as fellow members of the security force hurried toward the hall leading to the freight elevator, too. Thankfully, they were smart enough not to dash out into the open and expose themselves to the invaders' guns.

Invaders, Larkin thought. That was exactly what they were dealing with here. Fellow human beings—fellow Americans—who had wound up in a hellish situation through no real fault of their own. But from the looks of things, that tragic situation had warped their brains until they didn't want to do anything except lash out at the residents of the Hercules Project. Their minds were full of hate and the lust to kill.

At the moment, however, they weren't shooting anymore, so Larkin took advantage of the opportunity to replace the magazine he had emptied with a full one. When he had done that, he risked a glance around the corner and saw that the elevator doors were closed again. He didn't believe they would stay that way for very long.

"People from the surface?" Jill called across the hallway's opening.

"Nobody else it could be," Larkin replied.

"It sounded like they were well-armed."

"They've got a lot of guns, anyway. Don't know how good they are."

"As long as they throw bullets, they're dangerous."

Larkin couldn't argue with that.

"Have you seen Chuck?" he asked.

"Mr. Fisher?" Jill shook her head. "No, I haven't. I'm surprised he's not here with you."

Larkin was surprised, too, and he thought that Chuck Fisher's absence didn't bode well. Fisher should have heard any alarm that went out, and Larkin couldn't imagine him not showing up immediately to see what the trouble was. The only reason he wouldn't, was if something had happened to him and he *couldn't*.

"Since you were ready for them and kept them from getting off the elevator, maybe they'll give up and go back up to the surface," Jill suggested.

Larkin thought about that, but only for a second before he shook his head.

"They didn't get down here quite fast enough to take us by surprise," he said, "but what do they have to gain by going back up? It's no fit existence up there. They've all got radiation sickness already, and sooner or later they'll either die from it or starve to death. They'd probably just as soon go out quicker and kill some of us in the process."

"But they don't gain anything by that!"

"Maybe they just want to be more comfortable in the time they have left. Or maybe they haven't given up hope yet, even though the odds are against them. Or maybe they're just mad and want to hurt somebody. No matter what they want, we can't let them in here."

"We'll stop them," Jill said.

Larkin hoped she was right. But they were going to have a fight on their hands first.

* * *

Inside the elevator, Charlotte Ruskin was breathing hard, trying to fight down the terror that had filled her when the guns started going off. Even though she had killed three men herself in the past hour, she hadn't been prepared for the earth-shattering roar, the choking stench of gunpowder, and the overpowering feeling that the world was coming to an end around her.

Even though the shooting had stopped, she couldn't hear anything. She wasn't sure her hearing would ever return. She looked at Nelson, saw his lips moving, but couldn't make out the words. She was no lip-reader, but gradually she realized he was asking her if she was all right.

She nodded. The people from the surface were packed in so tightly there'd been no chance of a bullet penetrating to the back of the elevator. She wondered if that was why Nelson had made sure the two of them were back here. The others were—what was the old-fashioned term?—cannon fodder.

He put his mouth next to her ear, and she was a little surprised to hear him saying, "We have to try again! That's why I brought this along!"

He reached under his shirt and brought out something she didn't recognize at first. For a second she thought the red cylinders fastened together with duct tape were sticks of dynamite and wondered if he was crazy enough to set off an explosion down here?

Well, why not? What did they have to lose?

Then she realized they weren't dynamite at all. They were road flares, the kind the police set out when there was an accident. There was no telling where he had gotten them. During the more than eight months that had passed since the war, he'd had time to wander all over the devastated countryside.

"Give me room, give me room!" he shouted at the other people in the elevator. Charlotte's hearing *was* coming back. The survivors wedged themselves aside. Charlotte caught at Nelson's ragged sleeve.

"Be careful," she told him.

He just grinned over his shoulder at her, then said to the others, "When this goes off, we go out right behind it, understand? They won't be able to see us, so they'll be shooting blind. We go out and we don't stop until they're all dead."

That brought a cheer from the others. Nelson's back was to Charlotte, so she couldn't tell what he was doing with the flares. But then he jerked a nod at the man crowded up next to the elevator controls. The man must have pressed something, because the doors started to open again.

Charlotte just had time to wonder about something—wouldn't *they* be shooting blind because of the flares, too?—when Nelson tossed them out, and a hellish red glare erupted and seemed to swallow the whole world.

Chapter 38

Larkin saw the bundle of taped cylinders come flying out of the elevator to bounce along the short hall and out into Corridor Two. He thought they were explosives and yelled, "Everybody down!"

A huge fear for Jill's safety filled his heart.

But then instead of blowing up, the bundle seemed to turn into the flaming heart of the sun instead, and Larkin knew he'd been wrong. They were highway flares, and they were so bright he couldn't see anything else.

He knew what was going to happen, though, so he shoved the .45 around the corner and began pulling the trigger as fast as he could while he swung the barrel from left to right. Slugs sprayed through the hallway, but a deathstorm of lead came right back at him. He sensed the bullets flying through the air as much as heard them.

There were too many of the invaders. Some of them had to be down, but others took their place. Larkin didn't know if the other security forces could hear him, but he bellowed, "Fall back, fall back!"

His eyes had squeezed shut as he was emptying the Colt. Now he opened them to tiny slits as he turned and ran away from the hall. His vision had adjusted a little, so he was able to see where he was going, even though the red glare lingered along his optic nerves and in his brain. There was a small common area not too far away, where residents of Corridor Two could get together. Larkin stumbled into it and dropped behind one of the benches to use it for cover.

The survivors from the surface were boiling out of the corridor now, firing pistols, rifles, and shotguns. Some of them howled like wild animals, others shouted curses or just yelled incoherently. As they swarmed past the still-burning bundle of flares, they blocked the hellish light, so Larkin began to be able to see better. He rammed home a loaded magazine into the Colt and aimed over the back of the bench.

Boom. Boom. Boom.

The evenly spaced shots took down three of the attackers, spilling them limply to the floor. They drew attention, though, and Larkin had to duck as slugs and buckshot hammered the bench. More of the crazed intruders charged toward him, firing as they came. He knew his position would be overrun within seconds.

Then another figure leaped through the haze of gunsmoke that was tinted red by the flares. Shots spurted from the Glock Jill held and drove some of the attackers off their feet. She burst through their ranks, spinning and firing as she whirled through the air. A man's head jerked as blood and brains flew from it. Another twisted around from the impact of a slug in his chest. Larkin rose up and fired past Jill, his bullets shredding another of the attackers.

She leaped behind another bench and crouched there, breathing hard as she looked over at her father. Larkin nodded in thanks.

Gunfire roared along the corridor as the people from the surface scattered in their murderous rampage and the residents fought back. Larkin raised his voice over the racket and called over to Jill, "Are you all right?"

"Yeah, I'm fine, Dad. Look!"

Larkin turned back to the elevator hallway in time to see Charlotte and Nelson Ruskin dart out of it and run in the other direction, toward the Command Center. So those two had been reunited, just as he'd thought, and now they were on their way to cause even more trouble. If they reached the Command Center, there was no limit to the damage they might do. They might wreck enough equipment to put the whole project in danger.

"Son of a *bitch*!" Larkin said as he surged to his feet. "We've got to stop 'em!"

He took off running after the Ruskins. He knew without looking that Jill was right behind him.

Charlotte panted as she tried to keep up with Nelson. He had grabbed up a rifle that one of the other men had dropped, a military-looking weapon—Charlotte didn't know what they were called—and held it in front of him at a slant across his chest.

"What are we . . . going to do?" she managed to ask.

"I remember the Command Center from the tour we took. Moultrie will be there. If we can get our hands on him, we can force the bastard to do whatever we want."

"We should kill him! He locked you out!"

"That would be a waste. Look out!"

Two men in the red vests of the security force had popped into sight in front of them. Both men were armed and tried to raise the pistols they held. Nelson skidded to a stop and brought up the rifle, firing three swift shots before the guards could get off even a single round. They both flopped backward as the bullets tore through them.

Nelson grabbed Charlotte's hand and tugged her on. They ran past the dying men, who were gasping out their last breaths.

"What about the people who came down here with you?"

Nelson shook his head. "They're on their own. They knew it might be a losing battle. But they're getting to strike back, and that's all they care about. I want to take over this place so we can bring down even more of them and wipe out everybody! That's why I need to get my hands on Moultrie."

He was insane with hatred, Charlotte thought—but she felt her lips curving in a savage grin right along with his.

In this world, what was left but madness and revenge and death?

"There's the entrance to the Command Center," she told him, "straight ahead!"

Threadgill tried to push himself up from Trahn's chair. All the surveillance cameras were down, along with the computers, so he couldn't see what was going on out in the project, but he could hear the rattle of gunfire and knew hell was breaking loose. He needed to be there, doing what he could to help.

He had lost enough blood, though, that he was too weak to stand. His muscles simply refused to obey him.

"Trahn," he mumbled. "How're the computers doin'?"

"They crashed again," Trahn said as he hovered over a keyboard. "I forced another restart. Maybe they'll reboot this time."

"They damned well . . . better," Threadgill said.

"Oh, my God!" Trahn exclaimed. "Mr. Moultrie!"

Graham Moultrie, clad in hastily pulled-on jeans and T-shirt, shouldered Trahn aside and reached for the keyboard. He stopped before he did anything and stared at the monitor.

"Five minutes," he muttered.

"Sir?" Trahn said.

"It'll take at least five minutes for the computers to be up again. How many reboots is this?"

"It's the second one."

Moultrie nodded. His face was drawn and tense, but he seemed composed. "Let's hope that does it," he said. "The electrical grid is intact and emergency systems are running. That'll hold us until the system is fully functional again."

Trahn heaved a sigh of obvious relief. He said, "I knew you'd be prepared for any contingency, sir."

Moultrie smiled grimly. "Don't count on that yet. We're under attack from the surface."

"What?" Threadgill again tried to stand up. "I gotta go help—"

Moultrie put a hand on his shoulder. "You're hurt, Adam. You've done enough already." He glanced at the body on the floor. "Is that Jeff Greer?"

"Yeah. When I got here to see what the alarm was about, he shot me. I didn't have any choice but to kill him."

"Was Charlotte Ruskin with him?"

Threadgill found the strength to shake his head. "Didn't see her. How about you, Trahn?"

"She . . . she was here," the technician said. "She and Greer forced me to open the hatch at the top of the elevator shaft. They had an access card for the override."

Moultrie looked even more haggard at that news. "Where did they get it?"

"I don't know, sir."

"It must have come from Chuck Fisher," Moultrie said with a frown. "Chuck wouldn't have given it up unless . . ."

"Oh, hell," Threadgill said as Moultrie's voice trailed off. He was thinking the same thing: Fisher wouldn't have given up his access cards as long as he was alive.

"So Charlotte Ruskin was trying to reach the surface and find her husband," Moultrie said. "That's the only thing that makes sense. And now Ruskin and some of those other survivors have made it down here and are attacking the project—"

"That's right," a voice came from the doorway. "Your arrogance has caught up with you, Moultrie, and now you're gonna get what's coming to you!"

The men at the console turned their heads to look at the entrance, where Nelson Ruskin stood with an A.R. 15 in his hands and his wife beside him, pointing a pistol at them.

Charlotte stalked forward, being careful to stay out of the line of fire, and said, "You! Trahn! Send the elevator back up."

"I . . . I can't!" Trahn said. "The computer's still rebooting. I don't have any control."

She paused and looked down at Greer's body. "Jeff . . ." she said quietly. "I'm sorry."

Moultrie was standing so that he partially blocked Threadgill from the Ruskins' view. Threadgill reached deep inside and finally found the strength he needed to move. The intruders either hadn't noticed him or didn't realize he was armed. He came up out of the chair and swung his left arm, hitting Moultrie's upper arm and driving the man aside and down. Threadgill's gun came up and belched flame.

The AR-15 roared as Nelson Ruskin frenziedly pulled the trigger four times. One bullet went past Threadgill and shattered a monitor behind him, but the other three smashed into his chest. Threadgill's finger clenched spasmodically on the trigger and his gun went off again. The wild shot struck Charlotte Ruskin just above her left eye and snapped her head back. Her knees buckled. She was dead by the time they hit the floor, and she pitched forward on her face.

"Nooooo!" Nelson Ruskin howled. He tracked the rifle toward Moultrie, jerking the trigger as he swung the weapon. The bullets found Charles Trahn first. Trahn scrambled to get out of the way but was too slow. A couple of slugs tore through his body and exited in sprays of blood. He crumpled to the floor next to Greer and Threadgill, who had also collapsed from his wounds.

Moultrie would have been next. Ruskin charged across the room toward him, eager to kill. But before Ruskin could pull the trigger again, Larkin and Jill rushed into the Command Center and opened fire. Ruskin stumbled forward as the bullets pounded into his back. Great blossoms of blood appeared on his shirt. Some of the slugs bored all the way through and whined around the room, most of their force spent by their lethal passage through Nelson Ruskin's flesh. The AR-15 slid from Ruskin's hands and clattered to the floor. He reached out blindly, as if trying to get his hands around Graham Moultrie's throat, then sank to his knees and rolled onto his side. A crimson pool spread around him.

Larkin kept his gun trained on Ruskin as he told Jill, "Check on Charlotte."

Only a couple of seconds went by before Jill reported, "She's dead, Dad."

"I'm pretty sure Ruskin is, too, but keep an eye on him anyway."

Having said that, Larkin lowered his gun and hurried to Adam Threadgill's side. He knelt next to his old friend.

"Damn it, Adam."

Threadgill's eyes fluttered open. "P-Patrick . . ." he managed to say. "You need to watch out . . . for Ruskin . . ."

"He's done for, buddy," Larkin said quietly. He put a hand on Threadgill's shoulder and squeezed. "Thanks to you."

"Nah, I didn't . . . but I guess . . . it doesn't matter."

"No," Larkin said, trying to keep his voice from choking. "It sure doesn't."

"What matters . . . is that you tell Luisa . . . that I . . . I love . . ."

Threadgill didn't have the strength to go on. Larkin leaned close to him and whispered, "She knows, Adam. She knows. But I'll tell her for you anyway."

"Thanks . . . Patrick . . . Semper . . ."

"Fi," Larkin grated out as Threadgill's last breath rattled in his throat. Larkin knelt there for a long moment, head down, before he dragged in a deep breath and came to his feet.

Gunfire continued elsewhere in the project. Larkin

needed to be there. He looked at Moultrie, who was ashen but apparently unhurt, and said, "You all right, Graham?"

Moultrie nodded. "Thank you, Patrick."

Larkin turned toward the door and jerked his head at Jill. "Come on, kid. There's more work to do."

Chapter 39

The computer system finished its reboot approximately fifteen minutes later. All systems came back online, although some of them were glitchy. By that time, the shooting had stopped. All the invaders from the surface were dead: fourteen men and seven women.

So were nine of the Hercules Project's residents, six members of the security force and three so-called civilians. Those casualties included Chuck Fisher, Adam Threadgill, and Charles Trahn. Two dozen more residents were wounded, some seriously.

Larkin and Jill had come through the fighting without a scratch. Larkin's heart was full of pain from the death of his old friend, though.

With Fisher's death, Larkin found himself unofficially heading up the security force, so the report came to him of noises from the elevator shaft. Somebody was banging around up there. Larkin went and listened for himself. He knew right away what was going on.

He found Moultrie in the now up-and-running-again Command Center and told him, "Some of the survivors have managed to climb down the elevator cables and they're on top of the car now, trying to bust through it with what sounds like shovels and axes."

"They're not going to be able to, are they?" Moultrie said. "It's solid steel. They'd need a torch to cut through it, and even if they happen to have one, we're not going to give them the chance to do that."

"What do you think we should do, Patrick?"

Larkin pointed with his thumb and said, "Send the car back up. The hatch is open. They can scramble back out before they get caught. Then we bring it down and close the hatch. We're back where we started."

"Only the atmosphere down here has been breached and exposed to the air from up there."

"I'm sure you've checked the radiation readings by now. Just letting some surface air down here hasn't made them go up, has it?"

Moultrie shook his head. "No, we seem to be safe where that's concerned. And the scans for any other sort of contaminant have come up negative. The only thing that got down here that's still dangerous are the bodies of those dead maniacs—and we have an incinerator to deal with those."

Larkin grimaced. He knew Moultrie was right. Burning the corpses was the best and safest way to dispose of them. It still seemed a little harsh to him, anyway, despite the fact that he himself planned to be cremated if possible when his time came.

Moultrie sighed and said, "I should have taken your advice more seriously, Patrick. You knew that freight elevator was a weak spot in our defenses, and I didn't shore it up enough. I won't make that mistake again. I need someone to take Chuck's place, and I'm hoping you'll agree to accept the job."

"As head of security?"

"That's right."

The offer didn't come as a surprise to Larkin. It wasn't a responsibility he would have ever sought out on his own, but it also wasn't something he could turn down. Somebody had to do the job, and he was as qualified as anybody else down here. *More* qualified than most.

"All right," he told Moultrie. "I'll do it."

"Thanks, Patrick. I'll rest easier at night, knowing that you'll be watching over all of us. Now . . ." Moultrie turned to a keyboard and typed for a few seconds. He took a handheld tablet from his pocket and tapped a couple of icons on its screen. "I'm sending the elevator back up, as you suggested. When it comes back down, you can arrange to post as many guards there as you'd like, around the clock."

"I don't know if they'll try to get down that way again," Larkin said. "They had to have somebody on the inside helping them to make it this time. If it hadn't been for Charlotte Ruskin—"

"Someone else down here might decide to turn traitor," Moultrie broke in. "You're going to have to be on the lookout for that, too. I'm counting on you, Patrick, to ferret out anyone who might be disloyal to the Hercules Project."

"Sure," Larkin said, but even as he spoke, he felt a faint stirring of misgivings. It was easy for such efforts as Moultrie described to turn into a witch hunt. That could do more harm than good.

"And just to make sure those bastards on the surface think twice before they try anything else . . ." Moultrie did more tapping on the handheld tablet.

"What are you doing now?"

"Closing the hatch," Moultrie said.

Larkin frowned. "Doesn't seem like the elevator's had enough time to get all the way to the top—"

"It hasn't."

"But that means—" Larkin's heart thudded hard in his chest. For a second he couldn't speak. Then he said, "If the hatch is closed, those people on top of the car won't have anywhere to go when it gets to the top of the shaft."

"No, they won't. But you saw how insane they all were, Patrick. All they wanted to do was slaughter us, like they were some sort of crazed horde."

"They're sick and scared—"

"And a danger to the project." Moultrie set the tablet aside and put a hand on Larkin's shoulder. "How many of them did you kill, Patrick? Several, I imagine."

That was different, Larkin thought. That was in battle. It wasn't tapping an icon on a screen and standing idly by while people were crushed to bloody paste between two unyielding slabs of steel. Larkin could only imagine the stark terror that had gripped those people in the shaft as darkness closed in around them and the elevator car continued grinding upward . . .

And by now it was probably over, he realized. None of the blood would seep into the sealed elevator car. There would be no signs to haunt the residents of the project. Those poor bastards were gone just as much as the ones chucked into the incinerator soon would be. Gone and forgotten.

But Larkin wasn't sure he would ever forget the faint, satisfied smile on Graham Moultrie's face as the man sent those people to their doom.

Chapter 40

Larkin lifted his arm and used his sleeve to wipe sweat from his face as he entered his apartment after a shift on patrol duty, circulating through the project to make sure everything was peaceful. The heat was worse than usual today. It had been like that off and on for several weeks, enough so that people were talking about how it was hotter than it used to be. Some of them speculated that it must be summer on the surface.

Larkin knew that wasn't the case. Or maybe, technically, it was. But either way, it didn't matter. With the thick layer of earth, steel, and concrete above them serving as insulation, the climate at the surface would have no effect on conditions inside the Hercules Project.

The situation was worrisome enough that he said something about it to Susan when he found her in the apartment's small kitchen. She nodded and said solemnly, "I know. And it's not just the heat, Patrick. We've had a big jump in the cases we're seeing of asthma complications and other breathing problems. The air's just not as good as it was."

Larkin knew what she meant. On occasion, he'd

found himself having trouble catching his breath, and he knew there wasn't anything wrong with his lungs. It was almost like there wasn't enough *air* in the air.

"You should say something to Graham about it," Susan went on.

"I don't know. I'm not a scientist . . ."

"But you're the head of security and basically his second-in-command down here. If there's a problem, he should have told you about it."

Larkin shook his head. Susan had said that he was Graham Moultrie's second-in-command, and he knew other people thought of him that way, too. But ever since the attack from the surface led by Nelson Ruskin, Moultrie had changed. He didn't even pretend to listen to anyone else's opinion these days. He just gave orders and expected them to be carried out without question. Everything he did was for the good of the project and their continued survival, he claimed, and Larkin supposed that Moultrie actually believed that. But sometimes Larkin wasn't sure that was all there was to it.

Sometimes it seemed like Moultrie just wanted to shut down anybody who might disagree with him. More than once, Larkin had gotten the impression that Moultrie was keeping things from him, important things.

Like the way the life-support systems in the bunker were working.

Larkin might have mentioned that ill-at-ease feeling to Susan, but at that moment the walkie-talkie clipped to his belt crackled and his daughter's voice said, "Dad? You there?"

He knew that Jill's security shift was beginning as his ended, so she was on duty now. She probably wouldn't be calling him right now if it wasn't security-related, so he wasted no time unclipping the walkie-talkie and bringing it to his lips.

"I'm here, kid. What's up?"

"Got a situation brewing down here in the bunker. You mind coming down?"

Larkin cocked an eyebrow. Jill didn't ask for help very often, so her "situation" had to be something fairly serious.

"I'll be right there," he told her, then put the walkie-talkie back on his belt next to the holstered 1911.

"Should I come with you?" Susan asked.

"No, you stay here."

"She's my daughter, too, Patrick." Susan's tone was a little sharper than usual. "And if it's trouble, you might need some medical assistance."

She had a point there, he thought, but at the same time he wasn't going to put her in harm's way if it wasn't necessary.

"I'll call you if I need you," he said as he turned toward the door. From the corner of his eye he saw how her features tightened in anger, but he couldn't do anything about that right now.

Their apartment was on the same level as the lower bunker, so he didn't have to go "down there," as Jill had put it, just out the door, through the foyer, and into the huge, open living area. The sound of raised, angry voices drew him immediately toward the other end.

A crowd of close to a hundred people had gathered in front of one of the staircases. A man had gone up several stairs and turned so he could face the others and address them. As Larkin came closer, he recognized Chad Holdstock, who had been Jeff Greer's friend.

There was no proof that Holdstock had been part of the plan hatched by Greer and Charlotte Ruskin to allow the survivors from the surface to invade the project. Holdstock had denied even knowing what the two of them were plotting, and there was no evidence to say that he was lying. Larkin didn't trust the guy anyway.

After the bloody attack, the malcontents among the Bullpenners had been pretty quiet. Larkin didn't expect it to stay that way, though, so he wasn't surprised when he saw that Holdstock was trying to stir up the crowd.

Jill stood off to the side but came toward him when she spotted him. Larkin nodded toward the assemblage and said, "Looks like we've got some rabble-rousing going on."

"I'm worried that they're working themselves up to a riot," Jill said.

"What do they want now? To have another election?"

Since both of the residents' elected representatives—Charlotte Ruskin and Jeff Greer—were dead, the idea of the residents having any input into Moultrie's decisions seemed to have died, too. The whole thing had been a fraud to begin with, Larkin knew, and Moultrie had dispensed with even keeping up the pretense. It wouldn't surprise him if the Bullpenners started agitating for new representatives, even though it wouldn't do them any good.

But Jill shook her head and said, "It's not that. It's the food."

Larkin frowned. "What about it?"

"People don't like the new rationing regulations."

Larkin's frown deepened. Everyone down here had known all along that it was necessary to keep track of how much food was consumed. Even with the livestock and the hydroponic garden, their supplies weren't limitless. Moultrie had estimated that they could have full rations for eighteen months, and if the project remained closed up longer than that, some sacrifices might have to be made. It hadn't even been a full year yet since the war.

"Nobody told me about new rationing regulations."

"They just went into effect today," Jill said. "Supplies for people who live in the Bullpen have been cut by thirty percent."

"Wait, that's not right," Larkin said. "What about everybody else?"

Jill shrugged and said, "Just before I went on duty, Trevor and I received a message that our available supplies were being reduced by 10 percent. I don't know if there was any change for you and Mom and the other people who live in the silos."

Anger stirred inside Larkin. Susan hadn't said anything to him about a change in their rations, but maybe she hadn't had a chance to. Or maybe they weren't being asked to give up anything, while the people who lived in the Bullpen and the main halls were. If that was the case, the unfairness of it grated at him.

"That's what has Holdstock and these other folks so worked up?"

"Yes. Did Graham say anything to you about this, Dad?"

Larkin blew out a breath. "I don't think he tells anybody much of anything these days, unless it's his wife."

"Well, maybe you should say something to these people."

Larkin didn't consider himself any sort of public speaker, but he knew Jill was right. Holdstock's loud, angry complaints were bringing shouts of agreement from the crowd. Larkin couldn't really blame them for being upset, but there were better ways to deal with that than inciting a riot.

He moved into the rear of the crowd, shouldering a few people aside. "Hey!" he shouted. "Holdstock! Wait a minute—"

Holdstock spotted him—Larkin was taller than most of the people in the crowd—and pointed. "There's one of Moultrie's Redshirts now! Tell him what you think of Moultrie trying to starve us out!"

Larkin wasn't wearing the red vest of the security force. He had left it back in the apartment. But by now everybody in the Hercules Project knew who he was. For a little while, he had been regarded as one of the heroes of the battle against the surface survivors, but that goodwill had faded fast, as it always did where the public was concerned.

The people around him began yelling and shoving at him. Larkin dropped his hand to the butt of the gun on his hip. He had no intention of drawing it; he just didn't want anybody else making a grab at the weapon.

But somebody saw the move and cried, "Look out! He's gonna shoot us!"

"Grab him!" another man urged. "Pull him down before he kills us all!"

Larkin kept his right hand on his gun and swung his left arm in an attempt to clear some space around him. His fist backhanded one of the men with a solid thud that sent the man flying backward. But more surged forward to take his place, and suddenly Larkin was surrounded by a crazed melee, with most of the punches directed at him.

"Dad!" he vaguely heard Jill calling to him. "Dad!"

He knew she wouldn't stand by and let him be stomped and kicked to death, which was what the mob seemed intent on doing. And it *was* a mob now, no doubt about it.

Larkin knew his daughter. She would open fire to save him, and that would escalate the violence even more . . .

With the suddenness of a sucker punch, darkness fell.

And down here far underground, it was such a complete absence of light that it took the breath away. Everyone froze, stunned by the unexpected blackness that had swallowed them. That shocked silence and immobility lasted a couple of heartbeats, then people began to scream and lunge around blindly. Bodies rammed into Larkin, but at least they were just panicking now, not trying to kill him anymore.

Anyone who fell, though, might wind up trampled to death anyway. Larkin bellowed at the top of his lungs, "Stop! Everybody be still! Just stop where you are!"

The commands seemed to get through to some of the mob. Other voices called out, urging calm. Gradually, the screaming and milling around came to a halt. Larkin heard a lot of harsh, frightened breathing

What he *didn't* hear was worse. The life-support systems gave off a low hum that filled the project around the clock.

But the absence of that hum was like an alarm bell going off. The last time it hadn't been present was when the computer system had crashed during the attack from the surface. Even then, the lights had remained on.

Now it seemed as if everything in the project had shut down. All the things that kept everyone alive . . .

Less than a minute had gone by since the lights went out, although it seemed longer. Larkin forced his brain to work and remembered the small, battery-powered flashlight he had in his pocket. It was part of his equipment as a member of the security force, just like the walkie-talkie and his gun, and he always had it either on his person or within reach. He slid his hand into his pocket, found the light, brought it out, and thumbed it on.

His eyes had already had time to react to the darkness, so the shaft of light was a little blinding when it shot out. Larkin squinted and looked away from it. Several people exclaimed reflexively. Larkin aimed the flashlight at the ceiling so the light would bounce and spread out.

A palpable sense of relief filled the air. Nobody liked being stuck in the dark.

At least for the moment, the near-riot was over. Everyone was too worried about the power going off to think about the food-rationing situation.

"Dad!" Jill worked her way through the crowd to Larkin. "What happened?"

"I don't know," he told her. "But I intend to find out. You have your light, don't you?"

"Of course."

"Then help these people back to their quads. Then go to the apartment and make sure your mother's all right."

"Where are you going?"

"To the Command Center," Larkin said. "I want some answers."

Chapter 41

Larkin had just reached the landing where the staircase turned, halfway between the lower bunker and the main level, when the lights recessed along the top of the walls flickered a couple of times, then came on and stayed lit. He had been guided so far by his flashlight, but he turned it off now.

He stood there for a long moment, listening. When he felt as much as heard the low, powerful hum that meant the generators and the life-support equipment were working again, he closed his eyes for a second and heaved a sigh of relief. They weren't going to have to evacuate the project, at least not yet. That would have been a nightmare, although it was possible since the blast doors at the main entrance could be opened by hand once Moultrie physically unlocked them with his master key.

That would have meant all the residents would be fleeing to the surface—and they didn't know what dangers might be waiting for them up there.

Despite the fact that things seemed to be working again, he still wanted to know what had just happened. Like everything else in the Hercules Project, one man would have the answers: Graham Moultrie.

The Command Center was buzzing with excitement and activity when he got there, and the hubbub of conversation among the people on duty had an anxious note to it. Andrea Marshall spotted him and called, "Patrick! Do you know what just happened?"

"I was hoping somebody here could tell me," Larkin said.

Andrea shook her head. "It took us all by surprise, too."

"Graham in his office?"

"I *think* so . . ."

Larkin didn't wait to hear more. He strode through the Command Center to Moultrie's office and knocked on the door.

For a moment, there was no response. Then Larkin heard the electronic lock on the door buzz, and Moultrie called, "Come in."

When Larkin entered the room, Moultrie nodded and went on, "I thought that might be you, Patrick. I recognized your knock."

"Maybe it was a little heavy-handed—" Larkin began.

"Not at all. I also figured you'd be the first one to come see me." Moultrie was sitting behind his big desk, surrounded by monitors, computer terminals, and other equipment. He leaned back in his chair and said, "You like to stay on top of everything that's going on down here."

"I don't think I've been staying on top of it enough. Something's going on, Graham. I was considering asking you about it anyway, but with everything that's happened today, I have to."

"The power going out, you mean?"

"And the riot that almost broke out in the Bullpen over the new food rationing."

Moultrie sat forward, suddenly tense. "Riot?" he repeated. Clearly, he hadn't heard about that yet.

"Don't worry, it got broken up when the lights went out and everybody started panicking about suffocating instead. But once they get over being scared, they'll be mad again about the food."

Moultrie waved a hand dismissively and said, "They'll get used to that. There'll still be enough for everyone to survive."

"Yeah, but I don't think they signed up for a subsistence diet," Larkin said. "At the moment, though, I'm more worried about the power and the life-support systems. It's hotter down here than it used to be, Graham, and the air's not as good. Plenty of people have noticed that, too, and I expect they're not happy about it."

Moultrie clasped his hands together on the desk in front of him and sighed. "It's been that obvious?"

"It has."

"I was hoping people would think . . . Well, I don't know *what* I was hoping. That it wouldn't come to this, I guess."

"Come to what?" Larkin said. He couldn't help but hear the hollow note of dread in his voice.

"The life-support systems are failing."

Larkin stared at Moultrie for a long moment, then shook his head. "That can't be. You worked everything out ahead of time."

"I did the math," Moultrie snapped. "All the experts I hired did the math. But this is uncharted territory, Patrick. Nobody ever tried to support this many people in a completely sealed environment for this long before."

"It hasn't been completely sealed the whole time," Larkin pointed out.

"The breach from the surface was a short one. We've been monitoring for radiation and contaminants, and the levels are so low they're well within the normal range. The breach elevated them so slightly that it might as well have not happened."

Larkin couldn't suppress the reaction he felt to that statement. He burst out, "Well, then, my God, why don't we just go back up to the surface?"

"I said the range is normal down here." Moultrie's voice was hard and flat now, revealing that he didn't like to be challenged, which Larkin already knew. "It's still too high at the surface."

"It wasn't too high for Ruskin and the others to survive."

"You *saw* them, Patrick. You know what they were like. Is that the sort of existence you want to condemn our people to?"

"Of course not. But we don't know *why* those people were in such bad shape. The worst of them could have been poisoned by the radiation from the blast itself, not the residual radiation. We know that Ruskin was somewhere around here when the bomb went off. He must have been down in a storm cellar or something like that to have made it through. And he was in better shape than some of the others." Larkin cast his memory back. "What about Earl Crandall? He didn't seem sick. He could have come here from somewhere else, somewhere where things aren't as bad."

"And your point is?" Moultrie asked.

"If Crandall could come here and still be all right, it stands to reason we could leave the project and head west, to where the damage and the radiation aren't as bad. Sure, the infrastructure will be heavily damaged and the technology will be gone, but we'd learn new ways of doing things. A lot of us have the necessary survival skills, and we can teach and help the ones who don't."

That was the most the normally laconic Larkin had spoken at one time in quite a while. He could tell from the stony look on Moultrie's face, though, that the argument hadn't done any good.

"When the time comes, that's what we'll do," Moultrie said. "But it's not that time yet."

"Then when? When the generators and the life-support systems fail entirely?"

"They're not going to—" Moultrie broke off and slapped a palm down on the desk in obvious frustration and anger. "Damn it!"

"They *are* failing, aren't they? Not just the life-support systems, but the generators, too."

Moultrie looked away, unable to meet Larkin's eyes for a few seconds. Then he said, "Again, no one has ever undertaken anything like this before. The wear and tear on the equipment has been more than we anticipated. We've been having to shut down some of the generators for a while each day, and when we do that, we have to take some of the life-support systems off-line as well, so as not to put too much of a strain on the other generators. We're doing that on a rotating basis, so nothing is down for too long at a time."

"Like the old rolling brownouts we used to hear about," Larkin said.

"Exactly. But there's a solution."

"What's that?"

"We need generator parts to replace the ones that are wearing out. Honestly, best-case scenario, we could use some more gas to power them, too. If we can keep the generators running, we can patch up the life-support systems enough to get by."

Larkin had to stare again. "There's not enough gasoline?"

"Blast it, Patrick, you know as well as I do that not everything was completely in place when all hell broke loose. If I'd just had another month to prepare, even two more weeks . . ." Moultrie sighed and shook his head. "We had enough of everything on hand to survive in relative comfort for almost a year, didn't we? And it's not like everything is going to run out tomorrow."

"But it's going to get a little more dicey the longer we stay down here."

Larkin's words weren't really a question, but Moultrie shrugged in eloquent response anyway.

"All the more reason to risk moving back to the surface—"

"No! I won't abandon the project until I'm absolutely certain that it's completely safe."

"Nothing in life is completely safe, Graham," Larkin said quietly.

"Maybe not, but I won't do less than my absolute best to protect my people."

Larkin didn't care much for the way Moultrie said *my people* like that, as if they were his subjects rather than his tenants. In a sense, that's what he was: a land-lord. Not a king or an emperor.

Larkin didn't want to get into that. Instead he said,

"How do you intend to get parts for the generator and more gasoline?"

"I said we weren't all going up to the surface." Moultrie smiled a little. "I didn't say that nobody could go."

Larkin's brain was still reeling a little by the time he got back to the apartment—not only from the dangers Graham Moultrie had revealed to him but also the plan that Moultrie had concocted to counter those dangers.

Susan was waiting for him. He could tell she was trying not to look anxious, but she wasn't doing a very good job of it.

The first question she asked was that of a mother. "Is Jill all right?"

"She was fine the last I saw of her," Larkin replied as he put his arms around his wife and drew her against him. "If there had been any more trouble, I'm sure I would have heard."

Susan moved back a little and tilted her head to look up at him. "Patrick, what happened? Why did Jill call you, and did it have anything to do with the lights going out a little while later? I don't mind telling you, I was scared."

"So was I. I wish I could have been here with you."

"But I felt my way around and found a flashlight, and then it wasn't *quite* so bad. But I was still so worried about you and Jill . . ."

"Let's sit down, and I'll tell you all about it."

They settled onto the love seat. Larkin enjoyed the warm, companionable pressure of her hip against his.

He couldn't imagine life without her, and he hoped he'd never have to experience it.

For the next few minutes, he told her about the near-riot caused by the new food restrictions. Susan shook her head in answer to his question about that and said, "No, I haven't heard anything about our supplies being cut. Thirty percent for the Bullpen and ten percent for the people in the main halls, you said?"

Larkin nodded. "Yep."

"Well, that's just not right! It should be the same for everybody."

"I agree with you. I got into that a little when I went to talk to Graham, but there are bigger problems to consider."

"The power going out, you mean."

"Yeah." Larkin made a face. "Turns out that he didn't have everything figured out quite so perfectly as everybody thought, including him. The life-support systems have developed some problems, but the real trouble is the generators. They're wearing out, Susan, and even if the guys who maintain them can keep them limping along, they're going to run out of fuel before we're ready to go back up to the surface."

Her eyes widened. "But . . . if the generators don't work . . . we can't stay down here." Her voice took on a shaky note. "We'll all suffocate in the dark . . ."

His wife had a steel core, Larkin knew that. She could deal with bloody injuries and life-and-death situations as well as anyone. But this was different. The possibilities Larkin was talking about tapped into the sort of primitive fears every human being had lurking deep inside. No matter how far humanity progressed, within the heart of everyone was a prehistoric creature peering at the eternal darkness and everything bad hidden within it.

"That's not gonna happen," he said as he tightened his arm around her. "We're going to do something about it before things ever get that bad."

"We?"

"Well . . . some of us. Graham has decided to send an expedition up to the surface to scavenge for the things we need." Larkin paused, knowing he couldn't dodge the rest of the news he had for Susan. "And I'm going to lead it."

Chapter 42

Larkin expected an argument, and he got one.

"Are you crazy?" Susan demanded as she paced back and forth in front of him. "It's too dangerous for the rest of us to go up to the surface, but *you're* going."

"Someone has to," Larkin said calmly. "And it's not like this is the first time I'll be doing something dangerous."

Susan swung around sharply toward him. "I know! You always volunteered for every insane mission that came along."

"And I came back safe and sound from all of them. Well, mostly," Larkin added, thinking of a few scars and stiff muscles he had brought back with him.

"Getting shot at is one thing. I suppose you know how to guard against that about as well as anyone down here. But what about the radiation and all the other things up there that can kill you?"

"We have a dozen hazmat suits. Moultrie had them stored down here in case anyone had to go into possibly contaminated areas and work on equipment. They'll provide a decent level of protection from radiation, and they should filter out any biological hazards. I'll be fine."

"What about the . . . the people up there?"

Susan's voice held a note of horror. As someone in the medical profession, she understood quite well on an intellectual level that the people from the surface who had attacked the project were just suffering from various diseases and medical conditions. But that prehistoric part of her brain had recoiled from them in fear and disgust. Larkin knew that because he had experienced the same thing.

"The motion sensors haven't detected anything up there since right after the attack, except a few stray anomalies that probably weren't human. Even those seem to have gone away. The survivors who were left, they've either moved on somewhere else or . . ."

"Or died," Susan finished for him.

"The shape they were in, some of them are bound to have passed away by now," Larkin agreed.

"What if they just pulled back? What if they're still close by and see you and the others moving around?"

"We'll be better armed than they are," Larkin said confidently. "Chances are, if that happens they'll steer clear of us. They probably don't want any more to do with us than we do with them."

"And you're sure of that."

"Nothing in life is certain, babe."

She glared at him for a moment, then sat down beside him again. He took that as a small victory.

After a couple of minutes of silence, she asked, "Who's going with you?"

"I'll have to ask for volunteers, of course."

"I can tell you who's *not* going with you, Patrick."

"Jill," he said before she could go on. "Yeah, I already thought of that. She'll probably want to, but I'm in command of this mission, so I have the final say on who stays and who goes."

"She's going to be very angry with you."

"Hey, she's been angry with me before. Remember that guy in high school . . . what was his name?"

"Danny," Susan said.

"Yeah, Danny. She was convinced she was in love with him, and when I told her she wasn't, she threatened to move out."

"And then she broke up with him a week later."

"After breaking his finger when he wouldn't take no for an answer." Larkin sighed in satisfaction. "That's my girl."

Susan leaned against his shoulder. "But she's still not going with you."

"Not a chance in hell," Larkin said.

The heat and the staleness of the air grew worse over the next few days, though not unbearably so. Rumors ran rampant throughout the project, though, and the level of anxiety was high. Most people didn't know what was going on, and naturally, most of them assumed the worst.

Without going into detail, Larkin put the word out among the security force that he was looking for volunteers for an urgent, vital mission that might involve a high degree of risk. He didn't say anything about it to Jill, but he wasn't the least bit surprised when she got wind of it anyway. She confronted him one day in the Command Center.

"What's this about some secret mission?" she asked.

"If you're looking for volunteers, Dad, you know you don't even have to ask."

"Yeah, I know," Larkin said. "Which is why I *didn't* ask."

Jill's eyebrows drew down in a puzzled and maybe a little bit of an angry frown. "What do you mean by that?"

"I mean you're not going."

She drew in a sharp breath. "Just like that."

"Yep. Just like that."

For a moment she glared at him, then said, "Mom put you up to this, didn't she?"

"She didn't have to. It just so happens I'm in complete agreement with her. You'll be staying here."

"Because you think I can't handle myself if there's trouble?"

"You know better than that," Larkin scoffed. "You're staying here because your mother, your husband, and my grandkids are staying here. I can't afford to be worrying about them while I'm trying to take care of business on the surface. And I won't worry if I know you're down here looking after them. Besides, you have enough medical skills that they might come in handy down here."

"So you're just trying to butter me up to get your way."

Larkin grinned. "Is it working?"

She didn't answer that. Instead, she asked, "So the rumors are true? You *are* going up to the surface?"

"A small group. There are some things the project needs, and we're going to look for them."

"It's a scrounging party?"

"That's right," Larkin said with a nod. He looked

around, saw that no one else was in earshot at the moment, and went on, "We need parts for the generators as well as more gasoline if we can get it."

"The generators are failing, and that's why the life-support systems haven't been working at full capacity?"

"You got it, kid."

Jill frowned and asked, "Where are you going to find parts? Everything got blown to hell."

"We were on the outer edge of the blast wave. Not everything was destroyed. Some buildings are probably left, and what was inside them will be, too. There have to be some vehicles around, as well. Generators are basically gasoline engines. We can get some parts off cars and trucks that the engineers can rig to work. That's what they've told Graham, anyway."

Jill was thinking now. He could tell that by her expression. She said, "You can siphon gas from the tanks of any vehicles you find intact."

"Yeah. We might even find some underground storage tanks that are still all right, like at that convenience store a few miles west of here."

"You're going that far away from the project?" she asked in surprise and a certain amount of alarm.

"We'll go as far as we have to in order to get what we need," Larkin told her. "We'll take enough supplies for a few days."

"This could turn out to be very dangerous. If you take me along, I'll have your back. You know that, Dad."

"I know," he said. "But like I told you, it's more important for you to stay here and keep an eye on things." He hesitated, then added, "I'm not sure I completely trust Graham anymore."

That surprised Jill, too. "You don't? But without him—"

"I know, I know. We'd all be dead. Nobody's disputing that. But he's said and done some things—" Larkin thought about the way Moultrie had killed those surface survivors who had tried to break through the top of the service elevator. Jill didn't know about that, and right now she didn't need to. "Let's just say that he worries me. Too much power can go to a guy's head."

"And the way he changed the food rationing without any warning was kind of, well, harsh." Jill nodded slowly. "I guess I see what you mean. All right. I don't like it, but I understand. I'll stay here to guard against any more trouble. But you have to promise me you'll be careful up there."

"Of course. Just like I always promised your mother."

"And you didn't mean it then, either, did you?"

Larkin couldn't argue with that.

A day and a half later, Larkin had his team assembled. He was taking eight men with him, so that three of the hazmet suits could remain down in the project if they were needed. He had only male volunteers, but if anyone gave him any trouble about that, he could honestly say that Jill was the only woman who had offered to come along. And if they wanted to accuse him of patriarchy, they could go right ahead and do so. He didn't give a damn.

To keep more rumors from spreading, they assembled in the middle of the "night" when most of the project's residents were sleeping. They would use the service elevator to reach the surface. Ruskin and the other survivors had gotten in that way, so it stood to reason Larkin and his team could get out.

He looked around at the other eight men in the hallway. Graham Moultrie was there, too, with his hands in his jeans pockets and a solemn expression on his face.

Larkin wished the hazmat suits weren't made of bright yellow plastic. The colorful outfits would make them easier to spot on the surface, especially in the gray, overcast environment. That was what Moultrie had on hand, though, and the protection the suits offered was important, at least until Larkin could determine what the conditions were up on the surface.

They were taking along instruments that would allow them to monitor the air quality and radiation level. If those things were close enough to safe, they would remove the hazmat suits and stow them in the packs they were taking along. If they ran into trouble, it would be a lot easier to move around in a hurry without the bulky suits on.

Larkin had put some thought into selecting his team. Two of the men were engineers whose normal job was maintaining the generators and life-support systems. They would be able to tell what was needed and what they could make work. Larkin had had a long talk with them to make sure they were aware of the dangers they might encounter on the surface. Both men were willing to run that risk.

The other six members of the team were, like Larkin, members of the security force. Three of them carried pump shotguns. The other three were armed with AR-15s, as was Larkin. Each man, including the two engineers, also had a semi-automatic pistol holstered at his waist, over the hazmat suit. With the protective gloves they wore, handling the guns wouldn't be as easy as it would have been otherwise, but until they determined what the surface conditions were, they were going to err on the side of caution.

Unfortunately, caution had some inherent trade-offs, as Larkin well knew.

As they gathered in front of the service elevator, Moultrie said, "On behalf of everyone here in the Hercules Project, I want to express our appreciation to you men. This is a dangerous mission on which you're embarking, but one that's vital of the survival of everyone here."

"We know that, Graham," Larkin said, his voice muffled by the plastic helmet of the hazmat suit. It sounded odd to him in his own ears. "We'll stay in touch as much as possible, but we may wind up going out of range of the walkie-talkies."

"Do what you need to do," Moultrie said with a grim nod. "Just bring us back what we need to keep going."

Larkin returned the nod. There was nothing left to say. The group had gone over the plan, such as it was, until everyone knew exactly what they were doing. Unfortunately, under these circumstances, there were simply too many unknowns to take into account.

They were going into hostile territory, and they would have to play things by ear until they saw what it was like up there.

Even through the suit, Larkin heard the rumble that told him the hatch at the top of the shaft was opening. The elevator door slid back. The nine men trooped into it, carrying their weapons and packs.

Earlier, Larkin had had dinner with Susan, Jill, Trevor, Bailey, and Chris. The kids didn't know what he was going to be doing, but the adults did. Even though Larkin didn't intend it as such, there was an unmistakable feeling that this might be the last time they would all see each other. It had always been like that when men went off to war, he supposed, no matter how far back you went in history.

Later, when the two of them were alone, he had held Susan for a long time, each drawing strength and comfort from the other.

Then he had saddled up, figuratively speaking, and left to do the job that had fallen to him.

Now the eight men turned to face Moultrie, who gave them a smile of encouragement. Larkin pressed a button on the elevator's control panel. The door closed, and with a slight lurch, the elevator started up toward the surface.

Chapter 43

The elevator opened in the rear wall of a large basement that had been used for storage when this place was a missile base. On the far side of the space was a broad ramp where trucks had backed down into the basement so they could unload. Larkin wasn't clear on how the giant Nike Hercules missiles had been loaded into their launch silos, but at this point it didn't matter. The tops of those silos had been sealed up and covered with tons of earth, so no one could ever go in or out that way.

When Larkin stepped out of the elevator, holding the AR-15 ready in case of trouble even though sensors reported nothing moving around up here, he couldn't resist the urge to tip his head back and look upward. The building above this basement had mostly collapsed into it, leaving piles of rubble everywhere and open air above.

He was looking up at the sky, Larkin thought. For the first time in almost a year, he was gazing at the heavens again, as man had done from time immemorial.

Unfortunately, there wasn't a damned thing to see. For one thing, it was night, and for another the thick overcast that had hung above the earth for months was still in place. The gloom was thick as mud. There was too much debris down here for the team to move around safely without any light, so Larkin let the others emerge from the elevator, then said, "We'll wait right here for morning."

That was part of the plan they had all gone over ahead of time, so no one was surprised. If the others were anything like Larkin, they were eager to get out of here and back onto the surface, but they all knew it would be better not to show any lights that could draw attention to them.

The engineers, doubling as environmental techs for this mission, busied themselves taking readings, gathering their samples, and then going back into the elevator to check them so the lights they used to see the instruments wouldn't show. Larkin tried not to hover over them, but he couldn't stop himself from asking, "How does it look?"

"The air quality has a slightly higher particulate level than usual," one of the men responded. "That's probably due to the massive quantities of ash that were lifted into the upper-atmosphere as a result of the nuclear explosions. That ash has been circling the planet, carried by the upper-level winds, but slowly settling back to earth ever since."

"It wouldn't have all come back down by now?"

The man shook his head. "No, it may take a couple of years, maybe even longer, before the so-called nuclear winter is over. By this point, you probably won't be able to *see* what's in the air, but if your helmet was off, you could smell it, like you were in the vicinity of a big forest fire."

"And that ash is radioactive," Larkin said, trying not to sound dispirited.

The other engineer said, "Yes, but a lot of things in our normal lives were radioactive. It's a matter of how much. By now the radiation from the contaminants in the air, as well as in the soil and the debris that's left, has decayed to the point that it's not extremely hazardous."

"You're saying we can take off these suits and breathe the air?"

"Well," the man said, shrugging, "short-term exposure should be fine. If you were to spend years living in these conditions, your risk of developing cancer or some other form of radiation-related sickness would be somewhat higher than the normal, everyday risk in our old lives, before the war. But probably not dramatically so."

"But don't go taking off that hazmat suit just yet," the first man said. "Give us a chance to take some more readings once we're actually up on the surface, just to be sure."

That made sense, Larkin thought. Again, they were going to be careful instead of reckless . . . although a big part of him wanted to yank that helmet off right now.

The three hours or so until dawn were some of the longest of Larkin's life. And when morning finally did arrive, the blackness faded to gray at such a gradual pace it was almost indistinguishable. Only when Larkin realized he could see the piles of rubble in the basement did he understand that the time had come to move out.

The men were more than ready. They had sat down in the elevator, but when Larkin told them to get ready, they scrambled to their feet as quickly as they could in the bulky suits. He studied the wreckage in the basement and picked out a path through the rubble to the ramp, which appeared to be intact. Turning his head a little, Larkin said to the others, "Follow me."

He led the way across the basement, up the ramp, and into the open. Setting foot on actual ground, rather than steel or concrete or tile, made another thrill go through Larkin. He paused and looked around while he waited for the rest of the team to climb up out of the basement.

Larkin had seen the aftermath of numerous wildfires in his life, and that was what the scenery around the Hercules Project reminded him of. Gray, barren hillsides met his gaze no matter where he looked. The scrubby trees that had covered so much of the landscape around here were all gone, except for a few twisted trunks with dead branches extending from them like skeletal fingers.

The buildings had been flattened by the concussion of the nuclear blast twenty miles away. Here and there a small piece of cinder-block wall stuck up from the charred ground. The brick wall along the perimeter, which should have been visible, was nowhere to be seen. Larkin looked in the direction of downtown Fort Worth, but in the persistent gloom the horizon quickly faded to a hazy nothingness.

The clouds overhead were thick and gunmetal gray as they scudded slowly along, driven by a chilly wind. The sealed suits protected the men from that wind and retained their body heat, keeping them comfortable. Right now, though, Larkin wouldn't have minded feeling the cold on his face. It would remind him that he had climbed up out of the ground and was walking on the earth again like a man.

He turned to the two engineers, who were studying their instruments. "How's it look?"

"The readings are consistent with the ones we took

down in the basement," one of the men reported. "I think we should stay suited up for a while, though, just to be on the safe side."

A surge of recklessness welled up inside Larkin for a moment. He had survived the greatest disaster to hit the planet since that asteroid had come along and wiped out the dinosaurs. He was sick and tired of playing it safe.

However, the more pragmatic part of his nature won out. He nodded and said, "We'll keep the suits on while we take a look around."

Larkin could tell where the main road leading into the project had been. Some of the asphalt was still visible. He led the men along it toward the county road. As they came closer, he saw the rusted hulks of hundreds of cars, trucks, vans, and SUVs along the route where people had tried to flee. Some of them were overturned and lay on their tops or sides. Others were scattered haphazardly in the ditches, as if a giant hand had picked them up and flung them around. The blast wave had done that, Larkin knew.

"Most of those vehicles look burned," one of the engineers said. "The heat from the explosion probably ignited the gas in their tanks. We're not going to find anything useful here."

Larkin nodded. He had suspected that would be the case while hoping it wouldn't be. They wouldn't be able to grab what they needed and get back down into the project in a matter of hours. They were going to have to range farther afield.

"We'll head west along the county road," he said. "How far do you think we'll need to go in order to find usable parts and gasoline?"

The man just shook his head helplessly. He didn't know the answer to that question any more than the rest of them did.

"Let's go," Larkin said. He started winding his way through the wrecked cars along the county road. From time to time he glanced inside one of the vehicles, knowing what he was going to see: the charred remains of the unfortunate people who had been caught out here, trying futilely to get away. Sometimes there was an almost complete skeleton slumped over a melted steering wheel. More often there was just a jumble of blasted-apart bones.

Larkin had seen plenty of bad things in wartime . . . but never anything like this.

He didn't let himself think about that. As always, he concentrated on the job at hand.

Something moved up ahead. Just a flicker, but that was enough to make Larkin bring up the AR-15 and tighten his finger on the trigger. He didn't have a target, though. Whatever it was had ducked back out of sight.

The other men had noticed his reaction and responded accordingly, lifting their weapons as well. One of the men asked, "Did you see something, Patrick?"

"Yeah, but it seems to be gone now. And before you ask, I didn't get a good look at it. Couldn't tell what it was, except that it wasn't very big."

Another man, a fellow in his twenties named Wade, said, "At least we haven't seen any aliens or mutants or zombies yet."

"No, and you won't, because they don't exist."

Wade said, "There's usually a guy in the books and movies who says something like that, and he's the first one who gets eaten."

"Not today," Larkin said. "Come on."

They moved ahead. He didn't see anything else suspicious. The line of wrecked and burned-out cars stretched as far as he could see along the road, which was never more than a few hundred yards at a time because of the terrain. He knew this area very well, but it was difficult to tell exactly where they were because everything looked so different. All the houses along here had been destroyed in the blast. Here and there he saw what he thought were the remnants of foundations.

He thought they had gone close to a mile from the project's entrance when he called a halt and told the two men with the instruments to take more readings. After a minute or so, one of the men said, "The levels are holding steady. If anything, they're down slightly."

"Does that mean we can take these suits off?" one of the men asked.

"Not yet," Larkin said. "It's not hurting anything to wear them."

There was some grumbling about that, but nobody objected too much. Undoubtedly, in each man's brain lurked some fear of the environment up here on the surface. It was human nature to accept what their technology told them . . . but also to be a little leery of believing in it too much.

The sky brightened a little more. The sun was climbing higher, even though Larkin couldn't see it. A long ridge rose to their right. Larkin knew that up ahead was a road that climbed to the top of that ridge, and from that vantage point they could see for miles. He wanted to get up there and take a look around.

Where that other road turned off, there had been a

small convenience store and gas station. Maybe the tanks there still held some of the precious stuff.

As they trudged on, some of the vehicles they passed began to look as if they were in somewhat better shape. They didn't appear to have been burned as badly. Larkin thought that was an indication their gas tanks hadn't exploded from the sharp spike in temperature, even though the heat had peeled most of the paint from the outside of the vehicles. The group had brought along mechanical siphons and some plastic gas cans. Larkin called a halt and pointed to a car with the windows all blown out but not much fire damage.

"Check the tank in that one, Wade," he said.

The young man got out the siphoning equipment and unscrewed the car's gas cap. He slid the tube down into the tank and worked the pump. Larkin saw gas climbing through the tube. Wade grinned and stuck the other end of the tube into one of the gas cans. The flow improved.

"We got it, Cap," Wade said. "You want me to go ahead and fill up this can?"

"Yeah. Get as much as possible out of there. We have a dozen cans. As soon as we fill them, we'll head back. No point in going any farther."

Larkin glanced at the top of the ridge again. He wanted to get up there, but if it wasn't necessary to accomplish the mission, they wouldn't risk it. Not today, anyway.

The gas in the car's tank filled two and a half cans before it sputtered out. Larkin and his men moved on, searching for another vehicle that looked promising. As they left, though, he glanced into the car, saw the half-intact skeleton in the front seat, and wished he could say thanks to whoever that person had been.

Then he saw the car seat strapped into the backseat and had to tighten his jaw as he turned away and kept moving. He felt his heart slugging harder in his chest. The grief and anger over what had happened to the world would overwhelm him if he allowed it to. He forced himself to concentrate on the goal instead.

They passed a creek that flowed between rocky banks on both sides of the road and passed underneath it through a culvert. Up ahead, maybe a mile away, was the convenience store and the road that led up to the ridge.

Larkin was thinking about that when gunshots suddenly exploded behind him.

Chapter 44

He twisted around in time to see several men charging out of the creek bed, where they had been hidden by those rocky banks. They carried rifles, and as more shots erupted, Larkin saw that a couple of his men were down. He cursed himself for leading them into an ambush. The sheer barrenness of the landscape must have convinced him, at least subconsciously, that no one was around to threaten them.

That reaction lasted only a fraction of a second, however. Then the AR-15 was at his shoulder, spitting fire as fast as he could pull the trigger.

The group from the Hercules Project was better armed and outnumbered the attackers. They opened fire along with Larkin, and the ambushers, clad only in rags, went down with blood welling from numerous wounds in their gaunt bodies.

Larkin knew these men, shot up as they were, would no longer be a threat, but there could be more of them. He kept his rifle ready as he swiveled back and forth to check the creek on both sides of the road. No more attackers emerged, but that didn't mean he could stop worrying. Armed survivors could still be hidden out there.

Meanwhile, he had men down. He shouted through the helmet, "A couple of you check those wounded men while the rest of you stay alert!"

They formed a circle around the men on the ground and the two who knelt to see how badly they were hurt. After a minute or so, one of those men reported, "Blakely is dead, Patrick. Herring doesn't seem to be hurt too bad, though."

"You're sure about Blakely?" Larkin asked, his voice curt with anger.

"I'm certain. He was shot right through the heart. Looks like Herring just got a graze on his side, though. Hard to be sure in this damned suit."

"Get it off of him, then," Larkin ordered.

"Does that mean the rest of us can lose the suits, too, Cap?" Wade asked.

"Stop calling me that. And yeah, let's take the suits off. One at a time, though, and the rest of you stand guard while that's going on."

Larkin waited until all the other men had taken off their hazmat suits before he lowered his rifle, unsealed his helmet, and pulled it off. The smell of ashes immediately filled his nostrils. An underlying chemical tang made it even more unpleasant.

But for all its faults, it was still real air, breathed under an open sky, and that meant something to Larkin. Judging by their expressions, it did to the other men, too.

"We can live up here," Wade said, a slight note of disbelief in his voice.

"Yeah," Larkin said. "It may not smell very good, but it won't kill us."

"Right away," another man said bleakly.

"Hell, that's always been true of a lot of things," Larkin said. "How does Herring look?"

The man working on the wounded man didn't look up from what he was doing as he said, "I've just about got a dressing in place. I cleaned the wound and gave him an antibiotic shot."

Herring was conscious. He said in a voice strained from pain, "I'll be all right, Patrick. I'll be back on my feet in just a minute, and then we can get on with the mission."

"Not you," Larkin said. "You're going back to the project and wait for us there. Jenkins, you'll go with him."

The man putting the dressing on Herring's side nodded. "Probably a good idea. Who knows what sort of infectious agents might be floating around out here? He needs some actual medical attention."

Herring started to argue, but then one of the other men called urgently, "Larkin."

Larkin had just finished peeling off the hazmat suit, leaving him in jeans, sweatshirt, and a lightweight jacket. He'd had to set the rifle down in order to do that. He snatched it up again when he heard the note of alarm in the other man's voice.

Another survivor had climbed out of the creek bed and was coming toward the group from the Hercules Project. He moved at a steady walk, however, instead of charging, and although he was armed, his rifle was slung on his back and his empty hands were in the air. Larkin recognized him immediately, even though it had been months since he'd seen the man. He couldn't forget the old army jacket, the long white hair, and the beard.

The man was Earl Crandall, who had come down the

stairs with Nelson Ruskin to tap out messages in Morse code with Larkin on the other side of the blast door.

"Hold your fire, boys," Crandall called. "I told those fellows they'd be fools to bushwhack you, but they didn't listen to me. I'm not looking for trouble."

"How do we know that?" Larkin asked as he kept his rifle trained on Crandall. "Maybe you just hung back to see how it was going to play out."

A faint smile tugged at Crandall's mouth. "Maybe. That'd be the smart thing to do, wouldn't it? But as it happens, I'm telling you the truth, mister."

"Did you tell Nelson Ruskin he'd be a fool to attack the project, too, Crandall?"

The man's bushy white eyebrows rose a little in surprise. "You're the guy who was down there talking to me in code," he said. "You seemed like a reasonable sort."

"Yeah, so did you," Larkin said. "Or maybe that was just in comparison to Ruskin."

Crandall made a face and shook his head. "Nelson was a little crazy by that time, I'll admit it. After what he went through, not knowing if his wife was dead or alive, and then seeing so many people get sick and die . . . It was hard on the guy."

"It was no picnic for anybody else," Larkin pointed out.

"No, it wasn't. I wasn't around here from the start, but I've heard and seen plenty. I know how bad it was."

Larkin was careful not to let his guard down, but at the same time Crandall interested him. He said, "If you weren't here for the war, what are you doing here now?"

"I grew up in these parts. Rode my bike back here from West Texas after the big blast. I knew there might be some people who'd survived, and I wanted to help them if I could."

Wade said, "That's crazy. You came back even though you knew it might kill you?"

"Hey, that's what people do, son. At least they do if they're following the better sides of their nature. Anyway, I waited until the radiation levels had gone down some." An actual grin appeared on the man's face. "I ain't a complete doofus."

Larkin gestured with the AR-15's barrel toward the dead ambushers and asked, "Who are they?"

"Some of the remnants of the bunch that was with Ruskin. When Ruskin and the ones who went down with him never came back, we figured they were all dead. Same thing with the next batch. After that . . ." Crandall shrugged. "The ones who were left didn't have the stomach for anything else. Some of them moved on. Most of the rest died. There are still a few holdouts in these hills. The ones I was with spotted you earlier this morning and followed you. They wanted to kill you, steal your gear and any supplies you have. You can't really blame 'em. When you've been dying by inches for months, it does something to your head."

"But it didn't do anything to you?" Larkin said.

"Life I've led, I should've been dead twenty years ago. So I don't worry too much these days, just try to help out where I can. Okay if I put my arms down now? Standing like this is getting a little tiresome."

If he'd wanted to, Crandall could have opened fire on them from the creek bed, Larkin knew. Besides, he trusted his instincts, and they told him that Earl Crandall meant them no harm. He might even be willing to help, if he was telling the truth about the way he felt.

"Go ahead and put your hands down." Larkin motioned with the AR-15 again, toward the project. "Do you know what that is, the place where we came from?"

"The Hercules Project. Sure, Ruskin told me all about it. That's where he was supposed to wind up when the big bang came. His wife made it, but he didn't. Is she still alive, by the way?"

Larkin shook his head and said, "No, she was killed in the fighting when Ruskin attacked the place."

"Really? Well, son of a bitch. That's a shame. I reckon he really did love her and just wanted to be together with her again. Or maybe I'm giving him too much credit. He really was pretty loony there at the end."

"How in the world did he survive?"

"Storm cellar. Just luck he found a house with one of them in the back yard. It had a good thick door, too. Still got hot enough in there it nearly killed him. Cooked his brain some, I suppose, and burned so much of the oxygen out of the air that he nearly suffocated. He laid down there for a couple of days before he was able to crawl out. All this is what he told me later, of course. I wasn't there to see it. But I don't know of any reason he'd have to lie about it."

Neither did Larkin. Probably, Ruskin had been telling the truth.

By now, Herring had started walking slowly back toward the project, accompanied and supported by Jenkins. The rest of them would take Blakely's body back with them when they returned, Larkin decided. The man had a family, and they deserved to see him into the incinerator in whatever fashion they deemed proper.

"You fellas are scroungers, aren't you?" Crandall went on. "After gas and maybe some other supplies?"

"Maybe," Larkin said, although it seemed rather useless to deny it when they had gas cans sitting out in plain sight.

"You're wasting your time."

"What makes you think that?"

Crandall gestured toward the plastic cans and said, "You're siphoning gas from cars to fill those when there's a whole tanker truck of the stuff less than a mile from here."

Larkin caught his breath but tried not to let the surprise—and hope—he felt show on his face.

"What are you talking about?"

Crandall half-turned and pointed. "That little store up yonder a ways. As best I can figure it out, a gas truck was there making a delivery the day of the war. The truck was empty when I found it, but the underground tanks were full. The truck's pump still worked, so I pumped it back up into the tanker. Just luck it was all mechanical, nothing digital for the EMP to wipe out."

"And it's still just sitting there?" Larkin asked.

"Some of the boys used it to fill up every time they got an old car running. A lot of them drove out of here, headed for someplace they hoped would be better. Probably won't be, but people have to try, don't they?"

Larkin had said much the same thing himself on more than one occasion, so he knew what Crandall meant. Right now, he was more interested in the information the man had just given them.

"We need that truck and the gas inside it," he said. "Why did you tell us about it?"

Crandall's shoulders rose a little and then fell. "I

don't know. Maybe I was hoping that if I helped you out, you'd let me down into that place you've got."

"Don't trust him, Cap," Wade said. "If he's got gas, he could've gotten back on that motorcycle he mentioned and ridden out of here a long time ago."

"Sure I could have," Crandall agreed. "But maybe I had something else in mind."

"And what might that be?" Larkin wanted to know.

"I thought maybe you'd invite me down there for a cup of coffee." Crandall's grin widened. "Like Joni Mitchell said, sometimes you don't know what you've got until it's gone. And you don't know what you're going to miss the most, either."

Larkin shook his head. "We can't let you into the project."

"Why the hell not? Ruskin wasn't the only one who was supposed to be down there who didn't make it that day. The others are all either dead or gone, so I know you've got the space and supplies. And I just did you a solid by telling you about that tanker truck."

"We were headed that direction anyway. We would have found it."

"Maybe. Or would you have turned back before you got there, once you filled up those gas cans?"

That was exactly what Larkin had been thinking about doing, so Crandall had a point. Now that they knew the tanker was there, they would push on to the old convenience store. It wouldn't take all of them for that chore, either.

"Wade, Rodriguez, Adams, you come with me," Larkin said without addressing Crandall's suggestion. "The rest of you take Blakely's body back and make sure Jenkins and Herring get there okay, too."

"We're goin' after that truck?" Wade asked.

"That's right."

"And taking *him* with us?" Wade nodded toward Crandall.

"Can't really stop him from coming along without shooting him, now can we?"

Wade looked like he didn't mind that idea, but he didn't say anything.

"You won't regret this," Crandall said. "You'll find that I'm a good guy to have on your side . . . what is your name, anyway, buddy?"

"It's Larkin. Patrick Larkin."

"Pleased to meet you in person this time."

Some of the other men looked like they agreed with Wade and wanted to argue with Larkin's decision, but they didn't say anything when he told them to get moving back to the project. Larkin turned back to Crandall, nodded, and said, "Let's go get that gas."

Chapter 45

The concussion from the nuclear blast had knocked down the convenience store's walls, except for a few remnants on the west side of the building. Everything inside it had burned or melted, including the people. The gas pumps and the awning that had been over them were gone. Larkin thought it was lucky the underground tanks hadn't ignited.

The hillside north and west of the store had been covered with a housing development, he recalled. All those dwellings were gone now. Only a few vestiges of foundations remained to testify that dozens of families had lived here once. Looking at what was left, it was like those days had been centuries earlier, instead of less than a year.

Larkin and his companions hadn't encountered anyone else in the time it had taken them to cover the mile from the site of the ambush. Wade had muttered several times along the way that Crandall might be leading them into a trap. Larkin didn't believe that was the case, but he couldn't rule out the possibility entirely. That was the main reason he had split his force. If Crandall was trying some sort of trick, the whole group from the project wouldn't be wiped out. The others would get back and be able to tell Moultrie what had happened.

The air of desolation around the entire place was overwhelming, though. Larkin didn't see any threats, just the old tanker truck parked next to what remained of the store's walls.

"With the road full of cars, we'll have to drive in the ditch," he commented. "It'll be slow going."

"You can get there," Crandall said. "Might have to push down a fence or two along the way, but the truck's big enough to do that without any trouble."

Larkin looked at the smaller road that led to the top of the ridge. Since he was this close, he wasn't going to turn back without taking that look around he wanted.

"Wade, Rodriguez, you guys guard that truck," he said. The third man was one of the engineers, so Larkin told him, "Adams, you scavenge the parts we need for the generators from some of these cars."

"It may take a while to find everything we need," Adams said.

"That's all right. Crandall and I are going up to the top of the hill."

"We are?" Crandall said.

"That's right. Unless you know of some reason not to."

The man shook his head. "It's fine by me. Good view from up there." He paused. "Too bad there's not much to see."

"Be careful, Cap," Wade said. "I still don't trust this guy."

"I'm always careful," Larkin said. "Just ask my wife. On the other hand, don't."

He and Crandall walked along the side road, which went up and down a couple of smaller hills before climbing to the top of the ridge. As they headed in that direction, Crandall asked, "Why does the kid call you Cap? You have military ranks down there in the project?"

Larkin shook his head. "No, that's just him. I don't know why he decided to do it, but it seemed like more trouble than it would be worth to break him of the habit. We're both members of the project's security force, but it's not set up like a military outfit. More law enforcement."

"I was just curious. It sort of suits you, Larkin. Guys like you may be as close to Captain America as anybody the world has left." Crandall was silent for a moment, then said, "Speaking of that . . . have you made contact with other survivors anywhere else?"

"We picked up some shortwave transmissions fairly early on from some foreign country. People who knew more about it than I did seemed to think they were coming from Brazil. They stopped after a while, though. If there's been anything else, I don't know about it. What about you?"

Crandall frowned over at him. "Me? I don't have access to any sort of technology other than my rifle and my bike, man."

"You said you came here from West Texas. There must be quite a few people still alive out there."

"Some," Crandall admitted. "Probably a lot less by now. With all the tech fried and people having to get by on their own survival skills . . . well, you seem pretty smart. You ought to be able to make a good guess on how that worked out."

"A lot of starvation and dying of infection after minor injuries, right?"

"Yeah, boy. The food in the stores ran out in a hurry, and with no more coming in, folks were left eating whatever they could get their hands on. I don't imagine there's a dog or cat left west of the Brazos unless it's feral and stays far away from humans. And any kind of sickness, even a plain old cold, was fatal more often than not. That's one reason I left. Just couldn't stand to watch it all fall apart anymore. So I headed for a place where I knew things would be even worse." Crandall let out a bark of laughter. "I never claimed that all of my decisions in life made sense. I got some exes who would testify to that."

"What about now? Maybe they've tried to start doing some farming. Or is the soil too contaminated?"

"Don't know. I've never been a farmer. But it seems like something worth trying."

"One of these days," Larkin mused. He was thinking about the Hercules Project's hydroponic garden and the rabbits and chickens that had supplemented the food supplies. Seeds and livestock. Those were the keys to the future. Those and . . .

"Did the sun ever shine while you were out there? Did it rain?"

"No sunshine," Crandall replied, shaking his head. "But some days it looked like the clouds were thinner, almost like the sun might break through. Man, it would be good to see some blue sky again. We got a little rain now and then. Not much, mind you, but that part of the country was never noted for being very rainy to start with. I mean, it's West Texas, man. It's hot and dry. Or I guess now it's cold and dry."

"But could you grow anything? Would it be fit to eat if you did?"

"If you had a really green thumb . . . maybe. But it'd take somebody who knows more than I do to tell you if you could eat it."

While they were talking, they had almost reached the top of the ridgeline. A few more yards and they were there. Larkin stopped and took a good long look around. He remembered that on clear days, it had been possible to see downtown Fort Worth from here, although it was at least ten miles away to the east.

That wasn't true anymore, at least not today. Visibility was no more than a mile in any direction. Then a persistent haze took over. That was probably from the ash still in the air, Larkin thought. The ash that stunk in his nose at this very moment.

His disappointment must have shown on his face. Crandall said, "Didn't see what you wanted to see?"

"I'm not sure I ever will again," Larkin said.

By the time they got back down to the convenience store, Adams had pulled a canvas bag full of parts off several cars that now had their hoods up. He hefted the bag and told Larkin, "I think we can adapt these to the generators. If not, we know now that we can come back out here and try to find more."

"And we can do it without the damn hazmat suits next time," Wade said. "It stinks out here and it's cold, but somehow it beats bein' locked up underground." He shook his head. "That's too much like, well . . ."

"Being buried?" Larkin suggested.

"Yeah. I know logically that bein' down there is the

only thing that saved us, but still . . . we're human beings, Cap, not gophers or worms."

Crandall nodded and said, "Folks aren't meant to live under the ground. We came out of the caves too long ago for that."

"I wouldn't be too sure," Larkin said. "If we'd really left the caves behind, we wouldn't have lobbed all those bombs at each other, would we?"

None of the other men had an answer for that.

Adams climbed into the cab of the tanker truck, taking the bag of parts with him. It had already been hotwired in the past, so all he had to do to start it was twist a couple of wires together. The engine coughed and rumbled to life.

"Rodriguez, ride shotgun with him," Larkin said. "And I mean that literally. The rest of us will walk. Take it easy, Adams, and don't get stuck anywhere. We don't have any way to pull the truck out if you do."

"I'll be careful, Patrick," Adams said over the noise of the engine.

Larkin, Crandall, and Wade led the way toward the project. The truck rolled along slowly behind them.

After a while, Crandall said, "Does the fact that you're letting me come along mean I get to go down into the project with you?"

"That's not up to me," Larkin said. "Graham Moultrie will have to make that decision."

"I remember hearing Ruskin talk about him. He's the head man down there?"

"Yeah."

Crandall chuckled. "As you can imagine, Ruskin wasn't that fond of him."

"Moultrie did what he had to do," Larkin said. He

didn't mention the misgivings he had started to have about the founder of the Hercules Project. He still wanted to believe that Moultrie's actions were meant to protect the residents.

As if Crandall had read his thoughts, the man said, "Yeah, a lot of people start out that way. Then they find out how much fun it is to have so much power."

Larkin didn't say anything. He had enough trouble wrestling with his own doubts without putting them into words.

They passed the site of the ambush. The dead men had been pulled over to one side. Larkin saw something scurry around the corpses and then vanish into the creek bed. He lifted his rifle and said, "What the hell was that?"

"Rats," Crandall said. "Big mothers, too. I guess only the biggest and the strongest survived."

"Or the radiation changed them," Wade said. "Now they're mutant rats."

Larkin said, "I think I saw one earlier, but I didn't know what it was. And stop talking about mutants, Wade, especially when we get back down to the project. You don't want people to start panicking over nothing."

"Giant rats aren't nothin', Cap. That's something to worry about when we come back up here. By then there's no tellin' how big they're gonna be."

Larkin just shook his head and kept walking. After a moment he said to Crandall, "Sorry about your friends back there. They didn't really give us a choice."

"Oh, hell, I know that. I wouldn't call them friends, either. They were kind of like those rats. Scavengers. Can't blame them for it, at all, but it doesn't change what they were, either." Crandall was silent for a moment, then went on, "You're thinking about moving back up to the surface, aren't you?"

"I don't believe a day has gone by when I didn't think about it," Larkin admitted. "Most of us down there, we didn't go in thinking that we'd be there the rest of our lives. At least we hoped we wouldn't be. A year, maybe two, and then it would be safe to come back up and start over."

"In this?" Crandall waved a hand to indicated their surroundings.

Larkin looked at the hell-blasted landscape and shook his head. "No. This part of the world isn't ready yet. Maybe it won't be for a long time. But you came from someplace better." He turned to look at Crandall. "You can take us back there."

For a couple of heartbeats, Crandall didn't respond. Then he said, "Now I get it. You help me, I help you. But there's nowhere to go, Larkin. Nowhere good, anyway. It's not some damn paradise out in West Texas. Life out there is hard and brutal."

"But better than here."

Again, Crandall was silent for a moment. Then he shrugged and said, "Probably. But not as good as you've got it down in that bunker. Hell, man, you should just stay there as long as you can. Come out long enough to look around for what you need, like that gas."

He jerked a thumb over his shoulder at the truck creeping along behind them.

"Some people might want to do that," Larkin said.

"But not you."

"If we're being honest . . . no, I don't. You say it's a hard, brutal life out west, but I can't believe it's any more hard and brutal than it was a couple of hundred years ago when the first settlers started across there. Sure, a lot of them died, but a lot survived, too, and made new lives for themselves. Better lives, to their way of thinking."

"So you want to be a pioneer, like in the old days."

"Well, you know what they say." Larkin smiled. "The more things change, the more they stay the same."

Crandall laughed. "Yeah . . . like some guys being as stubborn as mules."

"You sound like you've been talking to my wife," Larkin said.

The truck had to go so slowly, navigating through the ditches where they were shallow and cutting through what had been fields before the war, that it took quite a while to get back to the project's entrance. They didn't encounter any trouble along the way, although Larkin remained alert for it. When they reached the remnants of the asphalt road, they followed it up to the collapsed building that housed the service elevator.

Larkin waved at Adams to indicate that he should park the truck by what was left of a wall. Adams did so and then killed the engine. He and Rodriguez climbed down, bringing the bag of parts with them.

"You're coming with us," Larkin said to Crandall. "It'll still be up to Moultrie to decide whether or not you can stay."

"Guess I can't ask for any more than that."

They went down the ramp into the basement. The elevator stood open. Larkin kind of hated to get in it and descend once more into the earth, but his family was down there, and they were more important to him than anything else.

What kind of life would it be for all of them if they

left the Hercules Project and struck out to the west? Would it be fair to Bailey and Chris to take them away from the comforts and advantages they had, sparse though those might be? Could they all survive out there? Plenty of the old pioneers hadn't, Larkin reminded himself. The West was littered with thousands of unmarked, forgotten graves.

But if nobody tried, nothing would ever get better. And they had to start over *sometime*. The supplies stored down in the project wouldn't last forever and couldn't be replenished fast enough to keep up with the demand. Another year at most and there wouldn't be any choice in the matter. Maybe it would be better to make the attempt now . . .

Those thoughts went through Larkin's brain as the elevator descended slowly. He still hadn't reached a decision when it stopped and the door slid to the side, opening into the short passage off Corridor Two.

Any consideration of the future vanished abruptly from Larkin's brain as he stiffened, his hands tightening on the rifle he held. Alarm surged up inside him. He exclaimed, "What the hell?"

Somewhere not too far off, gunfire echoed through the Hercules Project.

Chapter 46

Larkin charged out of the elevator with the other men close behind him. Adams dropped the bag of engine parts. They rattled and clanked as the bag hit the floor.

Larkin followed the sounds. They were coming from the direction of the Command Center. No one was in the corridor, and the deserted look of it just increased the worry he felt. Something was badly wrong, and the only thing he could think of was that the Bullpenners, led probably by Chad Holdstock, had rebelled against Moultrie and tried to take over.

Were there enough of them to do that? Larkin knew it was possible, especially if they were able to break into the armory and get their hands on a good supply of guns and ammunition.

From the sound of it, that was what was going on. The racket was that of a full-fledged battle.

"What's all the shooting about?" Crandall asked a little breathlessly as he ran along with Larkin and the others. "I thought you folks all got along down here!"

"Not even close," Larkin snapped. Up ahead were double metal doors leading into the long foyer that ran between the end of the two corridors. A silo was at each end, with the entrance to the Command Center in the middle. Larkin turned a little as he ran, hit the right-hand door with his shoulder, and bulled through it.

The gunfire came from his right. He swung in that direction, saw men falling back from the Command Center entrance, firing rifles and handguns as they retreated toward Corridor One. More men, some of them wearing the red vests of the security force, poured out of the entrance and fired at the ones who were fleeing. Larkin took in all of that in a split second and knew where his loyalties lay.

Then the world was yanked right out from under his feet.

Because his daughter was among those retreating.

Larkin came to a dead stop. Across that distance of fifty yards, his stunned gaze locked with Jill's. She had a pistol in her hand and was laying down covering fire, fighting a rearguard action as those with her tried to get away. For a split second they looked at each other.

Then a bullet slammed into her and twisted her around. Larkin saw the blood fly. Jill went to one knee, then staggered up and stumbled after the others.

Rage erupted inside Larkin. He didn't know what was going on here, didn't know which side was in the right, but he knew one thing.

Those sons of bitches had just hurt his daughter.

He brought the AR-15 up and opened fire.

Even with the red haze of fury clouding his brain, he didn't send bullets lancing wantonly into the men just outside the Command Center. He fired low instead. Some of the slugs ricocheted up into the crowd, but for the most part they just forced the men in the red vests to throw on the brakes and then scramble back through the opening.

"Cap, what are you doin'?" Wade demanded as he caught at Larkin's arm. "Those are our guys!"

"So are the ones they were shooting at," Larkin said as he lowered the rifle slightly. "And one of them was my kid!"

The group that included Jill had vanished through the doors at the other end of the foyer. Larkin had been able to tell that she was moving fairly well, so he hoped she wasn't hurt too badly. He had to find out, so he told the men with him to find their friends and family and keep their heads down until they found out what was going on.

Then he rammed through the doors again and loped along Corridor Two toward the foyer at the far end, where he could get the elevator down to his apartment. First, he would make sure Susan was all right, then he would try to find Jill and check on her.

The thud of rapid footsteps behind him made him glance over his shoulder. Earl Crandall was there. The man said, "I'm coming with you, hoss. I realize we haven't known each other long, but you're the closest thing to a friend I got down here!"

Larkin wasn't going to waste time arguing with him. Not when the world he had known for almost a year seemed to be falling apart with no warning.

Just like the world before it had done . . .

A door up ahead on the left side of the corridor opened a few inches. Larkin angled the rifle in that direction but held off on the trigger. He was glad he did when he saw a woman's terrified face peering out at him. She jerked back and slammed the door.

Crandall said, "I've seen a few other folks peeking out

at us after we went by. Looks like everybody's hunkered down, Larkin. Shit must've really hit the fan. Was everything all right here when you left?"

"I thought it was," Larkin said. "I guess I just didn't know."

Even though he was hurrying, his brain was working even faster. What he had seen back there had disoriented him, but he was sure of one thing: Jill never would have thrown in with Holdstock and the other malcontents who had rallied around him. So if it hadn't been the bunch from the Bullpen who'd been fighting with the security force . . . then who was it?

Larkin and Crandall reached the far end of the corridor and pushed through the doors there. Larkin's rifle was ready, but Crandall still had his slung on his back, where it had been all along. He asked, "You want me to cover your back, Larkin? I don't want to break out the hardware unless you're sure you trust me."

Larkin didn't hesitate. He said, "Yeah, I trust you. And if you give me any reason to regret it, I'll kill you."

"Fair enough," Crandall said with a grim smile. He brought the rifle around and let the sling slip down off his shoulder. It was an old deer rifle, Larkin noted. Not the greatest weapon for fighting a battle . . . but nearly 250 years earlier, a bunch of patriots had won a revolution using their era's equivalent.

They hadn't reached the elevator leading down to the apartments in Silo A when the door to the apartment on this level swung open. Jim and Beth Huddleston lived there, so Larkin wasn't surprised to see Beth step out.

He was shocked to see the gun in her hand, though: a Smith & Wesson .38 caliber revolver that she pointed at him as she said in a shrill, hysteria-edged voice, "Stop right there, Patrick Larkin!"

Larkin stopped and made a slight motion with his left hand, hoping Crandall would understand that he was telling him not to open fire. "Beth?" he said. "I don't know what's going on here. I'm all confused. Where's Jim? Have you seen my wife?"

Beth sneered and said, "Jim called me on the walkie-talkie and warned me about you. He said you tried to kill him and the others. I'm not surprised. Your own daughter was with those lunatics trying to overthrow Graham Moultrie!"

Damn, Larkin thought, would the world ever stop lurching around under his feet? Beth Huddleston was not only holding a gun—she who hated guns and had argued stridently against the Second Amendment at every opportunity—but now she sounded like she supported whatever it was that Moultrie had done now. She'd always hated Moultrie. To her warped, throwback way of thinking, he was *The Man*—and she took that ridiculous notion seriously.

What would make her turn around so quickly and completely?

Larkin started to get a glimmer of an answer to that question, but he didn't really have time to ponder it right now. Instead he said, "Beth, you need to put down that gun. I know you don't want to hurt anybody."

"Who's that with you?" Beth's voice quivered, less from fear than from rage, Larkin thought. "He's one of those awful people from the surface, isn't he?"

Crandall said, "I'm not looking for any trouble, ma'am—"

"Things are going to be different now," Beth interrupted as if she hadn't heard him. "Everything is going to be all right. We're going to get rid of all the bad people, and then there'll be plenty for the rest of us."

Those words made a chill go through Larkin. He said, "What are you talking about, Beth?"

The gun in her hand didn't budge. Larkin had been waiting for her hand to start to shake. But for someone who probably had never held a gun before, Beth was remarkably steady as she said, "The food. There's not enough. It's going to run out in less than a month unless there are fewer people to eat it."

"That's crazy. There should be enough for another six months, at least."

"No. There would have been, if Graham had had more time. But then there was the war . . ."

Under his breath, Crandall said, "This is some bad shit, Larkin. It sounds like she's talking about culling the herd."

"Yeah." Larkin had thought the same thing, and it put a cold ball of unease in his stomach. "Listen, Beth, I don't know what happened while I was gone, but I'm sure everything can be worked out."

Beth shook her head. "There's only one answer."

"Moultrie promised you and Jim that you'd be among the ones left, didn't he?" Larkin had gotten a hint of that earlier, but he was sure of it now.

"Well, it's only right that we are," Beth said with a note of defensiveness in her voice. "Jim has always been supportive of him, and I've come to appreciate that he's just trying to look out for us."

"He bought you off." Larkin couldn't keep the scorn out of his voice, even with the gun pointed at him.

"He didn't have to. We're better. We've always been better. We deserve to live." Beth sniffed. "It's only right. The people who are smarter, better educated, they have to survive and run things. You can't let normal people decide things for themselves. They'll do it all wrong.

I mean, my God, look at some of the politicians normal people have elected!"

As always, arguing with Beth Huddleston was a waste of time, Larkin realized. She was as much of an elitist as she had ever been, although the world's circumstances had changed drastically. People who thought they were better than everybody else would always try to seize power sooner or later, though, no matter what their circumstances were.

"Just what is it you want, Beth?" Larkin asked. "What do you hope to accomplish by pointing that gun at me?"

"I'm going to hold you here so Jim can come and get you. He'll take you to Moultrie, and they'll decide what to do with you."

"Look, I want to talk to them, too. You don't have to threaten me—"

The silo elevator opened. Larkin darted a glance in that direction, saw Susan stepping out. She looked all right, didn't appear to be hurt in any way.

But then Beth jerked the revolver toward her and Larkin saw her finger whitening on the trigger. He leaped toward Susan, praying that he could knock her out of the way in time.

The gun in Beth's hand blasted just as Larkin grabbed Susan and forced her back against the wall. He expected to feel the .38 caliber bullet smash into his back, but instead there was no impact.

When he looked around he saw Beth on her knees, cradling her right hand against her body and sobbing. The gun lay a few feet away. She didn't look like she was interested in making any attempt to retrieve it.

Crandall picked up the pistol and tucked it behind his belt, then said, "I used the barrel of my rifle and knocked her hand up just in time. May have broken her wrist, though. I'm sorry about that."

"Don't be," Larkin told him. "You saved either my life or my wife's. Thank you, Earl."

"That shot's liable to bring more trouble. Where do we need to go?"

Larkin glanced at Susan. "Have you seen Jill?"

"No," she said. "I was on my way to their place. I didn't know you were back, Patrick." She gave him a brief but fierce hug. "Are you all right?"

"Yeah. What the hell's going on down here? How did it all fall apart so fast?"

Susan shook her head. "I don't know. Jill came by earlier and said that there might be trouble. She told me to stay in the apartment with the door locked and to keep one of your guns handy. Then she left. I tried to do what she said and wait there, but I just couldn't . . ."

She didn't know that Jill had been shot, he realized. He was still hoping the wound wasn't a bad one, so he decided not to say anything just yet.

Instead he took her hand and said, "Let's go see if we can find her."

"All right. Patrick . . .?" Susan's voice held a tentative note. "Who's this?"

She was looking at Crandall, who smiled back at her.

"A friend," Larkin said, knowing that would have to be enough of an explanation for now. "Come on."

Chapter 47

Bailey had tear streaks down her face when she opened the door of the Sinclair family's living quarters in Corridor One, and seeing that made fear shoot through Larkin's heart.

"Grandpa!" the girl cried. "Grandma! Mom's hurt!"

"What?" Susan said. She rushed into the apartment.

When Larkin started to follow her but then hesitated, Crandall said, "Go on, man, don't worry. I'll stand watch out here."

Larkin jerked his head in a curt nod and said, "Thanks." He hurried after his wife, leaving the door open behind him.

Jill was on the love seat, stretched out as much as she could in its confines, with Trevor kneeling on the floor beside her. Her shirt was pulled up about a foot, revealing a bloody gash in her side where a bullet had plowed a furrow. Despite the blood, Larkin felt a surge of relief go through him. He had seen plenty of wounds like that during his time in combat. They left the victims stiff and sore, but as long as the bleeding wasn't too bad and the injury was cleaned properly and kept that way, it wasn't serious.

Just painful as hell, as was evident by the pallor that covered Jill's pinched face.

"Oh, honey!" Susan cried.

Trevor glanced up. "Thank God you're here. I think I've got the bleeding stopped, but I'm not sure what to do now—"

"Get out of the way," Susan said, her voice brisk as her training and experience took over. "This is something I know how to deal with."

Bailey stood to one side, her arm around her little brother's shoulders. Chris had been crying, too. Larkin went over to them and said, "Don't worry. Your mom's going to be just fine. I know what I'm talking about. Anyway, your grandma's the best nurse in the world, and she's gonna take good care of your mom."

"Dad?" Jill said, her voice showing the strain as much as her face did. "Dad, I have to talk to you."

"No, honey, it can wait—" Susan began.

"No, it can't," Jill broke in. "I'm sorry, Mom, but it can't."

Larkin went over and knelt beside the love seat. He leaned closer and said, "I'm here, kid. What do you have to tell me?"

"Moultrie's gone crazy, Dad. He came on the loud-speakers and announced that because of food shortages, half of the people down here would have to leave." Jill paused and took a couple of deep breaths. Larkin knew she was fighting off the pain of her wound. "Then he started reading off names. He said they had been chosen by lottery, but most of them were people who have complained about him in the past. He's getting rid of his enemies. Or at least, the people he considers enemies."

"This so-called food shortage that nobody ever heard of until today . . . is it real?"

Jill shook her head. "I don't know. Maybe nobody

knows except him. But it wasn't just Bullpenners he's kicking out . . . My name was on the list, and yours was, too."

Larkin's jaw clenched. While he'd been up on the surface, fighting to get the things the project needed to keep going, Moultrie had been plotting to get rid of him and his family. Because the power-mad son of a bitch knew he and Jill would never leave without Susan, Trevor, Bailey, and Chris.

"What happened after he made that announcement?"

"Just what you'd expect. Things went nuts. Holdstock led a delegation from the Bullpen up to the Command Center to talk to Moultrie. But some of the security force . . . opened fire on them." Jill swallowed hard. "Holdstock and another man were killed. The rest of them fell back. When the members of the security force who weren't on duty heard about that, we went to see what was going on. Some of the Bullpenners who'd been with Holdstock came with us. But when we got there—"

"They started shooting at you, too," Larkin broke in. His face was grim as he nodded. "Because Moultrie made sure that only guys who would be loyal to him were on duty in the Command Center. He has to have been planning this for a while. And that's another reason he sent me up to the surface. If I hadn't volunteered, he would have maneuvered me into it somehow. He knew I'd never go along with this purge crap."

"Dad . . . how is it up there?"

"We got a whole tanker truck full of gas, plus some parts that will probably work as replacements for the generators. The environmental readings are good enough that people can survive without the hazmat suits, and they ought to be better the farther away from the Metroplex you get." Larkin shrugged. "It wouldn't be easy, but there's at least a chance folks could get away from the worst of the damage and find a place to live. To start over."

Trevor said, "Then for God's sake, why don't we do that?"

Susan said, "But we wouldn't have medical supplies or a school or even the limited amount of technology we have now. And what would we do for food?"

"We'd have to take some things with us," Larkin said. "Those medical supplies you mentioned, and enough food to keep us going for a while. As for the technology . . . people used to survive without it. I guess we'd learn how to do that again."

Looking up at him as her mother finished applying a dressing to the wound, Jill said, "We'd need a leader. That would be you, Dad."

"I don't know if I want that sort of responsibility—"

"Whether you want it or not, you know good and well you're the right man for the job."

"She's right, Patrick," Trevor added.

Susan straightened from what she'd been doing and said, "If you're really talking about leaving, quite a few people will want to go with you if they think they can live up there. That would solve the problem of not enough food here, wouldn't it? There's no need for more violence."

"If we can get Moultrie to listen to reason."

Jill said, "I'm not sure we can do that. When he started reading off names and saying they had to go, he sounded sort of, well, unhinged."

Larkin rubbed his chin and frowned in thought. "And he doesn't know yet what conditions are really like up there, because nobody has reported back to him from our mission. For all he really knows, he would be sending people out to their deaths."

"He doesn't care about that," Jill said. "I told you he's gone crazy."

Larkin thought about the people Moultrie had sent to their deaths on top of the service elevator when the surface hatch was closed. Moultrie had been going around the bend for a while, and Larkin knew now he should have spoken up sooner.

But it wasn't too late to prevent a bloodbath down here. He had to do what he could to accomplish that.

"I'll go talk to him," he said as he stood up.

"To Moultrie?" Susan asked.

"Not without me," Jill said as she started struggling to get to her feet. "I'm coming, too."

Susan put a hand on her shoulder and said, "No, you're not. After losing that much blood, you need to rest—"

"But Mom—"

"Listen to your mother," Larkin said. "She knows what she's talking about."

"I'm not six years old!"

"But you *are* hurt," Trevor said as he moved in to perch on the arm of the love seat, "and your parents are right. You stay here with your mother." He glanced at Larkin. "I'll go with you, Patrick."

Larkin shook his head. "I appreciate the offer, but you need to stay here and keep an eye on things. I'll feel a lot better about it if you do."

"I don't mind helping—"

"That's how you can help me the most right now."

Trevor looked like he wanted to argue more, but after a second he shrugged and nodded. "All right. I understand."

"That guy Earl who came back with me, he's been living up there. He can explain to Moultrie how things are, if we can get him to listen. And then we can ask for volunteers to come with us. None of that 'list' bullcrap. Nobody should be kicked out if they don't want to go."

"You'll never get Moultrie to go along with that," Jill warned. "He's using this as an excuse to get rid of people he thinks may give him trouble, either now or in the future. That's why you and I were on the list, Dad. He knows we won't stand for him hurting anybody."

For a moment, there was a bitter, sour taste under Larkin's tongue. He had stood for Moultrie murdering those people, because he'd considered it a time of war. The survivors had wanted to break into the project and slaughter anybody they could. That *was* war, damn it, and Larkin would never lose a second of sleep over the men he had killed in combat.

But what Moultrie had done was over the line, and Larkin could see now that was just the first step in the man's descent into madness.

He remembered reading Conrad's *Heart of Darkness* many years earlier, and he had seen *Apocalypse Now*, as well. He was murmuring, "The horror," when someone knocked on the door.

Everyone in the room stiffened. Larkin swung his rifle toward the door. Trevor picked up a semi-automatic pistol from a table. Larkin motioned for him to stay beside Jill and Susan and told Bailey and Chris, "You kids go back in the bedroom."

Crandall had been standing guard in the corridor and Larkin hadn't heard any shots, so he figured the man from the surface was the one who'd knocked on the door. But he didn't take any chances, holding the rifle ready as he went to the door and swung it open.

"You got company," Crandall said. He stood there alertly with the deer rifle in his hands as he leaned his head toward the woman who was next to him.

Deb Moultrie.

"Deb," Larkin said. "What the hell—"

"Graham sent me to talk to you, Patrick," she said. "Can I . . . come in?"

"We can talk out here," Larkin said, his voice curt. He stepped into the corridor and swung the door closed behind him. "What does he want?"

"He's hoping you can put an end to the trouble."

"Funny. I was hoping the same thing about him. I was gone less than twelve hours, Deb. What happened down here in that time?"

Her face was pale and drawn into tight lines under the red hair, which was pulled back at the moment and fastened into a ponytail that hung halfway down her back. In a plain shirt and jeans, she didn't look like a fashion model anymore. She said, "Graham was trying to postpone this confrontation for as long as possible, but someone—probably one of the workers in the commissary—found out about the supply situation and leaked the information to Chad Holdstock."

"Then it's true?" Larkin asked tautly. "The food is running low?"

"Dangerously low. I . . . I knew there might be a problem, but even I didn't know how bad it really was . . ." Deb took a deep breath. "Graham wasn't cutting corners, Patrick. I swear he wasn't. He just didn't have time to get as ready for the disaster as he led everyone to believe."

"Because that would have meant he'd failed, and he didn't want to admit that."

"I don't know what he thought, and anyway, it doesn't really matter, does it?"

Larkin shrugged. "I guess what's important is that folks are going to start starving to death, unless your husband gets rid of a bunch of them."

Anger flashed in her eyes as she said, "It's not like he's going to line them up against a wall and shoot them!"

"He will if it comes to that," Larkin said with utter conviction that he was right about Graham Moultrie. He thought about Jim Huddleston and added, "He's probably got enough guys backing his play to make that happen, too."

Deb shook her head, but Larkin could tell that she wasn't completely convinced she was right about what her husband would or wouldn't do. Whether she wanted to admit it or not, the fear that Larkin was right lurked within her.

"So what does Graham want from me?" Larkin went on. "Why did he send you here?"

"To ask you to come and talk to him. He knows you have a lot of friends here. He wants to convince you that he's only doing what's necessary, so that you can make everybody else understand."

Larkin snorted in disbelief. "I'm not going to do his dirty work for him."

"You can make people see that they need to negotiate, though, instead of trying to kill each other."

Was that really worth a try? Larkin was dubious, but he supposed anything that might prevent more bloodshed shouldn't be ruled out.

"All right," he said, "but you're coming with me. Your husband's bunch won't start shooting if you're in the line of fire."

"He doesn't have a *bunch*," Deb snapped. "We're all still on the same side. We're all residents of the Hercules Project."

Larkin wished that were still true, but he couldn't make himself believe it.

Just like he hoped he was right about how having Deb with him would keep Moultrie's men from gunning him down.

Chapter 48

August 21

Susan tried to talk him out of going to parley with Moultrie. Trevor and Jill both wanted to come along. Larkin just hugged the grandkids, shook hands with Trevor, ruffled Jill's hair like he had done when she was a little girl, and kissed his wife.

Then he and Deb walked toward the Command Center, with Earl Crandall following and keeping an eye out behind them.

An air of tense, hushed anticipation still hung over the project. Larkin didn't know what was going on down in the Bullpen, but he would have been willing to bet they were nursing their wounds and trying to figure out a plan for attacking the Command Center. He wanted to head that off if he could.

He had an ace in his hand to play. He knew that conditions on the surface were suitable for human survival, despite the hardships they would encounter. The solution seemed simple enough to him: let anyone who wanted to leave the project do so, giving them enough provisions to hold them for a while. Larkin had a hunch quite a few would choose that option. Then the ones left behind would have enough supplies to hold out for a few more months.

Maybe by then, the ones who had left would have a settlement established somewhere west of here. They could come back for the others and lead them to their new home . . .

Larkin was getting ahead of himself and knew it, so he shut down that line of thought. Stopping the killing here today, that was the main thing.

The three of them went through the doors at the end of the corridor and turned toward the Command Center entrance. Several guards in red vests were posted there. Instantly, they tensed and lifted their weapons.

"Hold your fire," Deb called. "I've brought Patrick Larkin to talk, just like Graham wanted. Let him know we're here."

"That's one of those mutant survivors from the surface with him, Mrs. Moultrie," a guard said. "We can't risk—"

"What the hell is it with you people and mutants?" Larkin interrupted. "This is a friend of mine, Earl Crandall. He's as human as you or me, and he knows about conditions on the surface. I do, too. I've been up there, damn it. Bring Moultrie out here and I'll tell him about it."

One of the guards spoke low-voiced into his walkie-talkie. He listened to the squawking response, then said, "Graham says we're to bring you in."

Larkin shook his head and put his left hand on Deb's shoulder as she started to take a step forward. He still held the AR-15 in his right. "We're staying here," he said. "Moultrie can come out and talk to us."

The guards didn't like that. They were all men that Larkin knew, men he had worked alongside. But there was a subtle difference now, a slightly different cast to their faces. He knew that was because they had all made a decision that put them on the opposite side from him.

Even so, he'd been right about their unwillingness to shoot as long as Deb was with him. One of them ducked back through the doors while the others continued to point their weapons toward Larkin and Crandall.

A couple of tense minutes went by. Then the doors opened again and Graham Moultrie stepped out.

He wore his usual friendly smile as he said, "It's good to see you again, Patrick. I was hoping to hear your report from the surface under better circumstances, but at least we can move forward from here."

Moultrie sounded as affable and reasonable as ever, but Larkin knew better now. It was a pose, pure and simple, to get what he wanted.

"Why don't you let Deb come back over here," Moultrie went on, "and then you can tell me all about what you found up there." He looked past Larkin at Crandall and added, "I see you brought a . . . souvenir."

"I'm no damn souvenir, mister," Crandall snapped.

"This is Earl Crandall," Larkin said. "He's the one who translated the Morse code for Nelson Ruskin. And he helped us find a tanker truck nearly full of gasoline."

Moultrie's eyes widened. "That much gas? That's

wonderful. It'll keep the generators going for a long time. Assuming you got the parts we need for them, too."

"Maybe," Larkin said. "Don't know for sure yet. But there's a good chance of it. I'd say the generators and the life-support system are less of a problem now than the food supplies."

Moultrie's expression tightened. "That's not my fault," he snapped. "I've been trying to figure out a way to fix the situation. But the only way—"

"Is to cut down on the number of people depending on those supplies," Larkin said. "Isn't that right? And you'll get rid of the extra folks any way you can, whether it's booting them out of the project or putting them in the incinerator."

Moultrie took a step forward and clenched his fists. "Damn you," he grated. "You don't know what it's like, having all this responsibility. Having to decide who has to die so that others can live."

"Having to be a god, you mean? Since this is the Hercules Project, I guess that would make you Zeus. You're all powerful, and the rest of us are just puny mortals."

"If that's what it takes!" Moultrie shouted as his control began to slip away from him. "I've said all along, I'll do anything I have to in order to protect this project."

"Even if it means killing everybody, one by one, until you're sitting down here by yourself, lord of all you survey." Larkin paused. When Moultrie didn't say anything, just stood there red-faced and glaring, Larkin went on, "Luckily, you don't have to do that. I've been to the surface. People can live up there, Graham. It won't be easy, but they can live. Let me take the ones who want to go. That'll give you some breathing room down here and time to figure out what you want to do next."

That proposal sounded eminently reasonable to Larkin, but he could tell by the look on Moultrie's face that he wasn't going to agree. That would mean splitting up the residents, with him in charge of one group and Larkin, however reluctantly, leading the other. Moultrie wasn't going to relinquish even that much power.

Moultrie shook his head and said, "I've already announced who has to go."

"Some of them may not want to, and some of the folks you didn't pick might decide they'd rather take a chance up on the surface. You have to let people decide for themselves."

"No!" The cords in Moultrie's neck stood out from the vehemence of his reply. "No, I'm in charge here. *I* make the decisions. I created this place. I made it happen, nobody else. You'd all be dead without me!"

"That's true," Larkin said, "but now it's time to move on."

Moultrie shook his head. "Never!" He twisted abruptly and snatched a rifle from one of the guards. "Never!"

"Look out!" Crandall yelled. He started to lift his deer rifle, but Deb turned and grabbed the barrel, lunging against him and forcing the weapon up. Flame spat from the barrel of the rifle Moultrie held as he sprayed shots along the foyer. Larkin heard slugs whine past his ear and threw himself forward. From the corner of his eye, he saw Deb slump against

Crandall. A crimson flower bloomed on the back of her shirt.

Then he landed on the floor and the AR-15 bucked against his shoulder as he fired. He squeezed off three rounds, saw Graham Moultrie jolted back as the shots slammed into his chest. Moultrie lived long enough to drop the rifle and gasp, "Oh, God! Deb . . ."

Then his eyes rolled up in their sockets. He fell to his knees, swayed there for a second, and pitched forward onto the floor.

The guards stared in disbelief. By now Deb had sagged to the floor as well. Her blood stained Crandall's old army jacket where she had fallen against him. Crandall had his rifle pointed at the guards, and Larkin covered them with the AR-15, as well.

One man sighed, bent over, and put his rifle on the floor. The others set their weapons aside as well.

"I guess it's over," one of them said bitterly.

"You're wrong, hoss," Crandall said. "I got a hunch the new world's just getting started."

It had been a showdown Patrick Larkin never wanted. But in that split second as he lined his sights on Moultrie and squeezed the trigger, he had realized that it never could have ended any other way. Everybody was the hero of his own story, Larkin had read somewhere, and he was sure Moultrie felt the same way, that he was only doing what was necessary, no matter how many people died in the process.

Time would tell which of them was right, Larkin supposed.

He looked around the basement at the 197 people

assembled there, all of the adults and most of the kids wearing backpacks. Many of the adults were armed, as well. All of them had decided to take their chances on the surface. Everyone left down in the corridors and silos and the lower-level bunker had decided to remain. It was a free choice, influenced by no one. Larkin had made sure of that as much as he possibly could.

He'd had a chance to take inventory of the food supplies. He had split it up, 50 percent for the people leaving the project, 50 percent for those staying behind, even though more than half of the residents were heading for the surface. Larkin was confident they would find food up there. As soon as they located a good place, they would plant crops, and they were taking along some of the rabbits and chickens, as well. There would be some lean and hungry days ahead, no doubt about that, but they would make it.

The engineers had replaced the failing parts on the generators, and the project's gasoline supplies had been replenished from the tanker truck. Larkin and his group would be taking the truck and the rest of its valuable cargo with them, though, because they needed gas for the older, still-working vehicles they had scavenged to make the pilgrimage westward. Right now, those vehicles were fueled up and waiting for them.

Earl Crandall had come from a small town called Cross Plains; that would be their destination starting out. They would move on from there, if and when they needed to.

Larkin had sent the service elevator back down once everyone was here, so he was a little surprised when he heard its door open. He turned around and saw Jim

Huddleston standing there. Huddleston's face was set in grim lines.

"Decide to come with us, Jim?" Larkin asked.

"You know better than that. I just wanted to tell you . . . some of the people in the group staying behind have been talking about organizing and electing a new leader. Beth wants the job." Huddleston took a breath. "And you and I both know, when Beth wants something . . ."

"She usually finds a way to get it." Larkin shrugged. "If that's what she wants, I wish her luck. She may wind up regretting it, though."

"I just thought you should know that if she's running things down in the project, you and your people . . . well, you won't be welcome back here. If you try to come back, there's liable to be trouble."

"Jim, if there's one thing I can promise you, it's that nobody's going to want to come back here, unless it's to help you folks out. You're going to have to move back to the surface eventually. If we can, we'd be glad to give you a helping hand."

"I guess we'll have to wait and see when and if that day comes. Until then . . ."

Huddleston stuck his hand out.

Larkin hesitated; he couldn't deny that. He didn't like Huddleston, had very little respect for the man. But there was no point in being a jerk, either. He gripped Huddleston's hand hard for a second and meant it when he said, "Good luck."

Huddleston nodded and went back into the elevator. The door slid closed. For the brave souls here in the basement, the Hercules Project was over. They were moving on to something they hoped would be better.

As they left, they would walk past two graves. Larkin hadn't wanted to put Graham and Deb Moultrie into the incinerator. He and some of the others had dug the graves, fashioned markers for them. Moultrie and Deb rested on a hilltop, looking out over the project. Someday, grass and flowers would grow again on that hill, Larkin hoped. He would probably never see it, but that day would come.

He looked around again. Susan was there, summoning up a smile. Jill, still looking a little pale from the wound she had suffered, but strong and determined anyway. Trevor and the kids, setting off into what was a vast unknown for them, but unshakable in their family bond. The widow, daughter, and son-in-law of Larkin's old friend Adam Threadgill, reminding Larkin that he wished Adam was here to see this day. It might never have come without him, because he was the one who had told Larkin about the Hercules Project in the first place. Wade, Rodriguez, Adams, and the other men who had gone with Larkin on that first mission to the surface were here, too. Like him, they knew they could make it up there. And Earl Crandall, who would show them the way on his motorcycle, a new friend, but one of them now.

"Patrick," Susan said. "Look at the sky."

Larkin tipped his head back and gazed up through the ruined building at the thick gray clouds overhead. At first, he didn't see what Susan was talking about, but then . . .

There was the smallest of gaps, a tiny crack in the

overcast, really, but behind it for a second, maybe two, Larkin saw a sliver of blue sky before the clouds came together again.

That was enough to tell him it was still there. Hope was still there.

Larkin stepped out to lead the way up the ramp into the light.

Connect with Us

Visit us online at
KensingtonBooks.com
to read more from your favorite authors, see books
by series, view reading group guides, and more.

Join us on social media

for sneak peeks, chances to win books and prize packs,
and to share your thoughts with other readers.

facebook.com/kensingtonpublishing
twitter.com/kensingtonbooks

Tell us what you think!

To share your thoughts, submit a review,
or sign up for our eNewsletters, please visit:
KensingtonBooks.com/TellUs.